Lone Escort

Alaric Bond

Cover artwork shows details from *"A British frigate hove-to with her jollyboat preparing to pluck a man from the sea"* by Thomas Buttersworth 1768-1842. This work is in the public domain in its country of origin and other countries and areas where the copyright term is the author's life plus 100 years or fewer. It has been identified as being free of known restrictions under copyright law, including all related and neighbouring rights.

Thanks (as always) to Tessa James for editing.

Publisher's Note: This is a work of historical fiction. Certain characters and their actions may have been inspired by historical individuals and events. The characters in the novel, however, represent the work of the author's imagination. Any resemblance to actual persons, living or dead, is entirely coincidental.

Published by Old Salt Press. Old Salt Press, LLC is based in Jersey City, New Jersey with an affiliate in New Zealand. For more information about Old Salt Press titles go to www.oldsaltpress.com

For Janet and John

Other novels by Alaric Bond

The Fighting Sail series

His Majesty's Ship

The Jackass Frigate

True Colours

Cut and Run

The Patriot's Fate

The Torrid Zone

The Scent of Corruption

HMS Prometheus

The Blackstrap Station

Honour Bound

Sealed Orders

Sea Trials

and

Turn a Blind Eye

The Guinea Boat

The Coastal Forces series

Hellfire Corner

Contents

Lone Escort

Chapter One

The brig was running towards the rising sun with a fair wind on her tail as Lovemore, in his favoured place on the forecastle, peered into the growing light. He was on watch, but little had been required from any hand for some while and, rather than join the group yarning aft, had wandered forward to station himself where he now stood.

Or perhaps lounged would be a better description; the seaman had one foot resting on the low bulwark and was slouched over it in a manner decidedly relaxed and verging on the slovenly. His face had not seen a razor in days and the wind, which was indeed fair, flowed through an unruly mop of dark curly hair. Neither his posture nor appearance would have passed muster aboard a man-of-war where Lovemore had learned his craft, but the *Merriweather* was a merchant and her more relaxed regime suited him fine. Besides, though apparently at ease, Lovemore's mind was unusually alert and, as the creeping rays steadily revealed more of his surroundings, he noticed everything of importance.

For a start, there was no sign of land, which was just as it should be. An hour or so before, the mate had been certain they were in the Channel and now reckoned Falmouth to be off their larboard beam. And that may well be the case although it remained beyond the horizon, which was a pity as it would have been pleasant to glimpse England after so long away. But the mate could have been wrong, no great error in navigation would have shifted them closer to Start Point, or any of the other hazards that littered the area. They might even have missed the Channel completely and now be running straight onto a lee shore several miles to the north, or have already grounded on the Scillies, as some fool of an admiral did over a hundred years before. So Lovemore was actually quite pleased to find them surrounded by a healthy measure of water.

The increasing light picked out several other vessels and Hacker, at the main, was currently relating these to the quarterdeck when Cranston joined him.

"Aye, this is the Channel, sure enough," his mate confirmed as he rested alongside. The subject of their exact position had been in debate for so long it was a relief to have it settled. Both were experienced seamen and could feel the slight chop that would doubtless grow as the day progressed, and both were equally aware their journey home, the one that had begun almost a year before and on the other side of the world, was almost at an end.

Almost, but not quite; they were bound for the Pool of London: there were a good three hundred miles to cover before finally dropping anchor and in a voyage that had already seen several thousand, this last leg could turn out the most dangerous. French privateers regularly put out from Brest or the Cotentin Peninsular in the hopes of snaring a merchant such as themselves, and there was always the chance of running into a blockade runner; a lone enemy warship escaping the watch still placed over all enemy ports. The *Merriweather* was both fast and reasonably armed for her type; attributes that allowed her to sail independent of convoy or escort. But though she might defend herself against one of the lighter French raiders, she would fare less well against a combined attack, while meeting almost any size of enemy warship was bound to end with her capture. To be taken so when almost in sight of home was a fate as bad as any grounding yet there was another, equally terrible, that threatened homebound merchants or, more specifically, their crews. Because of this, the small cluster of shipping before them was now the seamen's sole source of interest, especially as the light grew stronger and more detail was revealed.

"One of 'em might be Navy," Cranston supposed as he peered under the leech of the brig's jib. Lovemore followed his gaze; there were five vessels in sight, three were most likely fishers and the fourth possibly a trading smack, but the last was undoubtedly a warship and, though probably British, no less dangerous on that account. Currently she was a good way off but beating in their general direction under topsails and staysails alone and the lack of effort, combined with a distinctive rig and sail pattern, was enough to confirm both her class and nationality.

The Royal Navy had a constant need for trained hands so British warships rarely missed the opportunity to raid a homecoming merchant and press some, occasionally all, her experienced hands. And this one looked to be a frigate; a type that relied on speed as much as firepower. To achieve both meant maintaining a highly skilled crew, so trained manpower was constantly in demand and something the *Merriweather* could be expected to provide. Even if the warship already had a full complement, it seemed likely they would receive a visit.

Lovemore and Cranston had sailed together for many years, so the exchange of a worried glance was enough to convey their fears, and both resumed their inspection without a word. The frigate was still a good distance off their larboard bow but her course, along with the present wind, suggested a tack was imminent, after which she would be passing close indeed.

"Think the skipper's aware?" Lovemore asked, finally breaking the silence, and they both glanced back to the brig's small quarterdeck. The master was indeed present, as was the mate, although both appeared unaware of the danger and were chatting amiably. Then a further shout from Hacker at the masthead cut into their conversation.

"Belike the frigate's about to alter course," he bellowed, and both officers looked up, then forward at the vessel concerned. Cranston and Lovemore wriggled impatiently as their betters exchanged comments and then, finally, there was action.

With a chorus of orders, the brig came alive; the rest of the watch on deck appeared, more sail was added, the braces manned and she began to turn several degrees to starboard. Her speed increased with the additional canvas and more so as the wind crept onto her quarter, so when Cranston and Lovemore returned from their work and considered the warship once more, she seemed less of a threat. For by then she was in the midst of her tack and, if all went well, should pass safely a respectable distance off the *Merriweather*'s stern.

"Reckon we're clear of her now," Lovemore stated guardedly.

"Aye, I'd chance," Cranston agreed. "'Sides, they may be heading for Falmouth.

"Falmouth?" Lovemore questioned.

"Aye, to pay off," the second seaman confirmed. "In which case they won't be needin' no extra bodies and we're in the clear."

It was a long shot perhaps but, when combined with their recent change of course, enough to make both relax. Then they noticed something to renew their concerns.

Rather than completing her manoeuvre and settling on a fresh westerly course, the frigate had continued to turn until set to intercept. And as she did, more sail was shaken out until the warship began to lean with the wind as she gathered speed.

"Blighter's steering to cross our hawse," Lovemore remarked in horror. It was a classic ploy and the opening gambit of countless single ship engagements even though the frigate was an ally and should present no threat. Both men immediately looked back to the quarterdeck where their officers appeared aware of the problem and were deep in discussion.

"We might run," Cranston remarked, turning back to his friend.

"Aye," Lovemore snorted. "Steer deeper into the Channel, though that would bring us closer to the French coast; given the choice between the Navy and a Frog privateer I know which I'd choose."

"Turn back into the wind, then?" Cranston suggested.

"To what end? Yon frigate's fair placed off our bow and I'd wager can cut into a breeze faster, and closer, than us."

Both turned their attention to the brig's rig. Freshly set up with new line and canvas the *Merriweather* would have the heels on most small warships on any point of sail. But the years at sea had taken their toll; her canvas was patched and out of shape, cordage had stretched and much of her tackle was worn through.

"Steer for the shore then," Cranston blustered in desperation. "We might make a port further east; Charlestown or Plymouth even."

"Wouldn't do no good, they'll just follow us in. You an' I'd be better off finding ourselves a decent hidey-hole to wait them out."

But now it was Cranston's turn to scoff. "Ain't much chance of that," he snorted. "We's well laden; you'll never find an inch of space below, and the Navy can rummage as well as any revenue man."

"Well we got to do something," Lovemore muttered. The

4

frigate was now under all plain sail and made a stirring sight with the sun shining through her stiff, fresh canvas. Were they taken, serving aboard her would have benefits over many warships; a better chance of prize money for one, and more space below along with the more interesting missions. However Lovemore had become accustomed to the merchant service and was in no rush to return to a man-of-war. Besides, he had first left England over two years before, there were folk on land he wanted to see, a fair sum in wages to be claimed and he had been looking forward to a simple rest. But even as they watched, the warship was creeping closer, white spray now steaming from her bows as she relentlessly closed on their path. And then came the briefest puffs of smoke; a warning shot, no more, and probably just a blank charge. It would be enough though, and all aboard the brig knew the signal foolish and possibly fatal to ignore.

With a brief order from the quarterdeck, the brig turned slightly and began to spill her wind. The frigate luffed up and took station across her bows and a small boat could be seen being lowered from davits at her stern. Cranston and Lovemore watched in silence as their own craft creaked to a halt. The frigate's crew soon had one boat in the water but were making a dog's dinner of launching a second which was being swayed out amidships and seemed to have fouled its tackle. The larger craft swung precariously aloft while those beneath struggled to free the tangle. Neither seaman could say if it were a launch or a barge, nor did they care. For it was roomy; far too roomy for the handful of crew that finally clambered aboard. And when it did begin powering towards them their spirits dropped further, for the rowers were indeed few, and there was more than enough space left to take them all.

* * *

Aboard the frigate, Brotherton, the duty midshipman, watched from a safe distance while his betters discussed the situation.

"A stroke of luck, what?" Captain Wheatstone was standing next to the binnacle and positively beaming; an expression guaranteed to instil grave doubts in the lad, who was relieved to see it directed at the first lieutenant. "A few stout hands will do very nicely and our arrival at Falmouth should not be delayed any."

"Indeed, sir," Lieutenant Leyton beamed obsequiously. "Truly fortunate, truly fortunate."

They were an odd pair, Brotherton decided as he carefully avoided catching either's eye. Wheatstone was almost impossible to age; he might be no more than thirty, although the thick jowls and perpetual red nose made him look considerably older. But, however ancient, his leaner and somewhat prim second in command must top him by a good ten years and it was equally obvious the older, more experienced, yet junior man, was acting as a form of superior nursemaid to the captain.

That being the case, Leyton's ingratiating manner was made more nauseating still for, to everyone apart from the captain, the first lieutenant was stiff and exacting; a fellow not to be trifled with or crossed in any way. It was an attitude that intensified with the declining importance of those addressed until, when reaching the level of one such as Brotherton, it became positively hostile. So to see Leyton fawn in such a way was even more sickening and intensified the midshipman's dislike.

HMS *Tenacious* remained hove to and broadside on to the brig; her guns might not have been manned but none aboard the merchant could ignore the threat such a position conveyed. *Tenacious'* jolly-boat containing Hedges, the senior midshipman, and a detachment of marines was already approaching while her launch, with their master-at-arms and ten stout hands aboard, followed behind. And Brotherton supposed sighting the merchant might be considered fortunate. It was rare for any warship to be fully manned and the few that were must allow for future injuries and illnesses to deplete their stock. However, the midshipman was young and had yet to accept the policy of seizing men expecting a homecoming, then forcing them to fight for their King. Even if the obvious unfairness were overlooked, they would be exchanging better wages and more lenient punishment for a world where danger was positively sought, pay would not be due for at least six months and discipline was harsh and enforced with rope's end, lash or noose. But despite his age, Brotherton was hardly naïve; he came from a naval family, *Tenacious* was not his first ship and much had been learned since leaving home eighteen months before. Given time he might put the needs of the service above concerns for his fellow man although that was by no means certain. He glanced at his captain, currently watching as the merchant was boarded and actually licking his lips in anticipation. One day he might even evolve into a character similar to Wheatstone although deep inside the lad hoped not.

* * *

"I have need of men for the King's service," Midshipman Hedges announced after hauling himself, unaided, aboard the *Merriweather*.

Styles, the merchant's master, had stepped forward to meet him but did not offer his hand. "We're homeward bound," he said, "and have been abroad these two years and more." His tone was soft and without expectation but some objection must be raised before the injustice continued.

"And you will find little has changed in the time," the midshipman replied with a callous smile. The master regarded him with mild interest; such a rank was usually the preserve of young men, yet the officer before him must be well into his thirties. "You will assemble your hands and I shall make my selection," Hedges continued.

"We're bound for the Pool, I have to see my ship there safely," Styles countered, again with little hope.

"You have wind enough for any number of British ports before and might find fresh hands," the midshipman sniffed. "Now do not delay me longer, and if I consider you to be selling short I shall see your craft stripped of her cargo and soundly searched."

* * *

Within minutes the frigate's launch had been secured alongside and her crew were joining the trim rank of marines already standing in line along the merchant's bulwarks. Their crisp uniforms of red and white were picked out by the early morning sun, making the iron faces appear even more imposing, while before them, and far less impressive, huddled a cluster of downcast seamen.

"Skipper didn't put up much of a fight," Cranston grumbled to Lovemore from the middle of the group.

"What did you expect?" his mate sniffed. "Nothing he could say and nothing he could do against that." He nodded to where the frigate still lay, dormant but threatening, across their bows.

"I've chosen the best seven," Hedges announced to Guppy, a master-at-arms. "Take the marines and see them back to the ship. I shall follow shortly though first must speak with the captain. You have the men's records I assume?" he added, turning to Styles.

Guppy, a bullet-headed man with a prominent jaw, made for the group standing in the merchant's waist and treated them to a broad, toothless grin.

"Alright my merry lads, get yourselves in line." He was as smartly dressed as the midshipman though in a far more functional uniform; but no amount of decoration or gold lace would have hidden a bully of the first order. His black eyes alighted on the nearest hand, an ill-shaven Irishman with mottled, pockmarked skin and a tangle of red hair. "You first, Ginger."

"Name's O'Grady," the seaman replied flatly. "And I'm no friend of your King."

"And I doubt he cares much for you neither," the master-at-arms told him, drawing close and speaking directly into the man's face. "But you'll serve him nevertheless and in any way I choose. So, can you hand reef and steer?"

"Well enough." The seaman was vain enough not to deny it. "Though I'll never make a reliable hand," he added as Guppy made a note on a small block of paper. "You'll never know where you are with me, nor what I might be doing behind yer back!"

"Is that right?" the warrant officer asked, apparently impressed.

"True as I'm standing 'ere," the Irishman proclaimed with a sideways smile to his mates. Guppy appeared to accept this and even went to move on, so when he turned suddenly and delivered a hefty slap across O'Grady's mouth with the back of his hand, all were as surprised as the Irishman.

"And you'll never know what I'm doing behind yours," Guppy confirmed with a sneer.

"Is there a problem, Mr Guppy?" the midshipman asked from further aft.

"Not any more, Mr Hedges."

There was a brief muttering from the crowd that instantly stopped as Guppy's attention returned.

"So," he began, "you may as well form a line and there'd better be no more trouble."

And after the brief demonstration of power, the rest went meekly enough. Even Lovemore, whose anger and disappointment remained as strong, found himself dutifully clambering over the brig's top rail amid a line of equally despondent shipmates. But before he dropped into the launch below, he paused. On the far horizon was a faint line of grey, the barest hint of his home country.

"First and last taste of home we'll be getting," Cranston, muttered, following his glance.

"Don't you believe it, lads," a member of the launch's crew told them, not unkindly. "We're bound for Falmouth; you'll be home in no time and probably sick of the sight of it afore long."

"'Cause a sight is all yer gonna get," another confirmed through yellowed teeth. "There won't be no shore leave, not with the pile we got for officers."

Lovemore said nothing but settled himself on a thwart and looked across at his new home. The frigate was smart enough and well set up with taut lines and what looked like a fresh suit of sails. Her paintwork glimmered in the early sunlight, the jet black of her hull broken only by a strip of bright ochre that picked out her gun ports and gave the impression of both speed and power. He had served aboard similar in the past and preferred the type to any other fighting sail but, with England barely over the horizon, a fresh cruise had been the last thing on his mind.

"Aye, we'll be in 'arbour a while yet," the seaman continued as he pushed past and prepared to release them from the *Merriweather*'s side. "Awaiting a convoy, or so they says," he added more confidentially, perching himself on the rubbing strip.

"So what're the officers like?" Lovemore enquired in equally low tones while keeping a weather eye on the master-at-arms who had dealt so efficiently with O'Grady.

"Rum lot," the seaman replied, then spat into the water. "Captain's no seaman and too fond of the cat, but it's his monkey you wants to keep clear of."

"You mean yon jaunty?" Lovemore enquired, nodding towards Guppy.

"Na, that's jus' a regular bastard," the seaman corrected. "I'm talking about the first lieutenant; he's sommat special."

* * *

It was a sentiment Midshipman Brotherton would have been in total agreement with, although little about serving aboard *Tenacious* pleased him and he was starting to doubt anything would. When given the chance to join a frigate he had jumped at it, especially after spending so long aboard a liner that showed remarkable reluctance to put to sea. For frigates were the most active of rated ships and, at a time when fleet actions seemed strangely out of favour, still regularly met their enemy counterparts in combat, usually emerging victorious and often with a pot of prize money for their trouble. And *Tenacious* was a well-found example; freshly set up, fully manned, and rumoured to be departing on a particularly active commission. But his short spell aboard had already revealed one major flaw; though soundly built and well provisioned, she was badly officered and, as a result, had a sullen and surly crew.

Such defects might be addressed and corrected by a capable commander; someone who would inspire his officers and consequently the men. Someone to set an example, a standard they might follow and so forge the vessel into an efficient fighting machine. But it was obvious even to the youngster that Wheatstone was no such man, and neither was his first lieutenant. And if two senior commissioned officers were unable to address the problem, no slip of a midshipman would have a hope.

Though ostensibly a stickler for discipline, Captain Wheatstone actually took little interest in the people and gave others too much discretion in their care. In addition to the cat which had appeared nine times in five days, starters and rattan whips were used with sickening regularity while there were other, more subtle, punishments that Brotherton was equally aware of. Such a demonstration of force might be necessary when breaking in a crew of raw recruits, but *Tenacious'* lower deck contained a large proportion of experienced hands who would have responded well to a leader they could trust. And however much Brotherton told himself he lacked the experience to judge, it seemed an important asset was being wasted.

Of course, Wheatstone was not the only captain to manage his ship so, and neither could he be considered unique in depending heavily on his first lieutenant. In the past, both arrangements would have been considered normal but attitudes and practices had changed significantly of late, something that Brotherton was well aware of, despite his tender years.

For the midshipman was quite an expert on the Royal Navy. His earliest memories were of a household run by bells and whistles and staffed by former seamen; even their butler had once been a coxswain. He was the fourth Brotherton to go to sea; his father had recently been made rear admiral and, though he tried to keep his parentage secret, being part of such a dynasty had given him useful insight.

With its recent increase in size and successes, the Royal Navy had risen significantly in the public's estimation and a new manner of command was emerging. The life remained hard and probably always would be, although greater understanding was now common between officers and men. Only recently certain long-established punishments had been discontinued and, though the discipline could never be considered lenient, there was more consideration in its application. But not with Captain Wheatstone and Lieutenant Leyton, Brotherton silently conceded; with that pair in charge, they were still sailing in the previous century.

* * *

The impression of a well-served ship stayed with the pressed seamen as they were decanted from the launch. The *Merriweather* had been at sea so long there was hardly a fresh piece of line aboard her, while every thread of canvas had worn through to almost nothing. In contrast, the frigate's cordage appeared new and every metal fitting positively gleamed although a ship can be judged by her boats and he recalled the mess made when this particular example launched hers. That, and what he had already heard of her officers, had sown the seeds of doubt; trim and slick she may appear, but he was yet to be impressed by his new home.

But there was no time to consider further; almost as soon as the last had been brought aboard they were led below to be met by the cheery faces and ribald comments of their new shipmates. The old guard encircled the newcomers, staring at them as if they were strange, exotic animals and adding the occasional prod to gauge their quality. Chances were strong a good proportion had been pressed themselves, either for that ship or another in the past, yet no sympathy was shown for their fate, but rather a wicked glee that others had been caught in the same net.

"Alright, stand aside there," Guppy ordered, breaking into the pack and restoring a degree of order. "Get into line an' I'll allocate messes." Lovemore glanced uncertainly at Cranston; both had served in warships and knew the routine. Matters such as enlistment, mess allocation and kit distribution usually fell to the first lieutenant – the man he had been warned about and was strangely eager to meet. Yet,

11

since coming on board – indeed from the time their own ship was seized – they had not seen anyone more senior than a midshipman or the master-at-arms. And the latter seemed to be in charge now, or at least thought himself so.

Guppy had seated himself behind a desk and, with all the authority of an entire rating committee, was beckoning the first man forward to sign or mark the muster book.

"You next; make a smudge, Curley," the man demanded when it was Lovemore's turn, emphasising the point with a nailless finger dabbed on the ledger between them.

The seaman stepped forward, collected the pen and examined it carefully before making a clear and practised signature on the yellowed page.

"What kind of a name is that then?" the man asked after staring at the ledger.

"The one I were given," Lovemore replied coldly, "Mr *Guppy*."

The words echoed about the berth deck causing a measure of laughter from the waiting men. But the master-at-arms was not amused.

"Mess with me, matie, and you'll regret it," he said, raising his eyes and the seaman immediately looked away. Whatever the rights of the matter, Guppy was correct; a warrant officer could ruin the life of any ordinary hand without even trying. And if what Lovemore had learned about the ship's senior men was true, he would be well supported.

A moan broke the silence and all eyes turned towards O'Grady. The Irishman's nose had started to bleed again and a thin trickle of blood was running onto his shirt.

"You, Irish; get yourself over here!" Guppy demanded, and the seaman lurched across. It took less than a second for a smudge to be made on the page, then Guppy regarded the two men afresh.

"Wainwright!" he called, without looking around. A stocky seaman appeared from nowhere. "Your mess is several light as I recall?"

"Yes, Mr Guppy."

"Well take these an' see this one's cleaned up – fellow seems to have had some sort of accident."

"Mind if I goes an all?" Cranston, the next in line, asked. "Lovemore an' I is tie mates."

"Are you now?" Guppy remarked as Cranston scratched at the

paper. "Well there'll be none of that aboard *Tenacious*; this is a King's ship an' proud of it."

"He said we're mates, nothing more," Lovemore stated firmly.

"I only has your word for that," Guppy snorted. "An' I for one ain't takin' no chances." He cast a cynical look at Cranston. "You can go with Robson's lot, they berth for'ard an' are a different watch."

Cranston shrugged and followed an older seaman while Lovemore and O'Grady made their way aft with their new mess captain.

Guppy watched them go with a measure of satisfaction. "An' if I ever catches the two of you together, you'll be sorry," he added.

Chapter Two

In the two hours Tom King had been walking, the weather had changed considerably. What started as a gentle spring afternoon was now all but forgotten, dull metallic skies had replaced the light sunshine while a crisp offshore breeze cut through the April air like a razor. From his perspective on Beachy Head's summit, he stared out at the grey sea beyond and beneath. The cliff's height made him feel both alive and delightfully vulnerable. There was more than fifteen feet between him and the edge, and it would take a strong wind indeed to carry him over, yet still he knew himself recklessly close. However, a lifetime at sea had taught him much about the weather's fickle ways, while more recently he had learned of constant rockfalls in the area, yet it was with a measure of reluctance that he took a step or two back before continuing to inspect his natural element.

For that is what the sea had become and his current dependence on land, one that included a family, house and fine estate, only highlighted the fact. Since opting for a life afloat nearly twenty years before, so much of his time had been spent under the sea's capricious power that the brief pauses ashore stood out like grit in cheap flour. And mostly these had been forced upon him, mainly through a lack of employment, pressing personal matters or, on more than one occasion, being in the hands of his enemies. However this current spell had been different, far longer and totally of his own volition.

The wind continued to blow although it bothered him little. King's watchcoat was old and more than a little battered yet it had become a favourite for all but the most formal of occasions. He knew without her saying a word that Aimée disapproved of the thing and indeed the patched cloth and resewn seams were hardly fitting for a man of his financial and social status. It had also seemed pointlessly heavy when he left the house but now was coming into its own and kept him tolerably warm, as it had through countless hours spent on deck in the past. The watchcoat was also one of his last links with the Royal Navy. He still had one full-dress uniform and two frock tunics which had not been worn since they moved to Sussex and were unlikely to ever see the light of day again. They hung in his dressing room surrounded by any number of fine suits ordered though never taken to, along with various pairs of shoes and boots that owed more to fashion than practicality. Apart from the tunics, two hats, a sword and several tattered books on navigation, he was a fully fledged landsman, although there remained yet one more link to the past that was not so easily dismissed.

King's left sleeve was empty, his arm having been removed after injury and the complications of infection. Several years had passed since and, if not fully accepting of the wound, he had at least become accustomed to it. That he had been a lieutenant when injured meant his naval career could continue and progress through the intermittent stage of commander to post captain with relative ease. Within service circles such an injury was relatively common; similar had been suffered by many far more illustrious than him, and so could almost be seen as honourable. Civilians viewed it differently, however, and, despite Aimée's assurances, King sensed several of the bland and shallow faces that dominated their current social circle privately regarded him as a cripple.

The black dog who always accompanied him on such walks had set up a group of seagulls and was now barking joyfully at their angry departure. Her name was Beth and, even though King rarely used it, that did not mean they lacked fellowship. The Labrador's company was as essential to King's walks as any old coat or occasional glimpses of the sea and they had come to understand each other well. He gave a shrill whistle and the animal instantly bounded away in search of further sport. From her, King's eyes returned to the distant water and this time saw something worthy of note.

It was a small ship-rigged vessel and how he had missed her before was a mystery. Currently she lay a good six miles off and to the south-west, beating towards him on the larboard tack – clawing for the chalk cliffs on a course that would have been dangerous had her wind been elsewhere. He watched, entranced, while old instincts quietly awoke. She was also carrying more canvas than was wise; clearly whoever commanded her was desperate for the security of land – that or a quick death against its rocks.

He contemplated the sight a second longer, then lifted his eyes and took in the dim shape a little way beyond. This was a schooner, a large one, and seemingly with similar intentions. She, too, was under heavy sail although carried more spars than was usual in a craft of her type. This clue was enough to capture him totally and, without conscious thought, King took a step closer to the cliff edge.

A glass might have been of use although he found the things hard to manage and besides, the sight of a former naval officer carrying a telescope with him on a walk was mildly pathetic. Yet even with unpractised eyes he found himself discovering more about both vessels. His attention returned to the nearest, which he now realised was a packet; the lines were becoming more discernible as she raced towards him, the distinctive Post Office pennant blowing stiffly in the breeze. Less than seventy feet in length and rigged for speed – even close-hauled the craft made good progress and was a stirring sight on such a dull afternoon.

King guessed she would have been on the short passage from her home base in Falmouth to Dover, another Post Office station, after which there was no telling her final destination. His mind ran on; packet vessels were usually well-found and popular berths for officers seeking a more regular life than the Royal Navy offered. Their hands were also better provided for; in addition to generous and regular pay, they benefitted from reasonable living conditions and protection from impressment. There was, however, one major downside to service in such craft.

Their role was to deliver mail and important passengers anywhere the union flag flew and in doing so they undoubtedly helped maintain Britain's grip on the current war. But to be truly efficient they must sail at speed and in all weathers, with no waiting for favourable winds or storms to clear. The current conditions were not so bad yet still King sensed this particular craft had difficulties far beyond the heavy breeze.

The larger vessels, those making the regular run to South America or New South Wales, carried specially designed brass nine-pounders known as Post Office guns, but even they relied more on outrunning anything they could not match in combat. And the vessel before him was well under two hundred tons; the most she could be expected to mount was a broadside of four or maybe six light long guns. Enough to deter something the size of a large rowing boat perhaps, but not the enemy currently on her tail.

King turned to the second vessel; it was still little more than a dim shape a mile or two beyond but even in that short time his senses had sharpened. The schooner was more heavily built, would be better armed and was undoubtedly a privateer.

Quite what had persuaded her commander to seek prey so

close to his enemy's shore King could not guess, although the act was by no means rare. And really it meant little that the British ship was in home waters; she might be in sight of land and could probably spot the various batteries strung out along the shoreline but, at such a range, they were of little use. With no other shipping in sight, it should be a relatively easy matter for the Frenchman to pluck her from under the very noses of his enemy. Even as he watched, two small puffs of smoke erupted from the schooner's bows, the opening shots in what would be a short encounter that King feared could only end one way.

He glanced about, suddenly desperate to share the event, but apart from the dog, currently investigating a rabbit warren, the cliff tops were empty, while the sea still only held the single dismal sight that soon drew his attention once more. In a career that had held its fair share of success, King had also known the bitterness of defeat and, watching silently, could guess at the British captain's despair. The packet still lay a good way beyond the range of any battery while the Frenchman crept ever closer and, even he watched, despatched two more shots from her bow chasers.

From such a distance there was no telling how well the privateer's guns were laid but being under fire at all must weigh heavily on the packet's crew. Were he in the British commander's position, King supposed he might try to rally his men; with little chance of gaining sanctuary there was still one card left to play: even so light a vessel might yet luff up and face her enemy. A broadside of light shot might not make much of an impression on the hull of such a beast, while the likelihood of scoring an important hit on the schooner's top hamper was slight indeed. But the chance must surely be taken and preferable to running for a refuge that would always be out of reach. And then, as if he had transmitted the thought, the packet's captain did react.

With a savage lurch to starboard that sent her hull rolling and every piece of canvas fluttering in disarray, the packet turned sidelong on its pursuer and lay wallowing for a moment in the choppy waters. Still straining to catch the exact details, King was transfixed. There was no discernible change in the schooner's sail pattern, yet he was sure the Frenchman had baulked slightly when faced with even token resistance and, for a moment, King wondered if she too would turn beam on. A broadside from what was likely to be far heavier pieces must tell for the packet, but there was also the risk she would be disabled. Despite the apparent isolation, there must be others aware of the situation and warships within semaphore range on hand to deal with the intruder. Alone and unencumbered she could depart in safety, for few could match her on such a stiff breeze, but even so sleek a vessel must be caught were she attempting to tow a prize.

The British captain was not intending to rush his shots, which was wise as his vessel was still recovering from her turn. Some attempt was even made to stabilise the rolling hull with the wayward canvas, while every second the oncoming Frenchman was proving a better target. Then, just as King was sure the privateer was due to fire her chasers once more, the packet spoke.

From such a distance the effect seemed impudent; in apparent silence, six small jets of smoke were released, only to be instantly carried away by the wind and it was hard to imagine the iron shot not being treated similarly. There was a sudden uproar as the dog began to bark frantically and the first drops of rain started to fall but King's attention remained fixed on the far-off encounter.

Just as the broadside was due to strike, the privateer released yet another barrage from her forward facing guns and for a moment he could see nothing in the confusion of fire and smoke. Then the Frenchman's jib billowed out and, robbed of the pressure forward, the entire craft luffed up and began to stagger in irons. King could not tell what harm had been caused; with luck, the bowsprit itself had carried away but even setting a fresh sail would take time and the packet was not intending to wait. The smaller vessel must have taken to the wind even as her enemy's damage was reported and already was gathering speed as it headed for what King assumed was the protection of a nearby shore battery.

The dog was continuing to bark and, turning, King saw she was being taunted by a positive flock of seagulls hovering just above her head. He gave another whistle and the animal responded, leaving the birds, and heading gratefully for her master. King turned from the sea, cast his stick forward, and began to stride along the cliff edge, his dog gambolling about him as the rain steadily increased. Already there was a reasonable distance between the packet and privateer, the latter had started to recover but was plainly injured and could be of no more danger to the British ship. If the French captain had any sense he would beat a retreat before serious warships were summoned. King grunted in satisfaction, it could hardly be called a victory yet watching the avoidance of defeat had been stimulating in itself, and the feeling stayed with him as he strode along the path that led to his home and a totally different world.

* * *

Cranston would have much rather joined Lovemore's mess. The pair had been tie mates for several years despite his friend having gone through a series of odd obsessions. When they first met, Lovemore had been a brilliant musician, playing the flute with a rare skill. But his ability and interest in music disappeared almost overnight to be replaced with a religious fever that came close to alienating the couple. One long voyage to New South Wales had ended that particular fixation although it was almost immediately replaced with another; crochet. For a while every member of their mess had been equipped with a variety of gloves, scarves and other assorted woollen goods before that also mercifully ceased. However Lovemore had always been a seaman – not the most skilled, perhaps, but a solid shipmate who had never let him down and being separated was proving far more painful than he had expected.

And not only did he miss him, and O'Grady, but their mess seemed far jollier than the dull lot he had been lumbered with. Most of his new companions were experienced hands with only one, a youngster by the name of Longdon, being a first voyager. The rest obviously knew their craft and Robson, the mess captain, was a boatswain's mate. Quite why the man was sharing with common hands was a mystery, it being far more usual for petty officers to mess together. But during their first evening, when supper had been eaten and all were waiting for the time when they could sling their hammocks, he learned more.

The ship had made harbour in good time and picked up a favourable anchorage. Divisional watches were yet to be officially abandoned although Cranston could still look forward to at least four hours' sleep that should be uninterrupted. But his fellows seemed in no rush to bed down and rather more interested in interrogating their new member.

"So you've been aboard a man-of-war before?" Robson asked as he chewed, open mouthed, on a piece of cheese.

"I've sailed in a few," Cranston agreed warily.

"What about frigates?" Houghton asked in a strong Yorkshire accent. He was one of many aboard that hailed from the north but lacked the warmth Cranston had come to associate with such folk.

"Frigates, liners, sloops," Cranston admitted.

"So why were you aboard a merchant?" Robson again.

"Been in too many scrapes and had my fill of fighting."

"Then you seen action?" the senior man clarified and Cranston considered him.

"You could say. I also spent a goodly time in the hands of the French."

"Captured?" Houghton grunted.

"That's the usual way," Cranston agreed.

"When were that then?" the mess captain asked.

"Few years back, at the start of the present war."

"Then you must have escaped," Robson persisted. "Boney an' his lot gave up exchanging 'bout then."

There were five other men around the mess table though they seemed content to let two do the talking.

"I got out with another hand and a bunch of officers," Cranston informed them. "Captain Banks, as he were then, and a lieutenant named King, though he's a captain now an all, I hears."

"I know of 'em," Robson admitted with what might have been respect. "It were quite a show by all accounts."

"'Appen," Cranston agreed dryly; he had already noticed how the north country expression was approved of by the others. "Lovemore were with me an' all, it was him I came aboard with."

"Oh aye?" Robson grunted, "I were going to ask about the two of you. What Guppy says, true is it?"

"True? You mean about him and me being more'n mates?" The mess captain gave a silent nod and Cranston sighed. "No, it ain't true."

"Said so," another who had yet to speak piped up in triumph. "Said it were just old Guppy sounding off."

"Aye, an' ah said it didn't matter either way," Houghton agreed. "But a new fellow comes into yer being, you need to know where you stands."

"Well you know now," Cranston told them sharply. "So what's the deal with Guppy?"

"Guppy's the jaunty – the master-at-arms," Robson clarified. "An' about as bad as them kind usually is."

"'Cept he got a lot of support," another added.

"I hears the captain's a tartar," Cranston remarked, his voice suitably low.

"Him an' the first luff," another, from the foot of the table, agreed. "Neither of 'em are happy 'less the cat's good and wet."

"An' they don't care nothing for us an' our scrag," yet another agreed.

"Must admit, I tasted better," Cranston sniffed. The beef had been well past its best and almost cold, while the peas were as hard as bullets. But what he had disliked most about the meal was having to eat in near silence. This was not due to a rule of the ship; other messes had been far more vocal and there was even a measure of laughter from some. But when he started to make conversation all he got were stern looks and grunts.

"It'll be Peter Warren after today," Robson allowed, "an' 'opefully a deal better than that they gave out at Sheerness."

"Fresh ain't all it's cracked up to be," another mused from further down. "I'd rather good salt horse than anything wi' blood in it."

"What we've been given of late weren't even that," a new voice added. "But at least we can vittle up proper now we're at Falmouth."

"So, the scrag's bilge an' the captain's a bastard," Cranston summarised conversationally, "anything good about this berth?"

"Some of the officers ain't so bad," a fair-haired man suggested.

"I'd like to know who," his neighbour retorted. The man sported a dramatic scar on one cheek that seemed to glow in the flickering lantern light.

"There's only one lieutenant at present," Robson stated, taking control once more. "We're still waiting for a couple more but some of the middies are older."

"I noticed one. It were him what boarded my ship."

"That would be Hedges; forty if he's a day," Scarface agreed, "and still in the cockpit."

"Likely to remain there an' all, number of boards he's been up against."

"Sounds like you got a right bunch," Cranston grunted. Being pressed so close to home had hardly been welcome. There were things he had wanted to do ashore, people to meet and coin to spend. But if it had to happen, if he must serve aboard a man-of-war again, why did it have to be a ship officered by tyrants and in a mess filled with grouchers?

"You ask me, the whole damn lot of 'em aren't worth a light," Robson declared. "An' I should know, I've served with the best."

"Aye," Houghton agreed with a measure of reverence. "Robson here were alongside Nelson hisself."

The mess captain nodded complacently while the others looked on with respect.

"Well that were fine for you both," Cranston supposed.

"His honour looked after his men," Robson told him harshly.

"Plenty do that," the new man retorted. "You may've been unlucky for all I know but Nelson weren't the only one with a thought for the lower deck. An' there are a good few what does so today."

"I'll not hear a word spoke against 'is Immortal Memory," Robson told him with a heavy sentimentality that contained more than a hint of menace.

"An' you'll not hear one from me," Cranston agreed. "But like I say, he weren't the only good apple in the barrel."

From further aft, some of the men were beginning to sing but there was no sign of merriment or even a lightening in the atmosphere amongst his new messmates.

"You don't respect Nelson, you're not going to be happy here," Houghton told him coolly.

"I told you, I've nothing against the cove," Cranston sighed. Amid the voices aft he could detect O'Grady's penetrating, yet out of tune, tenor; the others seemed to be having a high old time, it was just a pity he'd been lumped in with a bunch of Moaning Marys.

* * *

"Mister Croft 'as called to see you," Aimée announced, meeting him in the boot room as he was unbuttoning his sodden coat.

"Croft?" King repeated in surprise.

"Yes, he 'as been here some while," she confirmed. The dog was drinking noisily from her bowl and King's ears, never the most sensitive, had to strain to pick out Aimée's words. "I did not know what I should do with 'im."

"But you made sure he was comfortable?" King checked, boot in hand.

"Of course I did, Thomas," Aimée exclaimed, her mild accent rising to the fore. "Do you think I am totally the barbarian? I have placed 'im in the morning room, but he would not be given tea."

22

King eased off his second boot, flung the pair in the corner and tossed his coat and hat on top. His body servant would deal with them, in fact the man should have been there to meet and help him although he barely noticed the omission in his excitement. King had not seen Croft in almost a year; last heard of, his former first lieutenant had opted for the Impress Service but, wherever he had come from, the contact with his old life was welcome.

"Have you given him tea?" he asked. Aimée shook her head and sighed.

"I told you, Thomas, he would not take any. And you have been away for so long, I did not know what to say."

"You could have sent for me," King countered, fighting to keep frustration from his voice.

"How, when I did not know where you had gone? I never know," she added with a hint of reproach. "You go off for so long a time and only say where when you return. Sometimes it feels as if I have a husband who is at sea as much as home."

King paused with his hand on the boot room door. "Aimée, I'm sorry. I needed a walk and to get some fresh air."

"It does not matter," she replied, her eyes falling slightly, "and I am sad the air in this 'ouse is not to your liking."

"I mean it, I'm sorry," he insisted. "And we will talk about this later, first I must go and see Croft."

"Yes of course," she agreed, adding, "first you must speak to your friend."

But he had already left.

* * *

The morning room was where they took breakfast so was usually lit by an early sun. It had been brightly furnished to Aimée's specifications with a light teak dining table, two pine dressers and a beige silk rug. But in the current weather, and with dusk close by, it seemed gloomy and the uniformed figure that sat on one of the hard, upright dining chairs, especially so. However, Lieutenant Croft rose as soon as King entered and did appear genuinely pleased, the expression on his weathered face coming dangerously close to a smile.

"Good to see you, James, I'm only sorry to have kept you waiting," King exclaimed, extending his hand as he crossed the floor.

23

"It was no inconvenience, sir," the older man replied softly. "Mrs King has entertained me well and I was glad for the chance of rest."

"But what brings you here?" King enquired, motioning his guest to sit once more, and taking a seat himself.

"I happened to be in the area, or nearby at least," Croft explained. "Visiting a former shipmate and chanced you would not object to a caller."

"You are always a welcome guest," King replied with transparent honesty. Croft had lost none of his dour countenance although his face was slightly softer – which was probably due to the lack of salt air, King supposed.

"Thank you, sir, but I did not wish to presume."

"Again I say, I am sorry not to have been present; can I send for some refreshment?"

"I would not put you to trouble."

"Nonsense," King said, rising and reaching for the servant pull. "We can take tea and perhaps a slice of cake, and then you will stay for supper. Why, I can have a room made up for you as well if that would serve. You are at Deptford, as I recall?"

"That is correct, I have rooms there."

"And not taken a house?" King questioned. A lieutenant's share of prize money was considerably less than that of a captain, yet still he should have received a reasonable return from their previous commission.

"I have no need of one," Croft replied and King nodded in understanding. "I must however return," the older man continued, "though a spot of tea would be welcome." He reached for his watch and flipped it open. "The evening post leaves The Bull at six and it is a fair step."

"Then I will see you taken in good time so we may have chance to talk," King announced while noting the rain was now beating against the windows. "And you will not get quite so wet."

The door opened and a young girl entered.

"Bring tea, Sarah," King directed, "and see if Mrs King will join us."

The girl bobbed once before leaving in silence and King's attention returned to his guest. The man was several years his senior in age but appeared far older, even though he still sat ramrod straight and several inches from the chair's back.

"So what news?" King asked. "You opted for the Impress Service, or so I remember."

"I did," Croft agreed, a little awkwardly, "though have to say it did not suit. Finding hands for the Navy is worthy enough but did not suit my temperament."

"You surprise me," King mused. "As I recall you were always the master when it came to managing hands."

"I may have been once," the older man agreed, "and perhaps it is different aboard ship. Those that came my way were no more willing, but at sea there is little else to do except obey. On land, matters can be different and there were too many lawyers to deal with for my liking."

"I can imagine," King acknowledged. "But you are still in uniform, so ready for a posting perhaps?"

"I am and have been for some while."

"Would that I could help you, but my name carries little weight with the Admiralty and I have no plan for serving again myself."

"That is not why I am here," Croft assured him hurriedly. "There is news of Cooper and I wanted to be sure you were aware of it."

King's expression changed to one of concern. "He is well I trust?"

"Well and a free man once more," Croft confirmed.

"Why that is excellent! Though I had heard him in Verdun."

"No longer – free and safe in England; I received this from him not five days past." Croft reached into his tunic pocket and produced a small sheet of tightly folded paper which he handed across.

"A bold escape," King muttered after spreading it awkwardly on the table. "I trust he did not break his parole."

"It would appear not," Croft replied, taking the paper back. "There was an account in the *Naval Chronicle*; it seems he and several others were being transferred to another prison. They were escorted by a series of guards who saw them through each sector; one of the officers neglected to ask for their word of honour, and Cooper's party took full advantage."

"Strangely lax," King grunted, although he had travelled a fair distance himself when a prisoner of the French and could understand how such a thing might occur.

"Seven made their escape in all and only three were recaptured; the rest are all now in England."

"And those caught?"

Croft closed his eyes. "A spell in Bitche is about the best that can be hoped for."

"Still, good to hear that Cooper is home," King added quickly. "I must confess to not keeping up with matters of late."

"Do you not read the *Chronicle*, sir?" Croft asked.

"I subscribe of course," King admitted, "but am several months behind."

"I hope to visit Cooper next week," the older man continued. "He is in Essex and, I assume, still without employment."

"A good officer, and young," King mused. "I should chance he shall find a berth with ease."

As soon as he spoke the words King realised his blunder; James Croft was an equally fine lieutenant but possibly twice Cooper's age and also without employment; for him the road to a posting would be far narrower. Fortunately at that moment the door opened admitting the young servant with a tray.

"Will Mrs King be joining us, Sarah?" King asked as the girl set her load down and began to sort its contents.

"She hopes to later, sir," she replied, "but says you'll want to talk about ships and things first and such things bore her. Will you take tea, sir, or chocolate like the captain?"

Croft agreed to tea, then refused milk, sugar and all offers of cake. Sarah passed across the frail bone china cup and saucer which he accepted with a clumsy, gnarled hand.

"He says he has tried for a posting," the older man continued when the girl had left, and placed the crockery on the table where King guessed it would remain. "As have I, but the past season has been a healthy one and such opportunities are few."

King guessed the man's meaning; a lack of fleet actions and less combat of any kind had combined with improvements in medical care to create a Royal Navy that was surprisingly healthy. The only obvious chance for employment lay with new vessels or replacing an officer promoted or due to retire.

"But you do wish to return to sea?" King checked. When the pair first met he had regarded Croft as nearing the end of his career; the man had been efficient but lacked vigour and was very obviously marking time. The change fresh opportunities and a potent new ship

26

brought was amazing and apparently established, for he answered promptly and with feeling.

"I do so, sir, and the sooner the better."

"As an executive officer?" King continued feeling mildly guilty. There was little reason for his questioning; he knew of no position for Croft and neither did he intend to return to sea himself. The enquiry was taken seriously though and, more than that, his guest appeared to be reading unintended implications.

"I would welcome the chance, sir," he continued eagerly. "And aboard any vessel you had in mind. Even a spell as a more junior man would not be disagreeable."

"Oh, I have nothing to offer you, James," King told him quickly. The look of disappointment was enough to melt the hardest heart and his guilt grew. "Though I might enquire," he added. "There may be those with positions likely to become vacant who would value a reliable man."

"I would appreciate it indeed," Croft replied only a little deflated, "as I am sure would Mr Cooper."

"I will think on it," King promised. It was good of Croft to remember Cooper, especially when the younger man was by far the more employable of the two. "And who knows, someone might be glad of both your services; you worked well together, it would be a shame to break up such an excellent team."

"Forgive me, sir, but I think it was the three of us," Croft said, colouring mildly at his presumption. "I have never served under a captain as sound as yourself and doubt I ever will."

"Kind of you to say so, James," King replied. "It was indeed a favourable combination."

* * *

The thought played about King's mind after Croft left for Eastbourne and returned in force when he and Aimée were safely in their bed. His earlier exercise combined with the excitement of meeting up with a former shipmate sent him straight to sleep, but later, in the quiet hours of early morning, he snapped awake.

There was nothing strange in this; even after so long ashore sleeping all night – indeed, sleeping in a static bed, in relative silence and beside a warm body – remained a novelty and probably always would. Yet this time his brain was in turmoil and it was all he could

27

do to stay between the sheets and not get up for more exercise.

Which was out of the question, of course; what was permissible and almost expected aboard ship simply would not do on land. And he was undoubtedly a landsman now, with a landsman's responsibilities, and besides, Aimée would only wake and worry. But though he may feel pressed into a mould, he could have few regrets; there must be officers aplenty who envied his position and would swap in an instant. He might carry a wound, but prize money had also come his way; many of his rank and lower were on the beach and eking out a sorry existence on half pay with far greater injuries. As it was, he had this house and its grounds along with two small cottages, several fields and a tavern to provide funds for the rest of their days. And were that to fail there remained a considerable sum invested that should maintain them comfortably on the interest alone. And then, of course, he had Aimée.

He recalled the fact with a tinge of guilt as she moved gently in her sleep; how typical of him to remember her after assessing his financial assets. Despite all appearances, Aimée was not his legal wife; it would have taken a good deal of influence and far more money than even King possessed to arrange such a thing. Yet the pair were as devoted as it was possible to be, and he regarded her as his greatest piece of fortune. Tolerant and forgiving yet with spark enough to keep their relationship fresh, she had also provided them with a child, a boy currently sleeping peacefully in the next room, and was quietly confident another would be joining them shortly. King had never actively yearned for a family but with Aimée such a thing seemed natural and was in no way against his wishes. Young Robert was still in dresses and yet to reach the stage when they might dig ponds together or build shelters in the woods, although the time could not be long in coming. And if a secure life on land with a chance to watch his family grow also depended upon wearing uncomfortable clothes, making small talk with neighbours and countless other mundane activities he was blatantly unsuited to, he supposed it a price worth paying.

Beside him Aimée moved again; her breaths had been regular and deep but now they lightened slightly. King tensed, hoping she were awake while also dreading she might be, then he took the plunge.

"Aimée?" he asked in a voice soft enough to be ignored. There was no response, the breathing remained as constant although King now knew she was conscious. "Aimée, I have to tell you something."

She stirred slightly then was still.

"I want to go to London." He paused for a reaction and, finding none, continued. "I want to call on the Admiralty and see if I might find a command." There was still no response but now the thoughts had taken control and he had found his flow. "It may be foolish; I am sure there will be nothing for me. And it could be that a one-armed captain would be of little interest to the current board. But I feel I must ask, for if I do not, I know I shall regret it always."

The silence was almost comment enough and for a moment he hoped she had not heard and was still asleep. Yet equally he felt compelled to continue.

"You must understand, this is not against you. I am sure I shall return and can then know myself a land animal for ever more. But if there were the chance of going back to sea, I simply must take it."

Aimée turned slightly and then he felt a hand rest gently upon his arm.

"There was no need to say anything, Thomas." Her voice was soft – barely a whisper in fact –and continued more quietly still. "I already knew."

Chapter Three

"We raised Falmouth in good time," Wheatstone announced to Leyton in the privacy of the great cabin, "despite our little diversion. And are actually over complement, a rare state indeed! With a sound ship and the prospect of a ripe voyage ahead, I think it occasion enough for a celebratory dinner."

Tenacious had anchored as dusk was starting to fall and, now bright spring sunshine was heralding a new day, her captain seemed in an unusually jovial mood.

"I think that would be very apt, sir," Leyton replied cordially.

"We had better hold it in the evening though," Wheatstone continued. "I am due to call at the port admiral's office at ten and hope to return forthwith but it would be better not to rush things, what?"

The captain's dinners were legendary and not entirely to Lieutenant Leyton's liking. He was never one for heavy red meat, particularly when served almost raw as Wheatstone insisted. Even the wine, which was usually excellent, could hardly be enjoyed as a clear head was essential when dealing with a man like Captain Wheatstone. But starting late was a good point as it meant this particular dinner could not go on as long as some. Indeed, it must surely be over by midnight; those that began at three, the customary hour for dining, were usually just as well provided for and often ended no earlier.

"Very good, sir," Leyton agreed. "I also will be ashore."

"Is that so?" Wheatstone enquired with a noticeable lack of interest.

"I have to call at the victualler's office and upon the dockyard superintendent but shall be sure to alert Mr Sturridge."

"Do that, will you? And I understand the purser is planning a buying spree for the gunroom; you might ask if he can find us some beefsteaks," Wheatstone continued. "Those at Sheerness were well below standard, belike the West Country will provide better."

"I am sure he will be pleased to," the lieutenant assured. "Mr Dennison has a good eye for such things."

"Maybe so but I shall not tolerate any of his bargains," the captain grunted. "Remind him he is buying on my account and I only require the best."

"Very good, sir."

Leyton was several years older than his captain and had a far greater knowledge of the sea and it's ways; something that was relatively easy as Wheatstone's expertise roughly equated to that of a competent midshipman. And by being both better informed and able to convey his knowledge in a sufficiently subtle manner, Leyton had secured himself the position of Wheatstone's permanent first lieutenant. It was an arrangement that had suited both parties over several commissions; Leyton, who had long since given up hope of commanding a ship himself, was prepared to settle for having control through another while Wheatstone lacked both the desire and sensitivity to become a true seaman. His ambitions were far more basic and mostly concerned the many ways a captain might acquire wealth.

And these were numerous indeed; in addition to a generous salary, Wheatstone also benefitted from the largest share of prize and head money, generous commission from any specie he was able to transport and, despite recent changes, a liberal allowance for a positive band of servants that might or might not exist. His current position had been achieved with minimum effort but a good deal of personal pressure from a well-connected family and there was no reason why his career should not continue to prosper under the same support.

There was one downside, however; though Wheatstone could effectively buy popularity with the Admiralty, he was unable to achieve a similar trick with his lower deck. *Tenacious* had barely been in commission a month and had travelled just a few hundred miles yet already the first signs of a discontented crew were starting to make themselves known. It was something Wheatstone remained unaware of and Leyton refused to acknowledge, although there was little either of them could do to ease the situation.

Though competent at many tasks, the first lieutenant knew himself weak when it came to dealing with those on the lower deck. And without some understanding there could be no respect. Consequently he was inclined to delegate all matters concerning the general hands to more junior men and encouraged his captain to do the same. It was a coward's trick of course, but one he was forced to play, and the elderly first officer secretly feared this commission would end like the others, with their ship paying off in time to avoid an outright mutiny.

But if he could not make the people happy, he might at least keep them under control and Leyton was determined to see they were by enforcing the strictest discipline. Such a line was easy to take with even a caring of commander, for rarely did a captain enquire about the misdemeanours of individual men. Some offences brought to him for punishment might merit light investigation, but he was more likely to take his executive officer's recommendation. And by no stretch of the imagination could Wheatstone be called a caring commander, so Leyton had a free hand.

"There is the extra lieutenant joining us as well, sir," he reminded Wheatstone.

"Indeed so; and I shall enquire for a third when with the PA. That fellow Durham was more nuisance than he was worth; I had to let him go, even though it left you short on the journey here."

In fact Wheatstone's instant and totally unfair dismissal of the unfortunate Durham had been more than a minor inconvenience, coming as it had on the very eve of their departure from Sheerness, although Leyton knew better than to comment further.

"We managed well enough, sir," he assured him.

"It is the pity this Taylor could not have arrived sooner," Wheatstone continued. He had been preening himself in a strip of polished metal fixed to the bulkhead and was now reasonably satisfied with the result. "Our journey from the Nore would have been sufficient to gauge his quality and the fellow might have gone the same way should he have failed to impress."

"Mr Taylor comes with excellent references," Leyton soothed. "It is his first commission as a lieutenant though past commanders have praised his qualities highly."

It was a mild enough statement, but one Leyton would not have made had he thought more carefully.

"Past commanders?" Wheatstone asked, turning, his expression instantly changing from agreeable contemplation to one of outright anger.

"I meant he would seem to have given satisfaction aboard previous vessels," Leyton added quickly.

"Did you indeed?" the captain snapped.

This was another of the complications of dealing with a man like Wheatstone, Leyton decided. He could no more manage a ship than he could his temper and both traits were equally as dangerous.

"What is good enough for one may fall far short of my requirements," the captain continued in an increasingly loud voice. "And it will be my standards that this Mr Taylor will have to meet, nothing less. Anyone not able to cut the mustard shall not be tolerated." He paused and gave his first officer a significant look. "Anyone, Leyton; do I make myself clear?"

* * *

Below deck, the atmosphere was slightly more congenial and both Lovemore and O'Grady were reluctantly settling into their new home. The mess captain, a Yorkshireman with a strong accent, seemed a reasonable sort as did the others. All were experienced hands well used to the regime aboard a man-of-war who quickly detected fellow spirits in their new messmates. Of course, both would far rather be heading up Channel aboard the old *Merriweather* but that not being the case, they were adapting to the change with an acceptance common in their breed. Nevertheless, despite being amongst professionals and aboard a ship clearly on the top line in many aspects, both harboured doubts and, later that day when standing in line for a place at the heads, were able to share some.

"There's little wrong with the ship and nowt with her people," Lovemore mused. "Scran could be served a little hotter I suppose but I've known worse, yet something don't feel right."

"Officers ain't nothing to shout about," O'Grady grunted.

"Aye, that's probably it," Lovemore agreed. "A vessel might be sound in all senses but you can't do nothing without a decent bunch aft."

"Chanced upon the skipper yet?" O'Grady asked and Lovemore shook his head. "Nor me, though far as I can tell he's something of a flogger."

"Which would explain much," Lovemore sighed. "If the captain's crank, the rest'll follow – I seen it before and too many times."

Both men were off duty and preparing themselves for a long wait. Only four seats of ease were provided for the entire lower deck and a glance over the partition had revealed all were currently occupied by solid looking fellows who appeared to have taken up

33

residence.

"Our divisional mid. seems straight enough," Lovemore supposed. "But the jaunty's a bastard."

"Guppy?"

"Aye, that's the cull."

"Don't seem very different to most," the Irishman mused.

"Gave you a bloody nose if I remembers," his friend pointed out.

"Sure, but it's the nature of the job," O'Grady grunted. "You wouldn't expect someone in his position to be any different."

"Maybe so, but to suggest there were anything between me an' Cranston..."

"Ah, take no notice," O'Grady soothed. "Your man probably didn't want too many from the same batch appearing in one mess."

"Then what's wrong with sayin' so?"

"Only the one lieutenant, far as I can tell," the Irishman continued, "and he seems all wind and water."

"Can't do much without a strong first luff."

"I hears another's joining shortly."

"That might make a difference," Lovemore supposed. "Though I still says it takes a decent captain to make decent officers, and decent officers to make a decent ship. So far I can't say I'm too impressed."

"Alright lads?"

It was a younger voice, so the owner had no moral right to address them so, yet neither man objected; instead, both stiffened guiltily as their divisional midshipman approached.

"Right enough thank you, Mr Brotherton." Lovemore flashed a warning glance at O'Grady. The lad had crept up unnoticed although his face bore the look of youthful innocence and there was nothing sinister in the act. He also appeared to share the hands' objective and, equally it seemed, would have to wait.

Being a junior officer, Brotherton was entitled to more private facilities and could relieve himself in one of the enclosed roundhouses set next to the seamen's shared open-air accommodation. But the door to the tiny room was firmly shut and, to Lovemore and O'Grady's certain knowledge, had been for some time. Having to wait for such a basic need helped to erode their difference in status and in no time they were talking on a far more equal basis.

"Settling in, are you?" Brotherton enquired as he glanced longingly at the closed door.

"Well enough, thankee," O'Grady allowed, "though if you'll pardon me, they seem a rum lot."

"The mess?" Brotherton asked, mildly surprised. "You've got a sound enough man in Wainwright, he'll see you straight and won't stand any nonsense."

"He were meaning generally," Lovemore added.

"Are you talking of the hands?" Brotherton asked.

"Them, an' some of the officers," O'Grady clarified.

"I cannot comment on my fellows," Brotherton stated firmly, although both men noticed a hint of understanding in the lad.

"Of course not, but could you tells us a bit more about the captain?" Lovemore suggested.

The boy shrugged. "Not much, I haven't been aboard a great deal longer than you. We commissioned at Sheerness and only worked up on the way here. But I know him to be well connected at the Admiralty and believe Mr Leyton gives excellent support."

A successful action or perhaps some history of happy commissions might have impressed the seamen more.

"Runs a tight ship, does he?" Lovemore asked, watching carefully.

"He's strict, to be sure, as is the first lieutenant," Brotherton conceded, "though there's little strange in that."

"An' the pair of 'em are floggers..?" O'Grady chanced.

The midshipman gave a weak smile and nodded. "We've had nine at the grating," he admitted softly, "with a fair few due to answer charges shortly."

O'Grady whistled and Lovemore pulled a face. "That's rich," he said.

"It's the start of a cruise," Brotherton reminded them. "And neither the captain nor Mr Leyton are only down on the hands; believe me, no one's getting a soft ride."

"It were the impression we got," Lovemore admitted.

"There're plenty of strict skippers in the Navy," the boy pointed out.

"An' a fair number of first luffs to boot," O'Grady added.

"None of us will be minding strict, as long as they're fair," Lovemore declared.

"That's right," the Irishman agreed. "You can take a lot if

you're treated squarely."

"I cannot speak for that neither," Brotherton told them. There was movement from within the roundhouse and the midshipman was suddenly eager to end the conversation. "But stick to your duty and obey orders and you should fare well enough."

"Then that's alright then," O'Grady supposed, rolling his eyes. "We've nothing to worry about."

* * *

Tenacious truly had a fine stateroom Wheatstone decided, and not for the first time. The generous width of stern, common in her type, made for a glorious sweep of glass aft which, in turn, let in a decent amount of light, even so late into the evening. And his stewards had done a tolerable job in dressing the quarters; his dining table, now fully extended, positively glowed beneath many hours of waxing, the deep shine reflecting light and sparkle from the silverware and full placement of cutlery. But then dining was something Wheatstone took extremely seriously; Leyton claimed his parties were the talk of the entire fleet and he saw no reason to doubt it. From the pantry there came the scent of roasted potatoes and other vegetables; it was customary to serve a fish dish before the main, but Wheatstone always specified broth, if only to combat the aroma. Besides, the facilities for cooking aboard a frigate were limited with its cooking pots frequently being reused; he wanted no chance of the excellent sirloin being contaminated by remains of broiled cod or a soused salmon.

And then there was the wine. He had received good news from Garston, the port admiral; *Tenacious* was to be blessed with passengers. Not paying ones perhaps but he should see an agreeable return in another form and the news had persuaded him to open a twelve of hock that had been in store for almost a year. Such a white could not last much longer and was just the thing to ease in his principle guest. It would be followed by a case of claret he especially revered; one of only nine left that must last the rest of the commission, yet that, too, should not prove a waste. In addition, malmsey was on hand as an aperitif and any amount of port for later; four bottles had already been broached and now sat in wide-based

36

decanters. All in all, it was a good effort and Wheatstone felt uncommonly genial when Leyton arrived with the first of his guests. For entertaining was one of his favourite pastimes and he sensed this would turn out to be a memorable evening indeed.

* * *

"They're starting to arrive, get ready to go with the soup," Sturridge ordered as he wiped his hands on a cloth and glared about the tiny pantry. The vegetables for his main course had been cooked in the galley and now lay warming in the holding oven and he had requisitioned the ship's three large spirit stoves for the steaks. The raw meat sat in a red, coagulating mass perilously close to the frumenty that was for the officers' dessert. Once most of the soup was drunk, he would order his assistants to assemble the sides and start some proper cooking.

"And the first shall be last, and the last first," Sturridge muttered to himself. It was vital the captain received his meal piping hot, so the initial steaks would be for junior men and, being at the end of service, may not be fully warm when they reached the table. But there was little else he could do with limited space and equipment while the captain's insistence on every shred of meat being served undercooked hardly helped. Sturridge held his hand over a pan perched above one of the stoves. It was a long way from temperature and would always be cooler than he would have liked but years of experience had taught him to compromise. Everything would be done in time; it always was. Sturridge might have been something of a perfectionist when it came to food but, on first becoming Captain Wheatstone's cook, had quickly realised the standard need not be high. The only person likely to complain was the captain himself and, providing he had taken enough wine, that was relatively unlikely. In a few hours the evening would be over and, shortly after, its strain should have joined that of countless other such functions and be all but forgotten. Although at that moment Sturridge could not conceive of such a thing and his only concern was getting the captain's steak exactly right.

* * *

"Your table is looking particularly splendid, sir," Lieutenant Leyton observed when they had shaken hands. He had been delayed on his shore errands and only just made the ship in time. Even now the older man felt slightly flushed, although nothing in his complexion compared with that of Wheatstone's.

A continual intake of wine and port meant the captain's face was never exactly pale, yet now it positively glowed. And there was something else; he seemed animated and excited. Leyton was certain no more than his usual excess of drink had been taken yet still the similarity to a child at Christmas was unavoidable.

"Indeed, I am anticipating a momentous evening," Wheatstone beamed, and it was clear it would take very little to provoke him to dance.

"The beefsteaks Dennison acquired look to be prime, I only hope Sturridge can do them justice," Leyton remarked cautiously. "It is a shame the new man will not be here to enjoy the meal."

"New man joined us after breakfast," Wheatstone snapped. "Fellow by the name of Taylor; damn it, you spoke to him yourself!"

Leyton closed his eyes for a second. "I am aware of that, sir, I was meaning our additional lieutenant; the replacement for Mr Durham. Did Admiral Garston give any indication as to when one might be expected?"

Wheatstone stared back blankly. "I really could not say; his other news rather took me by surprise."

"Other news? Pray do tell, sir," Leyton urged. From his expression and general demeanour, Wheatstone must have learned something marvellous indeed. As far as he had known, their forthcoming mission was basic escort duty; challenging enough but hardly inspiring. Perhaps that had been cancelled and they had been granted a cruise?

"No, it will have to wait," Wheatstone replied, his eyes unaccountably turning to his sleeping cabin. "But you will learn more shortly," he added, "and well before the evening is out."

More officers were appearing; soon there was quite a crowd and Leyton was surprised Wheatstone made no move to meet them. Then the door to the sleeping cabin opened, a solitary woman appeared and a hush fell as she stepped confidently into a room now reasonably filled with men.

38

She was modestly dressed; a simple frock with a single strand of pearls at the neck being the only jewellery. Her audience had been ashore so recently they were hardly starved of female company, yet the face was so startlingly attractive that all became instantly transfixed. For she was truly a remarkable sight; the woman's hair – tied up in the modern manner – was a shimmering copper while her eyes appeared deep and luminous even from a distance. And she was undoubtedly beautiful.

"Gentlemen, you will allow me to present *Tenacious'* newest recruit," Wheatstone announced as he stepped through the small group and reached out towards the vision. "Miss Amanda Lévesque."

The woman smiled easily while her gaze travelled about her admirers and it seemed, to Leyton at least, as if she were examining and assessing each individually.

"Miss Lévesque will be accompanying us on our forthcoming voyage," Wheatstone added through a dripping grin. "And I think you'll all agree, will make a welcome and attractive addition to our company."

Chapter Four

Brotherton's place was at the very foot of the table and it was one designated to him by protocol as he, and Vernon to his right, were the most junior present. But the demonstration of his lack of status hardly bothered him as it seemed he was to be rewarded with an excellent meal. Moreover, the position gave a good view of both the captain, seated opposite if many feet away at the head, as well as those to either side. And even though the main course had yet to be served, Brotherton had already learned much about his superiors.

All were talking in a highly animated fashion and, as they started to slurp their way through an undistinguished ham and pea soup, there were several outbursts of unaccountable laughter. Vernon was barely in his teens and seemed overawed by the occasion; he even appeared intimidated by the senior midshipmen that sat between them and their betters. But Brotherton had long since decided he was going to enjoy himself and examined his fellow diners in more detail. Beyond Hedges and Owens, the senior midshipmen, there was the purser, master-at-arms, the surgeon, both marine officers and Manton, their sailing master. After them came the upper echelons of Lieutenant Taylor, who had only arrived that morning, and Lieutenant Leyton with Captain Wheatstone himself seated at the very head. Then next to him, and equally facing the lads, was an unexplained guest; a young and unusually attractive woman. Brotherton had been late in arriving and was still uncertain who she might be, but it was clear her presence raised no objections from those nearby and he certainly had few complaints about the view.

Despite his unusual vantage point, the meal was not so very different to others Brotherton had attended aboard his last ship. Only Guppy, immediately next to Hedges, was something of a surprise. He was undoubtedly a warrant officer although the master-at-arms was not usually considered of quarterdeck rank, so rarely found a space at such events, and his presence had definitely been noted by others.

That was nothing to the subtle stir created by the mystery female, however. To dine at a captain's table was by no means limited to officers and men; women were frequently invited. Depending on the circumstances, they might range from officers' wives or sweethearts, through more distant acquaintances and ending with those of a far lower order presumably intended to provide additional entertainment. It was hard to fathom exactly where this particular vision ranked and even more remarkable that she was the only female present; again there were no set rules but it would take a bold woman to appear amid a group of males without support from others of her gender.

Of course, he could have found out more by simply asking Hedges on his left. Both he and Owens had been amongst the first to arrive and doubtless knew more as they were now swapping knowing glances and the occasional muttered comment. But Brotherton had quickly learned that to show ignorance aboard *Tenacious* was an invitation for ridicule and preferred to concoct his own explanation.

The woman would be the daughter of an important dockyard official, or possibly even the port admiral himself – why not? Captain Wheatstone had invited her in an attempt to impress both his superiors and the frigate's senior officers and was now doing exactly that by drinking too heavily and making a thorough ass of himself. She would be appalled and was bound to return with stories of drunken debauchery causing Wheatstone and possibly several others to be instantly replaced. Brotherton allowed himself a private smile; it was fantasy of course, but any chance that this commission might suddenly take a turn for the better was worth considering.

* * *

"You see, my dear, the only way to manage a ship effectively is to separate officers from men," Wheatstone stated while trying, unsuccessfully, to see down the woman's dress. "Officers are gentlemen and appreciate the finer things in life." He gestured vaguely at the bawdy rabble before them. "Whereas seamen are merely peasants; important in their way I suppose but incapable of appreciating anything of quality."

"What exactly?" the woman asked, and Wheatstone was momentarily stunned by the complexity of her question.

"I beg your pardon?"

"What do they fail to appreciate?" she elaborated.

"Why, good food," Wheatstone replied at last. "You should see the stuff consumed on the lower deck, though they eat it up like animals, so they do, and would ask for more if I gave them liberty. And wine; blackstrap's the closest most of 'em get, and I wouldn't give you tuppence for the rum they're so fond of. Shall you take a little more of this excellent hock?"

Her glass was almost full, but Wheatstone contrived to add extra before addressing his own empty glass and treating it equally. The surplus from both spilt onto the polished tabletop.

"Give them wine as good as this," he continued while peering myopically at the label, "and most would only swill it like lemonade."

And so saying he drained his glass.

* * *

The beefsteaks arrived shortly afterwards together with tureens of fresh vegetables and bowls of roasted potatoes, along with smaller dishes containing fried onions. The glorious aroma reached Brotherton's nostrils as soon as his plate was set before him and immediately the lad's spirits rose. The potatoes were all but monopolised by his betters; he was only able to secure one, and that was hardly large, but the lack was more than made up for in cabbage, carrots and fresh green peas. And the meat, though barely cooked and decidedly tepid, was of an excellent cut. Fresh beef was hardly novel in a ship accustomed to petty warrant victuals although the steak before him was from no ration bullock. He glanced about, uncertain if he should start but all about were laying in with a will and he quickly joined them.

And it was only when he was halfway through his meal and was pausing for a rare sip of wine, that Brotherton became aware of something amiss further up the table. The distance in status between him and those at the head might have been vast but he had an excellent view and was even able to catch something of Captain Wheatstone's comments over snatches of inebriated laughter.

For some reason his host had found fault with his meal and was publicly berating the cook; the man had been summoned from his pantry and was now cowering in humiliation while Wheatstone delivered a first-rate dressing down. Brotherton had no idea what might have raised such anger when his own food was perfectly acceptable and any served higher up the table would probably be better. But whatever the case, the cook sped off with a reddening face

42

and clutching the captain's plate. Brotherton took some more wine and found it to be good indeed, then returned to his meal. Sometimes it was hard to understand, let alone judge, his betters.

* * *

"Over cooked!" Sturridge gasped when he reached the sanctuary of his pantry. "The finest steak money can buy, an' it ain't hardly seen the 'eat yet the cull complains it's over cooked!"

The two stewards who had been scraping the pans for every last remnant of fat exchanged glances before looking back to their master.

"We've more, Mr Sturridge," one suggested, nodding towards the small pile of congealing flesh that lay on one side and had been reserved for their own use later.

"Aye, I suppose so," the cook conceded. "Take the thickest and get one of them pans back on the stove. And it's got to be hot – red hot," Sturridge added. "No one's gonna say I can't seal meat proper!"

"That'll take a while," a steward remarked as he placed a pan over the flame. Sturridge briefly touched the cold metal and grimaced.

"Then he'll just have to wait," he said. "An' much good may it do 'im!"

* * *

"And what can I do for you, young fella?" Dennison asked.

"It's me hammocks," Longdon, a boy volunteer, announced as he held up two canvas bundles. "My divisional midshipman says they're not up to standard."

"Not up to standard?" the purser exclaimed, snatching one from the lad and knocking the other from his hands where it bounced onto the dark deck of the orlop. "Why there's nothing wrong with this one."

Dennison had rolled the hammock out and in the poor light it did seem sound enough.

"It's the holes round 'ere," Longdon explained, pointing to where the nettles attached to the canvas. They're starting to fray and a couple have torn."

43

"Have they indeed?" Dennison huffed. "Well you can tell your young gentleman that hammocks cost money, and if he wants to reach into his own pocket to provide new, he's welcome."

"So what am I to do?" Longdon asked pathetically. He was barely sixteen, this was his first ship and he had hardly been aboard her a week, yet already was finding himself in what appeared to be an impossible dilemma.

"Do?" Dennison demanded. "Why I have just told you!"

"But Mr Hedges says I must change them."

"I might have known it would be Hedges," Dennison grunted. "But it makes no difference. All will be issued with fresh hammocks on the first of next month; until then you will simply have to be careful." He stopped, considered the boy for a moment, then continued in slightly softer tones. "Unless you wish to help me out in some way?"

"Help you out?" Longdon asked.

"Yes, a little light work, when off watch." Dennison seemed to be sizing the boy up. "Nice strong lad like you will do well, and I'll see you gets a pair of brand-new hammocks well ahead of the others."

Longdon regarded the older man uncertainly. "I don't know," he began.

"Won't be too taxing," Dennison assured. "Several of the other lads drop by from time to time; my boys, I calls 'em. We gets on well, like a family almost."

"No." The word seemed to be plucked from him without his willing it as he snatched the hammock from the purser's hands. "Thanking you kindly, but I'll wait for new to be issued."

"Then it's a mistake you'll be making," Dennison warned while watching appreciatively as the boy bent to recover the second hammock. "The offer remains open and you don't want to run afoul of Mr Hedges."

But Longdon was already leaving.

* * *

"It will be a straightforward northerly crossing," Wheatstone announced as he replaced his glass. "We shall be escorting a substantial convoy and sticking with it as far as Halifax. But after that, I think matters might become a deal more interesting..."

It had not been his intention to discuss ship's business with his officers but, after disciplining Sturridge, he felt a further demonstration of a captain's power was needed to impress his young guest. The woman was seated next to him at the head of the table and had said remarkably little, but then she had been unusually quiet since first being introduced at Admiral Garston's office. There was nothing so strange in that, Wheatstone decided; many were intimidated on first encountering a senior post captain: he was actually quite accustomed to such a reaction. Admiral Garston had briefly explained her story which Wheatstone now barely remembered – some nonsense about being let down in marriage by a Captain of Horse Guards who was the son of another admiral. Wheatstone took one more glance at the woman's front then wiped his mouth with the back of his sleeve; the fellow must have been an imbecile to miss out on such a prize.

Exactly why the wench hadn't chosen to travel in the greater comfort of one of the heavy merchants, Wheatstone could not imagine; presumably money had something to do with the matter. But he had never been one to turn down a good offer and the only thing on his mind was spending the next few weeks in close company with an attractive young woman. So far she had resisted his advances and there was, he supposed, a faint chance she might be a member of the Twickenham Set. But be that as it might, Wheatstone could be persistent when he chose and knew there would be time enough and further opportunities to test her resolve. After all, he was captain of the ship and the lord of all who sailed aboard her. It would be strange indeed if no benefit could be wrung from such a position.

To his right, Leyton was watching him like an attentive hound. His second in command must have some wine inside him yet remained just as composed and annoyingly precise. Wheatstone made a point of demonstrating full control whenever possible but had long since given up trying to impress the man; in truth, had he not depended on him so, he would have sent him packing long since. But the newly arrived Taylor was a far better prospect. Unless they were presented with a babe in arms for their third lieutenant, he was likely to be the lowest in seniority and was plainly eager to please. With a little care, Wheatstone should be able to mould the lad into an agreeable sycophant, for there was nothing he liked more than a little hero worship.

Taylor had definitely been drinking, but not to the extent that he was incapable. Instead, the wine had simply eased some of the nervousness from the youngster. And this was his first commission, Wheatstone reminded himself; yes, he would be easy meat.

"Might it be a cruise, sir?" the younger man enquired hesitantly.

"That is for me to know, Mr Taylor," he announced sternly.

"Well perhaps you might tell us when we can expect to depart?" the woman asked more softly.

"Aye, sir, that's something we'd all like to know." This was Manton, the sailing master, who was slightly behind them all in alcohol and had greater reason than most to ask. It was still early in the spring; the North Atlantic could be troublesome and shepherding a collection of merchants through its waters was not a pleasant prospect.

"Well, that is indeed the question," Wheatstone temporised, collecting his glass again and looking towards the pantry door. "What the devil is Sturridge doing with my steak? I asked for another, not the whole blessed cow!"

"And exactly how large is this convoy?" Marine Lieutenant Piper chipped in.

"Aye, and will it be a quick passage?" his deputy added.

Wheatstone snorted; he knew he had gone too far. Such direct questioning would rarely be tolerated at a captain's table, but the wine was flowing freely and suddenly no one seemed to be caring much about protocol.

"Mr Leyton shall tell you more," he all but snapped while reaching for a bottle and filling his glass yet again.

"We will be escorting three ships from Falmouth," the first lieutenant began. "And are ordered to join up with a larger force leaving Spithead a day or so before."

"And when would that be?" the sailing master persisted.

"Not sooner than a week from today," Leyton told him crisply, "but shortly afterwards, you can be sure of that. Once we receive news the main body has departed, *Tenacious* will put out and rendezvous with them in the Channel."

"That's assuming we can find 'em," Hopper added with an inane grin. The surgeon was sitting further down the table and had no business listening to senior officers' conversation. The fact that he felt able to join in might be explained by his rosy complexion and the pair of empty bottles before him.

"I doubt that to be a problem," Leyton replied coldly. "It will be a large concern, at least sixty ships."

"That is indeed a significant number," Taylor mused.

Wheatstone cast a glance at the girl on his left; she seemed to be taking everything in but had hardly touched her wine.

"Such a fleet will need a considerable escort," Manton, the sailing master, pondered.

"And it shall have one, be sure of it," Leyton replied. "Though probably not of the size usual when protecting a southbound. We expect a rear admiral at the least to be in command."

"Then it is surprising that one has not been announced," Piper remarked. Leyton hesitated; the escort leader must indeed have been appointed and doubtless the captain already knew his identity. But Wheatstone had not seen fit to advise him and Leyton felt reluctant to admit the fact to the table. He glanced across in the hope of rescue, but the captain's attention had returned to the front of his guest's dress.

"I am sure Captain Wheatstone will inform you when he thinks fit," Leyton temporised.

At the mention of his name, Wheatstone seemed to spring into life. "What is Sturridge playing at?" he demanded, staring over the heads of his officers. The rest of the table had all but finished, yet his replacement steak was still to arrive and he was vaguely aware the lack of food had made the wine go to his head. He supposed it might have been slightly foolish in sending the first back, especially as he had been looking forward to the meal.

"Shall I summon the cook, sir?" Leyton enquired.

"Yes, do that," Wheatstone sighed, then added, "No, wait, here it comes."

Sturridge was indeed returning and with an obviously hot plate. The cook pushed past the stewards preparing to clear the other diners, ignoring the ribald comments from some junior officers as he went. Wheatstone checked the rest of the table; there were still greens remaining and a goodly share of potatoes had been dutifully left. The steak was set before him and he grunted in mild appreciation; the thing was barely brown and several onions fried in its juices had been added. The cut also looked a deal thicker than the one previously served and, as Sturridge stepped away without a word, he began to help himself to vegetables.

"We expect to victual while in Falmouth," Leyton continued, "and hope to be taking on another officer."

Wheatstone rather rudely reached in front of his guest for the mustard; now that he had a decent meal before him all intentions of impressing the young woman were suspended.

"A further lieutenant?" Taylor suggested.

"As you well know," the captain snapped while spooning the last potato onto his already crowded plate. "And one that will doubtless be senior to yourself."

The young man took the news well; there may even have been a hint of relief on his face.

"I think that is enough for now," Wheatstone growled, picking up knife and fork, and finally addressing his meal.

"We will doubtless learn more in due course," Leyton continued, having missed the captain's comment, "though I believe the troops we shall be escorting are ultimately bound for Quebec, to reinforce the garrison there."

Now Wheatstone began making an odd guttural sound; either he wished to add to the conversation, or stop his deputy from saying more but, with a mouth filled with rare beefsteak, neither was possible.

"And in addition to the men, there is bound to be a fair number of civilians," the first lieutenant carried on oblivious. "Wives and families of the troops although doubtless a few government officials will be thrown in for good measure."

"Something that will doubtless benefit them greatly!" Piper added to the merriment of others at the table.

But there was no laughter from Wheatstone, only a guttural cough and suddenly all eyes turned to him. He attempted to speak and, for a moment, looked likely to expel his current mouthful to do so. Then, after an elaborate swallow, there was a small spasm as he drew breath, and it was then that he began to choke.

* * *

Brotherton was the first to notice, even though he was probably the furthest away. For some time he had been vaguely watching those at the other end of the table. Leyton was holding forth while the captain concentrated on his food and the woman to his left looked alternately bored and disgusted. It was clear the ship's commission was being discussed and the few words that came his way were enough to keep him interested, although the look of panic that suddenly filled

48

Wheatstone's bloated face told him far more.

An uncle had once choked on a chicken bone during Sunday lunch. Brotherton had not been long out of dresses at the time but still remembered the commotion that erupted, apparently from nowhere. And it was the same now: as soon as the captain began to rock back and forth in his seat, eyes wide and mouth gaping, the lad knew what was about.

Others were less quick to pick up. As Brotherton rose and began to make his way to the head of the table, most merely turned in their seats and there was even drunken laughter from some while the woman drew back as if frightened of infection. By the time he was halfway there, the two marine officers had also risen, Taylor, the new lieutenant, was beating the man firmly on the back while Leyton shouted for the surgeon. And Hopper actually arrived before him, his side of the table being less obstructed, but the medic was barely able to keep upright and appeared incapable of rational thought.

"We must clear his airway," Leyton instructed.

"Of course," Hopper agreed thickly but did no more.

By then the captain's face was deep red and darkening further. He seemed constantly in the midst of a single, silent, retch yet the effort was having no effect other than to encourage streams of saliva from his mouth. Brotherton hesitated; it seemed obvious Wheatstone would soon be unconscious and he itched to take a hand. In his uncle's case, the bone had been removed although exact details had never been explained. Whatever blocked the captain's windpipe would surely be accessible; the surgeon would know more yet was doing nothing while Taylor's constant thumping only made the situation appear more dramatic and vaguely gruesome.

Brotherton supposed he might step forward, but to what purpose? Did he intend thrusting a hand into his captain's mouth? There were surely more senior men available for such a task. And what if he made the situation worse? What if his captain were actually to die; would he be held responsible? And still, he hesitated; his arrival had gone unnoticed, there being too much of a distraction elsewhere, while Wheatstone's spasms were starting to lessen. Soon he would be unconscious and then death must be inevitable. Death, in the midst of a dinner party; could there be anything more terrible and less expected? Yet the more he watched, the more such a conclusion appeared inevitable.

He looked about in desperation; most were watching their

captain with various levels of interest, while only the new lieutenant made any attempt to help. Even the stewards, undoubtedly the soberest of them all, remained motionless and Mr Sturridge, standing at the pantry door, appeared almost amused. Brotherton felt the first signs of panic and then sense took over.

No, he would not intervene; he had already discovered *Tenacious* to be a ship where initiative was firmly discouraged. It was a notion shared by others and probably significant that the only senior man to be intervening was a newbie. The captain was quieter now; his substantial form had slumped forward across the dining table and one fist was thumping redundantly on its gleaming surface. And then, as the beating gradually grew weaker, Brotherton did move, although it was merely to return to his seat.

Chapter Five

In addition to four impressive stone columns, an armed sentry guarded the Admiralty's main entrance. On noticing the uniform of a senior post captain – or maybe just his empty left sleeve – the marine private held the door back and, once inside, much was as King remembered. The hall was large and generally square with a high and decorated ceiling that supported a massive hexagonal candelabra. Corridors led off in three directions and there was a generous and, mercifully, lit fireplace to one side that took the chill from the April morning. A line of messengers stood nearby subtly warming themselves and one, somewhat reluctantly, approached.

"Captain King to see Captain Abbott," King announced.

"Very good, sir," the man replied, apparently saddened by being unable to show King to someone of greater significance. "Your appointment is for ten?" he asked.

"It is," King replied gruffly, resisting the temptation to consult his watch. He had spent the past twenty minutes pacing Whitehall and should be quite certain of the time.

"Then perhaps you would follow me?"

King knew it customary to tip messengers; the Admiralty servants carried a modicum of power and could show their disdain by leaving a candidate too long in the officers' antechamber or taking a deliberately circuitous route if some consideration were not made. But King would have none of such nonsense; he was by no means set on resuming his naval career and, should he fail to arrive on time, would simply announce the reason to Abbott. Possibly sensing this, the man led him past the hated ground floor waiting room and directly up to where the Lord Commissioners of the Admiralty regularly sat.

The Board Room was large and rectangular; three windows to one wall gave good light and the deep chestnut panelling added elegance, as did the decorated ceiling and fine array of furniture that even ran to a stately longcase clock. An empty and cold marble fireplace stood to one side above which hung a selection of rolled charts, with one – a detailed diagram of the Channel – on display in an ornate frame. But the object that caught King's eye rested on another wall. It was a massive dial, similar in appearance to yet another clock but, rather than numerals, its single gilded pointer indicated the current state of the wind. Inside the dial was a map of Europe and King wondered briefly what momentous decisions had been made after referring to both map and dial.

His appointment was with an Admiralty captain, so it seemed strange to be taken to the Board Room and for a moment he wondered if his decision not to tip the messenger had been wise. But the man strode confidently past the long mahogany table and King followed.

To the far side, and almost disguised within the wood panelling, was a plain door; the messenger approached and boldly rapped against it before entering without waiting for a summons. Keeping close behind, King found himself in a far smaller office. It, too, was panelled but in a lighter wood while the room's more functional furniture retained the look of permanence and durability only found in pieces of considerable age. The central desk behind which a senior captain was now seated could easily have seen a young Drake or Hawkins despatched on their travels; even the wax candles set, unlit, in twin candelabras might have been made several centuries before.

The captain had risen to meet him and extended a hand as the messenger slipped quietly out unnoticed by them both.

"Tom King, as I live and breathe! Why I have not seen you since *Pandora* paid off!"

King hesitated with his hand outstretched. The name meant little to him and there was nothing familiar about the grey-haired officer, yet the man seemed to know him well. Or if not know, then at least remember.

"Forgive me, sir," he began, and the creased face smiled.

"Abbott," he beamed. "Harry Abbott. I was flag lieutenant to Johnston, the PA at Torbay when we took you in. We dined together with Sir Richard and the old boy; pair of them spent all their time rumbling on about St Helena as I recall. And there was another fellow present, name of Caulfell?"

"Caulfield, Michael Caulfield," King corrected; he remembered him well enough.

"That's the cove!" Abbott exclaimed. "Keep him in sight, do you?"

"I fear not, he passed some time back."

52

"Sorry to hear, sorry indeed," Abbott declared, although his face showed little emotion, "and own to not having followed his career more closely; there are just so many officers these days. I say you do remember the meal?"

"Of course," King lied. He could actually summon up little detail of the frigate's final days, or her unhappy end at the hands of the breakers, and had no memories of dining with anyone, let alone the officer before him. "I trust you are well?" he temporised.

"Oh, well enough," the man sighed and shook his head dismissively. "And I suppose it is not a bad life," he added, motioning King to a chair before seating himself. "Miss out on the fun you salty fellows have; I rarely put out for more than a day myself and never hear a shot fired in anger, though would chance I serve my country in other ways..." Abbott glanced down complacently at his uniform which, although undress, was immaculately cut and of the finest quality. "When Johnston hauled down his flag they made me commander at Chatham, then it were only a question of time before I won my second swab."

King nodded but said nothing. He had little time for career officers such as Abbott; the type were known for their eye to the main chance and had little true connection with the sea. It was an opinion he had held for some time, even throughout his own brief periods of shore duty in fact, and might be the reason all memories of the man opposite had been dismissed. But then the meal at Torbay must be all of ten years past, time enough to forget much. The pair of them had been mere lieutenants and he wondered vaguely what could have happened to make Abbott remember so clearly. Since then both had progressed to become senior post captains; the aim of every junior officer as an admiral's flag was merely a question of time. However, King felt every step of his journey had been earned by risking his life in countless actions and receiving not a few injuries on the way while, safely ashore and liberally cosseted, Abbott gained rank by simply mixing in the right circles.

"So, what brings you knocking on the Admiralty's door?" the man asked, suddenly businesslike, and King wondered if Abbott had guessed at the lapse of memory or, worse still, his mild contempt.

"I were wondering about a posting," King announced quietly.

"That comes as a revelation," Abbott replied without a smile. "Frankly, Tom we had rather counted you out."

"Truly?"

"As I recall you were offered a seventy-four when *Mistral* paid off," the man shrugged, "and it were turned down flat. The admiral will be joining us shortly, but I know that is on his mind and we may as well address the issue straight away."

King nodded. It had not even come to interview: he had declined a summons from the Admiralty which was undoubtedly the act of a retiring officer.

"I had been on the Cape Town station for some time," he explained, adding, "and seen a measure of action," with slight emphasis.

"Ah yes, dear Sir Home Popham." Abbott smiled gently and rested back in his chair. "Fellow's still making a nuisance of himself, of course, but there seems nothing anyone can do to stop him." He added a sly wink. "Friends in high places, don't you know? I tell you, Tom, if either of us had half his connections we'd have been flying a broad pennant long since and already have our seat in the Lords."

King had no illusions about his former Commander-in-Chief, but to hear any senior officer being spoken of so made him slightly defensive, especially by one such as Abbott.

"So now you've changed your mind and wish to forgo the pleasures of land?" he continued.

"Something of that nature," King agreed.

"Well, I have to say you are not alone."

"I did not expect to be." The interview was not going well; the man opposite may well have the remains of his seagoing career in his grasp yet not only had he forgotten him, King also found he disliked the cove intensely.

Which was probably for the best, he decided, also resting back. When he expressed a wish to return to sea, Aimée had been so understanding but, now back in uniform and seriously considering the prospect, he found it less attractive. Yes, it would be good to be active again, to manage a vessel and her crew, and know the close association of trusted officers; men who could be relied upon always made the best friends. But then there was the house, the estate and Aimée along with his growing family: all the things he had worked and suffered so hard for suddenly seemed terribly important and far too good to throw away on a mere whim. And especially so if it meant dealing with bucks like Abbott.

"No, there are ships at sea and never so many, but also a greater number of candidates wishing to be aboard them." The man

54

was playing with his fingers absentmindedly as he considered. "Were you to join the line I fear there could be a sizeable wait. And then it might not be an active command, or at least what firebrands like yourself consider so."

King's senses twitched, something in the man's manner was sounding a false note. He became alert, and then suspicious.

"It is no matter," he said as if coming to a decision.

"You do not wish for a command?" Abbott asked, mildly surprised.

"I happened to be in town and wished to enquire of the situation, no more," he replied, standing.

"Why not wait a while longer?" There was now an element of nervousness in Abbott's tone. "Admiral Trenchard is aware you are here and will be with us directly; it would be best to speak with him before coming to any decision." He smiled slightly and, with some surprise, King sensed the expression to be genuine. Then the door behind them opened and he turned to see a far older man enter.

Trenchard was wearing the uniform of a rear admiral but the splendour was dulled somewhat by a horsehair wig which was cheaply made and sat crookedly on an otherwise bald head.

"Forgive me, sir. I heard you'd put in but could not be here the sooner." He stumbled into the room resting heavily on his cane, but the gnarled hand that shook King's was surprisingly hard and firm in its grip. "I trust Abbott here has been entertaining you well enough?"

"He was explaining the prospects for command were poor," King announced, seating himself again. The uniform proclaimed him to be of particular importance, but King happened to know Archibald Trenchard was relatively junior and yet another land animal. Though of good stock and the son of a captain distinguished in an earlier war, the man had never served at sea. More than that, for the past twenty years he had been stationed at the Admiralty offices in Whitehall and mixing with warriors such as Abbott. In fact, now it was brought to his attention, Abbott would probably be emulating him in a few years' time. Still, there was something about the slightly crooked figure that did impress; King had met with grass admirals before, and this one had more presence and natural authority than most.

"What's that, Abbott?" Trenchard snapped as he headed for a seat beside him behind the desk. "Not trying to put Captain King off, I trust?"

"I was simply ensuring he would be fully committed,

Admiral," the captain explained calmly while making room for his superior. "Recent experience has shown not all officers applying for command stay the course."

"And I suppose you're not wrong," Trenchard agreed, slumping down heavily in the chair. But once seated he looked up and King was struck by his pale blue eyes which were amazingly clear. "I'll be honest with you, Captain, the war is not going particularly well for us, diplomatically at least. Oh, Boney's on the run alright and we have high hopes for Wellesley in Spain. But the Americans are playing up; complaining about our lawful retrieval of British hands from their ships and the King is behaving oddly once more. Then we have the mob; most have grown tired of the restrictions and commitments that come with any long-term conflict and are showing less support. Even some loyal officers are becoming restless and those commanding ships seem to be the worst."

The admiral was now fiddling with a paper on the desk and, were he not still talking, could easily have forgotten King was even in the room.

"It appears every ship leaving England is captained by a man of business, a member of parliament or – Lord save us – a peer. You would not believe the requests we have for home leave; it is a wonder any of them ever venture near the sea, let alone their commands."

"I understand, sir," King replied, and once more those eyes rose and fixed his.

"So tell me, how are you obligated? Not an MP I am glad to hear, but are you a farmer perhaps? Or any other ties to the land?"

"I have an estate in Sussex," King admitted, "though do not manage it directly."

"And a family, or so I believe?" Abbott was also now regarding him intensely.

"A child," King agreed, "with the prospect of another."

"Then I congratulate you, sir." Abbott had found a chair next to his admiral and gave a genial smile. "I had no luck in the marriage stakes, though might tell you confidentially, it was never an aim."

Trenchard flashed a disparaging look at his colleague while King simply nodded.

"And do you have strong feelings for your wife?" the admiral asked, his attention snapping back to the subject in hand.

"I-I..." King had not been so taken aback since a midshipman. He was accustomed to discussing naval matters with those of senior rank but human emotions were rarely touched upon.

"I am truly fond of her," King admitted finally. "Though should point out she is not my wife; there are difficulties in that direction."

"Really?" The old man sighed and flashed another look at Abbott. "Sometimes I wonder what this world is coming to…"

Both captains appeared awkward for a moment and King cleared his throat, but Trenchard did not dwell longer. "The main thrust is, are you willing to forgo your domestic arrangements and return to the sea?" he asked. "Even if it were a ship on blockade or maybe one that tarries long in harbour?"

"I had hoped for something a little more active," King chanced.

"That was what we expected," Abbott smiled again. "And frankly feared, for you were one of the more promising officers under consideration."

King blinked; until he had requested this interview no one at the Admiralty could know he had any intention of returning to sea, yet they were considering him for something. And suddenly he was keen to hear what.

"I came in search of a ship," he admitted. "Were it harbour bound; in ordinary or a guard, I might not be so eager. But blockade duty would hardly disappoint and, even if it be in home waters, I would not expect to abandon her for other matters."

"And what if she were not a liner?" the admiral questioned. "Is your heart set on a two-decker?"

"No," King replied truthfully. "I have yet to command a seventy-four but always considered myself a frigate man. In truth, something of that type would be more welcome."

The admiral exchanged a glance with Abbott. "That is good to hear, Captain," he continued, turning back to King. "And would you be ready to take up your duties immediately?"

"Immediately?" King questioned, taken further aback.

"We have a ship at Falmouth that lacks a captain. Fellow died suddenly in the strangest of circumstances and I own has caused no end of trouble. Surgeon asked to be relieved of his responsibilities and there are rumours her people are close to revolt," the admiral snorted and rolled his eyes before continuing. "Frankly there is not the time for an investigation, but whoever has her must act with all despatch and set matters right. Sorting a discontented crew is not the easiest of tasks in the best of circumstances and time is of the essence as she is required forthwith." Trenchard was eyeing him with open curiosity now and even Abbott seemed to be gauging the effect of every word.

"There is a vacant post for a lieutenant; the man appointed might name any available officer to fill this, but, as I say, we cannot afford delay. And equally we have to be certain not to be let down later." Now the eyes softened slightly, "Which is why Abbott was perhaps a little hard on you."

"I think I understand, sir," King said, privately reassessing his view of shore-based officers.

"Well, what's it to be?" Trenchard rasped and it was clear that, landbound or not, he had an air of command.

"I should be happy to accept the position," King replied more firmly.

"Delighted to hear it," the admiral grunted. "Abbott here will have your orders drawn up and perhaps you might advise us of your choice of officer but do bear in mind the fellow will also have to move sharpish." Again, the eyes sought his and for a moment seemed to mellow further. "I'll not beat about the bush, we're glad to see you back, King," he said. "Make a success of *Tenacious* and there may be other opportunities."

"*Tenacious*, sir?"

"Your new command," Abbott informed him. "A thirty-eight; Artois class and by no means new. But she's fresh from refit and I think will please you."

"Though her people might be a different matter, what?" Trenchard exclaimed in a bark.

"Indeed, sir," King agreed, his head just starting to spin. "And thank you."

* * *

With Lovemore and O'Grady allocated elsewhere, Cranston had been feeling decidedly lonely in Robson's mess. The only member who showed any measure of sociability was Longdon, a Kentish lad and a landsman volunteer. At sixteen, the boy was younger than most but had a fine physique with a mop of dark hair and clear brown eyes. He also carried himself like a natural-born seaman with a confident manner and wry sense of humour that Cranston, at least, appreciated.

But sadly his appearance hid an almost total ignorance of all things nautical; frequently he would be called upon to carry out simple tasks and, not wishing to disappoint, they usually ended in disaster. And the present problem was just such an occasion.

Mr Amon, the boatswain, was not one to intentionally give any hand too complex a chore but it was a fresh crew and one he was yet to know properly. So, on seeing Longdon on the forecastle, then noticing the labyrinth of line that had unaccountably been left and now littered much of the area, Amon assumed him capable. Longdon was directed to tidy matters and the boatswain left without further thought. The lad had set to with a will but in no time the problem had been made worse and, when Cranston chanced upon him, the entire foredeck was covered in tangled cordage.

"Trouble there, matey?" Cranston enquired genially and Longdon threw down the coil he had been attempting to sort.

"It's a jape," he announced. "Bloody string's got a mind of its own; someone's set me up."

Cranston paused and took in the situation. "No one set you up," he said. "And this ain't string, it's line which, like most things, has its ways; you just have to know them."

Longdon regarded Cranston with a mixture of hope and suspicion. "Well I don't," he admitted.

"Then I'll shows you," Cranston declared. "This is three-inch," he added collecting a length and holding it out for Longdon to see. "Size is measured about the edge but you'll never have to; next time you see a piece you'll just know. An' if you look closely you'll see it's made from yarn, which runs in three bigger strands what are laid up to give it strength."

The lad examined the line more carefully and nodded.

"This type is called hawser laid – there are others but we'll leave them for now. Hawser's pretty common and you'll note the strands twist in the same direction, like the steps on a spiral staircase."

Again Longdon nodded.

"They call that the lay and, if you goes against it, you'll never make a proper coil." Cranston stretched out the line and began to form it into several loops on the deck. "You see, if I goes this way, the rope bucks and turns, whereas the other," he added, taking the line back and winding it in the opposite direction, "will coil it smooth."

"Same way as a clock turns," Longdon exclaimed.

"That's the ticket," Cranston beamed. "Hawser laid line is twisted right-handed, so you coil it clockwise. You start with the bight, see – that's the free end coming from where it's made fast – and work in that direction laying each round flat on the one before until you reach the end. Then you turns the whole lot over so the bight is on top, ready to be used, and all remains neat and ship-shape."

"I gets it," Longdon agreed, nodding.

"An' you do the same when coiling lighter line, though you can do that in your hands." He reached for a length of one-inch and shook out the tangles. "You hold the coil so," he said, indicating his left hand, "and form it with the other, keepin' this thumb turned towards the bight. Again he held up his left hand and again Longdon nodded. "Then, when you winds it in, the coils will form as if they wants to."

"It's simple when someone tells me," the lad sighed.

"Most things are," Cranston agreed, "and I'll always tell you."

* * *

"I think the best we can do is keep very quiet, at least for the next day or so."

"Is that all?" Alice asked.

"What else did you have in mind?" her mistress replied. "Sure, the captain's dead and there are all manner of strange officers crawling about the ship; the last thing we need do is draw attention to ourselves."

"It wouldn't be so bad if we had more room," the girl supposed. They were in the late Captain Wheatstone's sleeping cabin, the area had been hurriedly made over to them on boarding the ship and, apart from the woman's brief appearance at the fateful dinner, neither had left it since. And it was indeed small, two iron cannon took much of the available space leaving enough for only minimal furniture. And, after several days' confinement, the pair were becoming fractious. "If we stays here much longer I shall go mad."

"At least we're being fed," the woman pointed out. "But I still say we should be as quiet as possible."

"Do you think things'll change then?" the girl asked.

"They might, when a new captain is appointed," Lévesque pondered. "Though the new one might not prove so accommodating as the last..."

"Oh, I'm sure you'll work your magic," Alice smiled wickedly at her mistress. "There ain't a man born you can't get 'round."

"I wouldn't be so sure; we're dealing with the Royal Navy and they aren't all like Captain Wheatstone."

"So he chucks us off? We'll survive."

"Sure, we'll survive." The woman was quietly positive. "But frankly I don't want to give this boat up; it's going to the right place and should be leaving shortly; we may not get such a chance again."

"Yes, but so are a lot of others; a convoy they calls it," the maid reminded her. "And with some as big as Indiamen." She was seated in the only chair while her mistress perched uncomfortably against a cannon. "Ah, an Indiaman; that's the way to travel. More space and light, decent food and company what can be pleasant as well as profitable..."

"But that way is closed to us," the woman stated firmly. "At least for the time being. We were lucky to escape at the end of the last trip, and frankly I haven't been feeling too safe in England of late."

The girl shrugged. "Everyone seems keen to get going; as soon as another cove turns up to be in charge we can be off."

"And until then we stay as quiet as possible," Lévesque repeated.

"Alright," Alice sulked. "But I'm having the cot tonight."

"Sure, but there's only the one and you had it last night. It's my turn!"

"I don't care," the maid announced. "That floor's as 'ard as nails, I'm 'aving the cot."

* * *

They had finished supper and the conversation in Robson's mess was proving as uninspiring as ever when Cranston pulled out his scrimshaw.

"It's not a Make an' Mend," Houghton told him firmly.

"I knows that," Cranston confirmed as he began scraping at a small piece of tusk. "But this is near enough finished; I can't see no one complaining if I does a bit now."

The rest of his mess grudgingly accepted this and continued talking amongst themselves. Only Longdon, sitting opposite at the mess table, paid Cranston any attention.

"Picked it up in New South Wales," the seaman explained when he noticed the lad's eyes on him. "Used to belong to a whale or

61

some such beast, but he don't need it no more."

"So what are you doing?" Longdon enquired artlessly.

"Doing?" Cranston repeated. "Why I'm decorating it." He held the piece up for him to see. It was less than seven inches long and bore the pencilled outline of a ship under sail that Cranston had been tracing out with a scraper.

"It's neat," the boy decided after a while. "What are you to do with it?"

Cranston shrugged. "Might sell it next shore leave, that or give it to a mate. But first it'll have to be finished," he added, returning to the work.

"If I gets a bit of bone, will you show me?" Longdon asked.

"I'll show you on this if you likes," Cranston offered.

"Truly?"

The seaman handed over the tusk and his metal scraper. "Jus' follow the line, don't try an' dig too deep. You goes over it again and again, that's how it works, see?"

The lad nodded seriously and, with the tip of his tongue between his lips, carefully guided the tool along the pencilled line.

"Make an' Mend, is it?" the voice was harsh and unexpectedly close. It made Longdon jump and drop both tusk and scraper.

"I'm teaching him scrimshaw," Cranston stated. He had seen Guppy, the master-at-arms, approach but not soon enough to warn Longdon.

"That right?" the warrant officer asked, his face inches from Cranston's. "Well, you ain't got permission."

"We're off watch; he don't need permission," Robson announced from the other end of the table. Guppy stood up and turned his attention to him. As a boatswain's mate, Robson was also a petty officer and, though slightly lower in rank, all knew Guppy must treat him with a measure of respect.

"I'm checkin' up," Guppy announced. "It's my job, and this fellow 'as 'istry."

"History?" Robson questioned.

"The man's a molly," Guppy sniffed, glancing down at Cranston in disgust. "So we should all be keeping an eye on 'im."

"He's no molly." The boatswain's mate was reassuringly positive. "I never come across a straighter cove in my life. Might have some strange ideas mind, but you got no worries on that account."

"So why's he payin' so much attention to the lad?" Guppy

demanded with a look of triumph.

"Because he's 'is sea daddy," Houghton informed him. "Been teaching any free time either of 'em gets."

"It's what we're supposed to do," Robson reminded him. "Bring the youngsters on."

To be taken aback in front of a crowd was an unusual experience for Guppy and he paused for a moment. "Well I don't know about that," he said at last while considering Longdon as if he had betrayed him in some way. "But I ain't gonna leave up." Then, on switching his attention to Cranston he raised his finger. "And I certainly ain't letting you get away with nothing, do ya hear?"

Cranston dutifully nodded and Guppy moved on, to the visible relief of all at the table.

"You wanna watch it," Robson told Cranston when the master-at-arms was well out of earshot. "Fellow like that ain't reasonable. Put a foot wrong and he'll come down on you – see if he don't."

Chapter Six

King already had experience of Artois class frigates and didn't expect *Tenacious* would be vastly different. They had durable hulls, were generally well designed and carried a reasonable armament. And the example he had been offered was fresh from refit so, as far as fabric was concerned, there should be little to worry about. But despite this he wriggled uncomfortably in his seat. The Hackney coach seemed to be taking an inordinately long time; they must have left the Admiralty half an hour before yet had still to cross the river and were generally making poor speed. If he were able to catch the two o'clock post it should get him to Eastbourne that night but, if missed, there would be little point in waiting and better to find a room in town. He sighed and squirmed some more; that would make him an entire day late in taking up his command which was an intolerable delay with so much to do. Since bidding farewell to Trenchard, a cloud of anxiety had been steadily building and grew further as he fretted until a shaft of clear sense finally broke through. It was foolish to take on so; the carriage would not run faster, nor would he solve any problem purely by worrying. Time had not been a major factor in his life for some while; few domestic appointments were unbreakable and none bothered him greatly so why, when a ship awaited, were matters suddenly different? But whatever the logic, and however hard King sought to remain calm, the seconds continued to race. He just wished the same could be said for the carriage.

He sighed again then removed his watch and was surprised to see only ten minutes had passed since leaving Whitehall; there would be plenty of time to catch the mail coach, plenty of time to raise Eastbourne and plenty of time to tell Aimée he would be leaving her to go back to sea. And it was the last point that finally forced him to sit back in his seat and draw breath, while grimly acknowledging the carriage was now travelling way too fast.

They had been apart before, of course, and at least with a child for company she would not be totally alone. The thought consoled him for a moment before he recognised the bigotry that had prompted it and felt truly ashamed. Next he would be telling himself that adding further to their family – an event he was unlikely to be

64

present for – would occupy her further. Which was also true although, again, hardly the thought of a caring partner. But at least she would be left in greater luxury than they had ever known in the past.

Over a year before they said goodbye to the tiny rented terrace in Alton and moved to a house to be proud of, with grounds, income and status. And though not officially his spouse, Aimée was known to all as Mrs King, wife of a distinguished naval officer with sufficient wealth and importance to defy anyone that disputed the fact. The thought consoled him slightly and, as the carriage finally began to cross the river, he was able to set his mind on other things.

His choice of lieutenant was one and must take priority. *Tenacious'* current first officer was listed as a William Leyton and the name meant nothing to him. He enquired of the man before leaving Whitehall but learned little other than he had an undistinguished record, was more than fifteen years older than himself and had passed his board when King was still a junior midshipman. The first fact was unsurprising and the last two caused him private amusement; were he still a lieutenant, Leyton would be ahead of him in both age and position. But King was a senior captain and able to choose another to join them as lieutenant, and there the seniority aspect did present a problem.

To his mind there were only two possible candidates for the post: Croft and Cooper. Both had served with him in previous commands and both were excellent officers who would have filled the post of second in command perfectly. Yet even Croft, King's former premier in two ships, would be junior to *Tenacious'* current incumbent while Cooper was far younger and many years out of the frame. Of course as captain, King could override convention; there was nothing to stop him appointing Croft as his executive officer and demoting this Leyton fellow but, however narrow-minded, bigoted or even plain blinkered he might be, there were some levels King would not sink to.

In which case it might have been better to have asked for Cooper. The pair of them did not go back so far but he was senior to Taylor, *Tenacious'* only other lieutenant, and another enigma. The ship might be sound in fabric but Trenchard had hinted at problems with her people, and Cooper had a reasonable temperament and would sort such matters. But King had served with Croft for longer, knew him better and trusted him implicitly; the idea of turning him aside to sail with anyone else was unthinkable and it would be better to have him as second lieutenant than not at all.

King closed his eyes and dreamed a little; with Croft as premier, Cooper second and himself in command any ship could be made to work, even if the unknown Taylor turned out to be hopeless. It was just a shame such an arrangement was not possible.

Of course, he was assuming Croft would accept the post of second lieutenant, he reminded himself with a start. The man had every right to refuse and could even be insulted by the offer. King had made his selection at the Admiralty; they would be contacting him directly, so one of the first things he must do on reaching Eastbourne was write and explain. He may not be able to sugar the pill greatly but might make it a little easier to swallow.

And then there was the surgeon. It seemed the previous man had left with amazing rapidity, although the death of Captain Wheatstone had been strange indeed; a choking accident and with the medic nearby. No formal inquiry was staged but an unofficial investigation considered it an unfortunate accident with no blame attributed. Yet still the surgeon had chosen to leave and done so with such haste that King suspected a measure of whitewash and possibly persuasion was used. Which, again, he could understand; *Tenacious* was a valuable ship and one due to put to sea almost immediately; little would be achieved by attributing responsibility for her captain's death although, even if the only thing he might be guilty of was not doing his utmost, he was glad to see the man gone. That still left him short of a surgeon, however, and the name that immediately came to mind, indeed the only person King would feel comfortable sailing alongside, was Robert Manning. And there lay further problems.

When last heard of, Manning had used his not inconsiderable prize money to set himself up in Bath where he was doing extremely well in partnership with an apothecary. The pair had invested in a small business offering various forms of water cures and treatments which were proving popular amongst the gentler classes. King was delighted his old friend had fared so well, but how could he offer a surgeon's berth with a remuneration of a few shillings a day to someone on course to becoming as wealthy as himself?

At least Manning would not be offended by King's offer, and it was one he knew he must make. The likelihood remained strong he would refuse at which point anyone Surgeon's Hall decided to send would do and King could assure himself he had tried for better.

They were approaching their destination now and he could see the line of mail coaches waiting. He reached for his watch again and was pleased to note there was at least an hour until he need board, time enough for a meal before starting the journey. He stepped out of the carriage and felt the sun, now warm, on his shoulders as he reached for the Jarvie's fee. If the weather remained fine it should be a pleasant trip to Eastbourne and, with spring now firmly in place, a better one down to Falmouth. And then the worries would really begin.

* * *

Brotherton was steadily becoming acclimatised to life aboard *Tenacious* and that evening was typical of what he had come to expect. Rather than the usual mixture of warrant officers and midshipmen, the frigate's cockpit was divided into two cabins of equal size with the starboard being for the exclusive use of her young gentlemen. Brotherton's portion of the dark, cramped berth amounted to the room needed to store his sea chest and that space immediately above where he might swing a hammock. Apart from similar areas for the others, there was just about room for a small, canvas-covered table, six rather dilapidated chairs and a single cupboard usually commandeered by the older men. They had just eaten a reasonable meal prepared by the gunroom cook, and two of Brotherton's betters were now taking snuff while Hedges, the senior man, smoked a thin, and highly illegal, cigar. Both vices were relatively unusual amongst midshipmen, but then *Tenacious* boasted a rare assortment amongst her young gentlemen – an epithet that, to Brotherton's mind at least, was stretching matters on both counts.

Only he and Vernon were in their teens; the rest being considerably older, and with the ship at harbour stations, most were at the table. Hanson was in his early twenties and had failed at least one board while Owens and Hedges appeared positively ancient. No one knew their ages exactly, or how often they had tried for the all-important step to lieutenant, and no one had dared ask.

Vernon was currently attending to some duty with the first lieutenant so there was no one of his level to talk with. And the senior three were also taking port, again an unusual act in what was traditionally a young man's berth.

"The new skipper'll have a lot to do, I can tell you that," Hedges proclaimed, glass in hand and sitting back as regal as any admiral. "The people need to be brought into line and Wheatstone had only just got started."

"They seem a pretty experienced lot on the whole." This was Hanson, youngest of the trio, and the one Brotherton disliked the least.

"Experienced, yes," Hedges allowed. "All can string a yarn and make two and two equal five. 'Tis fortunate we have a man such as Guppy about to keep them in line, else there's no telling what tricks they'd be up to."

"Guppy don't stand no nonsense," Owens agreed.

"Which is the right course." Hedges again. "Treat the people light and you're askin' for trouble. They'll take advantage and, on a rough night when topmen are needed aloft, all you'll get is excuses."

"I'm not so certain," Hanson countered. "Guppy's been chancing his arm of late, him and his corporals. A bit of discipline is all very well but they ain't always fair, and that don't make for a happy lower deck."

"Who says they has to be happy?" Hedges seemed amazed. "All we need is the job done and to hell with if they likes it or not."

"Well Wheatstone definitely had the right idea as far as victuals are concerned," Owens declared. "I hope whoever takes his place keeps a similar table; don't want any 'salt junk and sixpenny' thank you very much."

"I'll wager any dinner invitations will be directed at the Canadian totty." Hedges again.

"One can hardly place blame there." Hanson reached forward for another loading of snuff. "Fine figure of a woman; even her maid is comely enough."

"Staying with us to Halifax," Owens agreed. "I would it were longer."

"As the doxie told the admiral," Hedges smirked.

"I think I'm for bed." Brotherton stood but, as he drew his chair back and made for his own dark corner of the smoky space, the announcement drew nothing more than a nod from Hanson. He had nothing against the older midshipmen, nor young Vernon if it came to it; the lad was pleasant enough, if a little inclined to whine. But the evening had been like so many others and, even before the ship had properly put to sea, he was becoming bored with the general atmosphere in the cockpit. The only japes were smutty or childish while the berth itself was run like a poor imitation of a wardroom. He had thought a frigate would have had more life, yet *Tenacious* appeared as staid and stuffy as his old liner. Perhaps the new captain would make a difference? Certainly the ship needed something, or someone, with a bit more life in them.

* * *

"You are a slovenly oath," Leyton informed Cranston.

The seaman swallowed dryly but said nothing. He was standing in the half-light of the great cabin, hat in hand and head slightly bowed in apparent deference, although there was little respect in his thoughts.

"You are permitted one hammock for use, and one for spare, to be held in readiness," Leyton continued crisply. "Yet I understand from Mr Guppy that you have but one, and that has not been washed in a week."

Cranston raised his head slightly but could tell the first lieutenant was in no mood for discussion. He had indeed been issued with two hammocks and both were in reasonable order, but when Longdon joined he was given poor examples already heavily worn. The lad had sought to object but the pusser's attitude had worried him and so had taken the problem to Cranston. Being the soft-hearted fool he was, the seaman took pity and lent him one of his own. At the time, taking one of Longdon's substandard hammocks in exchange seemed petty in the extreme especially when fresh supplies would soon be available. But while exchanging kit was acceptable, it seemed a loan was not: Guppy, the master-at-arms, had noticed and promptly reported him for it.

"I know not what you have done with your second hammock," Leyton continued, "and frankly do not care. If, as I suspect, it has ended up aboard a bumboat it would only make matters worse. And I am not ignoring the fact that your remaining hammock is due for cleaning."

Cranston swallowed; he had been in similar situations before, though rarely, and knew himself weak when confronted by authority.

69

Those in uniform were inclined to use long words and had different values to honest men, yet still he felt right was on his side. And he knew enough to realise someone should be there on his behalf, even if only to accept the charge.

With the ship being one lieutenant down, Cranston had no senior divisional officer and Hedges, his divisional mid., was unaccountably absent. But Brotherton, from a different watch, appeared to be standing in his place and was preparing to speak.

"If I may say something in Cranston's defence, sir?" the lad began uncertainly as Leyton reached for the punishment book. The lieutenant paused and regarded the boy.

"Are you his divisional midshipman?" he asked, ledger in hand.

"No, sir, Mr Hedges is indisposed and has requested I stand in his stead. I have an explanation that..."

"If you are not this man's divisional officer you have no business here," Leyton announced before returning to Cranston.

"Under section two of the Articles of War and with reference to our late captain's standing orders you are accused of misappropriating His Majesty's property and general filthiness." He flashed a look at Brotherton. "And in the absence of any responsible officer you may answer for yourself," Leyton added quickly and with emphasis.

"I didn't do it, your honour," Cranston muttered softly.

"Are you saying that Mr Guppy is wrong?" Leyton demanded. Cranston shook his head.

"Or that I am wrong?"

"No, sir."

"Or perhaps you *do* have two hammocks?"

"No, your honour," Cranston flustered. "No, I ain't sayin' any of that – I lent one to..."

"Do you have two hammocks or not?" Now the voice was icy cold.

"If I may say, sir..." Brotherton began but was instantly silenced.

"No, you may not, Mr Brotherton! I have already explained, you have no place in these proceedings. Now hold your tongue or I shall see you removed."

"I had two hammocks," Cranston added sadly, "but gave one to young Longdon."

70

"And did he not have hammocks of his own?" Leyton demanded.

"Yes, sir," Cranston admitted.

"Then there is nothing I can say, all charges stand," the first lieutenant continued with what might have been a measure of satisfaction. "You are sentenced to eighteen lashes; take him away Mr Guppy."

Chapter Seven

"I don't see that it has anything to do with you," Taylor shrugged. The pair were in the frigate's gunroom which was normally the preserve of senior officers and the equivalent of a wardroom in larger ships. So really Brotherton had no right to be there, except Leyton had sent him down with a message for the third lieutenant and, as luck would have it, Taylor was alone when the midshipman found him. "It ain't as if Cranston's even in your division. So why did you offer to speak for him?"

Now it was Brotherton's turn to shrug. "Hedges said he wouldn't do it, and you know what he can be like."

"I know that, despite his greying hairs, he remains a midshipman," Taylor replied crisply, "and will do what any lieutenant tells him, even a yonker like me. If you'd mentioned it, I'd have had a word."

"Well I didn't," Brotherton replied bitterly. It was indeed fortunate that he had been able to share some of his concerns; no one in the midshipman's berth had shown the least interest. But now he had finally found a sympathetic ear, and one that belonged to someone with a measure of authority, the situation appeared just as hopeless.

With hindsight, talking to Taylor would probably have been the right course. He knew the man little better than any of *Tenacious'* senior officers but liked him a good deal more. Taylor could only be five years or so older than himself and was probably a mite inexperienced, yet Brotherton sensed he could be trusted, which was more than could be said for those above him. "Though likely it would have made no difference," he added gloomily.

"Oh, I don't doubt that," Taylor agreed. "Mr Leyton is not one to accept objections. I'm not saying anyone could have changed matters; if he wants to see a man flogged he will, at least that's how it's been so far this commission."

"And likely to stay so," Brotherton agreed.

"Well, that's to be seen..." Taylor mused. "Right now *Tenacious* is without a captain. Oh, I know Leyton is acting up but there are certain things he simply cannot do."

"What manner of things?"

Taylor relaxed in his seat and considered. "He cannot indent for certain stores for one or approve anything other than the most rudimentary repairs. And neither can he authorise temporary promotions but, more importantly, he cannot order a flogging."

"Can he not?"

"So says the law," Taylor confirmed. "Mind, there are a few prepared to disregard it even so and, with all punishments, most steer a wide course. Legally no captain can order more than twelve lashes yet that is often conveniently ignored."

Brotherton pondered for a moment. "So, Cranston cannot be flogged until the new skipper arrives?"

"Officially, that is so," Taylor agreed. "But when Wheatstone's replacement is read in there will be little to stop it – providing, of course, Leyton can convince our new master to agree. Until then he will just have to wait. And so will Cranston," the lieutenant added, "though in his case it will be on the punishment deck and he'll be wearing bilboes."

* * *

King was once more in a carriage but this time not alone, and the company was hardly welcome. Of course, he could have hired a private coach, or even taken his own; there was money enough for such an extravagance. But years of austerity, pricked only by the briefest periods of relative wealth, had left their mark and he supposed he would remain a save-all to his dying day. And because of this, rather than solitude and a chance to think, a modestly dressed mother now sat before him nursing her red-cheeked baby. He assumed the latter was teething as the creature's monotonous whining suggested some degree of pain which it was determined to convey to all present while a distinctive nursey scent was also being freely distributed. He reminded himself that young Robert, now many miles behind in Eastbourne, was capable of just such distractions and there had been countless times when King had fled to their garden or his precious Beachy Head. But escape had been possible whereas he was doomed to share the noise along with the carriage's limited supply of air, light and space at least until the next stop.

And there were others present, he reminded himself, looking

about. Next to the mother and child a thin, rather pious-looking gentleman sat reading a news-sheet and doing so with an occasional muttered tutting that was presumably intended to convey both intelligence and discernment. He had a space beside him that currently held his bag; a hefty leather affair and King regarded the area hungrily. To his side of the carriage sat two more portly gentlemen, the nearest of which was pressing hard against King's right, wedging him into the vehicle's hard wooden frame. Only the lack of a left arm prevented the situation becoming positively unsustainable and King knew it would only be a question of time before he broke the unwritten convention of carriage protocol in addressing his fellow passengers and demanding a rearrangement.

Such distractions were especially unwelcome as King had much to think about, although he was equally aware that, had he been alone and truly able to focus, his problems would be no easier to resolve. For so much would depend on what was found when he reached the ship. Apart from her rate, class and age, he knew little other than some probably inaccurate dockyard reports. But even a true assessment would be of little value as the actual fabric was not his main concern. For a vessel to be in service for the King meant she must meet a few basic requirements of seaworthiness, what interested him more was her crew, the men who served aboard her, and the reports of them were even more vague.

Which was not to be surprised at, he supposed as the man opposite produced a handkerchief and blew his nose generously. The late Captain Wheatstone could not have been in charge more than a few weeks and the ship herself had only travelled as far as Sheerness to Falmouth with her present company. King sighed and wriggled a little in his seat; if only Wheatstone had taken his fateful mouthful a few weeks earlier he would have had a far shorter journey.

And he might also have been spared the recent frantic rush; barely three days before he had returned to Eastbourne with the news that not only was he returning to sea, but a ship awaited him. Aimée had been distant at first but soon began addressing all the small but important details that were essential before he could depart. Above him now, on the roof of the carriage, were two cedar-lined chests filled with his uniform and linen as well as another, smaller trunk containing books and personal possessions. His body servant was currently assembling more along with the cabin stores necessary to maintain a senior captain for several months at sea and would be following in the next couple of days. It had been King's intention for them to travel together but, once he was able to go, there seemed little point in delaying. Far better to arrive at the ship and start work, even if it meant looking after himself for a spell. And really he could not stand the atmosphere at home; however much she might try to hide it, Aimée was wretchedly sorry to see him go, and even young Robert must have sensed something and kicked up a terrible fuss when he left to catch the post.

The memories brought on yet more feelings of remorse and King shifted again in his seat as he tried to dispel them. To leave all he held dear through need was bad enough but doing so by choice was inexcusable. And neither was there any logic to it; when he first chose to serve at sea it had been a means to an end; the Navy would feed and shelter him and, if all went well, he should leave with money, status and security. Yet with all three achieved, and the bonus of a loving partner and family – benefits denied the majority of seamen – he was abandoning all to return once more; where was the logic in that? Aimée was the sweetest person in the world; few could deserve such undying, undeniable love, least of all a pig-headed fool such as him. But the plain facts could not be ignored; however much he loved his wife, his family and their secure life on land, he remained a seaman at heart and would only be truly content aboard a ship.

The wrench from home had not only been unpleasant, there was also collateral damage; so distracted had King been he completely forgot to write to James Croft. The omission was inexcusable but, as Aimée had diplomatically pointed out, not totally out of character. He had done his best to rectify the situation by sending an express within the hour but feared it would arrive long after the Admiralty summons. He had little doubt Croft would accept the commission but how he reacted when discovering himself second lieutenant was to be seen.

Although that was by no means a certainty, King assured himself. This William Leyton fellow may well judge being sandwiched between two acknowledged friends too much of an inconvenience and resign, in which case there would still be time to enquire for Cooper and the old team could be restored. Yet again, such an arrangement appeared ideal and entirely logical. King supposed some senior captains would find little difficulty in disposing of an unwanted first officer; even if he preferred not to officially dismiss him, any number of ways might be found to be rid of the man and it could even be argued all would benefit from the move. But, as the coach rumbled steadily west, such a course seemed increasingly less likely. King owed this unknown Leyton nothing yet still felt a modicum of responsibility towards him. *Tenacious* had just been through a comprehensive refit, something her first officer would have supervised throughout, and then there must have been weeks – probably months – of preparation for her first voyage. To be outed at such short notice, then forced to hand over so much hard work to another, would be cruel in the extreme and King credited himself with rather more sensitivity.

The cries from the baby opposite were becoming more frantic, even rat-face seated beside her noticed and gave the pair a glance dripping with disdain. The mother was apparently unconcerned, however, and simply hoisted up the top of her dress and, without a measure of unease or embarrassment, began to feed her child. Which was the logical solution, King decided with respect and not a little shame. For sometimes the logical solution was not the easiest, and often required a measure of gumption.

* * *

Croft was indeed on his way to join the ship and had made far better progress than his captain. As soon as the official offer arrived he scribbled a hasty acceptance, then began to make preparations.

Which in his case were not so very great. He had taken two rooms in Deptford to be relatively near the centre of matters but, despite having lived there for over a year, had never truly settled. It took less than an hour to assemble what he would need for active service in one sea chest and two ditty bags, then arrange with his landlady for two more chests containing less personal possessions to be stored while he was away. This latter service was traditionally performed for a peppercorn charge on the understanding that, if the officer returned, it would be to the same lodging and, if not, the woman would be free to sell the remains of his estate. But Croft had no thoughts for what might go wrong or even returning, his sights were set on the future, and a rosy one.

From Deptford, it was a short walk to the packet station and there he was pleased to note a place would be available on the next vessel which would take him right to his destination. Travelling by packet cost considerably more than a mail coach and was not always faster, but Croft preferred the medium; managing his luggage was so much easier and besides, he was not exactly short of funds. He boarded after a hastily grabbed meal and, by evening, they were rounding North Foreland and looking forward to an uneventful passage.

Which was how matters turned out. Despite a wind that would have confounded many lesser craft, the packet made good time and, when she finally put in to her home port, Croft could look upon his new ship.

He had known immediately it was her; apart from a jackass and a couple of thirty-twos, there was only one other frigate and, he cautiously admitted, she did look particularly fine. Though marginally smaller than *Mistral*, his previous berth, she still carried a broadside of eighteen-pounders and her hull appeared every bit as sleek.

Which was nonsense of course, Croft told himself as the packet drew closer. Artois class ships were built to withstand the rigours of blockade or extended foreign service and sported stout timbers and lines that were serviceable if not exactly attractive. Few British craft could match the grace and stylishness of French or Spanish architects and those that did were either copied from captures or designed by royalist émigrés. They could, however, be depended upon to perform reliably in all weathers and had proved themselves more robust than their elegant enemies on numerous occasions. But Croft was viewing her through different eyes and, even with topmasts down and a service boat performing some form of maintenance to her rudder, *Tenacious* appeared beautiful indeed. And, more to the point, he was to be her first lieutenant.

* * *

King actually arrived that very afternoon and, in his haste to board his new command, did not wait for a boat to be sent but hired one of the quayside wherries. He did, however, have the presence of mind not to take his new officers unprepared and ordered the boat to approach *Tenacious'* larboard side, where he could board with minimal ceremony.

Despite this, and the limited time allowed, side-boys were hurriedly assembled and as King made the difficult passage up the frigate's boarding steps he could already hear the piercing, if breathless, strains of their whistles. The sound unnerved him slightly but he was determined not to rush; for a one-armed captain to board his ship unaided should set a good impression, whereas if he slipped, and needed to be hauled aboard like a landed fish, it would be a dreadful start. But the manoeuvre was carried out competently enough and when he finally took his first step on *Tenacious'* pine strakes, King could touch the brim of his hat with a sense of achievement. An elderly lieutenant with greying temples that he assumed to be Leyton greeted him. "Welcome aboard, sir!"

Salutes were exchanged and followed by handshakes. King noted Leyton's palm was surprisingly soft; if his new first officer had done any manual work in the last twenty years, he would have been surprised.

"You were expected, of course, sir, but we knew not when," Leyton explained when they were making their way up to the quarterdeck. "Perhaps you will permit me to present your officers?"

King's eyes flashed to the group already assembled by the binnacle and felt a wave of remorse when he noticed Croft amongst them.

"Of course," he replied, "although there is one I know already; Mr Croft, how good it is to see you."

"And I you, sir," the lieutenant agreed, stepping forward.

"You made excellent time," King muttered, striving to look his friend in the eye. Croft was standing next to Leyton and he was momentarily surprised at the similarities. Both men were of similar age and had the tanned faces of seasoned officers and both bore the same appearance of respectful attention appropriate to their rank. But was there something more in his former first officer's expression – perhaps a hint of censure? "I am sorry not to have been here to meet you," he added more softly, grasping the well-remembered hand.

"I took the packet and were fortunate," Croft stated levelly.

His old friend's manner was decidedly stiff but there was nothing unusual in that, King assured himself; Croft had always been a dry old fish, although his guilt remained.

"And this is Mr Taylor, third lieutenant."

King's eyes switched to a far younger man with baby-blue eyes and a ready smile. Soon more unknown faces were being brought forward and he quickly ceased the struggle to remember names.

"Perhaps you will order the hands assembled?" he asked when it was over, and Leyton saluted once more before signalling to a boatswain's mate. In no time the waist was being filled and King could turn and look down on a sea of equally new and nameless faces that were his crew. No one could tell what might be encountered in the future but he would be relying on this group of men as much as any officer. When all were gathered there was a moment of silence appropriate to the occasion, then King withdrew his commission from within his tunic.

He had performed the same ceremony on a number of occasions, and it was a very necessary one; by reading the commission aloud he was being officially appointed as *Tenacious'* captain and so making himself responsible for every inch of her fabric as well as the lives of all who stood before him. But as he read the words King was aware that, this time, there was a subtle difference.

This time he was taking command as an officer with some history; there would be those amongst his crew aware of his exploits, a few might know he had been present at several important fleet actions and others of his dramatic escape from the hands of the French. He continued to read but occasionally glanced down; many listening – most if he was honest – showed genuine interest in their new captain. Whatever Trenchard might have said, this did not have the appearance of a troublesome crew and he sensed it was one he could work with. But it was only as he finally came to the end that he realised the lower deck would also be expecting much from him. Those that had heard of his exploits would also know of the ships he had taken, the victories won and, more pertinent to them, the prize and head money earned. They would be anticipating the same and probably already spending the latter in their imaginations.

But even disregarding their expectations, and for whatever reason, King felt he was being welcomed. He folded the paper and replaced it in his tunic; some new captains might have chosen such an occasion to speak further but he felt that best left and turned back to Leyton. Croft was standing next to him, to all intents the loyal and supporting second lieutenant. Looking at them King wondered briefly if the lower deck would have been quite so welcoming if they knew how he treated his friends.

* * *

"There will be no talking with the prisoner," the marine private told them sternly.

"Is that right?" Lovemore asked, considering the man. "An' what you going to do, shoot me with yer musket?"

"I shall summon the sergeant, then you'll be for it," the youngster replied.

"Then it's a mistake you'll be makin'," Lovemore sighed as he seated himself next to Cranston and produced a cloth-covered bundle. "'Cause I've a stash here I'd be willing to share with the right sort of company..."

Cranston and the marine watched in silence as Lovemore proceeded to open up his package, finally revealing a tight block of dried figs. "There now," he said, considering them.

"Where they from then?" the marine asked cautiously.

"Bumboat," Lovemore replied. "And I ain't broken no laws in buying them."

"You ain't got no rino," Cranston muttered accusingly and Lovemore grinned.

"I cashed the ticket from my time in *Merriweather*," he admitted.

"What, the 'ole lot? And for a handful of figs?" Cranston was disgusted.

"I got a fair enough rate and clink left over. An' if I hadn't done it, I wouldn't have been able to get you these." He raised his eyes to the marine standing over them. "Which I'm happy to divvy if you've a mind," he added.

The private glanced to right and left, then gave a slight nod and Lovemore broke off a generous chunk of dried fruit which was quickly stowed in the sentry's leather satchel.

"So, you want the news?" Lovemore asked his friend.

"I hears the new skipper's arrived," Cranston grunted. He had been picking oakum for the past three hours and, taking advantage of the marine's sudden lack of attention, tossed the current length of used rope down and began to stretch his fingers.

"Yes, but do you know who?" Lovemore asked. Cranston shook his head as he tore a fig from the clump. "Tommy King!"

"Our old lieutenant?" Cranston gasped. "Well, there's a thing!"

"Could be good for you," Lovemore continued. "He and us go back a long way; all them weeks on the road in France, then pitched

80

up together in Verdun, to say nothing of what came afterwards."

"I'm on a charge," Cranston reminded him after considering the matter for a moment. "First luff has me written in the book an' I can't see King, nor Sir Dickie Banks hisself being able to do much about it."

"Maybe so, but it's still good news," Lovemore insisted. "Eighteen stripes ain't gonna hurt for more'n a week, and we'll have a decent captain in charge a darn sight longer. King's ships are happy ones; happy and successful. I'd say it's the best news we've had for a while."

"That's easy to say," Cranston shrugged as he helped himself to another fig, "but you've not got an appointment with the cat."

* * *

"From what you tell me, the ship is in good order, Mr Leyton." The words were true and had been prompted by a brief inspection as well as his new first officer's verbal report. Whatever plans he might have harboured for finding fault, Leyton seemed to have been doing an excellent job; there were no firm grounds to see him dismissed and King was unsure whether to be pleased or sorry.

"I should be happy to elaborate in more detail, sir," the man suggested. They were on the half deck after finishing the quickest of tours and King hesitated. Maybe it was age, but the journey seemed to have taken more from him than he expected. Now that he had reached the ship, read himself in, glimpsed his new command and exchanged a few words with Croft, all he truly wanted was the chance to rest. Rest and be alone; rare luxuries aboard any ship preparing for sea and, as King hurriedly told himself, only granted to captains of a suitably indulgent nature. Yet still he longed for the privacy of his cabin. His body servant had yet to arrive, he would appoint a gunroom steward eventually but for the time being could deal with himself well enough.

"I shall look forward to that, Mr Leyton, but perhaps in the morning; I have had a long journey. You will understand I am certain."

81

"Of course, sir," the man replied, although there was a measure of doubt on his face that King could not ignore. Leyton was plainly a man who liked to get things done and could already be drawing conclusions about his new captain; possibly wondering if King would turn out a laggard. After years of nursemaiding Wheatstone, he might be excused such an opinion, and King would soon put him right. But not then, perhaps in the morning.

And so he had broken away and made for his own quarters; the only part of the ship yet to be visited. He had served in frigates before and knew the captain's accommodation to be generous. Quite what remained of Wheatstone's furniture was still to be discovered of course but if there was a cot he would be satisfied.

The marine sentry came to attention as he approached and King supposed the man had reason to look surprised having only set eyes on his new captain a few hours before. Opening the door he stepped through to the coach. Two eighteen-pound cannon took up much of the space, but there was room for a sturdy desk, two small cabinets and numerous bookshelves, some of which still held an assortment of his predecessor's possessions. But the place needed no additional furniture and would make a suitable office.

On and into the stateroom, what many called the dining cabin. As a class, frigates varied enormously from the cramped, almost obsolete, jackasses to far more modern beasts that were built like scaled-down liners. *Tenacious* was closer to the latter and so offered accommodation verging on the palatial. King's new stateroom appeared not only large, it had an inordinately high deckhead and was well lit by the generous sweep of stern windows as well as a skylight. There was also a decent sized table, currently under a cover and closed up but King knew the design of old; fully extended it would seat twelve in comfort with more than enough space on either side to see such a group served. A further desk and a full-size chart table were set next to the larboard quarter gallery and there were even two heavy, upholstered chairs by the entrance to his bed space that looked wickedly tempting. He nodded to himself; this was excellent indeed and, again, no need for additional furniture. Providing Wheatstone's relations did not make a fuss he would be well set up.

Just the sleeping quarters to inspect now, then he might arrange for a steward to see to what possessions he had brought with him, before, finally, resting his weary body. The light deal door to his bed space opened easily and he stepped inside. Directly in front was the first of two cannon, then the hanging cot itself and beyond, a canvas washstand, while to one side stood a small table and chair, all of which were expected. What did take him by surprise were the two women immediately in front of the washstand and the fact that one was almost naked.

Chapter Eight

When he thought back on the incident, King decided it significant the servant girl, fully clothed and totally decent, had screamed while her mistress calmly reached for a robe lying over the hanging cot and casually covered herself.

"A gentleman would knock," she informed him coolly when this was done and the rebuke was sufficient to shock him out of his stupor.

"I am the captain of this ship," King announced, "and these are my quarters."

"Captain or not, I would have thought a King's officer would have some knowledge of good manners and possibly a little decency."

King blinked; now there was the chance to notice such things he discovered the woman to be quite fetching. Pale skin and high cheekbones suggested a measure of class while the tumble of auburn hair was well cared for and spoke of wealth and possibly an indolent way of life. Quite what she, or her servant, were doing in his quarters was another matter though. He supposed one, or possibly both, might be the wives of officers and, with Wheatstone gone, it was understandable that they should make use of the space. But that did not excuse the blatant disregard for his authority.

"I have no interest in your opinion and request you leave immediately," he said. The servant girl, mousey haired and shorter than her mistress, turned to go but, rather than follow, the woman folded her arms and treated him to a stern look.

"Neither I nor Alice are going anywhere," she informed him. "Our passage to Halifax is agreed and we have been granted this cabin to use as our own. So I suggest it is you that should be leaving."

"Nothing has been agreed by me," King retorted, "and I say again, I am captain of this ship."

"Well maybe you should discuss this with your admiral?" she suggested.

"Do you mean the port admiral?" King questioned. He could not imagine Cox, who was to command the convoy and a renowned misogynist, agreeing to such an arrangement.

"Indeed and the dearest of men. He instructed the late

84

Captain Wheatstone to grant us passage and I have no doubt will do the same to you. Now if you will excuse me, Captain, I am in the process of dressing and would appreciate some degree of privacy."

King drew breath; the past few days had been filled with so many mixed emotions that this felt like the last straw.

"You will not take that tone with me," he announced in a voice harsher than intended. "I have received no instruction regarding your passage and, should I do so, will protest most strongly. Women may only be carried aboard a ship of war by permission of the admiral commanding and, as *Tenacious* is to be sailing under Rear Admiral Cox, I can assure you no such consideration will be forthcoming. Now, you will oblige me by making yourself fully decent, collecting your baggage and leaving this ship."

It was an unnecessary broadside when a single shot would probably have served, and King felt instantly guilty. But, excessive or not, his words must have been on target and the look of defiance faded from the woman's face, to be replaced by something far more congenial.

"Perhaps you will allow me to explain?" she suggested and, when King had given a cautious nod, she turned to her servant. "Alice, would you leave us? I fear this might take some while."

* * *

"Whatever your personal situation, I fail to see how I may help," King said when she had finished. They had moved out of the sleeping quarters and were seated in the easy chairs in *Tenacious'* stateroom. Amanda Lévesque, as King discovered the woman to be, still wore the light silk gown and appeared completely decent, although there remained an element of awkwardness in the situation.

"It is only a passage to Halifax we require," she repeated for what must have been the third time.

King shook his head. "But why not a merchant?" he asked. "Most in the convoy are ultimately bound for Quebec but some shall be calling there and are more suited to passengers. The fare need not be excessive."

"It is not money I am concerned with." The note of defiance was returning. "What I cannot afford is a scandal. As I have explained, my husband-to-be turned out something of a scoundrel. And, I will make no bones about it, Captain King, I am not exactly in my first flush of youth. Gossip aboard such ships spreads like wildfire and many shall be travelling to Halifax; if it is generally known there that I have been jilted, the chances of another suiter will be small indeed."

"And do you so need a husband?" King asked. Now they had chance to talk, his impression of the woman was steadily improving although he remained conscious and mildly wary of a forceful personality at least equal to his own.

She smiled. "You know as well as I of a woman's place in society. I am not rich in myself but do have access to family money; any form of disgrace would see that come to an end and, though I might survive a year or two, in time should be destitute. And frankly, Captain, though I am not incapable of providing for myself, the idea of marriage did rather appeal. Obviously, once wed, all that I own would become my husband's, though I should have been certain of some degree of security, provided he proved himself trustworthy that is. However it seemed what honour my late fiancé did possess was insufficient to see us even as far as the altar."

"And I am sorry to hear of it," he said. "But perhaps if you were to sail under an assumed name?"

"Captain, we are heading for Canada, which is my home and a place I know well while the journey will take a considerable time. Do you think anyone could retain such a pretence aboard a crowded merchant? Were my story to become public knowledge, I should be the talk of Halifax which would be disastrous for my father's business. Captain Wheatstone was happy enough to take me, even though I sensed some form of payment in kind was anticipated. But if you will not show a measure of Christian charity, I shall simply have to go back to dear Admiral Garston, tell him of today's events and throw myself on his mercy. I am sure at least one respectable officer can be found who will sympathise with my predicament and not attempt to take advantage of it."

King bit his lip; his recent intrusion may sound less innocent when related and, though such a thing might not affect his career as such, Aimée would doubtless hear of it. "But where will you sleep?" he asked vaguely.

"The quarters I have already would seem adequate – providing all are prepared to be discreet," she added with a flash of eyes.

"And your servant?" he added, conscious he was steadily abandoning control.

"Alice will spend much of her time attending to me and might bed down on my floor. However, I gather Captain Wheatstone intended she sleep downstairs and was to give her your first lieutenant's cabin – a Mr Leyton is that not right?"

King nodded obediently. It was a reasonable solution, Leyton's cabin in the gunroom had its own head which would allow more privacy and, with the absence of a chaplain, they did have a spare berth.

"I am not certain," he said. It had been a busy day in a busy week and now the initial shock was over he was keener than ever to rest. "I suppose I could use the coach," he mused.

"It was what Captain Wheatstone proposed," she agreed, adding, "at least, that is where he said he would be sleeping."

"Then I suppose it might be made to work; Admiral Cox need not know and, if he does discover, I shall simply refer him to the port admiral here. Though, should I find the situation intolerable, you will still be transferred to a merchant."

"Then I must see you do not," she told him with a half-smile. "But there is one more thing to request; I would wish for a bed."

"A bed?" King questioned.

"Sure, it is how normal people sleep." Now her expression softened further. "Once they have grown out of their cots I am meaning."

King found he was smiling also. "And not unknown aboard ship," he assured her, "where they are referred to as bunks."

"Yes, I have noticed a tendency for sailors to choose their own terms when perfectly serviceable ones are available."

He raised his eyes. "I cannot answer for that but will ask the carpenter to provide you with a bunk – a bed," he corrected, "and have your cot removed."

She nodded her thanks and there was a pause. King could hear the sound of bare feet on the deck above, a steady thump as *Tenacious'* gunner attended to the housings of the forward cannon and the distant grumbling of a warrant officer berating some hand; common shipboard noises he was well acquainted with, yet they seemed almost out of place in such a domestic situation.

"If you will grant me this, I promise to honour your own

privacy," she added. "And, once we are underway, shall hardly be noticed. Though, heaven knows, you must have seen enough of me already!"

* * *

A frigate's gunroom took the place of a wardroom, which was a voluntary arrangement that shared the space provided for senior men to the best advantage. Each lieutenant or high-ranking warrant officer was allocated an individual cabin which, though not vast or particularly robust, gave a measure of privacy. These were set to either side of a central shared area where they could eat and socialise together and there was even a pantry and small galley that, in theory at least, could provide fresh hot food. It was usual for the first lieutenant to be the president of the mess and so be entitled to sit at the head of a permanently erected dining table and give judgment or wise counsel on the officers' domestic arrangements. And being that he outranked them all, these decisions were usually accepted without dispute.

Croft had carried out this duty aboard several other ships so, at first, it was hard not to make for the head of the table and instead adopt a lesser place to one side. Equally, when Lieutenant Leyton made a ruling, be it about the current state of their wine supply or the amount of fresh vegetables needing to be purchased for the officers' consumption, it felt awkward listening to another's opinion. And there was no doubt that on first discovering he was not to be *Tenacious'* first officer, Croft had been shocked and mildly put out, although it had not taken long to adjust to the arrangement. What he had told King on that rainy afternoon was correct; any seagoing post would have been welcomed as, after many applications, the alternative of a respectable retirement seemed far more likely.

Nevertheless, Croft had not wanted to retire, and still the idea appalled. Such a thing would mean a change far greater than any subtle alteration in status and one there could be no returning from. He should have no further excuse to rent rooms but must take on the responsibility of a house and all that entailed. And though he might function well as a sea officer, he was well aware of deficiencies in other areas; there would be servants to hire, a cook, a gardener at the very minimum, if he wished to maintain a place in society. With the money acquired through recent commissions, he need not worry for funds and could use his rank to assume the post of gentleman, although the idea of living on land and never again experiencing the cut of a salt wind was too terrible to contemplate. So when the call came, all such thoughts were gratefully dismissed and, though it felt strange to watch another of a similar age and temperament carrying out his former duties, just to be aboard a warship again made up for any resentment. Besides, as Croft watched silently from his place at the side of the table, he quickly decided that William Leyton was not doing a bad job.

They had different views on some matters of course; to his mind, Leyton was far too keen on distancing himself from the general hands, relying on junior officers, and the overuse of the punishment book, to instil discipline. And then there was the question of how he would get on with the captain...

After several incompetent commanders, Thomas King was the first Croft had felt able to respect yet, inspired and capable though he may be, the young man was not without faults and some took a while to accommodate. From what he could gather, it had been usual for Leyton to advise his previous captain to the extent that he had more or less run the ship; King would never permit such presumption, and neither did he respond well to any degree of pomposity. But that was something the pair of them could sort out and Croft would gladly leave them to it. To be at sea, aboard a warship and amongst men he was coming to know and respect was all he truly desired. Besides, his newfound freedom might allow a measure of relaxation on his part; there should be the chance for serious reading and perhaps he might enter more into the social life of the gunroom; something he had been unable to indulge in when second in command.

One of the stewards had entered and was currently speaking with Leyton. And it was a perennial complaint; it seemed mice droppings were common in the pantry but now small hairs had been spotted within a crock of butter. Croft watched with interest as the first lieutenant addressed the problem. Ultimately it would remain unsolved; measures could be taken but no ship was ever free of vermin and attempting to make it so would only bring disappointment and frustration. But not for him; Croft was quite content for others to deal with such issues.

* * *

Amanda Lévesque was keeping her word; since speaking with King she had barely moved from her quarters while her maid attended to laundry and similar tasks elsewhere in the ship. So when the girl finally tapped at the light deal door, she was especially pleased to see her.

"And how did your patter with the captain go?" Alice asked as she unbuttoned her apron and slumped into the only chair the small space held.

"Oh, well enough," her mistress told her primly. "Sure, Captain King is as most sea officers: pompous, opinionated and totally naïve."

"But we are staying aboard?"

"Undoubtably," Lévesque confirmed. "Our passage to Halifax is guaranteed and won't have cost us a penny."

"More to the point, it will have been done on the sly," the girl remarked with appreciation, "though I would still rather sail aboard an Indiaman..."

"Then it is the pity one is not travelling to Canada," her mistress sniffed. "Yet I should not have taken passage aboard even so. Sure, we have fleeced John Company enough in the past and their world is a small one. Names can be changed but not faces: it only needs one former conquest to spill and..."

"Don't bear thinkin' about," Alice agreed, "though one of the larger boats would have been better than this."

"Most are carrying troops, and those offering civilian berths are popular with army officers," Lévesque mused. "Some might be colleagues of those recently trimmed; several weeks in their company might have made remaining in England any longer appear relatively safe."

"'Tis a pity even so," the maid sighed.

"May I fetch you a glass of lemonade?" her mistress asked her.

"Lord bless you, I been over an 'ot iron most the afternoon."

"We have quite a supply; one of the captain's servants brought it after our little conversation."

"Then you did make a good impression," the girl commented with approval.

Lévesque reached for a pewter jug set on the table and filled two mugs before handing one to the girl. "We discussed some details of our stay," she continued. "I'm afraid you will have to sleep with the men."

"No novelty there," Alice smirked, "though I suppose you're meaning in them rooms downstairs."

"I do indeed," her mistress replied.

"Why can't I bed down here?"

"Because it would not be seemly, and I might need the space. But you will be getting one of the better cabins."

"I'd rather stay with you."

Lévesque cast a sidelong look. "There may be the odd exception," she said, and the girl gave a coy smile.

"Oh, and they will be making a door in that wall," Lévesque added, nodding towards the thin bulkhead that separated their quarters from the half deck beyond.

"That will be useful," Alice remarked, impressed. "And should make my comings and goings the easier."

"Sure, I think Captain King was more concerned with his own privacy," Lévesque murmured. "The alternative is for us to continually troop through his bed space and I could see that did not appeal."

"He were properly hooked then?" the maid smiled.

"Gobbled our story like a chub. Sure, men are such strange creatures, all bluster and puff but, once you get behind their armour, as manageable as any chit."

"Well, it sounds like you've worked your magic," Alice said, resting back in her chair and sipping at her drink.

"I think so," her mistress agreed. With the cot filled with laundry there was nowhere else to rest, so she leant against a cannon and drank also.

* * *

King was impressed despite himself. He had spent much of the previous day studying the ship's books including all records and notes from former captains as well as dockyard reports and general recommendations. Then, when he felt enough was known about her fabric, he invited Leyton to the great cabin. They had yet to fully victual and any reasonable first lieutenant should have an outline of what they might need. But possibly more importantly, he wanted the chance to speak to the man in private; discover exactly what was going on behind that stiff exterior and perhaps why he had been content to finish his career nursemaiding a fellow such as Wheatstone.

And impressed was definitely the right word. Despite his captain's untimely death, Leyton had accomplished a great deal and seemed uncommonly on top of matters. King sat back behind his predecessor's desk and surveyed the pile of ledgers Leyton had brought with him. Those stores a first lieutenant was permitted to indent for had been ordered and noted; these included the petty warrant victuals that kept *Tenacious'* crew fed from day to day, as well as other consumables such as soap, candles, tallow and the like. Other, deep sea, provisions were not within his remit and *Tenacious'* hold seemed particularly light, while she only carried a derisory amount of shot, powder and gunner's stores. But in each instance, Leyton had calculated the quantity required and made a pencilled note in the relevant ledger. Were King prepared to, he might send in all the standard requisitions expected of a captain about to sail without checking further or even moving from his desk. So yes, impressed summed up King's feelings perfectly, although equally he could not ignore a slight sense of disappointment. For if Leyton had failed at this first hurdle, he might still have found reason to see the man dismissed and allow Croft up as replacement; as it was, he looked like being stuck with the fellow.

"You've done well, Mr Leyton," he said, glancing up. "I could not have asked for more."

"Captain Wheatstone requested I undertook much of the work when we first put in," the older man replied deprecatingly. "After his passing, it seemed logical to continue."

"It must have come as something of a shock," King mused. "To lose your captain in such a manner."

"It was a surprise, to be certain," Leyton agreed without a hint of humour. "We had sailed together for many years; *Tenacious* was our third ship."

King nodded; he could understand such an association. If he had been able to appoint Croft as his second in command, the pair of them would have been in roughly the same position. But, from the few notes Wheatstone had made in the log and his personal journals, the man appeared to have been an utter fool. For all that, they might have been friends though King could still not understand why Leyton, clearly a competent officer, should have wasted time on the cove, let alone become a follower. King hoped the relationship between himself and Croft stood on a more equal basis.

"Has there been a funeral?" he asked; Leyton shook his head.

"Captain Wheatstone was from Dorset and had few family; an uncle has sent for the body and I believe there will be a ceremony in his home town."

"Which doubtless you will wish to attend," King supposed.

Leyton's expression remained set. "I have no idea when it might be and frankly had not thought to enquire."

"There remain four days before we are due to sail," King reminded him. "There may yet be chance."

"Thank you, there is no need."

Now that was a further surprise and perhaps an additional deepening to the mystery. But King moved on.

"Captain Wheatstone agreed to take a Miss Amanda Lévesque as a passenger; did you know of this?"

Now there was a change in Leyton's countenance, and he appeared distinctly uneasy.

"I knew nothing until she was presented to me the night Captain Wheatstone died," he replied, with a hint of defiance. "I have since spoken with the woman and received her story. If I may say, sir, the concept sounds highly irregular; were I consulted first, I would definitely have been against it."

King nodded; Leyton had spoken of being consulted in such a way as to suggest he was used to being involved in the captain's decisions.

"However, the accommodation suggested seemed appropriate," the older man continued. "And I did not wish to raise too many objections for fear of besmirching Captain Wheatstone's name and reputation."

Yes, that was reasonable, King supposed a little bitterly. Far better to let a new captain face such problems.

"Has there been any reaction from the people?"

"Regarding the women's presence?" Leyton clarified. "Nothing of any significance. A few lewd remarks when the servant girl was attending to her mistress's laundry, but they were swiftly dealt with."

That brought up another point that was far more pertinent to the health of the ship.

"Indeed, I wished to address that." King reached forward and

93

collected a small red ledger. "I note the punishment book is already well used; Captain Wheatstone made good practice with the cat, even in so short a period."

"We were working up," Leyton replied quickly, "and some things are better demonstrated than threatened, especially at the start of a commission. It was a matter where Captain Wheatstone and I were of one mind."

"At the start of a commission the men will be finding their feet," King pointed out.

"But if you'll excuse me, sir, should undue leniency be shown it must be paid for later."

King made no reply; Leyton's attitude was by no means rare and might even be considered the norm, despite recent reforms. King supposed he was lucky in that most ships he had served aboard had not made excessive use of corporal punishment while, as a captain himself, he had never felt a need beyond the occasional unavoidable case. And if his new first officer was of a different opinion, he would simply have to alter his ways.

"There is currently one awaiting your approval," the older man added.

"Indeed?"

"A man from the new intake who is definitely in need of correction," Leyton continued. "The master-at-arms reported him."

"That would be Mr Guppy?"

"Indeed, sir; a sound man and especially good in his post."

"I have noticed him on deck," King confirmed, "and observed his habit for carrying a rope's end."

"A starter," Leyton agreed quietly, "and as a form of encouragement, no more."

"When in the hands of a boatswain's mate, perhaps," King allowed. "But Mr Guppy is not a boatswain's mate, he is a master-at-arms. It is a responsible position and, though he must maintain discipline, there should be no need to rely on corporal punishment to exert his authority; you might care to mention that."

"I shall indeed, sir," Leyton confirmed.

"So, what charge did Mr Guppy bring?" King asked, moving on.

"General filthiness, sir, but that is more of a catch-all; the fellow appears to be a competent seaman but too fond of exhibiting his independence and we both thought he would benefit from being

94

taken in hand."

"I see," King mused. "We might speak of this later; there is much else to attend to. But I do not wish for this to be a flogging ship, Mr Leyton, and if that conflicts with the views of any aboard I fear it will be them that will be taken in hand."

Leyton opened his eyes slightly wider but made no comment.

"So, tell me more about the crew," King suggested, feeling his point had been made. "*Tenacious* is fully manned, I understand?"

"Indeed, sir; we had been fortunate, although I understand Captain Wheatstone enjoyed good connections with the Impress Service. Rather more ordinary than able, but fewer landsmen than is customary. And yes, we are currently over our recommended wartime complement."

"A rare thing to be sure; how did such a state occur?"

"We ran into a homebound merchant before our arrival at Falmouth," the older man replied with evident satisfaction. "Took seven of her crew and all prime seamen."

"And was the port admiral informed?" King asked. In cases where men were pressed at sea, it was customary to declare the fact on reaching the next home base; the ship concerned would usually be allowed to retain the extra hands but in cases where she was already well provided for they were redistributed to more needy vessels.

"I think not, sir," Leyton replied levelly. "Captain Wheatstone made no mention of having done so and the men remain with us."

King glanced down at the muster book. If that were the case it was a mild infringement of the rules and no one would blame him for turning a blind eye to it. He ran down the list of names and jumped slightly when two stood out.

"Cranston and Lovemore," he remarked, looking up.

"Yes, sir," Leyton agreed. "From the new intake; do you know of them?"

"I have served with men of the same name and they are hardly common. As I recall they were fine hands; a might flighty on occasions maybe but I should be glad to sail with them once more."

Leyton did not share the smile. "I fear one is down for punishment, sir," he said stiffly. "The man I spoke of."

Chapter Nine

Nearly all requested victuals had been stowed and *Tenacious* would soon be taking on shot and powder; once both were safely aboard, they only need top up on water before the ship could be allowed to leave harbour. And that day had been set for the following Thursday when, in company with three merchants currently at anchor to the other side of the bay, she would set off in search of the convoy. Cox's force was scheduled to leave Spithead the day before and, due to its size and the accuracy of semaphore communication, King had little doubt they would find it easily enough. And he was equally certain the water would arrive in time; so far everything his second in command ordered had been prompt and of a reasonable quality. In fact, Lieutenant Leyton had given him little cause to complain, even if it seemed the man himself might be holding a grudge.

When King was given the details of Cranston's case he summoned the seaman and questioned him personally, after which he found no difficulty in quashing the charges. Leyton was present and said nothing as the full story finally came out in all its tragic innocence. For a captain to overrule his first officer was a delicate matter but, with such blatant evidence, King considered it potentially more harmful to discipline if he allowed punishment to continue.

It was done as subtly as possible, of course; Cranston was dismissed and returned to the punishment deck and only later, when King finally addressed the entire ship, was the matter mentioned in public. And then it had been relatively easy; after an introductory speech that he hoped also to be a rallying call, King continued with slightly less formality. Most of the hands were unaware of the ship's intended deployment, so he had enlightened them in the broadest terms. The fact that they would be escorting a convoy brought little excitement; as a mission, it was one better than blockade duty but considerably inferior to the cruise many would have preferred. Nevertheless, the very act of sharing information implied a measure of trust that he hoped would be returned. Then there had been a few necessary promotions; to make up for deficiencies amongst the petty officers, two able seamen were to be rated boatswain's mates and a quarter-gunner advanced to gunner's mate – news that was generally well received. And then it seemed entirely natural to address the subject of punishments.

Which King did, as delicately as possible, making it clear that no indiscretions would be ignored, but equally he had little intention of turning *Tenacious* into a flogging ship. And, as a new captain with a new regime, he wished to start with a clean sheet so all current punishments were cancelled, on the provision that they would be reinstated and doubled if any offender transgressed in the following three months. King had been careful to check nothing so very great was in process. Apart from Cranston, there were only three stoppages of grog and the wearing of a wooden collar for a man convicted of repeatedly swearing, so the sparing of a new hand brought little comment. And neither did King think he had undermined the first lieutenant in any way but rather the reverse; again, it took little in the way of verbal skills to intimate that Leyton had been instrumental in seeking clemency for Cranston. Whether anyone was particularly fooled was another matter, but he had made his point and possibly Leyton had learned something from the episode.

But at least he had fewer concerns with Lieutenant Croft. Amid the rush of preparing *Tenacious* for sea he had found time to speak with his old friend. It was in the great cabin and, with his servant still yet to appear, the interview had been as private as possible aboard a wooden ship. And Croft had been as solid as King hoped; yes, he had expected to be first officer, but any seagoing position was welcomed, and the man had made a special point of saying how pleased he was they would be sailing together. The last point had touched King deeply for their relationship had not started well and even now he wondered exactly how much he had in common with the elderly officer whose attitudes and expectations tended towards those of the last century. Yet the empathy they shared was hard for King to ignore, as was their innate camaraderie. And it was gratifying to discover Croft felt the same.

* * *

"I trust your meal was agreeable," Lévesque told her maid.

"Very nice, thankin' you." Alice placed the covered tray she was carrying on the small table. "We was given mutton stew and it looks like you got the same," she added after removing the cloth. "Really, I don't see why you can't eat with us in the gunroom. Or with

97

Captain King if it comes to it."

"I should at least take my meal an hour earlier," Lévesque agreed.

"So, why does 'e keep you cooped up so?"

"Oh, I dare say I could go on deck more often," the woman pondered, "but prefer to keep my face hidden, at least until we have sailed."

"Maybe he'll ask you then?" Alice supposed, adding, "You 'ave the chair, I wanna try out the new bed."

Lévesque obediently moved across to the tiny table and seated herself. "I trust yours was warmer than this," she remarked after taking a mouthful.

"Pipin' hot," Alice confirmed with a grin, while bouncing on the straw mattress, "though the company were some'ow lackin'."

Lévesque gave a wry smile and continued to eat.

"There is an old man in charge who's got some sort of chip on his shoulder, and another 'bout the same age what don't say nothing to no one."

"And they are friends?" the woman enquired.

Alice shrugged. "They're both so quiet it's 'ard to tell. Though I shouldn't like to leave 'em alone with any sort of weapon."

"Anyone else?"

"Young lad name of Taylor, he's alright. An' some other coves – no idea what they all do. Oh and a couple of soldiers – marines I think they're called. Both have ruddy great plums in their mouths – and wanderin' 'ands, but I've come to expect that..."

"As long as you don't start liking it," her mistress warned.

"Don't mind 'em samplin'," Alice corrected, "but they're not getting nuthin' else for free, an' I ain't starting business till we're movin'."

"You sure you want to?"

"Don't see why not; all I need is a place to work and that can usually be found." She considered her mistress. "What about you?"

"Sure, I hadn't truly thought," the woman admitted. "We have fared remarkably well aboard Indiamen in the past so there's no reason why I couldn't sound out a few of the officers – sailors are supposed to be rich after all and all men are gullible."

"I wouldn't be so sure of that," Alice told her. "Most dress like scarecrows but you never knows what they got in the bank. Some of them we trimmed in Bristol looked 'alf-starved, yet they come up lovely once you put the twist on 'em."

"It's something to bear in mind I suppose." Lévesque prodded at her food with her fork. "Though you may be right; better to wait until we sail."

* * *

The shot was coming first; once safely stowed, when there was less chance of a spark, the powder would follow. And Cranston, revelling in his newfound freedom, was working the main yard falls. In this he was accompanied by Houghton, from his own mess. Lovemore and O'Grady were also close by at the fore, so they could exchange a wave when, as now, a fresh netting of shot was being attached. The work was monotonous but, with *Tenacious'* tackle being almost new, hardly taxing and Cranston was simply enjoying being in the open air; even hauling on a line made a welcome change from picking oakum.

"Let you out I sees." The voice came from behind and Cranston knew the owner without turning his head.

"That's right, Mr Guppy," he replied, his gaze remaining forward. The next net was almost attached; with luck, they would be given the order to haul shortly and it could not come fast enough for him.

"Got off light, if you asks me," the master-at-arms continued. "But then you will if you's a favourite of the captain."

"Former shipmate," Cranston corrected gently. "Served with him a couple of times, no more."

"That's not what I hears," Guppy continued, coming round to face the seaman. "Happen the pair of you go way back an' there ain't nothing you can do that's wrong in 'is eyes. Close friends are you?" he leered. "Spend a lot of time in 'is cabin?"

"You can think what you want, Mr Guppy," Cranston told him. The sailing master, by the hold, was ready to see in the next load and they were prepared in the barge below. "Though I'd be careful who you speaks to an' what you say."

"Why's that?" the warrant officer demanded, instantly suspicious.

"Haul taut!" The order was finally given, and Houghton took up the strain. "Hoist away – handsomely!"

Now he and Houghton were bearing down on the line, taking

turns to reach up beyond the other until the heavy netting appeared at the ship's side. It continued to rise until stopped by yet another call from the master's mate. "High enough!"

The load would now be swung in, before finally finishing its journey deep in the very bowels of the ship. Due to Houghton's silent support and the marvels of their tackle, Cranston could hold the weight easily with one hand while wiping at his forehead with the other.

"I said why's that?" Guppy repeated with more than a hint of menace.

"Because if what you say is true," the seaman sighed, "an' I got so much sway with the captain, I might just 'ave a word with 'im about you."

* * *

All was now safely stowed, they only needed water and the hoy was expected shortly. Once that was aboard they would be set for an early morning departure the following day. King collected the general orders from Rear Admiral Cox who had charge of the convoy escort and locked them in his desk drawer. They had arrived three days before and were plain enough; King had read them a number of times and felt he could recite every word if called upon. And the recent message from the semaphore station was no less vague; the convoy had left as expected and been sighted off Portland Bill. With the wind and glass steady there should be little trouble in picking them up. It was pleasing to note so much had been done in a short time and equally that Leyton was not the only one to work hard. Taylor, the new man, had been just as active while Croft was proving an excellent support to the second in command. Such an ability to change roles was rare in officers of any age and one that King appreciated greatly.

Sadly not all his junior men performed as well initially; on several occasions King noticed Guppy, the master-at-arms, continuing to overplay his hand and one of the boatswain's mates had been rather too fond of using his starter. He made his wishes known as subtly as possible and knew Taylor and Croft to be behind him; Leyton's support was not quite so obvious but slowly the new regime was being adopted.

And the hands were responding to a less severe approach. There were still the occasional problems; a small fight broke out between two watches while bread was being taken on board and a pressed man had attempted to hide away in a victualler. But in general the work was being done efficiently and with a far more positive attitude. *Tenacious* was fortunate in having a high proportion of trained hands; with a little care and rather more understanding, he felt confident of melding them into a crew to be proud of.

The one small fly in the ointment was finding a replacement medic. He had delayed contacting Surgeon's Hall in the hope of word from his old friend Robert Manning but as the days passed with nothing heard he was starting to lose hope. An application would surely provide him with a man trained sufficiently to carry out his duties, though King had hoped for better. To his mind a ship's surgeon should know more than simply how to wield a saw and the best treatment for the pox; he needed as great an understanding of his fellow man as any captain, and Manning had such qualities in spades.

A shout and the clump of his sentry's musket on the deck, followed by a far more genteel knock heralded the arrival of Leyton.

"The water hoy's in sight, sir," the lieutenant announced stepping into the great cabin. "Mr Steven, the cooper, has been alerted and has all empty casks ready to be filled."

Leyton was wearing an old, undress tunic as was sensible at such a time, yet still he managed to look well presented and, again, King was impressed.

"Very good. How was the water we took on at the Nore?" he asked, rising.

"Adequate," Leyton replied, "I could say no more."

"And how much water did you request?"

"Three tons, sir," Leyton replied with a hint of doubt. "Which should be sufficient to make up our requirements."

"Then what say we start a few of the old leaguers?" King suggested. "Nothing too obvious; see they are drained into the bilges, they can be pumped out later. But the hoys usually carry a little extra and I would rather be served with West Country water than the muck that has passed through London."

"Very good, sir," Leyton agreed although it was clear he had doubts and King noticed this.

"Is there a problem, William?" he asked.

"No, sir," the lieutenant began, "though such a thing might

101

not be in accordance with regulations."

"Oh, I am sure of it, though should rather take a risk and see the ship served with good water than do nothing and we all be poisoned. And it will be my risk," King added, "you will in no way be responsible."

"Yes, sir." This time Leyton seemed far happier to agree.

"Is there anything else?"

"If I may ask, sir, do we have news of a surgeon?"

"Nothing as yet I fear."

"And it has been several days," the lieutenant sighed.

King scratched at his chin. He had not been entirely honest with Leyton and to admit so now, after their last conversation, might give the wrong impression. As far as the first officer was concerned they were still awaiting a replacement from Surgeon's Hall, Leyton had no idea the position had been offered to Manning. "Our two surgeon's mates, how do they do?" he asked.

"Well enough, sir," Leyton replied. "Both could whip off an arm or a leg without trouble," he stopped as if suddenly remembering his captain's disability.

"Go on," King encouraged.

"And – and I am sure they may deal with the more basic ailments," the older man finished in a slight blush, "though neither could be called a surgeon."

King nodded; it was the impression he had formed after interviewing both. Plenty of ships had sailed with medical departments more poorly served and a competent fellow would no doubt be appointed and may do well. He simply wished the new man could have been Robert Manning.

* * *

Stations for leaving harbour were due to be piped and, on such a bright, clear day with the tide and wind in their favour, there could not be a better time. Lovemore sniffed the breeze appreciatively; the nearby land appeared lush and inviting while small trails of smoke could be seen rising from its houses and businesses. Despite the previous week's constant traffic to and from the various yards, few from *Tenacious'* lower deck had set foot on British soil and no official shore leave had been granted. There would be taverns and cat houses within half a mile of where he stood and, after being away from

England for so long, Lovemore could have handled a decent spree.

But it was not to be, they would be sailing that day and, though Eastern Canada was not so distant as New South Wales, it would still be a sizeable trip with no guarantee of time ashore at the end of it. Yet he remained a seaman through and through and would rather be underway than waste any more time at anchor, almost in touch of shore-bound pleasures.

Lovemore was once more on his favoured forecastle; ahead of him he could see the boatswain in the jolly-boat. They had singled up the night before and just finished raising topmasts and topgallants, now the warrant officer was checking their tophamper was correctly set up with yards properly squared. In Lovemore's opinion, one advantage of sailing with Captain King was the man's innate seamanship. Despite only the briefest times in which to put the ship to rights, much had been done aloft. *Tenacious* had only just come from refit yet several minor defects had been found and all were now corrected. More than that, improvements had been made; much of the new line was properly stretched and heavier mats had been fitted both to the topsail and topgallant yards. No ship would sail the sweeter for such provisions, but they should do so for longer and the foresight appealed to Lovemore's practical mind. Currently the boatswain's mates were leading parties in slushing the blocks; each sheave was actually self-lubricating due to the almost magical properties of the exotic wood they were turned from, but an additional layer of pig fat never went amiss. The wind-sails that had provided ventilation during their brief spell in harbour had also been struck and every brace, lift and halliard checked and coiled down where necessary, ready for their moment of action. Lovemore had served aboard vessels of all types and sizes; each was unique in their own way, but all shared the risk of confusion and uncertainty when they took to sea. *Tenacious* might be a new ship and one he had not volunteered for, with officers that had initially appalled and a lower deck lacking in spirit, yet he was strangely keen that she should prosper. Besides, there was a fresh man in command now, one he knew well and trusted totally. The hands had responded well to having a seaman in charge and, though a spell of escort duty in a warship would not have been his chosen future, he was phlegmatic enough to accept it as a better alternative to some.

Preparations continued; the gunner was currently inspecting the main battery of eighteen-pound long guns, seeing each was lying square in their ports and properly secured for sea while the wheel was being continually turned from hard over to hard over under the critical eye of the quartermaster. The captain had come on deck; Lovemore could see him further aft in conversation with the first lieutenant then, from the corner of his eye, he spotted something else.

A shore boat had put out from the nearby wharf and was making for them. It would be well known that *Tenacious* was about to sail so this might be important news or perhaps some last-minute instruction. Lovemore watched idly, it was a short trip and the boat was under oars. In the stern sheets he could see a midshipman and another figure, stouter and more formally dressed – possibly a civilian or some superior dockyard official.

"Looks like we got our sawbones." It was O'Grady; the Irishman also had a liking for the forecastle and had crept up on him unawares.

Lovemore nodded; that would be it. One aspect of *Tenacious* that had not impressed was her medical department which, even to his untrained eye, appeared something of a shambles. The boat was coming alongside now and both seamen peered down with ill-concealed curiosity. Yes, there was a midshipman alright and one Lovemore knew well. The lad had grown a bit in the intervening years but that was young Summers, or he was a Dutchman. During their escape from France the boy had been amongst their party and it was good to see him sound and apparently thriving. The other man was not so familiar, darkly dressed and wearing a large hat he was lucky to retain in such a breeze. One or the other – possibly both – looked to be joining the ship as there were several chests aboard the boat.

"Aye, that'll be the new surgeon," O'Grady confirmed. "An' a likely looking chap, not one of them youngsters what thinks they knows it all then finds some things forgotten."

"And it looks like we're gaining another youngster," Lovemore added.

Indeed the boy was clambering up *Tenacious'* larboard side and would soon be greeted by the captain himself, who had abandoned his sacred quarterdeck. But that was to be expected; the pair went back a long way and a shipmate – any shipmate – is always worth meeting up with. The surgeon was joining them now and for the first time Lovemore saw his face and knew who he was. And it appeared the captain recognised him as well.

* * *

"Pray do not misunderstand me, Bob," King found it hard to hold back the grin. "I would never look a gift horse in the mouth. But should you be here?"

Manning shrugged. They were in the coach of the great cabin to which King had almost dragged him as soon as his feet touched the deck. "I would not be anywhere else, Tom," he claimed.

"But your business, your practice?"

"My business shall run itself. The patients we attract are more there to be indulged than treated; few feel the need of a limb removed, which was always my speciality."

"As I have cause to know," King laughed. "But are you certain of what you may be letting yourself in for? We will be seeing this convoy to Canada, then who can tell? America is showing sign of dispute, I really could not say where we shall end up, or when."

"Then that will be little different to any voyage we have engaged upon in the past."

"And Kate?" King asked, suddenly serious. "She knows you are here? You are a family man now."

"She knows," Manning allowed. "And yes, I had not forgotten my commitments. In truth, we are still as close as ever though lead different lives and are the better for it. Besides, I might ask the same of you," the surgeon added.

"Of me?"

"You have obligations now as well, Tom; why you could not have been at Cuckmere more than a year since and here you are, up and off to sea. I doubt if Aimée's more than halfway through furnishing the place."

"It is something I have considered," King admitted. "The break was not an easy one."

"And possibly worse for her, if I'm any judge."

King went to protest but thought better of it; of all his friends only Manning had both the right and insight to make such a remark. And despite his natural reflex being to argue, inside he knew him to be correct. "Whatever, it is uncommonly good to see you," he replied at last, relaxing, and smiling once more. And then another familiar face attracted his attention.

It was Summers, his old midshipman from *Kestrel* and *Mistral*; he must have followed Manning and now stood awkwardly by the door.

"And you have brought young Summers with you!" he exclaimed, stepping forward to meet the lad. But perhaps lad was not the right word; Summers had grown physically since they last met and now sported a creditable amount of stubble on his chin. But the same enthusiasm shone in his eyes and, as King grasped his firm handshake, sensed not much else had altered.

"What with midshipmen's berths being in short supply, Michael has been living in our house a good while," Manning explained. "I brought him in case you needed extra. I believe he would serve in any capacity."

King turned back to the lad and considered making play; offering a place on the lower deck or perhaps as an officer's servant. But he noted the look of worried anticipation and took pity. "You will be a welcome addition to our cockpit," he said. "And when we make harbour, I shall be certain to see you put before a board."

"That would be fine, and thank you, sir."

King grinned at the new arrivals. "James Croft is with us and you'll find a couple more former shipmates on the lower deck, but *Tenacious* is no *Mistral*; she is hardly commissioned and has yet to truly settle. To be frank it is good to see some friendly faces."

A shout and the clump of a musket from the marine sentry signalled the arrival of another midshipman.

"First lieutenant's respects sir," the lad announced entering the coach and jumping slightly at the sight of an unknown midshipman. "We have received permission to get underway."

"Very good, Mr Brotherton, I shall be up directly. And you might take Mr Summers here and introduce him to Mr Leyton. He shall be joining us aboard *Tenacious;* I would be obliged if space could be made for him in the cockpit."

"Who is this Leyton?" Manning asked when the youngsters had left.

"He is my first officer," King told him hesitantly.

"But you said Croft was aboard," the surgeon questioned, and King nodded.

"That I did," he said.

Chapter Ten

The convoy was indeed a large one and had been easy to intercept. King made contact with the flag and paid his respects to Admiral Cox before handing over the three brigs under his care and taking *Tenacious* to her appointed station midway on the larboard beam. The weather was holding out well, they had a steady wind with only a light swell and by the afternoon had settled into the routine of convoy work. In fact, when Taylor came to relieve Croft at the beginning of the first dog watch, they might all have been at sea for a month.

"Anything unusual to note?" Taylor asked as he checked the traverse board.

"Nothing especial," the older man replied. "The larger vessels keep station well enough but there are a couple of brigs off our starboard quarter you'll need to keep an eye on and one especially has caused concern."

Taylor looked up and back and could immediately see the vessel Croft referred to; she was buff bowed and carried an assortment of sail that suggested a poor supply. The convoy was close-hauled on the starboard tack and even as he watched she luffed up, presumably involuntarily, and hung in irons.

"*Amphitrite*'s the closest escort," the second lieutenant continued. "She'll deliver a bottle should one be necessary but, if that be the case, prepare to drop back and cover her sector."

"Very good," Taylor agreed. When they first met he had been put off by Croft's abrupt manner, which was far too much like the first lieutenant's for his liking. But a week of working with the man had brought a change of heart. Though old for the post, Croft was undoubtedly a seasoned officer and had no objection to sharing his experience. Even in the short time, he had taught Taylor much.

"And there's a schooner further forward," he added now. "I've noticed her showing too much canvas and steadily creeping out of station. Penny to a pound Admiral Cox will signal us to give chase and drag her back."

"That would come as a pleasant distraction," Taylor grinned, glancing up at *Tenacious*' tophamper, "I have yet to see the old girl sail in earnest."

107

The frigate was under topsails and stays; in such a wind she could have added several knots to her speed with only slightly more canvas. It was frustrating in the extreme to be held back so, especially when they would probably need to maintain this snail's pace for several weeks.

"Should it happen, I would advise you to call the captain," Croft grunted.

"Call the captain?" Taylor questioned. "Just for the change of sail?"

"Especially for a change of sail," the older officer replied levelly. "And I should like to be informed as well."

"Very good, sir." Taylor's reply was automatic although it was clear he did not fully understand.

"You must remember, Captain King and I are also relative newcomers," Croft explained. "It was hardly a major voyage, but most aboard saw her down from Sheerness and have had some chance to sample how she handles. I'd say the captain is just as keen as you to show a bit of canvas and I would be equally interested."

"I understand," Taylor grinned.

"I'm sorry to be late, sir." It was a fresh voice and Taylor turned to see Summers, the new midshipman, join them by the binnacle.

"Technically you are not late, Mr Summers," Taylor told him not unkindly. "But standing orders stipulate officers should present themselves well before the new watch is called and there are barely minutes to go."

"Yes, sir," Summers agreed, mildly crestfallen.

"Very good, then we will say no more about it."

"Are you settling, Mr Summers?" Croft asked and the lad brightened visibly.

"Oh yes, sir," he beamed. "She's a grand ship, almost as fine as *Mistral!*"

Croft gave a nod in response and his expression had also lightened somewhat on speaking with his former shipmate. "I should chance you will come to prefer her, in time," he added.

The ship's bell rang out and the watch was called; Taylor officially relieved Croft, and Summers went aft to run the log while those of the starboard watch drifted below after being replaced by their larboard counterparts. Within minutes the ship had settled once more and all were accustoming themselves to their next period of duty. As a dog watch it would only last two hours, then they could look forward to the evening and their first night at sea for some while. And the view from the binnacle hardly changed; the brig that had been in trouble recovered and, probably due to her recent inattention, began keeping better station, while the schooner, though still carrying too much sail, remained relatively in place and appeared to have avoided notice from the flagship.

"I understand you have sailed with Mr Croft before," Taylor chanced when Summers returned from checking their speed and was wiping himself dry with some cloth.

"Yes, sir," the midshipman agreed. "He was the first lieutenant in *Mistral*."

"*First* lieutenant?"

"That's right, sir. And I've served with Mr Manning, the surgeon."

"Of course," Taylor replied, still digesting the information about Croft. "I recall you arriving together."

"When the captain called him he asked if I'd like to try for *Tenacious* as well, and fortunately there were space."

"Fortunate indeed," Taylor agreed. "And you are pleased to be back at sea?"

"Absolutely, sir," Summers beamed. "Though some of the other mid.s are right tarpots."

"Tarpots?" Taylor questioned. On becoming *Tenacious'* junior lieutenant he had been mildly disconcerted to find several of her young gentlemen to be older than himself but was surprised the matter was brought up so, especially on the very public quarterdeck.

"Yes, sir," Summers confirmed innocently. "There's only Vernon and Brotherton anywhere near my age; the rest are ancient – Mr Hedges must be close on forty!"

"A dastardly crime to be sure," Taylor murmured.

"Sail-ho! Sail off the larboard beam!"

All small talk came to an abrupt halt at the call from the maintop.

"What do you see there?" Taylor bellowed.

"Difficult to say, sir." It was Bovey, a West Country hand who would be fresh to his post. "I thought I'd caught a glimpse a moment or so earlier. She's gone for now but appeared to be making for us on a broad reach. Reckon she'll be in sight again in no time."

Taylor and Summers exchanged glances. They were still at the very mouth of the Channel; there must be a dozen reasons why a vessel should be steering such a course. But this was also dangerously close to the hunting grounds off Brittany where privateers were known to haunt. In theory there was nothing to fear from such a threat; *Tenacious* would be larger than the majority of such raiders and the convoy was adequately protected by other equally powerful escorts. But both ship and crew had still to settle down, and soon night would be upon them; it seemed almost rude to be interrupted so.

"I have her again now," Bovey's voice rang out once more. "She's small, though appears to be a warship – leastways, she's carrying royals. An' she's making to catch us."

"*Amphitrite*'s reporting her to the flag," Summers announced.

"We should do the same," Taylor ordered adding, "Messenger, advise the captain; say we have a suspected raider on the larboard horizon."

Summers chalked a note on the traverse board before summoning the signals party while the youngster that had been sheltering in the lee of the bulwark sped off on his mission. Taylor placed his hands behind his back and drew breath. The sunshine that had been with them so far that day had started to fade and a thin haze was forming on the horizon. They may well be in for some seriously bad weather but, whatever the situation, there would be no point in looking for the sighting; if Bovey could only just make it out from the maintop, some time must pass before anything became visible on deck. Yet a sail making directly for them was suspicious indeed, and the fact that it appeared to be a warship made it doubly so. The young man took a turn or two across the quarterdeck and sighed; if Captain King had truly been looking for a chance to test out his new command, he may well have found it.

* * *

Two hours later the new watch had been set but little was altered in the command group on *Tenacious'* quarterdeck. King had remained on deck after being advised of the sighting and with him were Leyton and Croft, both of whom had turned out on hearing the visitor was potentially a raider. Which now seemed more likely than ever; the warship had continued to close on them and, despite a sky now heavy with impending storm, could be examined from the deck.

110

She appeared to be a corvette; small when compared to nearly all the convoy's escorts, but agile and more than capable of taking even the largest of the merchants. And she was not alone; two sleek sloops trailed in her wake. They would be lightly armed with probably nothing more than nine-pounders, but faster and even more slippery than their leader. A studied attack from all three would have been difficult to defend in broad daylight; well handled, the small vessels would run rings around heavy frigates and their stately charges. And a night-time attack would be so much harder; especially one destined to take place amid what promised to be foul weather. Carefully spaced and using the oncoming storm as cover, it would be relatively easy for the French to cut out one of the merchants and, with a total lack of moon, the act might not be discovered until dawn.

There was still some doubt about the raiders' precise identity though; they might be French National vessels or the product of an especially wealthy and presumably successful private operator – possibly a collaboration of several. But though three light single-deckers was a small force to face eight frigates, two brigs and a liner, they still represented a major danger and one awkward to counter.

"Biding their time," Leyton muttered as he studied the leading ship through the deck glass. The French were on roughly the same course and just keeping pace while heavy cloud had darkened the skies well in advance of dusk. The first few spots of rain were also being felt and, without a word being spoken, all knew it would be a difficult night. "Though Admiral Cox could always despatch a couple of us," the first lieutenant added vaguely. "That might teach them a lesson..."

"To what end?" Croft enquired. "They would have the heels on *Tenacious* or any of our frigates and sending a brig would only lead to her destruction."

"How dare you, sir!" Leyton exploded. "Might I remind you that I am the first lieutenant? You will not contradict me on the quarterdeck!"

Croft made no reply and even stepped back a pace as if to acknowledge his lack of importance. And King also remained silent, for there was nothing he could think of to say that might ease the situation.

In general, he disliked quarterdeck comment although, ironically, was usually prepared to listen to Croft, a man he had served with and respected. And in this case, Croft was undoubtedly correct; the French would take great pleasure in leading any counter-attacking force astray. Once darkness fully descended it would only be a matter of time before they slipped past their clumsy opponents to gorge themselves on a convoy significantly reduced in defence. But Leyton was right in another respect: he was indeed the first lieutenant and Croft really should have known better.

King cleared his throat and looked about, conscious of the sullen atmosphere that had descended. Clearing for action might be a suitable distraction but it seemed an unnecessary fuss just to ease the tension between two officers. Besides, he had avoided doing so to that point for a very good reason.

Neither *Tenacious* nor her people had given him cause for disappointment; every manoeuvre had been carried out competently, even if most lacked the grace expected from a well-practised crew, while the ship herself, though stiff from the dockyard, was stretching her muscles and steadily coming to life. After a week of intensive exercise all would have bedded down into an efficient fighting unit but at that moment he was unsure how much could be asked. And it was their first night at sea – their first night under his command at least. The southern coast of Cornwall was thirty miles off the convoy's starboard beam; to have come across an enemy so soon into the voyage was unfortunate in the extreme. King pulled his watchcoat tighter as the rain increased then stepped forward to the break of the quarterdeck. He still nurtured a private hope the danger might pass – that the French would have a change of heart or the storm increase dramatically. If not, if combat became inevitable, there must still be time to knock down bulkheads and clear away the cannon, although that should surely not be for an hour or two and, he still hoped, possibly never.

He glanced down into the frigate's waist and considered his crew; they were expecting a fight and most apparently welcomed the prospect. The starboard watch was officially on deck; their larboard counterparts should have been below and resting or grabbing a hasty supper before coming up themselves at eight. But as King ran his eyes over the huddled bodies it seemed the world and his wife were present. Most were gaining what shelter they could under the slim larboard gangway while deep in muttered speculation. In the main they were new faces, although seamen aboard a man-of-war were the same the world over. He watched them with a mixture of condescension, respect and not a little affection. It would take more than a few drops of water to discourage a true tar. Obviously, he could clear the watch below away and instruct their petty officers to keep better order, but that was not in his nature.

He turned back and faced his officers. "What time is sunset," he asked absentmindedly, and both Leyton and Croft went to answer together.

"Five-and-twenty past seven, sir." And it was Leyton's reply that rang out, Croft having wisely deferred to the senior man.

* * *

An hour later it was all very much the same; the enemy was still off their larboard beam while the merchants – admittedly now sailing in better order – continued as before. Like a herd of zebra, they made slow, steady progress while seemingly pretending the lions stalking them did not exist. But the escorts could not afford to be quite so blinkered and King sensed it was only a matter of time before he must clear for action. Yet still he felt reluctant; there was time, and the chance danger might pass them by remained. And then he noticed something that made such a possibility even more attractive.

Until then Amanda Lévesque had hardly been seen. Throughout *Tenacious'* preparations for returning to sea she had kept a low profile and, apart from having to bed down in the coach each night, there were times when King even forgot the woman's existence. Once he had chanced upon her reading in the great cabin but she had left immediately and seemed content to stay in the sleeping quarters, even to the extent of taking her meals there. Her maid had caused slightly more trouble, and Leyton had shown great satisfaction in disciplining a steward for allowing her fresh water for laundry, although the couple's presence was causing few of the problems he had feared. But Lévesque had chosen that moment to appear and, though conservatively dressed in a generous overcoat, and despite making straight for shelter in a vacant spot next to the lee bulwark, the atmosphere on the quarterdeck immediately altered.

Owens, the duty midshipman, was casting the occasional glance and King sensed someone was bound to wander across and engage her in conversation while the entire signals party were staring openly. And it would not do, King told himself. *Tenacious* was a fresh ship, barely shaken down; soon she might be in the midst of a pitched battle and any distraction was to be avoided.

He made his move a fraction of a second before Owens; something the junior man noticed and wisely held back. Lévesque seemed unsurprised as he approached and they exchanged the usual courtesies, then King got straight to business.

"Madam I should warn you that we may shortly be going into action."

The woman nodded. "Alice has already said as much," she told him.

"Alice?" King asked.

"My maid. She has been speaking with one of your stewards."

King supposed such a thing was unavoidable; a maidservant was bound to converse with others of her ilk yet still the act was mildly annoying.

"And you will no doubt be requiring my cabin," she continued.

"It is likely, in which case a safe place will be found for you both."

"Sure, I shall be just as happy on deck, Captain."

"I am afraid that will not be possible," King replied. "If we go into battle this will be a dangerous place indeed; a station below the waterline shall be found."

"And will you be there also?" she asked.

"Me?" King's annoyance was lost amid his momentary confusion.

"Yes, Captain. If the deck is a dangerous place for a woman, it must surely be so for a man. Or are officers in the Royal Navy somehow granted immunity from enemy shot?"

"I do not have time for this," he snapped.

"No, I see that and am sorry," she said quickly. "I spoke in haste and was most rude, especially when you must have a deal on your mind; do please forgive me."

King blinked.

"It is just that the room you have provided, though generous and greatly appreciated, is a mite on the dark side. I have stayed there as much as I can, as I hope you appreciate, but on hearing we may be facing action felt some time in the fresh air might be allowed. I can, however, understand that my presence might be a distraction."

Her sudden change of course had taken King by surprise and he struggled for words.

"I shall return to my cabin forthwith. Should you need it, Alice and I will go to any part of the ship you feel advisable and undertake to keep well out of everyone's way."

"You might be of use," King began hesitantly. "Mr Manning, our surgeon, welcomes assistance."

"Thank you, Captain, but I know my limitations, and sick room nursing is well beyond them. Now if you will excuse me I shall not bother you longer."

Again King nodded and once more felt that, in some strange way, the woman had got the better of him.

* * *

"Decent fifth-rate should deal with any of them," O'Grady maintained from his position on the forecastle. "Or all at once, if it came to it."

Of the three, he had the least experience aboard a man-of-war, while the Irishman was also the one who trusted most to luck.

"Broadside to broadside, I'd say you was right," Cranston allowed, shivering slightly in the rain, and pulling his jacket closer.

"Though I wouldn't expect them to give us the opportunity," Lovemore added.

"Ah, the French ain't that clever when it comes to the sailing," O'Grady scoffed. "Nor much else if the truth be told."

"Usual French perhaps," Lovemore pondered. "Were they National ships I'd say we'd be safe enough. Since Trafalgar, Frog commanders have rather lost their spike."

"French is French," O'Grady shrugged.

"Curly's right," Cranston agreed. "Them'll be privateers; men of business with proper thoughts about prize money an' how it should be divided. You can forget a quarter share of nothing – if they take one of our merchants everyone aboard'll be set for life."

"And with a prize that tempting," Lovemore agreed, "they will not be easy to fight."

* * *

Summers was now officially off duty yet, like most aboard *Tenacious,* he had remained topside. But a stray midshipman on the quarterdeck is likely to be put upon and the lad had no wish to be sent for lookout duty at the masthead or any such uncomfortable position. So it was that he sought the shelter and relative sanctuary of the half deck and with Brotherton, his newly adopted friend, was studying the enemy through a larboard scuttle.

"You seen action before?" the younger man asked from behind while waiting for his turn at the peephole.

"Oh yes," Summers replied with more confidence than he felt. "Many times, both at sea and ashore."

"Ashore? You been in a landing party then?" Brotherton was amazed.

"I've defended against a landing party," Summers corrected.

"Successful was it?

Summers turned back and shrugged. "Standing here, ain't I?"

"So what's the score?" the younger man continued when he had taken Summers' place and was peering out. "That lot just going to sail next to us the whole voyage?"

"I should say not; we might be the more powerful force, but the French have the upper hand. They can attack whenever they wish, though only a fool would do so now when night's so close by."

"And we're the nearest escort," Brotherton agreed.

"Oh, that won't have much to do with matters. Soon as the sun sets they'll be off."

"Off?"

"Aye, I wouldn't expect them to stick around and signal their attack," Summers declared. It was a relatively new experience for him to be in the position of learned advisor and he had to admit to rather enjoying it. "They probably know exactly where they're going to strike already; the better privateers have set moves which they practise. Tonight's attack might be for'ard; they got sail in hand and, at the speed we're going, could reach the head of the convoy in under an hour. Or they may drop back, heave to and allow us to move on, then come up on our starboard flank and bother those on that sector."

"They'd go to so much trouble?" Brotherton questioned.

"Wouldn't be no trouble," Summers snorted. "Few hours work at the most, and probably no cause to fire a shot, nor face one in return. Find a sleeping merchant and run alongside; even the biggest might be boarded before you can say knife. Then all they need do is steer her away an' head south for home."

"But if an escort gets involved?

"Oh, that might make a difference. None of them would fare well against a frigate's broadside, but I doubt they'll give us the chance. Corvettes are slippery fellows at the best of times – I should

116

know I've served in them. They don't stay neatly in line and swap broadsides – can't afford to. And if a frigate tries something similar she'll find herself raked fore or aft, depending on the enemy captain's pleasure."

Brotherton had retreated from the scuttle and Summers noticed him give an involuntary shiver.

"And have you been in action afore?" he asked.

The lad shook his head as Summers took his place. "'T'aint nothing to it," he stated firmly as he looked again at the enemy. "Most times no one knows exactly what's going on; best thing is to listen out and obey anything meant for you."

"I'll be with the main battery; for'ard and to larboard."

"An' I'll be to starboard," Summers agreed stepping back. "So we won't be far apart."

"I done it in exercise," Brotherton announced. "Not in *Tenacious* maybe, but aboard the old *Splendid*, several times."

"And at sea?" Summers asked. "Live firing?"

The youngster shook his head. "Only in harbour; the old girl spent most of her time there. And it were always dumb show."

"You'll find live firing a mite different," Summers supposed. "And being in action's another matter altogether. It's the pity we've not had chance to practise."

* * *

Soon dusk began to merge seamlessly into darkness. And it was complete, King decided. Usually the sea reflected light enough to see a reasonable amount; shapes, if not colours, could be distinguished and starlight alone could bring ships safely into harbour. Fleet actions had taken place under such conditions but, in the driving rain and under a cloud-filled sky, the black cloak of night totally enveloped them.

He had cleared for action a few minutes before and now, with both watches officially on deck and the ship strangely bare and quiet, there was little else to do but wait for the enemy to strike.

"Who is at the masthead?" he asked and once more Leyton provided the answer.

"Bovey again by now, sir; he is well acquainted with his duties."

"I remember, from the West Country."

117

"Indeed. And Hacker is at the fore; new man but he seems to know his way about. With your order to change every half hour, we have to conserve the best for later."

King's senses were suddenly alerted; was there something in the first lieutenant's last comment: a vague criticism perhaps? The standard trick for lookout duty was an hour yet there was surely nothing so very strange in halving that, considering the circumstances? But Leyton had shown mild surprise when King gave the instruction, which obviously did not coincide with his own thinking. It was a small incident yet one that annoyed out of all proportion; the last thing King felt he needed was subtle criticism.

"You are familiar with the night signals?" he asked Hedges, standing nearby, in an effort to dismiss the thoughts.

"I am, sir," the man replied promptly, and King nodded in return. It was unusual to have a midshipman older than one of his lieutenants and *Tenacious* boasted three. With Croft and Leyton being far from young, *Tenacious* was in danger of being run by old men. But at least having Hedges as a signal midshipman gave a measure of maturity to the section. Now night was upon them Admiral Cox would be able to control his force to some extent using lights, rockets and flares, although there would be nothing like the sophistication of daytime communication. But the major disadvantage was rather more subtle; each signal sent or replied to would be obvious and must reveal the ships involved to a hidden enemy.

"Well, gentlemen, I think we might prepare ourselves for a busy night," King announced more generally. Having everyone on deck would be wearying indeed; the watch officially below might be dismissed and he could suggest some of his officers rest. With bulkheads down and the ship darkened, *Tenacious* would provide cold comfort although they might at least shelter from the rain and anything would be better than remaining on deck and staring into blackness. But as he was about to phrase the order, a cry from the foretop forestalled him.

"Deck there, I see movement!" It was Hacker, the new man, and clearly in earnest. More than that, he appeared to have spotted something Bovey at the maintop had missed. "Vessel off our larboard bow; I reckon she's trying to pass ahead!"

"How far off?" Leyton called, and it would have been better if he had used the speaking trumpet to focus his voice.

"'Ard to say, sir; probably two mile, maybe less."

The convoy remained close-hauled on the starboard tack; when last seen, the French had been on a similar course but must have manoeuvred. It would have taken little to simply add more sail, draw ahead of their prey, then tack and King was mildly disappointed that they should choose such an obvious move.

"Shall we signal the flag, sir?" Leyton asked.

"No!" King snapped, angry both at the suggestion – which was foolish in the extreme – and that Leyton should choose to make one. "Shake out the forecourse, and smartly now!"

A slightly crestfallen first officer passed the order on and soon there was a rumbling of feet forward as hands made for the shrouds. King knew the increase in speed would be negligible but was equally sure the French were not far ahead, there simply had not been the time to gain any distance. And though *Tenacious* would sail the faster under further canvas, showing her topgallants would also make her more visible.

"I have her now!" This was Bovey at the main. "It's one of the enemy sloops, I thinks, an' what looks like the other in her wake."

King shook his head; it was strange indeed for the French to attack so. By aiming for the head of the convoy they would surely be inviting attention; far better to go for the tail. With the current wind it should be possible to nip in quick, grab a prize and be away with the breeze on their quarter. Then a dreadful thought occurred: where was the corvette?

And was it significant that, as soon as King suspected the sloop attack to be a feint, he should catch Croft's eye? In theory the man should have been in the waist with his guns though he had reason enough to remain on the quarterdeck and King was glad of his presence.

"Flag and *Serpent* are for'ard," Croft said, clearly having come to the same conclusion. "If the sloops strike, they'll see them off."

That was undoubtedly true, in which case for *Tenacious* to come charging in would only add to the confusion. And if, as seemed increasingly likely, the corvette was planning a solo attack on the rear of the convoy, the escort strength there would be that much less.

So what should he do? King scratched his chin in thought. There had been every reason to abandon his station to investigate a sighting but turning away from a known enemy to go in search of one he *thought* might be there was far less excusable. Again he caught

119

Croft's eye, the older man's face was strangely lit in the glimmer from the binnacle but still King drew confidence from it. Croft knew him of old and must surely share his thoughts. And more than that, King sensed he agreed with them.

"Shall I prepare the larboard battery, sir?" Leyton again; he was still anticipating a meeting with the sloops and had no mind for any other course of action.

"No, Mr Leyton," King said, with deliberate clarity. "I do not intend proceeding further. Take us about, we are going in search of larger game."

Chapter Eleven

Even under minimal sail, *Tenacious'* speed increased with her turn and, when the wind came firmly on her quarter, the frigate began to positively thrash through the dark waters as she headed into a pitch-black night. To his right, King was aware Leyton disapproved of his actions and supposed he could not be blamed. After all, it was the duty of every first lieutenant to care for the ship, yet his new captain was apparently determined to send *Tenacious* into peril. Not only had they turned away from a recognised enemy but were now in danger from oncoming merchants. Admittedly the convoy should be a cable or so to larboard, but the longest any ship had been at sea was a couple of days and it would have taken no great error in station keeping to place a heavy trader directly in their path. If so, and on such a night, collision was almost inevitable and King could sense the man's tension as he fidgeted next to him.

He took a turn about the sodden deck and pulled his watchcoat closer. Yes, Leyton had every right to be worried; even now he must be wondering exactly why a madman had been appointed to command while doubtless cursing the day Wheatstone forgot to chew his food. But King could spare no further thought for him; Croft stood close by and, even though he must soon leave to attend *Tenacious'* guns, his presence was reassuring. He paused and stared up at where the maintop should be. "What do you see there?" It was proof of his growing anxiety that he allowed himself to bellow so, which was hardly becoming for a captain.

"Nothing to note, sir," the lookout replied after a pause. "I get sight of odd ships from the convoy now an' then, but no more."

King told himself not seeing an enemy was good, that it meant the merchants were safe. But as the minutes ticked by it also suggested he had been wrong in his assumption and taken *Tenacious* out of station for no good reason. If he remained on this course much longer they would come across *Amphitrite*, the escort that had been astern of them. To plough into her would be worse than running aboard a trader; a wasteful start to the commission and one he must be held entirely responsible for. Then Bovey's broad accent came through again, and this time it was to grant him absolution.

"Sail-ho! Sail on the starboard bow!"

There was something about the man's inflexion that told King they had found the privateer and he was tensing even as Bovey continued.

"Less than a mile off and steering to cross our hawse!"

A murmur of comment passed about the quarterdeck, but King cut through it with a curt order. "Look to your guns," he snapped at Croft, "the rest of you prepare for action."

If their masthead had only just spotted the Frenchman there was every chance *Tenacious* would not have been seen, coming as she was from an entirely unexpected direction. But the fact remained that an enemy warship was about to cross their bows; the Frenchman might not be carrying much in the way of heavy metal, but even nine-pounders would dig deep into a frigate's delicate prow.

So, what should he do, turn to starboard and allow the Frenchman access to the convoy? Or steer to larboard and attempt to head him off? The latter would be the more dangerous option as the risk of colliding with a merchantman would be far greater, while not knowing his opponent's speed made any form of calculation impossible. Still, it was King's job to keep raiders from his charges and there was only one way he could be sure of doing that.

"Take us three points to larboard, Mr Manton."

"Very good, sir," the sailing master replied, "three points to larboard it is."

"To larboard?" Leyton questioned.

"You heard me, damn it!" King snapped before turning his attention to Croft who was about to take up position in the waist. "Prepare starboard battery," he bellowed, "and you may fire when you think fit."

That was one advantage of having someone he could trust as gunnery officer; in such conditions, it was unlikely the Frenchman would be sighted for more than a second. By the time a broadside could be ordered from the quarterdeck the magic moment might have passed. Not only would Croft know exactly when to act, he had the confidence to do so on his own judgement. He and Leyton might share similar ages along with other characteristics and both had proved themselves efficient first lieutenants, but Croft was undoubtedly the better fighting officer and the right man for this particular task.

* * *

Lovemore and O'Grady were serving the same cannon, and both had long since been allocated tasks. Lovemore was to work the flexible rammer, a length of heavy rope that incorporated a lambswool swab to one end and a weighty piece of wood at the other; the former should purge every last spark from a recently fired barrel while the latter acted as a traditional rammer and would see the weapon firmly loaded. Using the length of rope to connect the two made the tool easier to use while alleviating any need to open ports on the lower decks and was one reason why the average rate of British fire was so high. And the Irishman had been given charge of the weapon's wadding and projectile; it would be up to him to have an eighteen-pound ball ready when required, that or one of several types of specialist shot designed to take out an enemy's rigging, tophamper or crew. The others had been assigned similarly and most were experienced when it came to ships' artillery. But, apart from an hour's exercise while becalmed off Dungeness, when neither Lovemore nor O'Grady had been present, there had been no gunnery practice aboard *Tenacious*. And now in the dark and the rain, they were to use her weapons in deadly earnest.

The idea appalled Lovemore, and he sensed the Irishman felt the same. Their cannon was a devastating weapon and one that required careful handling; badly managed it could be as dangerous to those serving it as any enemy, and these were not ideal conditions.

"What's the target, sir?" Wainwright, the gun captain, asked as Lieutenant Croft arrived.

"French corvette," he replied. "Expect to meet her off our starboard beam. And wait for my word."

They were turning again, merely a few points to larboard but, with the wind now being taken more fully on the beam, the ship began to list slightly; something her gun captains would have to make allowances for when laying their weapons. Though the chance of needing to seemed slight as they stared out into the utter blackness. How could mischief be planned in such terrible weather? Surely any seaman with a choice would be below decks and snugged down? Lovemore glanced across at O'Grady; both men were thoroughly soaked and, in the dubious light from the battle lanterns, appeared anything other than warlike.

"Alright, check your pieces." This was the voice of a

midshipman close by and all straightened at the sound. Lovemore flexed his rammer in his hands. The gun was already primed and loaded; all they need do was sight the enemy and take aim. The tackle men were ready with handspikes and there was another charge – six pounds of cylinder powder – safe and dry in the salt box while O'Grady had round shot by the score in the garlands.

"I have her!" This was the voice of Hacker, at the foretop, and all tensed, ready for more. "She's off our starboard bow but coming up fast on a broad reach. Less'n a mile off an' heading for a spot of dry; you should see her on deck any time!"

Still they looked and still it seemed impossible for anything to live in such weather; then the outline of a warship emerged from behind a curtain of rain. Suddenly the corvette was in plain view, well within range and with a reasonable portion of clear weather ahead of her.

"Be sure, lads," Croft's voice sounded out against the storm. "No point in firing at nothing."

Seconds passed; the French must surely have seen them but were holding their course. Then, as her foresail gave a flutter and she prepared to turn, Croft spoke again.

"Fire!"

It wasn't a simultaneous broadside; several seconds passed between the first and last discharge and there were moments of silence between. Yet each of *Tenacious'* cannon spoke which, considering the conditions and general lack of exercise, was an achievement in itself. But now the true test came; just as the shots should have been raining down on her, the corvette entered another patch of storm although that was of little interest to those at the guns. The officers might wonder about damage, or if their prey would change course – they had more immediate concerns.

And despite their inexperience, it was clear most knew what was about and were working with a will. At his piece, Lovemore was the first to attend the warm barrel sending his sodden sponge deep into the weapon's smoking mouth – turning the rope as he went and keeping his footing even as the ship gave an unaccountable lurch to larboard. Then the cartridge was ready and being offered up, followed quickly by O'Grady with round shot. A wad was added before Lovemore pressed all home, keeping pace with the barrel as those at the tackle heaved the beast forward. Wainwright, the gun captain, was there just as the carriage came to rest and had inserted the priming quill as all was being secured. The priming horn came next and, shielding the mixture of spirit and powder from the incessant rain, the Yorkshireman sent a generous dose down the touch hole. All now looked to Croft, standing close by. Their cannon was one of the first signalled ready, and in a time that would have done credit to a dry, daylight exercise. But it seemed the officer's attention was elsewhere. For the enemy had still not appeared and quite where they might be was anyone's guess.

"Sail! Sail-ho! Dead ahead and close to!" Hacker's voice made all turn and there was even a shriek of surprise from a younger voice forward.

"Braces there, braces!" Another shout, this time from a boatswain's mate on the forecastle and suddenly the ship was flung into the tightest of turns while the oncoming hull of a heavy merchant loomed ever closer.

"We're going to hit," an anonymous voice announced. "Damn it, we're going to hit!"

"Fend off there!" Taylor's order rang out loud above the sudden commotion and then, almost comically, *Tenacious* scraped past the larger ship, with only the snapping of lines to show how close their tophampers had been. Another cry from Taylor further forward sent a boatswain's party to attend the damage but Croft's attention was elsewhere.

"Attend your pieces!" he bellowed; to the gunners, it seemed the man had eyes everywhere and was ready for anything. There was still no sign of the Frenchman and, with the sudden manoeuvre, most had lost track of where he might be found. By now *Tenacious'* entire starboard broadside was ready but, without a target, there was little anyone could do. And the thought that somewhere in the blackness beyond, a potent warship stalked them was disquieting in the extreme.

* * *

Croft was equally unaware of the enemy's exact position but knew better than to reveal the fact, so when Summers approached to ask the obvious question, he swiftly diverted it.

"Never mind that, look to Osmond's gun; the salt box is open, their powder will be soaked!"

He turned away as the lad ran off to berate the crew and stared

125

out into the storm. If they had not needed to divert so it would have been a relatively simple matter to double back and find the enemy raider. But turning as they had – and from his position in the waist Croft only had a vague idea of the exact helm order – combined with whatever course the privateer might have chosen, left him literally in the dark. Captain King on the quarterdeck may have plans but the distance between the two men was far greater than the forty or so feet that separated them. Warning would be given if such a thing were possible, but Croft longed – oh how he longed – for a single glimpse; the slightest indication of where the enemy might be found and so be able to truly prime his men.

And it was not just the thought of releasing another broadside that filled his mind. So far they had been lucky and not been fired upon; *Tenacious* may even have inflicted significant damage and their opponent might, even now, be skulking away to tend their wounds. But that single broadside could equally have been ineffective, and he was uncomfortably aware that any enemy prepared to take on a superior force on such a night was not without spirit. At any moment the privateer might appear off their prow – or stern – and even a nine-pounder corvette could deal a hefty blow to a frigate if managed correctly. Should such misfortune occur there would be little *Tenacious* could do to return fire, and a severe raking would knock much of the frigate's stuffing from her. So yes, it would be pleasant to have even a vague idea of where they might be found, or at least be confident of an element of notice.

* * *

And King was just as unsure. Despite being on the quarterdeck and knowing the commands given to avoid colliding with the merchant, he too had lost track of his enemy. He sensed the Frenchman to be off their starboard quarter, although that was little more than supposition. But he had no doubt *Tenacious* was currently heading away from the convoy she had been detailed to protect and that was something he must correct. To do so may mean meeting with the corvette or another from the convoy, and then there was *Amphitrite*, the frigate that had the station directly astern of them. She may have shifted slightly in the storm or even sighted the enemy and be bearing up to engage her. But while all any of them could see was the dark, storm-filled night, there was little to be done. And King was grimly aware that so far he had achieved nothing other than to desert his own station and release one possibly ineffectual broadside; he really must do better.

"Take us about, Mr Manton." King's order triggered a dozen shouts and soon he felt the ship stagger slightly as the sailing master brought them through the eye of the wind. Then, with a creditable lack of fuss, *Tenacious* began picking up speed once more. Her deck heeled to the opposite tack while the taut lines gave out a slight thrumming and all began looking to their captain for further instructions.

"Continue round," King grunted. "I want to keep pace with the convoy."

"Shall I order the lookouts to be especially careful?" Leyton leant forward cautiously as if addressing a dog that might snap at him for no reason.

"No," King replied, trying to keep the anger from his voice. "They know the situation and will do well enough without our interfering."

The first lieutenant shrank back and King felt mildly guilty. It had been a reasonable suggestion; a rogue French warship was nearby who would be more likely to spot *Tenacious'* larger bulk than they would her. And one stray merchant had already been encountered; there were probably many others.

"But I think they are due to be relieved, are they not?" King added as a thought occurred. The new watch must have been called by now; such a thing meant little when in action, but he wondered if the lookouts had been changed according to his orders. Such a routine matter was the direct responsibility of the first lieutenant and, even in the poor light, he could see Leyton was unsure.

"I shall check, sir," the older man flustered, "and will see to it directly."

King sighed and glanced about, desperate to make something out in the gloom, but the night remained as dark. And then suddenly there was light – a flash of yellow erupted off their starboard quarter and so bright it might almost be tasted. Indeed King's mouth dropped as the colour turned to orange, then red before dying completely. The Frenchman was close by; not point-blank range but nearer than anyone had expected. And she had sighted *Tenacious* sufficiently to release a broadside. It wasn't quite a raking, but the frigate's vulnerable stern would certainly be in danger. And then the shots began to arrive.

* * *

The first struck their starboard quarter gallery and was quickly joined by others that peppered bulwarks and scantlings. A cloud of dust was instantly smothered by the rain but the vicious splinters were not so easily stifled. One found a soft target in the leg of a marine, who dropped his musket in surprise, another tore the shirt and skin from the chest of a gunner and a round shot dealt the barrel of a quarterdeck carronade a ringing blow that echoed for a moment and then was silenced. The starboard mizzen chains were also hit, though mercifully not destroyed, and another fortunate shot passed every member of the signals party, choosing instead to annihilate their store of flags and bunting. But other wounds were more deadly; two members of a starboard carronade's crew fell to the same nine-pound ball while a further round shot crossed the entire quarterdeck, missing binnacle, wheel and command group to pick off the twelve-year-old messenger crouching by the larboard bulwark. But though the blow had come unannounced, and all was confusion and terror for a moment, *Tenacious'* crew rose to the occasion.

In the waist, Croft, physically unaffected as were most around him, blew his whistle to summon the gun crews and, with Taylor, Summers and a slightly bemused Brotherton, directed the starboard captains to the threat. And Amon, the boatswain, who had been struck, appropriately it seemed, by a length of three-inch cordage falling from above, staggered to his feet and promptly ordered his team aloft. Some hands took to clearing wreckage or splicing line; others attended to the injured, strapping severed limbs with twine and canvas before seeing them below, while the shattered body of a seasoned hand who had seen action one too many times was heaved over the side and abandoned to his natural element.

And King, standing tall amongst the confusion, also reacted. For an enemy to take him by surprise was both deplorable and galling; even now, when the corvette's position had been so terribly revealed, he found his stunned eyes could make out little in the patch of squall that still hid her. But knowing where she had been was sufficient to give his gunners a better chance at striking back.

"Hold your fire, Mr Croft!" he bellowed, stepping forward. Then, without looking back, "Take her three points to starboard!"

Warrant officers backed up his orders but in the main their cries went unheard; the hands knew their craft and took up stations without further prompting. Braces were adjusted as the ship crept round and then came the incredible sight of their enemy's bowsprit, reaching out from amid the storm as if to rebuke them. That single spar was all the indication needed; their opponent was finally revealed and, more than that, shown to be in a vulnerable position with *Tenacious* about to cross the corvette's hawse.

"Fire!"

This was a far more impressive broadside and delivered just as closely as the one so recently received. Spurred on by their injury, the British gunners had put their all into that single action. Most fired together, only two of the quarterdeck carronades trailed slightly, although not by more than a second, and both had good cause.

For a moment the Frenchman was lit by British fire but by the time their shots landed, all was blackness. Still, even amid the storm, there came the sound of falling wreckage, a flash of canvas as it blew out in the wind and then, just as suddenly, a solid and more permanent light.

It came from the hull of the ship before quickly travelling up her masts where it burned proudly for a second and then was gone. But deep in the corvette, the fire remained and, as the warship staggered from such a killing blow, was soon lighting up her innermost recesses.

"Handsomely there!" Croft shouted at the straining crews. Sweat mixed with blood and rain as the gunners struggled to tend their monstrous weapons. *Tenacious* was continuing to turn, soon she would be close-hauled and creeping up the Frenchman's starboard side where the guns were unfired and must be a danger. But there could be no fear of the privateer striking back; the French had been fortunate in hitting them once but would never be so impudent again for, close to and with both in clear sight, the difference in their sizes was apparent. Croft glanced briefly to the quarterdeck where, lit by the enemy's blaze, King, Leyton and Manton could be seen quite clearly. The captain caught his eye and gave a brief nod.

"Fire!"

Again *Tenacious'* broadside spoke and, this time, the gun

captains had clear sight and could choose their target more carefully. The privateer lay less than two cables off and brilliantly lit by her own flames; all they need do was add to her torment.

And now the frigate was luffing up, steering intentionally into the wind to halt her progress. The afterguard and waisters did what they could to control her flapping canvas while the starboard gunners struggled to reload their weapons yet again. Croft turned away and caught the eye of Summers; the pair knew each other well enough to exchange a shake of the head. Both accepted the Frenchman was doomed. Another broadside would tell for her without doubt; if she did not blow she must surely strike. And though it were always better to be on the winning side, both were conscious of a mild feeling of anti-climax. For there could be little victory and no glory in accounting for a smaller foe.

Chapter Twelve

The corvette did not explode, but neither could she be saved. With the convoy still dangerously close, there was little that could be done other than allow the flames to claim her. The British did try for survivors; *Tenacious* hove to clear of the passing merchants and far enough away from her beaten enemy to be safe. Both cutters were then despatched with Hedges and Owen in command and each with stout men at their oars but, after searching for the best part of an hour without success, King had been forced to summon them back.

And now, more than a week later, the events of that night were merging into a single memory. Their damage had been addressed and repairs made; nothing fancy, the ship had been quite crudely patched in places but was once more serviceable. However, defects far more important than those to her fabric had been revealed which King addressed with a rigorous regime of exercise. Not everything was possible as the ship must still perform her primary task of escort but, when the storm finally eased, a reliable wind was found and, allowing for the creeping pace of a slow convoy, much could be achieved while still carrying out their duties.

The topmen were the first to be put through their paces; canvas was set, struck and set again, while the ship was made to tack and wear to such an extent that she occasionally turned entire circles. Having the men aloft gave the chance for experiments in different degrees of reefing and every officer, down as far as Brotherton and Vernon, was allowed to take command and see *Tenacious* through a series of prescribed manoeuvres under the sailing master's watchful eye. The gunners were also thoroughly exercised; like the frigate's topmen and foremast Jacks, they were mainly experienced hands and, after being bloodied in battle, had gained a degree of confidence that was bordering on arrogance. It was their officers' task, and Croft's in particular, to prick this blister of pride and see each knew their duties to the extent that serving their pieces became instinctive. Those of the starboard battery had accomplished more by having fired in anger and, after consulting with their divisional lieutenants, Leyton made changes to see the experience was shared.

This, as in all else associated with a first lieutenant's regular duties, he carried out with credible efficiency and King was no less impressed by the man's ability to manage the officers in general. But the fact remained Leyton had not been a sound support during the action, and King feared he never would be.

No blame could be attached for this, although equally it was not something that could be corrected, even by extensive exercise. In King's opinion, men were either fighting officers or not, and Leyton appeared to fall into the latter category. As a trait it was by no means unusual; aboard larger vessels a wardroom may contain several excellent officers who were well versed at handling a ship and often exceptional mentors for the younger men. In action, however, they were best given minor posts away from the need to think quickly and with dispassion. And lacking the spirit for combat was not something that carried any degree of shame; there were times in King's own life when he had been unable to summon up sufficient stamina to out-think an opponent or simply confound him with a lateral approach. Moreover, Leyton could hardly be criticised for failing to follow King's train of thought when such a thing frequently lacked reason, yet his shortcomings remained significant enough to be annoying.

And there were more; it was also proving impossible to cure the man of his fixation with punishment. Much had been done to limit the amount of starting with a rope's end, the favoured tool of persuasion for most warrant officers. After being taken in hand on more than one occasion, even Guppy was beginning to show a degree of control. But this had all been from King's instigation; Leyton apparently lacked any degree of sensitivity when it came to correcting the hands himself, and neither did he seem capable of inspiring others. He might pay lip service to his captain's stated policy for fair and equitable discipline but it did not meet with his approval and his daily list of minor defaulters remained high.

This, and all other irritations, were heightened in no small way by knowing there was another close by just as capable who could almost read his mind. King and Croft might be an unlikely combination, and one that neither would probably have chosen, but the pairing undoubtedly worked, whereas that of King and Leyton did not.

Which was a situation that could not be allowed to continue, King decided when he had finished a solitary supper ten days after the action. The time to consider had been necessary to avoid any rash decisions although now he regretted not having been more definite at the outset. If he had instantly rejected Leyton, Croft would be in his post and they might have a fresh and probably younger additional lieutenant; possibly even Cooper, had there been time. His concerns about *Tenacious* being run by old men would have been quashed and, as the crew's exercises continued, they might also be melding a truly efficient band of officers.

The convoy was currently south of Ireland; at the current rate it would be several weeks before they raised Halifax. He might apply for a replacement there, though it would be hard on Leyton to be ditched miles from home, and the chance of finding a decent junior on a foreign station must be smaller. But if, as seemed likely, *Tenacious* was retained under Warren's flag, he would have no hesitation in swapping the first lieutenant.

Nothing had been set in stone of course; there remained the chance they would be sent directly home. An eastbound convoy might be assembling even now and could be ready to go almost as soon as they arrived. But be it in Halifax or Falmouth, Leyton's time aboard *Tenacious* was limited, it was just a question of when and where he was dismissed.

* * *

The average lower deck hand enjoyed few liberties, but one was the right to choose his messmates. Applications to change messes were permitted and usually made directly to the first lieutenant. If the officer concerned was efficient and genuinely cared for his men, a reason might be requested and any suspicion of bullying, intimidation or coercion passed on to the divisional officer responsible to investigate. But if there were no objections from the new mess, and especially if the extra man made them up to an even number, permission would normally be granted. Yet despite it being a simple system and one that usually favoured the seaman concerned, Cranston was reluctant to approach Lieutenant Leyton; the man had been noticeably absent when accommodation was allocated and his recent acquittal from what had been shown to be a trumped-up charge might still rankle. Besides, the first lieutenant, with his dour countenance and fiery temper, was simply not an officer to approach unless absolutely necessary.

Yet life in his current mess was starting to depress him; despite making every effort at geniality, Cranston's only true friend was the youngster Longdon. The others were solid enough but lacked warmth and their formal mealtime conversations and equally sombre recreation periods simply did not suit his temperament. Once, greatly daring, he had suggested a round of Crown and Anchor only to have the proposal treated with something close to horror; the solitary concession any of them made to entertainment was an occasional tapping of a bare foot to O'Neil's fiddle and Cranston found himself longing for a spark of levity and the company of like souls to break the monotony. Yet still the spectre of Mr Leyton hung large and so he had approached Brotherton, a midshipman, instead.

"There's not much I can do," the lad sighed when Cranston confronted him. They were on the orlop; Cranston had gone down for a change of shirt and the midshipman had been speaking with the purser. "Mr Leyton will be in the gunroom now; you might send a message in."

Cranston pulled a face. "I'd rather not, Mr Brotherton; him an' me don't always see eye to eye. You couldn't have a word?"

The lad shrugged. "I might try; would you be coming to my division?"

"I would, sir," Cranston nodded eagerly, adding the honorific quite consciously. "Wainwright's mess; he only has the six an' two are old shipmates. It would suit me fine."

"Seven men don't make a regular mess," Brotherton pointed out, "there ought to be an even number."

"Well they ain't got a boy," Cranston pondered. "I could take Longdon with me. I know he's just as miserable an' would get on fine with Wainwright's lot."

"You say you've friends there already?"

"Lovemore an' O'Grady," Cranston confirmed. "Though you don't want to believe what Mr Guppy said, them's just mates."

"Oh, I don't take any notice of Mr Guppy," Brotherton confirmed with boyish honestly. "And I will see what can be done. Robson might not take too kindly to be losing two of his men."

"I don't think he'll mind that much," Cranston assured him. "We don't exactly get along."

* * *

134

The wind, a dry southerly, began to make itself known on the eighteenth day when Ireland was way off their starboard quarter and they were in the Atlantic proper. To that point the convoy had been making a steady pace but, once they were hit by what began as a solid and strangely warm breeze, all began to change. Several of the smaller merchants' sails blew out while other vessels, like the impatient schooners, began to pick up speed as if unintentionally. Despite the weather, King had not let up on his regime and *Tenacious'* crew, though thoroughly exhausted by the drills, were starting to pull as one. But by mid-morning there was no need for imaginary manoeuvres; the number of signals passing between flag and escorts was almost beyond counting and all on duty were kept more than busy chasing up and hauling back their charges. When the new watch was finally set the old sought sanctuary below, but it was only a momentary respite. With the wind continuing to build, quite mundane tasks became hazardous; even keeping on station caused the frigate to show a considerable list and, when she was called to tack or wear, it was difficult for the most seasoned to keep their footing.

Standing propped against the binnacle, King breathed in the hard, fresh air. Up Spirits had been piped fifteen minutes before and shortly they should be sending the lower deck to dinner. First though, he was taking a careful look about the convoy. One of the brigs was replacing a topsail and had dropped out of station as a consequence while a larger merchant seemed to be suffering from a jammed block and had a staysail flapping dangerously out of control, but nothing needed their immediate attention. As he checked on his charges, King was aware of Leyton close by and sensed the man was simply itching to suggest feeding the hands. It was probably a mark in the first lieutenant's favour that he was keeping his peace, yet still the tension between the two was almost palpable.

"Larboard watch to dinner," King ordered finally. It was usual to serve the lower deck as a whole, with a skeleton crew – the seven bells men – left to sail the ship. To divide them into watches would take longer, even if less time were allowed to eat, but with the wind continuing to build he needed men on deck. The alternative, delaying everyone's meal, would be more likely to cause discontent. Leyton clearly did not approve and gave the order in sulky tones, but there was nothing so very strange in that and King had no intention of pursuing the matter further.

And as matters turned out they managed to satisfy the

135

larboard watch while the starbolins had at least finished their beef when King was forced to call for all hands. The wind had grown yet stronger; there was still no rain but the amount of scud and spindrift being chiselled from the waves was sufficient to soak them all. And in the midst of everything one of the largest merchants had sprung a topmast.

Tenacious was instructed to assist but, in truth, there was little she could do; the heavy vessel was falling behind and soon would leave the protection of the convoy altogether. Unless some form of jury rig could be set up before nightfall, she would have to turn back; that, or continue the passage alone. Were it a smaller vessel, Admiral Cox might have allowed her to fend for herself but such a charge was not to be trifled with. Even ignoring the probable monetary value of her cargo, she could be carrying important dignitaries and possibly troops. So, whatever the reason and whatever happened, *Tenacious* must remain in company.

All hands would be needed to turn and King had two choices. He could tack; a well-found ship with a reasonably skilled crew should have no problem even in such a blow. But then *Amphitrite* was close on her heels and tacking placed an extra strain on any ship's rigging. In the current conditions the last factor would be a major consideration; it only needed one small accident – a block jamming or a sail to split – and they could hang in irons risking a collision. Or he could wear ship although, with a positive line of merchants to starboard, that option was equally fraught with danger. Wearing was less taxing on the tophamper but mishaps could still occur and, with the wind as it was, they might be pressed deep into the very heart of the convoy. But all the time the injured merchant was steadily falling behind with foremast visibly adrift and the rest of her rigging a tangle of line and canvas. *Tenacious* was the nominated escort so must be seen to respond, and the sooner the better.

"Prepare to wear ship," he snapped, and immediately all about sprang to life with the squeal of pipes and deep-throated roars. Manton, the sailing master, came hurrying on to the quarterdeck and Leyton, who had been by the taffrail stepped forward to join Croft, the officer of the watch. But King did not wish for assistance; he was getting to know *Tenacious* and felt he could handle the situation. Indeed, the very idea of passing the manoeuvre over to one of his juniors almost brought physical pain. Besides it was important he took command. Of late, *Tenacious* had been subjected to almost constant drills and he had shown a new, and presumably impressionable, crew he could be hard on them; now was the time to demonstrate he was just as strict with himself.

He looked to the wheel; Grigson was there with three mates assisting. Many years' service had tanned the man's face to a deep mahogany and his skills as a quartermaster were likely to be as ingrained. It would be Grigson who physically controlled the ship and so doubly important the pair of them worked in concert. King gave a slight nod and received a smart knuckled salute in reply. He turned and stared directly into the wind. It came at him, hot and hard; a constant force which he supposed was a mercy. Then, collecting the speaking trumpet from the binnacle, King prepared to go to work.

"Main clew-garnets and buntline! Mizzen brails!"

Despite lying under heavy reefs and staysails, *Tenacious* was travelling reasonably fast; there would be scant time for consideration once he began. King knew the theory and had performed such a manoeuvre many times; the main topsail must be kept just full with mizzen topsail and crossjack yards pointing into the wind. But never had he worked in such a gale, and never under such intense observation. Apart from his officers, all on deck, from topmen to waisters, were already watching him intently, as would those on nearby ships. But the eyes that most bored into his head belonged to Leyton, his first lieutenant.

"In mizzen, up mainsail!"

The ship was working easily to his commands; he drew breath.

"Man weather main, lee crossjack braces!"

Now *Tenacious* was being taken in hand and still seemed to be responding well. King's eyes travelled across to the nearest merchant to leeward. She was just in line so posed no danger, but there was another close astern and slightly to windward of her.

"Ease down weather clew-garnet. Down foresail!"

It occurred to him that *Tenacious* was like a freshly broken horse reacting to a trained hand; while he kept her under control she would comply, but the slightest hesitation or doubt and there was no telling what might happen.

"Stand by to take in foresail. Weather clew-garnets and buntlines."

The nearest merchant was now passing out of danger, but King still had his eyes on the one following. It would be close but, unless the other master panicked, or attempted something strange, they should be safe.

"Up foresail!" He paused and swallowed. "Stand by to set mizzen; let go the brails and haul out!"

And then it was over; despite the conditions, it had been a manoeuvre worthy of any primer and he could look every man on the quarterdeck in the eye. *Tenacious* settled on her new course while, to starboard and well out of danger, *Amphitrite* beat towards her as the straying merchant passed by to larboard. On the frigate's quarterdeck he could see a figure waving his hat in acknowledgement; it would be Solomon, her captain. King had never met the fellow, but the talk was he ran a tight ship and was an excellent seaman. He spared a nod for Grigson as the figure of an officer, heavily clad in oilskins, approached.

"If I may say so, sir, that was excellently done."

"Thank you, Mr Leyton," King replied, equally formally. "You may dismiss the watch below and see they finish their meal."

Chapter Thirteen

"I shall need the carpenter and the bo's'un," King announced the following morning, "along with any mates or assistants they may require."

It had been a remarkably uneventful night. The wind, which rose further after *Tenacious* caught up with the *Lady Camden*, finally started to dwindle at midnight. By then something of the damage had been tidied and it continued to decrease until first light when an initial appraisal could be made. But even from the British frigate's quarterdeck, it was clear this would be no easy repair. *Tenacious* carried a number of spare spars but none that could match the size required; it could be the *Lady Camden* was better equipped although the prospect of replacing a topmast mid-ocean was not an attractive one. But whatever was to be done must be decided so King had signalled his intention to board the merchant and speak with her master.

"I would recommend one of the cutters, sir," Leyton advised, and King suppressed a sigh; did the man seriously think he would be taking the jolly-boat? With the wind now more manageable, the sea had settled considerably but this was still the North Atlantic.

"Thank you, Mr Leyton, if you would make the appropriate arrangements I should be obliged."

King watched as the first lieutenant bustled off. When visiting another ship it was customary for a captain to take at least one other officer and it did not take him long to decide who.

"Cutter is being cleared away and Mr Amon and Mr Morales are making ready," Leyton reported on his return.

"Very good, I shall be in my quarters. Perhaps you will ask Mr Croft if he will accompany me?"

"Mr Croft?" Leyton repeated with a hint of surprise.

"Yes," King confirmed. "You are second in command so will attend the ship in my absence."

"Very good, sir." The reply was in a more level tone. "And will you require a midshipman?"

"I shall," King agreed. "Kindly send for Mr Summers."

Summers was a good choice; despite their greater age and experience, King had yet to be impressed by any of *Tenacious'* older midshipmen and the lad handled any small boat like he was born to it. His presence at the stern sheets did make conversation with James Croft less private but, with the carpenter and boatswain along with several of their mates also close by, actually made little difference. Besides, there was less need for protocol in a twenty-five foot cutter.

"How are you enjoying life aboard *Tenacious*, James?" he enquired.

"I like it fine, thank you, sir," the lieutenant replied. "She is well-found and blessed with a full and competent crew."

"And the gunroom?" King asked in a lower tone.

"Agreeable and supportive in the main." Croft's answer was quick and welcome. Many captains strive for what is commonly known as a happy ship, but the term usually refers to the lower deck; creating contented officers was far harder.

"There is no friction between..?"

"I find I am getting on with every officer," Croft interrupted with a smile, "and am only too pleased to be at sea again."

They were nearing the merchant now and King looked up at her towering bulk. The hull was resplendent in a fresh coat of paint but several cracks had begun to show above the wales and there was evidence of plaster having been recently applied. King had no idea how far the *Lady Camden* had journeyed, but it was clear she was coming to the end of her useful career and approaching either a sizable refit or the breakers.

"*Tenacious!*" Summers' voice rang out in reply to the lookout's challenge and the cutter swept under the big ship's stern to gain a lee from her hull. And then they were approaching the starboard entry steps.

King swallowed: this was the part he always dreaded. When in harbour, or if conditions were incredibly still, he might board some ships unassisted, and the tumblehome on the *Lady Camden* was temptingly steep. But they were in the North Atlantic and there could be no shame in showing caution. A whip would be needed to get him aboard which was always a humiliating experience, though preferable to being dragged up soaking wet should he slip.

It seemed those aboard the *Lady Camden* were aware of his

condition – that or a signal had been made from *Tenacious* without his knowledge – as a boatswain's chair was swung down unrequested from the main yardarm. King waited until the thing was in the boat, then stood awkwardly and allowed Croft and Summers to strap him in.

There was a welcoming committee to meet him on the merchant's starboard gangway, where he was shortly deposited. The ship's master was there, presumably with one of his mates, and several officers in British Army uniform. And as King clambered out of the hateful contraption he was also aware of a group of well-dressed women looking up with open curiosity from the waist. Then the master, a grey-haired man of less than average height, stepped forward and extended a hand.

"Name's Gilroy, Harry Gilroy," the captain informed him with an affable smile. King announced himself and was introduced to the others; the names meant little and were certain to be forgotten but he did pick up on their ranks which gave a measure of comfort. All present appeared sound in wind and limb and he had noticed a measure of pity and possibly distaste on several faces as he struggled to free himself. But though he might lack an arm, as a senior post captain in the Royal Navy, he outranked them all.

"Perhaps I might offer you shelter and some refreshment, Captain?" Gilroy suggested as he led him off the gangway.

"I should like my men to take a look at your tophamper," King replied.

"Of course, any advice would be welcome," the master told him when they reached the quarterdeck. "My own boatswain and carpenter have thoroughly inspected the damage and fear little can be accomplished, but your fellows may know more – ah, here they are now."

King turned to the welcome sight of Summers and Croft clambering up the quarterdeck ladder with Amon and Morales in tow.

"I shall see your artificers are shown the damage," Gilroy continued, "but perhaps you will join me in my quarters? There are a number of matters we need to discuss and it will be a mite more comfortable there."

* * *

As it turned out the captain's accommodation aboard the *Lady Camden* was disappointing. It was set aft and benefitted from an armed sentry at the door but there all similarity with that provided to Royal Navy officers ended. Rather than the splendid quarters King enjoyed, Gilroy's space was barely larger than the coach and, instead of elaborate stern windows, daylight came from the meanest scuttle imaginable and had to be supplemented by three sets of candles. The room was well furnished however and featured a central table as well as a narrow desk but lacked a cot; presumably one would be rigged at night, or Gilroy might have an even smaller ante-room off. Few senior Royal Navy commanding officers would put up with such scant provisions but then King reminded himself the merchant service was a very different proposition.

Trade could bring large rewards and especially so in wartime. He had no doubt *Lady Camden*'s officers were well paid and probably enjoyed a decent amount of personal cargo space; if this were carefully used they might double or triple their wages on every voyage. Gilroy must be over fifty so probably as close to retirement as his ship; when the time came he was likely to be an extremely wealthy man. And part of those riches would have been made by selling off his own quarters to paying passengers while living in reduced circumstances himself. But at least the area was free of cannon so, when everyone settled about the small table, there was just about room for all.

King was seated next to Croft, which was a pleasant change from Leyton's seemingly constant presence. Opposite them, four army officers had contrived to squeeze together and now regarded their naval counterparts with a mixture of curiosity and distaste while Captain Gilroy, who had dismissed his first mate, sat at the head with the authority of an elderly schoolmaster.

"I think we might begin by admitting there is little chance of our making an Atlantic crossing," he announced when all were settled. "Oh I know your men are inspecting the damage, Captain," he added hurriedly, "and if a miracle can be achieved there will be no one more pleased than me, but we have to face reality. Neither of us possesses a spar of the right proportions and I have no intention of risking my cargo and passengers with a jury rig."

King remained silent; that was yet another difference between the two services. If a destination were important there was little a Royal Navy ship would not do to raise it. But a merchant had more constraints; Gilroy would have been commissioned to see his ship and all aboard her to Halifax. How and when this was achieved would be totally down to him and time was not normally critical, so he could hardly be blamed for taking the safer option.

"One moment, sir," one of the soldiers protested. "Need I remind you that I and my fellow officers are separated from our men? How long will this diversion take?"

"That can only be estimated, Colonel Campbell," Gilroy replied with the confidence of one who held all the aces. "A lot will depend on our speed, of course, but I would estimate anything up to a week to make Ireland. Sadly we are too deep to take advantage of the facilities at Kinsale, but Cork will be open to us. So add another seven days as a minimum to see to our repairs there, then we might be ready to set off once more."

So in three weeks we shall be roughly in the same spot as we are now!" another officer huffed.

"Not exactly, Captain Crossland," Gilroy's reply was cold and measured. "In three weeks we should, and I emphasise the word, gentlemen, we *should* have a sound foretopmast and be able to face the Atlantic. But it might take longer," he added flatly. "There might not be a berth available and we cannot guarantee being able to access a suitable spar."

The army officers muttered together in mutual disgust, then turned their attention on King.

"And you, sir; Captain Kid is it?" Campbell grunted.

"It is Captain King, Colonel," Gilroy told him sternly.

King made no reply but knew enough about army ranks to place Campbell as a lieutenant colonel, the equivalent of a naval commander and considerably inferior to him.

"I assume you will be returning to the convoy," the officer continued, "might not you transport us?"

"I fear not, sir," King replied.

"But we are hardly a great number," the colonel assured. "What is it, Jefferson; nine men all told?"

"Plus wives and some family," another agreed.

"And our servants," a third added.

King shook his head. "I regret, gentlemen, there is not the space aboard a ship like *Tenacious*."

"But it need not be for long, sir!" Campbell protested. "Why, as soon as you regain the convoy we might transfer to other vessels and continue our journey – which, I might add, is on the King's service."

"I assume your ship will be able to catch the convoy," one of the junior men added with what might have been a smirk, and it was that last remark that tipped the balance. Until then King had held some sympathy for the soldiers' predicament, but the void between naval officers and their army counterparts had always been significant and this particular group, with their upper-class accents and domineering ways, was doing nothing to lessen it.

"My duty is to escort Captain Gilroy's ship," he stated firmly. "In which case, if he is forced to turn back for Ireland, I shall accompany him."

"But won't your Grand Admiral, or whatever he is called," Campbell flustered, "won't he wonder what has become of you?"

"Rear Admiral Cox despatched me to attend this ship," King replied flatly, "and, if it means following her to harbour, I surely shall; there are provisions for such an eventuality in my sailing orders."

"Well I calls it a damn poor show," another soldier grumbled. "Why, to separate an officer from his men is tantamount to siding with the enemy!"

"Indeed!" the fourth, who had remained silent to this point, agreed in an upper-class whine that was as painful as it was affected. "If one of us chooses to raise a complaint, it might fare badly for you, Captain."

"I would advise you to choose your words more carefully," King replied, fixing the man with his gaze. "I am a senior post captain in His Majesty's Navy; my rank is equivalent to that of a full colonel," he added with a significant look at Campbell. "Frankly, sir, no junior officer in my service would address me so and I will not tolerate such a lack of respect from anyone present."

All had the grace to look abashed, but King had more to say.

"And I have not separated you from your men. Why they are travelling aboard a designated troop ship while you and your families enjoy the undoubted luxury of the *Lady Camden* is not my concern, although those in authority may be more interested were it brought to their attention."

"I am sure my officers meant no disrespect, sir," the colonel hurriedly assured them all. "We are merely keen to reunite with our charges, and sincerely appreciate anything you can do to that end."

Gilroy had been a silent witness to the exchange but was

making little effort to hide his approval; King supposed even a few days in such company had been trying, so to see another bring his arrogant passengers down to size must be satisfying in the extreme. "If I may add a note of optimism, gentlemen," he said, his eyes still twinkling slightly. "When we are able to sail again, the *Lady Camden* should make a faster passage than that of our late convoy."

"And I take it we won't have to wait for another load of damned shipping to assemble?" the colonel grunted.

"I hope not," Gilroy replied with a glance to King. "I should not care to make such a passage alone, but if Captain King could be persuaded to accompany us, would have no hesitation. My ship is hardly young, but I feel she might still show a significant increase on our previous speed."

"That would be capital," Campbell exclaimed while looking apprehensively at King. "Would that meet with your approval, sir?"

"I have been ordered to escort the *Lady Camden*," King shrugged, "and *Tenacious* is required on the North American Station so, providing there is no lengthy delay, I think it might suit all our purposes."

"Then that is excellent indeed, sir," Campbell beamed, "and we truly cannot thank you enough."

* * *

"It's sprung right enough, your honour," Joe Morales, the carpenter, declared when King was finally free of the meeting. The man was well built with black close-cut hair and an earnest look in his dark eyes. King already knew he could be trusted; the fact that *Tenacious* was sailing at all after her engagement with the corvette was chiefly down to him and he was pleased to have someone so competent to call upon. "But then the spar is as wide-grained as can be," the man continued. "Not seen wood so rough since Old Jervie took control of the yards, if you don't mind me sayin' so."

"Can anything be done to strengthen it?"

Morales shrugged. "Most of the lads are former India hands an' one 'as served the King; they done a fair enough job with batons, but I reckon my mates could tighten it further. Might take somethin' with a reef then though I wouldn't want to trust it far."

King nodded; it was what he had expected and ironically good news; at least with the damage blatantly unsuitable for further

145

progress, the *Lady Camden* had every reason to turn back. And as a vessel carrying a valuable cargo – he was not including the army officers in this assessment – his duty was to see it safely to the nearest home port. Which would be Ireland, there could be no doubt of that for there was equally no reason to go the extra miles to England.

It did, however, present one drawback, he told himself when the carpenter had finished his report. He supposed it possible to ditch the unfortunate Leyton in Cork; there may a solid replacement available but unlikely. Any officer worth his salt would be seeking a post in one of the major naval ports and they were hardly likely to remain long enough to send for Cooper. But this was not the time to think of such things, he had to speak to Gilroy.

"It's as we expected, sir," he said, approaching the master. He was on the merchant's half deck with his first officer while Croft and Summers had appeared and were standing close by. "My men might be able to add some reinforcement but agree that you should proceed no deeper into the Atlantic."

"Then the sooner we make for Ireland the better," Gilroy supposed. The man had eyes that might have been made from blued steel and, though his skin was weather-beaten and his greying hairs undoubtedly thinning, there was more than a spark left in him. "You are certain you wish to accompany me?"

"I would not see you return alone," King replied. "'Tis a pity more support were not available though Admiral Cox was hardly blessed with escorts."

"The protection of one of His Majesty's frigates will be ample I am certain," Gilroy smiled in return. "But forgive me, when we were speaking earlier I could not be certain what were your own thoughts and what had been said to annoy our military friends."

"I am happy to see your ship to Cork," King confirmed, "and, providing a repair can be effected, will then accompany her to Canada. I dare say a small convoy will be formed, though would be sorry if further vessels slowed us in any way. What speed can the *Lady Camden* make?"

"She's a former Indiaman and has completed five trips to the East, which is more than most," Gilroy replied. "Yet there is still a fair amount of life remaining; with a decent wind she'll stay with any of your liners and has been known to give royals to others of her size."

King remembered the badly concealed lines of plaster on her hull. From what he could tell, the remaining tophamper appeared in reasonable order but the fact that one mast had already sprung was hardly reassuring.

"And what armament does she carry?"

"Standard for an Indiaman I'm afraid," Gilroy sighed. "Cannonades mainly, though we have a couple of long nines on the fo'c's'le."

It was what King had feared; he knew the HEIC cannonade of old, a strange blend of carronade and long gun. And, like so many compromises, it had the defects of both with none of the advantages.

"But my gunners are reasonably trained," Gilroy continued, "and, as you will have noted, we also benefit from several army officers aboard. Sure, if it comes to an action, I shall not want for advice," he added dryly.

Now it was King's chance to return a grin; Gilroy was a man he could deal with and that fact alone made what they were about to attempt more feasible.

"Very well, I shall send a working party across to see what can be made of your fore. Then we can make for Ireland. Is there anything you need in the way of supplies?"

The master laughed. "Thank you, Captain, but we are well provided for; indeed, I was about to make the same offer. Perhaps I can show my appreciation in some way? We have some excellent wine aboard as well as snuff and cigars; maybe a small contribution to your personal cabin stores?"

"I have all I need, thank you. But might I enquire of my officers?"

"Please do," Gilroy smiled. "I am sure we both remember being junior and poor! Which gives me a better idea," he added, starting slightly. "We carry a fair number of passengers in addition to the officers you encountered and all expect to be well fed. What say we organise a small reception? Bring those of your men who would appreciate a decent meal along with some female company and we will see them sated – at least as far as their stomachs are concerned!"

"Thank you, sir, that is a generous offer," King told him. "And one I hope we can take advantage of. But first I must make good my promise and attend to your foremast."

Chapter Fourteen

Darkness was falling when Morales and the boatswain pronounced the spar, if not exactly solid, then firm enough to take a reefed topsail. And with the wind continuing to die, the *Lady Camden* was able to add a maintop, the lower staysails and her forecourse and so maintain a reasonable speed, with *Tenacious* sailing protectively off her weather quarter.

Lovemore, on his beloved forecastle, was viewing their charge circumspectly when Cranston joined him. Now that the latter had changed messes the pair shared the same watch, and both would be on duty and topside officially in half an hour. But it was a pleasant evening and with the ship once more in motion they preferred the open air.

"So," Cranston began after he had seated himself next to his friend and the word hung for several seconds before he added, "going back, are we?"

"Happen," Lovemore agreed with equal languor. "But not England."

"That's what I heard," Cranston agreed. "The word is Ireland, and I own to never having seen the place."

"I has, though not to land."

"Reckon we'll get ashore this time?"

Lovemore shrugged. "More chance with Tommy King at the conn than most others."

"I could use a decent spree," Cranston declared with a sigh.

"Me an' all," Lovemore agreed. "And I'd chance Ireland to be as good a place as any."

* * *

"If we keep this pace, we should sight land well within a week," Manton, the sailing master, declared in response to Leyton's question. They were in the gunroom and those senior officers not on watch had just finished their midday meal.

"And are we bound for Kinsale or Cork?" Croft added casually while peeling an apple with neat efficiency.

"Cork," Leyton replied quickly. "Kinsale is rarely used these days; I am surprised you did not know that, Mr Croft."

"I am aware it is rarely used by the *King's* Navy, Mr Leyton," Croft agreed, cutting the fruit in half on his plate with a definite clunk, "though merchants do still favour it and is it not a merchant that requires a spar?"

For a second both men glared at the other, then Leyton continued in crisp, measured tones.

"The smaller perhaps, though you would hardly get a seven hundred tonner over the sandbar; isn't that right Mr Manton?"

Both officers looked to the sailing master like quarrelling children appealing to a parent.

"Sandbar at Kinsale might be a problem," Manton agreed cautiously. It was rare for the officers to bicker so and he could not help wondering what had caused the change. "Though one that can be managed if you judge the tide right. But there're two ruddy great rocks that'll take the bottom from a craft of any size; the Sovereign's Bollocks they calls them, and I for one would far rather Cork."

"Then everyone shall be happy!" Taylor declared, more in hope than expectation.

"I could do with soap and rosin," Dennison, the purser, announced from the foot of the table.

"And a decent draught of Brandy," Piper, the senior marine lieutenant added, raising his glass and examining its contents in the light from a candle. "Don't know where you got this firewater from, but I'm surprised it don't melt the bottle."

"I paid less than a guinea the case," Dennison informed them with an element of pride.

"Tastes like it," Piper snorted.

"Well, we'll probably be served a good deal better aboard the *Lady Camden*." Taylor's comment had been innocent enough so he was surprised when all eyes suddenly turned on him. "Did you not know?" he asked. "We are invited to dine."

"Dine?" Leyton seemed more angry than pleased; for the captain to take Croft aboard the merchant had been annoying enough, but now it seemed others were to be invited as well.

"According to young Summers," Taylor added quickly.

"Were you aware of this, Mr Croft?" Leyton demanded and all attention switched to the second lieutenant.

"Captain Gilroy did mention the possibility," he admitted,

glaring at Taylor, "though a date was not settled. I would chance it more out of politeness."

"She's a former Indiaman," Piper pointed out cheerfully, "so any meal aboard should be a fine one. And you mentioned women, did you not, Mr Croft?"

"There were ladies aboard," Croft admitted.

"Then let's hope they will be there also," the marine added.

"We don't know which of us are to be invited," Leyton reminded them sternly. "The captain has been known to select some strange companions."

"Well I'd wager he'll take Miss Lévesque," Taylor suggested quickly.

"And why should he?" Piper again. "According to young Alice, she declined passage with a merchant."

"Though was singularly vague as to why," Cross, the junior marine, added.

"Perchance the fare were too much," Dennison suggested.

"If she didn't keep nipping off to feed her mistress we might discover more from her maid," Piper grunted.

"I think it unbecoming to discuss a lady's private business," Leyton announced from the head of the table.

"To be honest I couldn't care if she comes or not," Taylor admitted. "I just hope I gets chosen."

* * *

But before any formal invitations could be made another distraction appeared and one far less frivolous. The sail was spotted less than four hours later and, though it drew no closer and presented little immediate threat, its presence was unwelcome. King had come on to the quarterdeck as soon as the sighting was reported and now, more than an hour later, his frustration was steadily increasing. In the past, when he had two sound arms and probably a stone or so less weight, he would have thought nothing of taking a trip to the top and looking for himself. But with the mystery ship still showing little more than topsails while sailing on what appeared to be a broadly similar course, he had to rely on his imagination.

"Reckon they'll know more aboard the *Lady Camden*," Croft said, nodding towards the stately vessel off their larboard bow. The merchant's masts were higher, and it was likely their lookouts could see slightly more. But even if the sighting were hull up and in clear view, King doubted they would be any the wiser. A little closer and they might discover something from the pattern and cut of the sails, but what would really identify their shadow was a change of course and there was no sign of any deviation.

"So what do you think?" King asked at last. In the main he mistrusted opinions, but with Croft as the officer of the watch and Leyton elsewhere, he felt inclined to make an exception. His old friend might lack imagination but had a wealth of knowledge and experience; more to the point, King knew him well enough to take his advice.

"It might be heading for England, sir," Croft suggested. "In which case they have every reason to be sailing on such a heading."

"You may be right," King said, pursing his lips. "But on the other hand, they will surely have us in sight. And holding the windward gauge as they do, could equally be biding their time."

"Biding their time?" Croft questioned.

"I am assuming them to be the enemy," King confessed.

Croft was silent for a moment. It was not such an outlandish suggestion; the sighting may well be a French ship, in which case she should be finding it as hard to identify *Tenacious* and her consort as they were her. From such a distance the pair could appear to be two juicy British merchants making a run for home or, just as easily, a couple of fighting sail on privateer patrol. "Do you think that likely, sir?" he asked at last.

"I am not certain," King admitted, "though it cannot be discounted."

"Of course not," Croft agreed.

Whatever the sighting was it remained invisible to those on deck, yet still King stared out in its general direction. He might be making something out of nothing but the mystery ship had sparked his instincts. The likelihood of it being an enemy was indeed slight but, should that be the case, it was performing just as he would expect.

Any raider with a modicum of sense would keep two sizeable vessels in sight and only approach as the sun prepared to set. Imminent darkness would give ample cover if their intended prey turned out predator while a night-time action between unequal sides usually favoured the single ship. And, given that an enemy this deep into the Atlantic was likely to be at least a heavy corvette and probably something as large – or larger – than *Tenacious,* it would not be an easy fight. The *Lady Camden* carried a token armament although her cannonades were more for show than purpose and, being as she was able to provide little in the way of speed or manoeuvrability, the merchant would prove more liability than asset. Such a prize, protected by a solitary escort was every privateer's dream, although he must not forget that a successful single ship action would not do his own career any harm. So perhaps, rather than a burden, maybe King should regard his charge as bait?

"There is considerable traffic from the Americas to England," Croft reminded him softly and King had to smile. The man was right and, once more, had brought him down to earth. There was far more reason for the mystery sail to be British – or at least neutral – than hostile. Croft knew him well and must have guessed how his thoughts would be flowing. The older man's lack of sensitivity meant he was generally far more grounded and, if the sighting were ten times more likely to be friend than foe, he would give ten times the consideration to such an outcome, which was probably the sensible approach.

"Well, there is little for us to do unless they show their hand," King supposed. "See the lookouts are replaced promptly and send for me if any sign of change."

And so he returned to his quarters, confident that *Tenacious* was in capable, if unimaginative, hands.

* * *

The call came a while later; by then the second dog watch had been set and Taylor was at the conn in place of Croft. With barely two hours to go before nightfall, the sighting had suddenly altered course and, after adding sail, was now bearing down on them with the wind firm on her quarter.

"There's royals going up now an' all," Harker, at the main, reported as those officers not on duty also began to gather on the quarterdeck. Even if the change of course had not announced the fact, for the mystery ship to show royals was a good indication that she was no merchant. There remained the possibility of her being a British vessel heading home and choosing to investigate *Tenacious* and her charge in safety, but King felt the odds had dropped from ten to one against her being an enemy and were more like even money.

"Make to the *Lady Camden*: 'enemy in sight to windward',"

King ordered and Hedges' signals party went to work with a will. It might be unnecessarily dramatic to identify the sighting so, but no harm would be done by Gilroy preparing for action. He would have passengers to consider after all. And neither would it hurt if he did the same, King decided. The last time they had seen action he had put off the moment but this was a very different situation. Then *Tenacious* had been fresh and untested with a crew to match but in the subsequent days considerable changes had been made. Now he felt he had a far more solid ship beneath his feet and, more to the point, one already bloodied in battle. He turned to Leyton who had claimed his place next to the binnacle. "And you may clear for action," he added.

* * *

By the time the sighting was visible from the deck and their masthead had identified her as a frigate, the sun was starting to set. From his position near the binnacle, King stared out at the faint smudge of grey and white off their starboard bow. They were no nearer to knowing the vessel's nationality for certain but he now privately regarded her as French. A Royal Navy frigate, or even a warship belonging to an inquisitive neutral, would have closed to check on them long before this; the fact that they had waited until now suggested whoever captained the sighting considered *Tenacious* and the *Lady Camden* to be potential prey.

King turned his attention back to his ship. They had finished clearing for action some time before and now, with guns prepared, the scent of slow match hanging in the air and all hands waiting patiently in the dying light, the scene aboard *Tenacious* was dramatic indeed.

A shout went up from the foremast lookout, "Signal from the *Lady Camden*!" Hedges was fumbling with his codebook while one of the hands read off the numbers. Then the midshipman looked up and reported. "They're wishing us good luck, sir."

"Very good, acknowledge," King directed. Ostensibly it was a wasted signal and Gilroy must be taking advantage of the last of the light to send it; if they were to communicate again that evening it would be with flares and lights. But Gilroy was an experienced master and, even after such a recent first meeting, one King instinctively trusted. And at least he knew he was not alone in judging the oncoming ship to be hostile.

Leyton was looking in his direction and showing signs of wanting to talk; King suppressed a sigh and took a step closer.

"What do you intend, sir?" the older man asked.

"What do I intend?" King repeated.

"The enemy," Leyton waved vaguely in the direction of the approaching frigate. "Are you proposing to meet it? Or should we stay by our charge?"

King shook his head. "I truly know not why you ask."

"I am second in command, sir," Leyton announced, puffing himself up slightly. "If you should fall it would be for me to continue the fight; I have a right to know – Captain Wheatstone always kept me informed of his intentions."

"I am not Captain Wheatstone," King informed him crisply. "I shall tell you everything necessary but in my time. Until then you shall refrain from posing needless questions; do I make myself clear?"

"You do, sir," Leyton replied and King turned away.

* * *

With the ship cleared for action and every hand alert to the current situation, beating to quarters was almost a formality. But until the order was given, Croft had had every reason to remain on the quarterdeck. He had, however, been a mute witness to the exchange between Leyton and the captain and afterwards felt it prudent to go to his battle station in the waist.

Fortunately, Summers and Brotherton were of the same mind and the three of them met up by the half deck.

"Will it be like the last action, sir?" Brotherton asked.

"In some ways," Croft replied. "Though the weather is a deal more pleasant and some degree of moon is expected."

"So we should see more when it rises," Summers supposed.

"We should see more before," Croft corrected stiffly. "The last few nights have enjoyed excellent visibility as you will no doubt have noted."

The two midshipmen nodded guiltily, and the older man continued.

"What will make a difference is we have no convoy to protect, but rather a single merchant ship. The *Lady Camden* has an excellent captain and some very competent officers but that will in no way

154

make up for their fragile foremast."

"So we cannot expect much from her," Summers clarified, "in the way of manoeuvres, I am meaning."

"We cannot," Croft agreed. "And neither will we be able to count on support from other escorts. I may tell you now, gentlemen, we were treated extremely lightly last time; our opponent was smaller and taking on considerable odds. We have still to judge tonight's enemy, but the chances are strong they will turn out at least as powerful as us. And with no merchant to consider, they can attack pretty much at will, whereas the captain will have to think for this ship as well as the *Lady Camden*." There was a pause while the second lieutenant treated them both to a stern stare, before turning on his heel and heading away to attend to his duty.

The two lads' expressions had changed from concerned expectation to downright alarm, something that Lieutenant Taylor could not fail to notice as he approached.

"Ready for the off are we lads?" he asked, clapping his hands together in anticipation. "Should be something of a fight if I'm any judge — so why the long faces?"

"It was Mr Croft," Summers explained. "He were just encouraging us."

* * *

An hour and a half later the sun had fully set but, with the help of early stars and exceptional phosphorescence from a mild sea, much could still be seen. *Tenacious* remained under minimal sail; she could have added three or four knots with extra canvas although King was content to let her keep pace with the merchant making steady progress off her larboard bow. But closing to starboard, and creeping towards his long guns' maximum range, the enemy frigate was showing no such reluctance. With the wind more on her quarter and a veritable cloud of spray issuing from her stem, she was undoubtedly commanded by a captain intent on close action.

Which was fine, King told himself as he swallowed dryly. After numerous reports from the lookouts, it was now established that the raider was French and at least as powerful as them. Vernon, one of the young gentlemen, had even identified her as a forty gunner of the type that could carry a broadside of twenty-four-pounders although, being little more than a child, could be expected to exaggerate slightly. But given that this would be more or less an equal fight as far as warships were concerned, all that remained to discover was which had the better crew.

"He will be within our reach in no time," Leyton murmured but King chose to ignore the comment. As a main armament *Tenacious* mounted Blomefield eighteen-pound long guns, popularly regarded as one of the most accurate heavy cannon made. But no weapon performs well at maximum range; even if the shot arrived on target its force would be close to expended and King had no intention of wasting a valuable opening salvo so. Besides, he was still unsure exactly what his opponent had in mind. The Frenchman was almost level and steering to creep up on *Tenacious'* starboard bow. Such a state of affairs could not continue for long; King need only increase sail and turn slightly to starboard to cross the raider's hawse — something the Frenchman was bound to avoid. And there was equally a danger of the two frigates battling it out broadside to broadside, which would be a waste of such manoeuvrable vessels. No, his opponent must have something more adventurous in mind and King was quite prepared to let him act first then react as necessary. But that did nothing to dispel the tension that was steadily gathering on the quarterdeck; something that he found all too easy to blame on his second in command.

He took a couple of paces back and forth then breathed deeply. Gilroy, in the *Lady Camden*, was maintaining a sensible distance off their larboard bow, more than enough to give room to manoeuvre if it were needed. He barely knew the man but sensed he could be depended upon not to panic and add sail or let off any unnecessary broadsides. Leyton, still close by, seemed likely to speak again at any moment and King was bracing himself for the next inane remark when something far more important caught his attention.

"Deck there, she's turning!"

The murmur of anticipation from those around him had given warning even before the masthead's call and King looked up to see the enemy was indeed altering course. From sailing on a broad reach the Frenchman was turning to larboard and appeared about to wear. In which case they were abandoning any hope of attacking *Tenacious'* bows and would be heading instead for her stern.

"Prepare to wear ship!"

He had issued the order without properly thinking it out but, even before Manton had begun taking them about, knew it to be the right decision. The only other option had been to tack, but that would take longer, and move *Tenacious* too far away from her charge. He waited while the ship passed through the eye of the wind, watching his enemy as she performed a similar manoeuvre. Soon *Tenacious* had settled on the larboard tack and had begun heading away from the merchant – something else that could not last for long.

"Take her fully to larboard; as close as she will hold!"

The Frenchman had also finished turning; soon the two ships would be heading towards the other on what would be close to a collision course. The only question was, whose nerve would break first?

"Ready larboard battery." he muttered.

It was the sensible choice; sailing as she was, *Tenacious* would be far more likely to turn to starboard than risk luffing up. But that was assuming the Frenchman held his course which, in his position, King would never have done. The gun crews had received their orders; those detailed to manage guns on either battery were moving across to the larboard pieces, leaving the bare minimum to stand by the frigate's starboard weapons. King swallowed again; the Frenchman had not reduced sail after his manoeuvre and was heading for them under courses. Even ignoring the wind, which was strong for such a sail pattern, to enter combat with mainsails set was a dangerous practice; the extra expanse of canvas was as likely to be ignited by the ship's own guns as any enemy action. But there was no doubt the raider was sailing fast as a consequence; it seemed King's opposite number had no fear of damaging his tophamper and was putting everything in to closing as soon as possible, which may be a clue as to the type of man he was dealing with.

The sudden flash of two red spears momentarily illuminated the raider's bows; the French were firing off their chasers, again almost a rash act as little damage could be caused by light weapons at such a range. But the distance between the two ships was reducing by the second; before long they would be close enough to exchange full broadsides and such heavy fire would truly make a difference.

And it was at then that King decided on his plan. As in the past, the idea had crept up on him even after he had made arrangements for completely different tactics. But though the ploy would be rash in the extreme, he had learned to trust his inner feelings – even to the extent of acting on them without thinking further.

"Belay my last – ready starboard battery!"

Leyton looked aghast for more than a second but he had also learned from experience, and in his case, it was not to argue with his new captain. Instead he bellowed out the order that sent the gunners back to the starboard battery. There were shouts and confusion and someone fell headlong across the deck but, as King surveyed the scene before him, he felt certain it was the right tactic.

* * *

"Why don't the bugger make up his mind?" Cranston asked of no one in particular as he stumbled back to the starboard gun he now manned with Lovemore and O'Grady. The actual choice of weapon meant little to him as he performed the same task on each, but there had been an excellent view of the oncoming Frenchman from his larboard station, and now all sight was lost.

"Steady there!" Croft's voice rolled out with calm authority: a solid stanchion in a troubled world. "Gun captains, attend to your priming!"

Wainwright, who was the first captain of the starboard gun, had already checked along the cannon's barrel; there was no enemy in sight or range, just the blue-black of night, yet still he removed the lead apron covering the firing lock and primed his weapon.

More shouts from the quarterdeck, then the thunder of feet as waisters and the afterguard attended the sails.

"We look to be movin'," Lovemore, rammer in hand, murmured.

"'Appen," Wainwright, at the breach, agreed. "Though it can only be to larboard, and that'll mean tacking."

"Bold move," Cranston agreed.

"But a foolish one," O'Grady snorted. "Only an eegit would tack so in front of an enemy."

"We knows the captain of old," Cranston stated, glancing at Lovemore. "He ain't afraid of taking chances, and most times they pays off."

There was creaking from both hull and yards, *Tenacious* was indeed turning into the wind and would shortly be right in its eye. Those at the guns exchanged doubtful glances; the ship certainly appeared to be about to tack, yet no provision was being made to catch the breeze, instead she was being forced round and to what must be an almost dead stop.

"Now, what in heaven's name..?" O'Grady began, glancing back to see if some fool of a midshipman had been placed at the conn. But Captain King could be seen standing as resolute as ever and, much closer to them, Lieutenant Croft seemed equally unmoved.

"Sight your weapons!" The single command was enough to bring order on the gundeck; not only did each captain begin to stare down their cannon's simple sights, the tackle men took up the strain while those with crows of iron placed them under the carriages and awaited instructions.

"Here it comes..." Cranston muttered under his breath. The ship might have been subjected to the most atrocious handling, but such an extreme luff did have one major advantage: Cranston now had the finest view of the enemy. And even as he watched, the dim outline of the raider's oncoming hull was creeping closer to his cannon's ark of fire as *Tenacious* continued to turn.

"Left, left, left..." Wainwright ordered, emphasising his instructions with a waving palm as the weapon was duly wrenched across. The ship was slowing all the time, but enough momentum remained to carry her further into the turn and it was his, and every other gun captain's, intention to have the target squarely in their sights when it finally came to a halt.

And the time would be soon, all at number eight cannon knew that. The enemy was considerably less than a mile off with her bows comfortably in range. Mishandling or not, King's sudden luff had been an inspired act; the raider had been about to manoeuvre herself and was taken by surprise.

"Sails are all ahoo an' in a right old raffle," Cranston declared with satisfaction.

Lovemore glanced across to where Croft and Summers were standing together, waiting for some command from the quarterdeck. Then, even as he watched, the second lieutenant touched his hat before turning to the battery.

"Fire!"

The gun captains pulled their firing lines simultaneously and, even allowing for the inevitable deviation in priming, *Tenacious'* main battery spoke as one. The gun crews moved in as soon as their breach tackle checked the discharge and, choking slightly from the smoke, began to attend their weapon.

It was done with the minimum of fuss and credible speed, soon Wainwright was sizing up his target once again.

"Looks like we're getting two in and no returns," Cranston told Lovemore. "Old Tommy King ain't lost 'is touch."

* * *

The feeling was similar on the quarterdeck. Though Leyton had winced visibly when King forced the ship directly into the wind the wisdom behind such lunacy was soon evident. Their opponent had indeed been preparing to turn and the unexpected manoeuvre caught them off guard.

But it was still long-range, King assured himself as the second barrage was released. With a little more pluck he could have waited slightly longer and given the enemy a true pounding. But there might not have been time; the Frenchman had been turning to deliver a broadside. He had not only countered that, but delivered two of his own and, though no damage was visible in the murky light, King must certainly have made his point.

"Frogs weren't expecting that, sir," Manton, the sailing master, told him with a measure of respect.

"I gather they weren't the only ones," King replied curtly. "Now lay her over and get us back on the wind."

Chapter Fifteen

Two broadsides are rarely enough to win a battle and, as *Tenacious* picked up speed and returned to her previous tack, King sensed his opponent would not be fooled again so easily. And so it proved; even before their canvas was fully tight, the Frenchman was manoeuvring. Either through common sense, or possibly guided by *Tenacious'* preparations, he wore onto the same tack and was soon sailing just off their starboard quarter. And despite being slightly behind in the race, the enemy ship also began taking in canvas.

"It seems we have not affected their sailing abilities." Leyton's remark might not have been addressed at him, but King heard it and flashed a warning look in the older man's direction.

A messenger approached and knuckled his forehead.

"Mr Croft is reporting the starboard battery prepared, sir," Owens announced.

"Very good." King looked across at the enemy; it was now about as dark as it would get, yet enough light remained to show the general shape of his opponent. The Frenchman was within their firing arc and another broadside might not go amiss, but the range remained long and he sensed it prudent to hold his powder. Then a slight movement in the opposing frigate's yards told him he was right.

"She's going about!" The call came from the masthead and confirmed King's suspicions while also explaining why they had finally taken in their courses; there had never been any intention of remaining on the starboard tack, the enemy was far more interested in slipping behind to get at the *Lady Camden*, and possibly raking *Tenacious'* stern in the process.

"Wear ship!"

There was no other option; to tack might turn *Tenacious* the quicker but must leave her chasing the Frenchman; if she could wear relatively smoothly they might yet keep pace. King glanced up at his own canvas, still quite visible in the gloom. Apart from the lower staysails, *Tenacious* remained under topsails alone.

"As soon as we are about, add the fore," he ordered. The extra canvas was unfortunate, but every knot counted.

Manton took them about efficiently enough; by the time they

were picking up speed on the larboard tack, the Frenchman was only slightly ahead. And Gilroy had the right idea, he was hanging doggedly to his original course and lay well off their starboard bow.

"Two points to starboard," King ordered, and the frigate began to creep nearer her charge.

"If only we had more speed..." It was Leyton again and King supposed he could not blame the man. Slightly more pace would certainly make any move on the Frenchman's part more difficult, but he remained reluctant to draw men from the cannon. "Perhaps topgallants, sir?"

"No," King replied flatly. "But you may prepare the larboard battery."

King felt a twinge of guilt; the last time he had given such an order it had been countermanded almost immediately. But this time he was sure the larboard guns would have the chance to speak, and relatively shortly.

"Enemy's steering to starboard," Manton reported. King looked up; sure enough, the raider was turning nearer to the merchant and was now all but running before the wind.

"Wear ship," King ordered once more. Now the extra pressure forward was coming into its own and *Tenacious* positively flew into the manoeuvre, barely slowing as her stern passed through the wind's eye. The Frenchman remained slightly ahead and was drawing away although not fast enough to shake them off entirely. They might still try for the merchant of course, but King could thwart any move by a further turn to starboard. Again it was little more than supposition, but he had already delivered two broadsides and sensed a third, even if it were answered, might just tip the balance. He glanced over to where the bulk of the *Lady Camden* could still be seen heading steadily east; in the near darkness it was hard to tell if the Frenchman had speed enough to reach her while avoiding *Tenacious* on her starboard quarter but King had the strong suspicion they would shortly find out.

* * *

"It's a race to be sure," Croft muttered to Summers as the pair of them surveyed the enemy off their larboard bow. There was little doubt the Frenchman was pulling away but, equally, the merchant's stern was effectively creeping down their starboard side; if the enemy frigate were going to make a move, it would have to be soon.

"Cartwright reports a damaged gunlock," Brotherton announced.

"Very well, he shall have to use the linstock, but make a note," Croft told him, and the lad went away satisfied.

"He's holding up well," Summers remarked.

"Doing admirably," Croft agreed, "I shall be sure to tell him so later."

"She's turning!" The shout had come from Taylor further forward and all stared out into the night. Sure enough, the vague outline of the French frigate was slowly changing; the ship had put her helm across and was finally making for the *Lady Camden* and, in the process, would be crossing *Tenacious'* bows. Both Croft and Summer looked back to the quarterdeck, but King was aware and a bellowed shout brought the waisters out and *Tenacious* began to lean into a tight turn.

"Less than a mile off," Summers commented coolly and the two ships manoeuvred in near unison.

Croft alerted the gunners then gave the midshipman a silent nod. This was going to be close.

* * *

"This is going to be close," Cranston, now at the larboard gun, muttered.

"Belike, but we've already given 'em a bellyful," O'Grady grunted, "an' there's plenty more if they wants it."

"Right a touch," the larboard gun's captain directed from his weapon's breach, and the carriage was heaved over. The enemy frigate had almost completed her turn, and *Tenacious* was close behind; in no time the pair should be on parallel courses and well within reach of the other.

"Fire!"

The order was perhaps a little premature, Cranston decided as the broadside roared out, but that was no bad thing; it would mean they had now delivered three salvos at the Frenchman and were yet to take one in reply, although such a situation could not continue.

"For what we are about to receive," Lovemore murmured as he swabbed out the warm barrel, and if all the gun crews were

163

working slightly slower than normal it was mainly due to anticipation.

But when the enemy's broadside was received it landed high. This should have been expected as *Tenacious* now held the weather gauge. But the French captain had the presence of mind to prepare for such an eventuality and a dose of bar shot flew amongst their top hamper, tearing through line and canvas, smashing tackle and tangling itself amid the British ship's shrouds. Debris of all kinds rained down; a heavy fiddle block landed squarely on the shako of a marine, accounting for both in one swift blow and there were numerous lacerations, bruises and broken bones amongst the general hands. And the ship herself suffered; shrouds and braces parted, the horse was ripped from below the mainyard and Drew, their foretop lookout, was never seen again. But in general *Tenacious* came through the ordeal and, more to the point, would shortly be in a position to release another broadside herself.

For the gun crews had done their work despite line, tackle or worse falling about them. Receiving the broadside might almost be thought of as a relief as they could be sure of another brief portion of life before the enemy struck again. In that time they would be sending yet another consignment of eighteen-pound round shot; their fourth which was a considerable amount when balanced against the single measure of bar they had endured. By those odds, victory was surely a formality.

* * *

The merchant remained on their starboard bow but, since the turn, *Tenacious* was creeping towards her larboard quarter and travelling faster. King noted this, as he did the damage to his tophamper, and that their larboard battery would shortly be able to send yet another broadside towards the enemy on their beam. In truth, so intense was his deliberating that the thoughts seemed in control of his very brain, analysing the various options even without him willing it. There would probably be time for one more salvo from each before *Tenacious* forereached on the *Lady Camden*, then his opponent might manoeuvre again. And when they did, what could he expect? The raider could turn hard and as near to the wind as possible in an attempt to close with the merchant; carefully timed they might rake his own ship in the process. Or they might add canvas and attempt to draw ahead of *Tenacious,* then turn on the two ships' bows with a similar aim in mind.

"Fire!"

Croft's order cut through his thoughts; the second lieutenant was keeping his head and continuing to send out simultaneous broadsides, which were the most effective in such conditions. King's attention returned to the enemy, now possibly drawing ahead slightly, which made him think the second option was more likely. They could expect further fire shortly, unless *Tenacious* had already caused significant damage. The night was conveniently clear with bright stars and a luminous sea; a small moon had started to make itself known in the east but, even with its help, it was still difficult to gauge his enemy's strength. She might have been sorely wounded or have shaken off ill-aimed shot as a dog might water; only fire would be visible in such conditions and there was no sign of flames.

And then King got all the fire he could have wanted; the Frenchman released her second barrage with a wave of blinding light and, once more, it was aimed high.

Looking up, he could almost feel the deadly shot as it shredded through his ship's precious rigging. Once more wreckage began to tumble from above but now it contained a more gruesome element. The boatswain, his party, and every available topman had gone aloft after the last barrage and several fell screaming to land heavily on the deck or in the dark waters beyond. But though later he would regret each and every casualty, it was the actual fabric of his masts that concerned King. He might blithely make plans for any eventuality but, if the Frenchman wrecked his tophamper, both British ships would be taken with ease.

King continued to assess the situation; Croft's men were serving their guns, it would be at least a minute before the first was ready and from what he could see aloft, and feel through the soles of his boots, *Tenacious* was holding her course. The *Lady Camden* lay about two cables off their starboard beam; he had been right in his earlier estimations, but what would the enemy do now? A figure approached; once more, his thoughts were to be disturbed.

"Beggin' your pardon, sir." It was the boatswain. The man was knuckling his forehead respectfully enough, but his eyes seemed distant and wild.

"What is it, Amon?" King asked.

"It's Morris, sir, one of me mates. He's fallen from the foretop and seems to 'ave been lost. Can't find 'im on the deck an' no one's seen sight nor sign. Scally and Howarth is missin' also."

"I can do nothing," King replied softly, there being something in the man's manner that overrode any irritation at being interrupted.

"I knows that, your honour..." Amon paused but still seemed shaken.

"How is the tophamper?" King prompted and the question seemed to jerk the man back to reality.

"Not good, sir. We've several lifts what needs replacin', shrouds by the dozen and some of them stays won't hold much longer, but that ain't the 'alf of it."

King waited.

"We took a low blow to the larboard forechains; they's pretty much done for, there's no support and it'll take a while to rig anything even temporary. Morales' lot is on it at the moment and she'll hold for a while, but don't you try no more o' your fancy tricks or you'll lose the 'ole mast."

"I see," King told him while inwardly his spirits fell. "Do what you can; I'll not put her under any more strain than I can help."

"Can we take in the forecourse?"

"Yes, and any stays'ls that cause risk, but try to maintain a balance, won't you?"

The man knuckled his forehead again just as Croft released another broadside. King stared out towards the enemy and tried, in vain, to see if any hits registered. Despite everything, it would appear his mind was being made up for him. Should the Frenchman press for a close action they might survive but, if any form of manoeuvring were needed, *Tenacious* would be unable to respond. Carefully handled, the enemy frigate might well account for them, while also taking the *Lady Camden*. And if he lost his foremast it would only make the raider's job easier.

* * *

He may have given a different impression, but Brotherton had yet to fully accustom himself to being in action. His first exposure, in driving rain and impenetrable black, had been horrific enough. At the time it seemed nothing could be so bad again, although at least the dark had kept some horrors from him. Now he could see more, and none of it was pretty.

Men had fallen to shot or splinter with some being brutally disfigured in the process. Yet strangely the quick deaths affected him less than the injured, especially those left to scream and plead before being dragged to the nearest hatch and roughly deposited below. Even those yet to fall, the men still actively serving cannon or carrying out makeshift repairs to fabric or rigging, made a terrible sight. The straining, swearing, desperate bodies were doing battle as physically as any hand-to-hand fighter; frightening men, brutally determined to give all they had and more. The scene would have been awful were Brotherton not personally involved, but this was also his fight, his battle, yet all the youngster felt able to do was keep watch and out of everyone's way.

A powder monkey roughly his age rushed past with cartridges slung over each shoulder and, standing aside, Brotherton envied him his mindless task. Then the lad tripped, fell headlong and lay sprawled while both canvas carriers bounced away. Brotherton seized one, but the other released its paper cartridge which was immediately stepped upon and torn open.

"Powder on the deck!" The shout came close to a scream as Brotherton made for a pail placed ready for such an emergency. A burly gunner reached it first and, in one fluid action, the bucket was swept up and its contents deposited over the spilt grains.

"Very good, Wilson," Brotherton muttered, this time in his best officer-like voice, but the seaman had much to do and moved on, leaving the lad to stand guiltily idle amid the chaos.

* * *

"I think the Frenchman's hit bad, sir!" It was Manton calling from the larboard bulwark; King immediately moved across and peered out into the gloom. "Her main tops'l is shivering," the sailing master continued, pointing at the vague image. "Belike she's taken a hit and has lost control, that or is planning to turn."

"And taking her time about it," King added as he gripped the top rail. In the dim light and amidst such confusion it was hard to be certain, but something was definitely amiss on the enemy ship. She could have received similar damage to themselves — likely, in fact — and were that the case, this would be the ideal time to take advantage

167

of such a situation. Except *Tenacious* was severely wounded and would shortly be slowing when Amon began reducing her canvas.

"They're taking in her main t'gallant!" Leyton announced as he joined them.

"So they are!" Manton agreed.

King turned to look up at his own tophamper. "Mr Amon!"

A faint cry came in return; the boatswain and his team were on the foremast and about to take in the lower sail.

"Mr Amon, do you hear me there? Belay striking the forecourse!" Little could be seen in the dark but King thought he heard the sound of conversation aloft.

"Won't hold for long, sir!" Amon's voice came through the din of battle.

"Half an hour?" King questioned and there was a pause.

"Happen," came the reluctant reply.

"Then hold off for now."

King glanced across; the *Lady Camden* was off their starboard beam; *Tenacious* had effectively protected her from the raider, which was fortunate indeed – he gave himself no credit – and those at the quarterdeck carronades were signalling their pieces ready. He and the others withdrew as another broadside was released, then waited for the smoke to clear.

"That must have hit 'em deep," Manton stated with rare appreciation. With the two frigates now so close it was almost a certainty, although *Tenacious* might expect the same at any moment. But rather than another barrage, the French ship did finally turn – although not to starboard, as King had been dreading. Instead, her hull was allowed to fall back with the wind and for one glorious moment, her stern was exposed.

"Blighters were waiting for our shot!" Leyton muttered and there could be no argument. The enemy frigate must have been hit far harder than any of them hoped, yet its captain still had the presence of mind to do nothing until *Tenacious* released her broadside. His consideration had won precious time for it would be several minutes before the larboard guns were served; the French might begin their escape and, with a wounded foremast chain, King could do little to stop them.

"Do you think they knew we were damaged?" Leyton asked; it was an unnecessary question, but this time King did not object.

"I haven't the faintest notion," he replied softly. "And frankly do not care."

"But if the mast will hold a while longer, we might still give chase!" Leyton protested.

"With a wounded forechain there's no telling," King replied, before turning away. The larboard guns would shortly be prepared and may release one last broadside at the departing Frenchman. But already the frigate was disappearing into the night, leaving them in peace to lick their wounds and he did not want for more.

Chapter Sixteen

The sun was shining with real warmth as King ambled down the cobbled street and he felt in no rush to return to the ship. They had made Cork within six days, which was reasonable going considering the wounded condition of both ships. And now, less than twenty-four hours later, work was well underway to see them take to the sea again. Both vessels were safe in the nearby river and close to their respective yards. There had been no commercial spars suitable to replace the *Lady Camden*'s topmast, but Gilroy had spoken to his people and one had been magicked from Dublin and should be with them within three days. King had no idea if the merchant's passengers had held any sway in the matter but, even if not, she was carrying a valuable enough cargo and he recognised that folk were inclined to act quickly when money was the motive. If the same attention were paid to fitting and rigging the spar, she should be ready to sail within the week.

Conveniently enough, that was exactly the time the government dockyard said they would need to attend to *Tenacious'* forechains. Morales and his team had already begun by stripping out the battered channel and constructing a suitable staging; when he had last seen her, his command had been secured to a wharf and bore little resemblance to the sleek ship that was steadily capturing his affection. There were other less vital repairs needed but these could be addressed at the same time and, if all went according to plan, they might not be so very late in arriving at Halifax.

Which, King assured himself, was remarkable indeed and he might almost feel inclined to congratulate himself, were it not for the inner doubt that had been present since taking command of *Tenacious*. It was one he had tried to suppress from the start and concerned his passengers, Miss Lévesque and her maid.

There had been no trouble from either woman as such, both stayed well out of the way during the recent actions and Lévesque herself was keeping her side of the bargain by remaining in her cabin – his sleeping quarters, King reminded himself – at most other times. Of course, it would have been cruel to totally deny her access to the deck and she came up occasionally to take the air but he was pleased to note this was usually during the quieter, evening watches and, as far as he knew, she had never tried to engage anyone in extended conversation.

All plans for a lavish reception aboard the former Indiaman had been cancelled due to *Tenacious'* damage, but King had hosted an informal meal for selected officers in the great cabin. It would have been churlish in the extreme not to invite the woman, and she had been a perfect guest, keeping up regular light conversation throughout and remaining friendly, yet also curiously distant. King had been especially pleased by the last point; they had not been at sea a month, although a lack of female company must be starting to tell on the younger men. Yet on several occasions he had watched her sweep away the first hint of an advance and in such a manner as to cause no offence.

It was also interesting to note that those who had been keen to try her virtue – and the marine officers led the field here – were now treating the woman with the same respect and consideration they might give to a favoured sister. Which was equally fine, he assured himself, although hardly explained the occasional noises heard through the thin partition that separated her quarters from his own. However tame her conduct may appear, and whatever measures were being made to disguise the fact, he was reasonably sure another person occasionally shared her accommodation at night.

To ensure his own privacy, a separate entrance to her sleeping quarters had been cut in the light bulkhead allowing the woman to come and go more or less as she pleased, but at every hour of the day a marine stood guard over both entrances. Any member of the crew seeking to join her would have been noticed yet, whenever he checked, there was no record of a visitor. Such evidence should have heartened him, as well as allaying what might be unworthy doubts, but did not. For King had built his career on trusting instincts as much as facts and, if he suspected Miss Lévesque of entertaining nocturnal visitors, he was reasonably certain she was.

The truth would doubtless emerge in time as few secrets remain aboard small ships on long voyages although why one woman's morals should concern him so was also a mystery. But whatever the reason – or lack of it – he sensed his passengers to be trouble and would be greatly relieved when *Tenacious* finally made Halifax and the pair left for good.

But these were not the thoughts to consider on such a day, for it was a truly splendid afternoon and his interview with the port admiral had gone well. Nothing had been confirmed although he now felt surer than ever that *Tenacious* was to be retained on the North American Station, which would be good indeed. There should be action aplenty in such waters and to serve under John Warren was an honour in itself. The only fly in the ointment was the matter of Leyton; Admiral Carson had been willing to arrange for an exchange but could recommend no one of any great quality as a replacement. Had more time been allowed he could have sent for Cooper, or another from England; as it was he had to choose between an unknown quantity and the current incumbent. And when doing so he must consider the other officers; Taylor was good but inexperienced and it would hardly be fair to lumber Croft with two junior lieutenants. So, annoying though he might be, they would have to stick with Leyton a while longer, for the man was at least efficient.

But those thoughts could also wait; it was a novelty to be ashore and King was determined to enjoy himself. Cork looked to be a particularly attractive place and, as there should be nothing pressing for his immediate attention at the ship, he was set to explore it properly.

Just over an hour later he had walked much and bought a small ornament for Aimée along with six wooden toy soldiers for young Robert when he came across a familiar figure. Croft was approaching; the man's slightly stunted gait was as unmistakable as his face, which bore its usual mixture of gloomy contemplation. But there was no mistaking the sudden lightening on noticing his captain, and King was inwardly moved by the compliment.

"Well met, sir," the older man announced and King could have sworn he was almost smiling. "Did you find the port admiral well?"

"I did and have news if you would care to hear it."

"I should like that more than anything," Croft nodded. "Perhaps we might take a dish of tea – it is surely too early for anything stronger."

* * *

With all long-term patients transferred ashore and the ship mercifully still, Robert Manning had decided it time for a thorough sort out. In addition to cataloguing and assessing the medical equipment, he had plans to set up a proper surgery and dispensary in what his predecessor had used as an additional cabin. With two assistant surgeons and three attendants, colloquially known as loblolly boys, there was manpower enough to address the medical side of the work and give the place a thorough clean but he had also been allowed a couple of general hands with painting experience to ensure everything was finished in time. And they were men Manning knew well; both Cranston and Lovemore had been present when he and several others made their audacious escape from Verdun. After sharing such an experience it was difficult to maintain the usual relationship between officer and men although such a distinction rarely bothered *Tenacious'* surgeon. Manning had risen to his current rank from being a loblolly boy himself and, though he harboured a secret hope to one day qualify as a physician, valued comradeship above status and was especially pleased to have his old shipmates assist him.

"You have a fair number of rats, Mr Manning, sir," Cranston announced when most of the furniture had been removed and they could properly survey the area.

"I had feared as much," the surgeon admitted.

"Not a lot we can do," Lovemore added. "This is their world, though we can patch where possible and generally try to keep the buggers out."

"Will that work?" Manning asked.

"Only to a point," Lovemore replied. "Full-size rat can chew through the side of a ship if he feels the need; only place free of vermin is the magazines and then 'cause they're copper lined."

"Could we not go for them, seek them out one by one and rid the ship of their presence?"

"You mean a rat hunt?" Cranston asked perking up.

"Wouldn't work," Lovemore scoffed. "Even if we got the lot – which I doubt – they'd be back aboard the next shipment of stores."

"Additional cats then?" Manning suggested but Lovemore shook his head again.

"Ship's got enough as it is; sometimes you can't sleep for the blighters yowling; get any more and they'd be a problem in theirselves."

"Might organise a fishing contest," Cranston suggested.

"Fishing?" Manning was surprised.

"Aye, get the youngsters organised over the gratings. A rat'll take bait as happily as any fish."

"And you don't need no hook," Lovemore agreed. "They just

clings on till you grabs 'em."

"It's an idea I suppose," Manning pondered. "At least it might reduce the numbers. Perhaps a prize for the boy who brings in the most?"

"Won't be no need for that!" Cranston grinned. "Let them keep what they catches, and they'll be more'n happy."

"Miller pie," Lovemore agreed with a lick of his lips.

"Or just toast 'em over the galley stove," Cranston suggested. "Anyway you do it, they cooks up luv-er-ly."

"I think we'll stay with sealing the holes," Manning told them more levelly. "You don't want Joe Morales to address it?"

Both men shook their head. "Carpenter's lot've got enough on their plates at present," Lovemore said. "Me an' Cranston'll sort it, an' add a lick of paint after."

"I remember your painting in Verdun," Manning grinned.

"Aye, Holby's Casino," Cranston agreed.

"Made a fair job of it, as I recall."

"Shame it only lasted the one night," Lovemore sniffed.

"I can ask my loblolly boys to help."

"Wouldn't be no need," Cranston again, "'less they've got painting experience. But we'd appreciate having one of our mates join us."

Lovemore nodded emphatically. "Aye, O'Grady – he'd be a real boon."

"O'Grady?" Manning questioned. "Has he done much painting?"

"Not that we knows of, but he'll get the work done."

"Aye," Cranston confirmed. "Captain said there's a chance of shore leave if the ship's sorted in time."

"And O'Grady's from Cork," Lovemore added. "There ain't nothing he wouldn't do to get a spell on land."

"And quickly," Cranston agreed.

* * *

They found a small hotel almost immediately and it had an empty dining room so the arrival of two senior naval officers was welcomed by the bespectacled owner. But when King requested plain tea for Croft and chocolate for himself, then all offers of cake or scones were refused, the man retreated and sent his daughter in to care for them.

174

"We've hardly had chance to talk," King remarked once they were seated and the girl had gone. "*Tenacious* has an excellent company, but tattletale is likely aboard any ship."

"Indeed," Croft agreed.

"So, while we have a modicum of privacy I would like to repeat how sorry I am it was not possible to make you my first officer."

Croft's expression relaxed slightly. "And I, in turn, repeat it is hardly a consideration. For me to be at sea again is enough and besides, Mr Leyton is carrying out his duties well I believe."

King nodded, that was certainly the case: apart from a tendency to be presumptuous, he could not fault the man technically. There remained, however, a subtle clash in their personalities that quite defied explanation and showed no sign of easing. But neither point could be mentioned to another officer, even Croft, and King moved on to other matters.

"Tell me, is Miss Lévesque's presence causing any problems?"

Croft considered for a moment. "I think not," he said at last. "To be frank I should say we hardly know the lady is aboard. Apart from the recent dinner, she takes most meals in her quarters and is rarely seen on deck."

The beverages arrived and Croft's refusal of milk caused the servant girl's eyebrows to raise slightly. Then they were left in peace once more.

"And her maid?" King prompted.

"She only eats her main meal in the gunroom and leaves early to see her mistress fed."

King nodded; that seemed reasonable enough; surely there was no need to worry further. "I am glad to hear of it, and is Mr Summers settling well?"

"I believe so," Croft replied. "He would appear to have teamed up with young Brotherton and I would chance the atmosphere in the cockpit is a mite healthier as a consequence."

"Would you consider him ready to stand a board?"

Croft sipped at his tea before answering. "I should say so, yes," he replied at last. "The lad is old enough and has the relevant experience, though I should be sorry to see him leave *Tenacious*."

"And you think he would, should he be successful, I am meaning?"

"That is very difficult to say," Croft mused. "Seagoing lieutenants' positions are notoriously hard to find."

"That is not my experience," King countered. "When I enquired of the port admiral there was no one he could recommend."

"You asked Admiral Carson?" Croft exclaimed and King immediately realised his mistake.

"It was mere talk," he hurriedly explained. "I was curious about the general situation."

Croft seemed to accept this and took another sip. "Well that might be for Cork, but in England it is very different," he said, replacing the cup, "as I can surely testify. When last I heard from Cooper he was still seeking a post, though Summers might have the lead on us both being the younger."

"I will put him forward when we reach Halifax," King mused. "If nothing else he would gain from the experience."

"And if he passes, then chooses to leave and seek a commission elsewhere?" Croft enquired.

"Then he will be lost to us," King smiled lightly, "though the service will undoubtedly have gained. And there are times when the good of the service must be our first consideration."

* * *

Amanda Lévesque was folding linen while her maid looked on.

"Will you be going ashore?" The girl was seated on the only chair in the small room and keeping a professional eye on her mistress's work.

"Of course," Lévesque replied placing a chemise on the growing pile. "Our bankers have offices in Cork."

"But can they accept Bristol promissory notes?" Alice asked. "Surely they must be presented at the bank of them what we bobbed?"

"Oh, they will be accepted," the woman gave a sly look. "Sure, 'tis one of the advantages of handling funds of such a nature, all are loath to offend me."

"I don't know how you get by so." Alice shook her head in apparent sorrow.

"And neither do I, but it seems the case. I shall pay a small premium for their trouble, and yet more to have the funds straightaways transferred to coin, but both are worth the expense."

"So will that be right away?"

"Oh, I am in no rush," the woman replied after considering for a moment. "Too much chance of being spotted. I shall delay a couple

176

of days and then only stay on land as long as I have to."

"Have you been to Cork before then?"

"Never even to Ireland," she admitted. "But we are still preciously close to England and many there would be glad to know of our presence."

"And just our luck for one to 'ave travelled," the girl agreed with a snort.

"Sure, it is a thrill I could do without."

"I can remember the time when you'd have liked nothing better," Alice smirked. "You'd have been down to the bank before the ship were fully docked, then off in search of further sport."

"Think you so?"

"I'm sure of it; a new town 'anded to you from nowhere, ripe for the picking and with one of His Majesty's warships standin' by to whisk us safely away afterwards. There'd 'ave been no 'olding you!"

"Ah, but that was then," Lévesque admitted as she collected another garment.

"So what is it now?" Alice asked, her playful smile still in place. "Losing your touch? Or just getting old?"

The woman looked up sharply. "Sure, I'm young enough to give your backside a tanning," she declared and the girl chuckled afresh.

"So what is it then?" she persisted.

Lévesque paused and looked vaguely at nowhere. "Maybe both. Or maybe I'm content with what I already have."

"Content?" Alice pulled a face. "I mean, what we got from the West Country were a fair enough 'aul, but still won't keep us long; not the way we spends."

The woman pulled a wry smile as she considered her cramped, dark quarters. "I don't see us living too well at the moment."

"When we gets 'ome I mean. You know 'ow the stuff runs through our fingers – and the more we gets, the faster it goes."

"Maybe, but I still think we have enough."

"Enough?" Alice was now clearly disgusted. "I don't think you an' me could ever 'ave too much coin."

Lévesque gazed at her fondly. "I wasn't talking of money," she said.

It was something that had become almost a ritual in most of King's commands and one he was determined to maintain aboard *Tenacious*. Each morning, whatever the weather and even if little had occurred the day before, King would hold a formal meeting with his first officer. They usually took place in the great cabin and in the past had involved Croft but, even with Leyton, the tradition continued, and probably with more reason. For, try as he might, King could not establish the same close relationship with the new man and, if it were not for the regular conferences, the lines of communication essential between captain and first lieutenant might eventually break down.

But on that particular morning there had been plenty to report and much of it was good. The work on *Tenacious'* forechains was well advanced and scheduled to be completed by noon, almost three days ahead of Morales' predictions. Other repairs connected with their recent action had also been attended to, the galley was totally reordered and Manning now had a smart sickbay with a proper dispensary that would also provide a measure of privacy for examinations. And the *Lady Camden* sported a fresh topmast with work well underway to see it fully rigged. In short, the only thing that might delay them leaving in the next few days was the arrival of three schooners from Dublin.

These were actually the only drawback. When Gilroy sent for the spare mast word got out that *Tenacious* would be sailing for Halifax and Dent, the port admiral at Dublin, had arranged for them to accompany her. It was a minor annoyance, no more, and when King received the news he was determined not to let it concern him. Schooners were fast vessels and, providing they were up to the crossing, should not affect the quick passage he had in mind.

"They might even prove advantageous," Leyton remarked when he was told that morning.

"In what way?" King questioned and the first lieutenant shrugged.

"We might station them at extreme points," he replied, "and so gain warning of any impending raider."

"We could," King allowed, "but that would also raise the chance of our being sighted in the first place."

"Indeed, sir," Leyton agreed although, as was so often the case, his words appeared as no more than lip service.

That the two men should hold opposing views on a small matter served as a good example of the gulf that lay between them, and King swiftly moved on.

"We expect all three by Wednesday night and will sail with the tide on Thursday morning, that is whether they are here or not."

"I understand, sir." Leyton's reply was perhaps a little stiff, and King accepted he had probably offended the older man.

"Then the final point is shore leave," he continued. When James Croft had been his second in command the morning meetings had taken far longer and often included refreshment but, with Leyton, King was simply keen to get them over.

"I think most officers have enjoyed enough time ashore," Leyton declared a little primly.

"I was thinking more of the people," King replied. "All have worked well and *Tenacious* is in better shape as a consequence."

"They have done their duty, sir, no more."

"If you recall, Mr Leyton, I did say leave would be granted if we kept to schedule and have no intention of breaking my word."

"You need not break your word, sir," the older man persisted. "Further work could be found and if not that, there is always exercise."

"No, I will not have it." King felt his anger rise and deliberately took a second breath. "We are in a secure enough port and have a high proportion of loyal hands, I think they might be trusted."

"They are the same hands we sailed with, sir, and several attempted to run before you joined us."

"When the cat was in almost constant use," King retorted. "Damn it, man, the ship has been secured to the quayside these past few days; has any man attempted escape?"

"Lieutenant Piper organised a most efficient picket..." Leyton began.

"Which could have been evaded with ease if any felt the need."

"Are you suggesting men under your command have no desire to desert, sir?" the lieutenant demanded.

"I am suggesting if a man is treated fairly he is less likely to try. And part of my definition of fairly is keeping my word."

Leyton swallowed but made no response.

"Larboard watch will be allowed twelve hours on Tuesday and, providing all runs smoothly, the starbolins will have the same the following day. Make it known that if any appear late, all in their

179

mess will be deprived of spirits for seven days."

"Very good, sir."

"And they will need coin," King continued.

"We are freshly commissioned," Leyton pointed out with evident satisfaction. "No pay will be forthcoming for at least five months."

"Indeed not," King agreed. "But there will be head money for the corvette that blew. It may not account for much but see every man is allowed half a guinea in expectation. Mr Dennison can work out the details and administer it as a loan."

"We do not have access to such funds." The man was almost whining now.

"I shall authorise what is necessary from my bankers," King snapped. "Now if there is nothing else, perhaps you will see to that immediately as we appear to have finished our business?"

* * *

Well, we kept to our side of the bargain," O'Grady muttered as the three men surveyed the finished sickbay. "Are you thinkin' the skipper will keep to 'is?"

"I should say so," Lovemore replied. "He were only a lieutenant when we knew 'im, but always treated us straight."

"Aye, you got nothing to worry about with that one," Cranston confirmed. "An' he says we're all getting 'alf a bean in advance, so reckons that'll be right an' all."

"Though I can't see that going far," Lovemore sniffed.

"You'd do a lot less with nowt," Cranston told him, "an' that's what you was left with after sellin' yer ticket to that bumboat."

"As I recall, I was buying a block of figs," Lovemore told him loftily. "Now why would a fella do a foolish thing like that?"

"Weren't all spent on figs," his friend pointed out.

"Have you got any more then?" Lovemore turned on him.

"Couple of shillin's p'raps."

"Well, will you listen to the two o' yer?" O'Grady demanded. "We got ourselves twelve hours in one of the nicest towns in Ireland. I'll show you around, and we'll get by fine on far less than ten bob."

"Will it be jus' the three of us?" Lovemore asked.

"I were thinkin' we might ask young Longdon an' all," Cranston said, scratching at his chin. "Kid ain't been nowhere yet, so can 'ardly be disappointed."

"I tells yer, it's a wonderful town," O'Grady assured them. "I'm a Cork man miself – more or less grew up in the place; you're in for a treat an' no mistakin'."

"So we'll get some home cookin' will we?" Lovemore asked.

"An' maybe a few comforts?" Cranston added.

"Can't offer you nothing like that, me folks are all gone, along with any friends more'n likely. But it's still a grand place and there's nothing to disappoint. The only thing you'll have to be careful of is fallin' in the Lee."

"The Lee?" Cranston questioned.

"It's the river; surrounds the place, so it does. Barky's more or less sittin' in it now."

"Can't see that being a problem," Lovemore muttered.

"No?" Well, there are a fair few bridges you want to be careful of when you've a skinful. Stream's strong enough to take you out to sea, that's if you don't sink to the bottom first."

"Well, we'll be alright," Cranston supposed. "Long as you jumps in after us."

"And why would I be doing that then?" O'Grady asked.

"Said it yourself," the seaman beamed, "you're a Cork man."

* * *

It was the second time King had been ashore and the second time he noticed someone from the ship. Also, as before, the town was blessed with the most delightful spring sunshine so as he stepped from his banker's offices with the heavy pouch of coin in his pocket, he was reasonably pleased to see Amanda Lévesque on the narrow pavement.

"Would you be returning to the ship?" she asked on noticing him.

"To be honest I had not decided," King admitted, returning her smile.

In fact he was taken slightly aback; ever since their first, unfortunate, meeting, Miss Lévesque had behaved with respect and politeness, yet still he felt she was keeping him at a distance. Now though, she seemed glad of his presence. "You have been making purchases, perhaps?" he added, nodding towards the small parcel she carried under one arm.

181

"I had some business to transact." She held the package slightly closer to her as if frightened he might seize it.

"Well, would you care to take some refreshment?" King asked. The hotel where he and Croft had talked was close by and he was in no particular rush. "Or perhaps you might assist me. I understand the town is famous for lace; I thought I might buy some but have no eye for such things."

"Thank you, Captain, but I really should return."

For a moment King debated; he could let her go, explore a little further, and perhaps find something more suitable for Aimée than the plaster duck already purchased. But there was something about the woman's manner that suggested she would rather he stayed and, so strong was the feeling, he decided to submit to it.

"Very well, then we shall go together," he announced and was strangely pleased when she quickly fell into step.

"I suppose I should be glad of your protection," King confessed with a grin when they had travelled a few paces. "I am carrying a fair amount of coin."

The remark was meant to be taken lightly, although it caused a different effect on the woman. "Coin? That is strange to be sure," she began, then added rather lamely, "why ever would you be needing coin?"

"Larboard watch will be given liberty tomorrow," he replied. "Eight till eight, though I fear some may stretch matters slightly."

"Then I am glad I chose today for my trip," she said. "Sure, the last thing I would want to run into is a lot of drunken sailors."

"Oh, I think you would be safe enough," King assured her. "Jack ashore can be a mite disconcerting but in the main means well."

"The ones I met in Bristol were not so."

"When were you in Bristol?" he asked as they paused to cross a road.

"A while back; some sort of fleet had come in and the town was awash with the most uncouth louts you could ever meet."

"I am sorry to hear of it but suspect you may have come across a very different type of seaman."

"Are they not universal?"

"To a point, but the ones you describe ply a separate trade to most merchants, and a Royal Navy tar is even more removed."

She might have wanted to enquire further but King had more to say.

"Most of my men will be wanting drink for sure but some money will be spent on luxuries; soft bread, butter, fresh milk."

"So that is where your coin will go?" she supposed. "And not women?"

"Oh, women without doubt, but I cannot blame them for that."

"You cannot?" she glanced sideways and gave him a penetrating look. "Why so?"

"A hand spends much of his time at sea with others of his ilk; on the rare occasions he is allowed on land, and in a place where his language is spoken, is it so surprising he seeks out female company? And twelve hours is hardly time to strike a normal relationship."

"Sure, I accept what you say," she allowed as they paused again to let a waggon pass by. "Though it hardly alters my impression; this world is made for men, run by men and for the benefit of men; women are barely allowed to exist in it."

King was silent while he digested this and they had travelled several hundred yards before he thought of a suitable reply.

"You seem very set in your convictions," he said at last.

"And why should I not be?" she demanded. "Have you not eyes in your head? Or do you simply choose to see what you will?"

"Miss Lévesque I fear..."

"You speak lightly of men taking their pleasures with prostitutes and consider little wrong in the practice; indeed you seek to excuse it. Yet how would you judge a woman who behaved so?"

His mouth opened but no words were forthcoming. This was hardly the conversation King expected or wished to take part in; he already felt mildly embarrassed with it being so public. And then she made it a good deal worse.

"Tell me, Captain; have you had affairs?"

The streets were by no means crowded but there were folk around who could listen should they choose.

"I, I have been married," he began.

"Have been?" she asked, picking up on his hesitancy. "So is the poor lady no longer with us?"

"She is no longer with me," King smiled suddenly. "To be honest I have little idea of her current situation. It was a while ago and we do not converse."

"Yet you speak of buying lace; pray who might that be for?"

Again he was lost for words although it seemed Miss Lévesque

183

had enough for them both.

"The fact is, men can behave as they wish; visit nugging houses, employ mistresses, attempt to bed whoever they will, and the cruellest they can expect is to be called a bounder."

"Hardly," King protested, but there was more.

"A woman who behaves so will be treated far worse while there remain places in England where the harshest and most humiliating punishments are dealt out for the mildest of such transgressions."

"I see," King muttered. It was at least a mile to where *Tenacious* lay trussed to the quayside and it would seem the time was to be well filled.

"And what happens when a woman marries?" she asked, though fortunately did not wait for an answer. "Sure, everything she owns, all her money, possessions, estates – even her name is taken by her husband with no room for complaint or protest."

"I do not think he requires her name," he suggested softly, but the comment went unnoticed.

* * *

Those going ashore were certainly dressed for the occasion; as the larboard watch gathered in the waist they looked far smarter than on any Sunday. Most wore their tiddly suits; white duck trousers with bold red waistcoats and crisp broadcloth jackets, many of which had pearl buttons and lace or ribbon sewed into the seams. Black or red silks had been tied with studied nonchalance about their necks, while hats of fresh straw or tarred cloth topped everything off nicely. The men moved stiffly in their unfamiliar finery, some of which was borrowed from members of the starboard watch, and their unaccustomed shoes made odd noises on the deck, threatening to trip them headlong before they even touched land. But, though most had been in London less than a month before, and their leave would last a bare twelve hours, all were keen to be off and explore the delights of the town.

And none more than the four almost first in line at the entry port. Cranston and his mates had missed breakfast to get the pitch and were already planning their time.

"Delaney's is the best bakers," O'Grady assured them, "least it was when I were last in these parts. Get any amount of cake so you

184

will, an' the softest bread ever baked."

The men were licking their lips in contemplation; such luxuries were worth forgoing half a pound of burgoo for.

"And after that?" Longdon, the lad, piped up.

"After that we'll sees what's about," Cranston told him in a fatherly air.

There was a shout from a petty officer on the quarterdeck and the crowd began to push forward; soon they were walking on solid ground, bodies swaying oddly to compensate for a lack of movement underfoot.

"It all looks the same," O'Grady assured them. "An' I knows it like I never left; I tell you lads, you're in for a day you'll never forget."

* * *

"Most are thoroughly incapacitated," Leyton announced stiffly. "One has a broken arm from falling off a flagpole and there are several cases of what the surgeon thinks to be barrel fever."

King nodded; it was what he had expected. But his second in command had more news to impart and was taking obvious pleasure in doing so.

"Marine Lieutenant Cross and his men have brought back six following summonses from the constables and Mr Piper is currently at the magistrates' court negotiating the release of seven more."

"If he experiences difficulties I should be informed," King stated softly and Leyton nodded in acknowledgement before returning to his list.

"Then we have twenty-nine cases of smuggling; most are concerned with drink but seven cats were carried aboard without permission as well as a suckling pig, two dogs and a sparrow in a cage."

"A sparrow?" King repeated in wonder.

"It had been painted yellow and was sold as a canary," Leyton stated with due solemnity.

"Is that all?" King asked without hope.

"It is all for now, sir, but frankly I cannot see how we can subject the town to the starboard watch tomorrow."

"We can because I said we would," King reminded him. "Besides, there isn't a port in the world that does not welcome the income provided by seamen on a spree."

"Indeed, sir? I'd chance we have found the exception."

"The fact is, they all came back, and that was the proviso."

"Not quite all, sir," the first lieutenant replied while folding his paper and tucking it into his waistcoat pocket. "Seventeen were late in returning to the ship and will appear at the next defaulters, and four remain absent."

King collected his watch. "It is barely nine," he pointed out. "That's only an hour adrift."

"An hour, or a day, or a week, it is an offence; unless they show soon they should surely be charged with desertion. And I should add that they were all from Wainwright's mess."

There was something in the way Leyton delivered this last piece of information that alerted King.

"Wainwright's mess?" he questioned.

"Yes, sir. A boy, Longdon, who probably knows no better, but he was in company with three older men; O'Grady, Lovemore and Cranston. The latter you will recall, I am certain."

"Yes," King agreed sadly, "I do remember Cranston."

"Indeed, sir," Leyton agreed with a final note of triumph. "He is the hand you spared from punishment on your arrival."

Chapter Seventeen

HMS *Tenacious* sailed on the morning tide two days later. The wind was fair, and she led four other vessels in her wake: a stately former Indiaman, two sleek schooners and a brig that looked unlikely to clear the bay with any certainty. The last was something that still stuck in King's craw; he had agreed to schooners, but this was a vessel of a very different ilk.

On seeing her the previous afternoon he had immediately protested to the port admiral, but the old boy had been emphatic. It seemed her master regarded his craft worthy of the North Atlantic claiming she only lacked a decent coat of paint – something that would be rectified on reaching her home port of Halifax. And meeting with the man made little difference; the *Mary Jane*'s skipper was a stocky Canadian with deeply tanned skin and an abnormally loud voice. But there was also such an air of honesty about the fellow that, when he swore a reasonable speed could be maintained, King found himself believing him. A later inspection of the brig's tophamper was not so reassuring but by then King had agreed to take the vessel under his care. It was an acceptance not without qualifications however; should she fail to keep up, the brig would be left to fend for herself and no time or energy could be spent helping with repairs.

Mildly pacified, King had sent out his orders for the convoy, then gratefully fled the confines of Cork Bay, conscious he was leaving behind many equally glad to see them go. And now, with the details of a town still reeling from two days of *Tenacious'* crew at leisure fast becoming blurred, he finally had time to consider what to do about Cranston.

The seaman and his mates had returned while Leyton was making his report and usually would have suffered nothing more than a minor and informal punishment. The three older hands were reasonably sober with only the boy showing any signs of excess. They had been delayed due to the supposed expertise of O'Grady; the Irishman claimed to know the town well yet failed to see them back in time. Again, it was a standard excuse that would usually have been accepted with the proverbial pinch of salt and King was still prepared to be lenient. After all, leave had been granted as a reward for hard work and nothing more was required of any man that night nor the following day. But without reference to his captain, Leyton had ordered Cranston to be restrained and when he investigated the matter, King found himself rather hoisted by his own petard.

Had he not been quite so adamant about keeping his word over granting leave there might have been room to manoeuvre but, when pardoning Cranston for the initial trumped-up charge, he had plainly stated further bad behaviour would attract double the penalty. It was a ludicrous situation; as captain of the ship he should have total autonomy, yet now was trapped by the very rules laid down by himself.

He turned from the taffrail and looked forward along the length of *Tenacious'* quarterdeck. Taylor had the watch and was standing with hands clasped firmly behind his back, an attitude copied by young Vernon, the duty midshipman, nearby. Manton was also on deck and reading the traverse board while Hedges and a team of signalmen were checking the newly installed flag locker. Could it only have been a month or so before that he had been on the cliffs at Beachy Head?

A lot had happened in the intervening time and much of it for the good. *Tenacious* had been in action twice and accounted for herself well enough; with a little more patience and practice she would soon be a crack frigate. And her people were still improving; not only had a new record been set when they recently set up topmasts, there was a better general feeling on the lower deck. It was something hard to define and impossible to log but meant a great deal to King.

So, how would that attitude change were he forced to punish Cranston? His instinctive answer was it must deteriorate. As far as punishment was concerned, most major crimes carried a set penalty and it was a brave, or foolish, captain who deviated from the considered wisdom. But there were no such guidelines for the manner in which a ship's discipline was administered. Some captains maintained a tight hold, coming down hard on each offender and never offering any leeway, while others preferred a more relaxed approach and were inclined to listen to reason and even excuses before acting. There were successful commanders and happy ships at both edges of the spectrum, but the one thing that would never be tolerated was injustice.

Despite harsh living conditions and expectations that often

bordered on that of a slave, the average lower deck exhibited a surprising degree of sensitivity. Few would accept a man being punished for a crime he had not committed and consistent unfairness, be it from the boatswain's rattan or a formal flogging, had been the cause of many mutinies. But equally the average Jack would not abide favouritism; if an officer showed unwarranted deference, be it in excusing unpleasant work or ignoring transgressions that should see him disciplined, the outcome was much the same and a strong atmosphere of revolt may result.

It was this narrow path that every captain must tread, and much would depend on the attitude or personality of the officer involved. King had long since learned this could not be assumed but must come from the man himself. This last point was equally important as, however unsophisticated a regular hand might appear, few were anything less than straightforward and all could spot a fraud at twenty paces.

But this hardly helped King in his present dilemma. As captain, it was within his power to punish Cranston in any way he chose. The charges against him might be quashed, upheld, or doubled and few would openly object. But should he make the wrong choice, should he judge the mood of the people – or his officers – incorrectly, he could be certain of repercussions from one or the other, and opposition from either side would hardly help maintain a happy ship.

* * *

The recent time ashore had produced far too many defaulters for the ship's small area of punishment deck so, considering the severity of their crimes and the fact that being in the Atlantic Ocean made escape unlikely, those awaiting review were allowed to return to their shipmates and resume normal duties. But despite this temporary freedom, when they gathered for their midday meal on the first day out from Cork a sober atmosphere prevailed over Wainwright's mess.

"I still says the fault's wi' me," O'Grady sighed. "If I hadn't been fooled so by that new bridge, we'd have been back to the barky with seconds to spare."

"No point sailing over your own wake," Cranston told him. "What's done is done; we was late, got caught and have to pay the price."

"That's alright for the rest of us," Lovemore pointed out. "A week without grog won't do no one any lasting harm. But you'll get that an' a whole lot more."

"It were a trumped-up charge," Wainwright maintained. "Everyone knows that; you won't find anyone supporting Guppy, not with the new skipper in charge."

"Guppy's not got nothing to do with it," Harris, a cockney, added. "First luff's got 'is teeth in and you know what a gullion 'e can be."

"But a charge was brought against 'im," Bovey declared. It was generally accepted the seaman had an understanding of naval law, even if the knowledge rarely kept him from trouble himself. "And punishment was previously decided. New captain decided to quash it, as is his right, but that were on the understanding Cranston kept out of trouble."

"We was all in trouble," Lovemore protested.

"But you weren't all on a warning," Bovey countered.

"So we lose a few tots of grog," O'Grady remarked, "an' Cranston here ends up being scratched by the cat – tell me that's fair."

"I'm not saying it's fair," Bovey sighed, "I'm sayin' it's the law."

"That isn't strictly true," Wainwright pondered. "Weren't Tommy King who charged Cranston with the original offence, it were Leyton. New captain: new regime."

"No arguing with that," Morgan, a Welshman, added. "Ship's been a better place since King took over. Put Guppy in his place straight away didn't 'e though? And 'e seems to 'ave the measure of old man Leyton."

"It were Leyton what confirmed Guppy's charges," Cranston grumbled.

"Man's a bastard through and through," Wainwright agreed. "Nothing he'd like better than seeing your backbone at the gratin'."

"That many stripes is nothing to worry about," Deerman, a German, muttered darkly. "I have had the same on two occasions and once the forty-eight."

"Yeah? Well, you probably deserved 'em," Bovey told him. "Cranston don't, and if they sends him to the grating the lads'll have something to say about it."

"Aye," Morgan agreed. "We's all behind you – to a man!"

Cranston nodded briefly but the reassurance was soon dispelled.

"Something to say about it?" Wainwright mocked. "Bleedin'

sea lawyer! What exactly are they gonna say and to who?”

"He's right," Lovemore confirmed. "Things 'ave been getting easier of late, but we still got to keep in line. First sign of rebellion and we'd all be up for a floggin', no matter who's in command.”

"So what's the captain gonna do?" Wainwright again. "Upset Lemon-Lips Leyton or go against the entire lower deck?”

"Well," Cranston stated with all the dignity he could muster, "I suppose we shall just have to wait and find out...”

* * *

"I think I should like to dine with the captain again," Lévesque announced after her maid had entered the tiny room.

"Would you indeed?" Alice sniffed. "An' when might that be?”

The woman shrugged. "Oh, he has yet to ask, but it is a while since he held a dinner party.”

"Dinner party? I wouldn't call eating ship food with a bunch of pauper navy men a dinner party!”

"Well, that's where you're wrong my girl." There were several sheets of paper and an inkstand on the table and she quickly moved them away. "I made enquires when we were in Cork; our Captain King is far warmer than we realised.”

"Wouldn't know from the state of 'is table," the girl grumbled as she set the loaded tray down in front of her mistress. "Or 'is wine cellar.”

"There's more," Lévesque continued. "I chanced upon him when collecting the last batch of gold from Simpsons. Gave him the line about women in a man's world – lapped it up like a puppy so he did. I'd say he'd benefit from a little training.”

"Well see you gives me good notice," her maid instructed. "Only I wouldn't want to go to the trouble of bringin' your food upstairs to find you eatin' in style next door.”

The meal was pork chops, part of a carcass the purser bought cheaply in Cork that had now reached the stage when it desperately needed eating.

"Lordie, not that old pig again!" the woman muttered as Alice removed the cloth.

"I'm almost lookin' forward to salt beef," the girl agreed. "So when you plannin' on dining with Sir Tom then?”

"He isn't a sir," Lévesque corrected, "just plain old Thomas

King but, not only does he have a bob or two, there's a spark of intelligence about the cove."

"You think so?" Alice pouted. "Just a patronisin' old sod if you asks me. An' you've dined with him afore, why d'ya want another go?"

The woman shrugged as she chewed on a piece of fat. "I might get something decent to eat," she supposed.

"I shouldn't bank on it. But it would be a turn up," Alice continued after considering the matter, "plucking a captain on his own boat..."

"I think he's ripe enough," Lévesque confirmed with a sly grin.

There were fresh vegetables with the meal although the potatoes were starting to blacken and were probably another of the purser's bargains.

"So how you going to do it?" Alice asked. Her voice was still low but now held a measure of respect.

"Sure, I haven't decided yet," her mistress replied. "But reckon he'll be worth the effort."

"A Navy officer will definitely be a first," the girl pondered while Lévesque preened herself slightly before taking another mouthful of pork.

"Yes," she agreed, "it should be a new experience for us both."

* * *

On a sunny afternoon with the ship back at sea and a good three hours before going on watch, there were few spots better than the mizzen fighting top. The place was rarely visited unless a change of sail was in mind, and with the steady southerly coming neatly on their larboard quarter, Brotherton was relatively certain not to be disturbed. They had been at sea a little over two days and all was going smoothly; their charges were currently in an untidy straggle to leeward with the *Lady Camden* to the fore and *Mary Jane*, the brig, very much the backmarker but, with a clear sky and an empty horizon, there was no cause for alarm. And even if one should drop out of station, shake a yard or sink, it would hardly be his concern — for the next three hours at least.

No studding-sails were carried on the mizzen so he was denied a bed of folded canvas, but Brotherton made himself comfortable enough on the smooth woodwork and, as the sun began to warm his face, quickly settled into a gentle doze.

Which was interrupted by the sudden arrival of Summers. The lad appeared through the lubber's hole and, seeing his friend resting peacefully, could not resist a firm prod to the side of his stomach.

"What the..." Brotherton yelled, rising suddenly. Then, on seeing Summers, added, "You bastard!"

"Charmed, I'm sure," the lad beamed as he removed his hat and pulled himself up and alongside. "Thought I might catch you up here."

"Only place you can get any peace," Brotherton grumbled. "At least I thought it was. So why you not on duty?"

"I swapped with Owens," Summers replied, his voice now slightly dreamy as the sun began to work its magic. "He's taken my afternoon watch and I'm standing the second dog today and first tomorrow."

"Lemon chops agree to that, did he?" Brotherton asked.

"Oh, I didn't ask Leyton," Summers snorted, "but Jimmy Croft gave the okay and he's as straight as they come."

"You served with him afore as I recall."

"Oh yes," Summers agreed, "but that doesn't cut no ice with Croft; he don't have favourites."

"Bit like Leyton," Brotherton supposed.

"In a manner," Summers agreed, "he just hates everyone."

"Sure hates me, and I'm up before him tomorrow."

"Before him?" Summers rose slightly in surprise. "You mean..."

"I mean I have Cranston's lot in front of the captain. I'm their divisional mid. so have to speak for them, and I don't think it's going to be pleasant."

"But if the captain's takin' defaulters, there's no reason for Leyton to be present."

"Oh he'll be there," Brotherton predicted grimly. "Cove wouldn't miss it for the world."

"Why do you say that?" Summers asked.

"Because I has a feeling he's going to get one over on the captain. And would rather not be around to see it."

* * *

The investigation of minor crimes was commonly presided over by the first lieutenant. Any subsequent punishment must be approved by the captain, but a man of such importance rarely took an active part. And many believed the detachment preserved the sanctity of a commanding officer's status; for how could a hand respect his captain when he had personally explored what could be a litany of shocking misdemeanours and then passed judgement upon them? Even the lowest of hands could appeal to the captain if he suspected unfairness and, if still not satisfied, then apply for official examination under court-martial, but it would be a fool who did either. For any captain worth his salt would be inclined to support his second in command, as would any court a captain; only in extreme cases would the appeal be granted and then the matter was rarely made public.

But King did not expect Cranston to object; whatever the sentence it would be accepted as part of a seaman's lot and endured in the same manner. Yet, neither did he wish for Leyton to be seen to nominate the punishment. To his mind, the whole matter had been blown out of all proportion and he was especially angry that his second in command was proving so obstinate. But then King must equally accept he was partly to blame. Had he not stepped in and pardoned Cranston initially, his eighteen lashes would have been all but forgotten by now. As it was he had blithely excused the man then, never guessing he would transgress again, foolishly, and publicly, announced the sentence would be doubled on further misbehaviour. And now what he had intended as a goodwill gesture had come back to bite him; Cranston was facing double the original punishment, while Leyton, for whatever reason, seemed determined to use the situation to score some form of personal victory over his commanding officer.

King had no real idea what was making his second in command behave so, but the act had sealed the first lieutenant's fate as far as he was concerned. Looking back he should have taken action when they were in Cork; even an incompetent replacement would have been preferable. But then he could not deny *Tenacious'* repairs had been supervised extremely well and it was hard to dismiss a man who carried out his duties with such competence. No, King decided, the fault was truly with him; he had been too soft-hearted although, as soon as they reached Halifax, he would definitely see the man

194

exchanged. And then Croft could be allowed to take his rightful place as first lieutenant and, together, they would make something of *Tenacious*.

He sat back in his chair and did his best to relax while waiting for the appointed time. Leyton had already dealt with the other defaulters; this morning's examination would only concern Cranston and his cronies. King supposed bringing such attention to the case might have been unwise, but then all of *Tenacious'* officers and most of her crew were aware of the significance so there seemed little point in subterfuge. Besides, he was suddenly sick of treading carefully, or making allowances, and wished for nothing other than the matter to be finished once and for all.

The clump of his sentry's musket from the outer door, followed by a muffled cry, drew his attention and he was standing, ready to meet the first lieutenant as he entered the great cabin.

"The defaulters are waiting outside, sir," Leyton informed him and, was he imagining it, or did the man's face show a slight paleness?

"We shall wait until ten," King replied briskly, and both men stood awkwardly until the distant clatter of the ship's bell ringing out four times permeated the peace of the stateroom.

Another clump of the musket butt, another shout from the marine, then the raucous counting of time from an uncultured voice; the door opened and Cranston, leading three other hands, was marched into the room. A pair of marine privates, their sergeant and a midshipman followed and soon the four miscreants were facing their captain.

"The charge is being late in returning from shore leave," Leyton recited formally. "How do you plead?"

After a simultaneous reply of guilty, Leyton calmly regarded the prisoners.

"Do you wish to speak?" he asked, and it appeared O'Grady did.

"It were all on account of me, yer honour," he declared while standing as smartly as any seaman could expect to. "I were conning us back to the ship and was just a little under the weather. There was an extra bridge that had been built since me last visit and I were banjaxed."

"Which is no excuse." King was speaking to the group as one. "You should all have been aware of the time."

That was indisputable, although O'Grady seemed eager to add

more, but Leyton continued before he could.

"Who is to speak for them?" he asked.

Brotherton stepped forward and stood to attention. "Mark Brotherton, divisional midshipman," he announced.

"And you know these men, Mr Brotherton?" King inquired formally.

"I do, sir," the lad confirmed, his voice quavering only slightly. "All joined recently but have caused no reason for complaint or correction."

"That is not true," Leyton's voice rang out harshly. "Cranston has already been charged with general filthiness, as Mr Brotherton is well aware."

Brotherton opened his mouth but was uncertain whether to continue.

"Carry on," King told him gently.

"Sir, they fought bravely in both actions, and Cranston, Lovemore and O'Grady have pleased Mr Manning in the repairs to his surgery. Mr Manning offered to be present but had other commitments."

"And how were the prisoners on return to the ship?" King asked.

"The men were relatively sober, sir," Leyton allowed, "though Longdon was far from well."

"He cast up in the Lee, so he did..."

"Silence!" O'Grady's explanation was cut short by a painful yell from the marine sergeant.

"I see," King began. "Well, I cannot pretend to be impressed by your actions but do accept such mistakes occur. You will all be denied leave at the next opportunity and are deprived of spirits for a further fourteen days. Dismiss!"

The word was repeated with force by the sergeant and the seamen were marched from the room. But Leyton remained, as King knew he would, and was equally unsurprised when he had more to say.

"That is surely not the end of it, sir?"

"As far as I am concerned it is," King replied firmly.

"But other charges are outstanding," the older man protested, adding, "as you are surely aware," with a possible note of censure.

"I am aware of the charges you brought against him previously," King stated with deliberate coolness.

"Which you chose to hold over," Leyton reminded. His face had now lost any sign of pallor and both cheeks were burning red.

"I chose to hold them over because I did not wish to pursue the matter further," King was equally conscious of a growing anger and was determined not to submit to it. "I have served with Cranston in the past so feel I know him as well as any man. And probably a good deal better than some of my officers."

"No captain should have favourites," Leyton stated hotly.

"No captain should receive unwanted advice from his second in command," King retorted. "Frankly, Mr Leyton your performance has pleased me in many ways, but I am not impressed by the attitude shown in this matter."

"I am thinking of the good of the ship, sir!" he was almost shouting.

"As am I," King snapped back. "And enforcing charges that were initially trumped-up will do it no favours."

"I do not regard them to be trumped-up," the man spluttered.

"Do you not? Why, I have made the most casual investigations and am convinced of it!"

For a moment Leyton was silent although King would have continued even if not.

"I am unaware if you were misled by Mr Guppy, or took it upon yourself to accuse the man, but assure you such a practice will not be well regarded if revealed at court-martial."

Now all colour was gone, the older man simply repeated the last two words to himself with an expression of total horror.

"And that is no idle threat." King's tone was lower now but just as intense. "You may come from a time when unfair beatings were tolerated and even encouraged, but that is no longer the case, at least in any ship I command. All punishments inflicted aboard *Tenacious* will be according to the law. I thought I had made that plain but it seems you need reminding."

"If you are unsatisfied with my performance I shall retire on reaching Halifax," the man sulked.

"That is for you to decide," King snapped. "But for as long as you remain first lieutenant, you will do well to remember my wishes. And that I am Captain of this ship."

Chapter Eighteen

Of course he had been wrong, King decided later; Leyton was entitled to protest against Cranston's punishment being conveniently ignored. And for all either of them knew, the lower deck may well take umbrage at their captain's apparent leniency. Yet still King sensed he had come to the correct decision, even if it had threatened *Tenacious'* delicate order of command.

But it seemed Leyton soon forgot the incident. Despite his bold statement, as the small collection of shipping edged deeper into the North Atlantic no further mention was made of retirement and he continued to perform his duties with total efficiency. If anything the relationship between the two men improved; often, when King came on deck to check their position or the convoy's performance, Leyton would be present and, after exchanging somewhat formal pleasantries, genuine conversation followed while the morning meetings grew less wearisome and began to show positive results. Following suggestions from Leyton, a subtle change in the messing arrangements – moving two groups that were known to argue and redistributing their members – brought a significant reduction in quarrels during mealtimes, while an additional wind sail rigged forward cured an outbreak of mould beneath the forecastle. The pair of them would never become friends, that much remained obvious, but it was as if the confrontation over Cranston's punishment had acted as a catalyst that brought them forward to some form of understanding.

"I must confess to never having made a crossing so far north." It was a crisp, bright morning when Leyton made the confession; the hands had eaten their breakfast and the watch on deck was currently at exercise, something both he and King were casually supervising.

"Have you not?" King enquired. "Though surely have been to the Americas?"

"Indeed, and was stationed at Halifax," Leyton confirmed. "I spent some time there and regard the place as my second home. But we transferred from further south and came by the Gulf Stream."

"I was not aware," King admitted. "And how did you find Halifax?"

"A pleasant place; Sir Richard Hughes was C-in-C in those days."

"I know of him though our paths have never crossed."

"Much of my time was spent with Moore, one of his lieutenants," Leyton continued.

"Graham Moore?"

"Indeed. When he was made commander there was the chance I might join as premier in *Bonetta*."

"Which would have been a good move indeed," King remarked. "Moore has done well, as would any of his followers. We fought together at Tory Island; he was a post captain then."

"And he has gone on to greater things since," Leyton added with a hint of regret. "Yet I remain a lieutenant."

King glanced at the man and seemed to see him in a new light. There were several King had served alongside who failed to advance; some left the service and more than a few died while, conversely, one was now a commodore and due to be made admiral at any time. Such were the ways of the service – of life almost – and he had rarely considered them until then. For why should he? His progression had been steady enough and was now at the point where he could walk his own quarterdeck as a senior captain, which was surely success in anyone's judgement. Those he had left behind would doubtless have wished the same for themselves and more than a few must have missed opportunities similar to Leyton's. And it was then that he began to understand the elderly officer a little better.

"Still, it is the pity you did not follow Moore," King told him gently. "He went on to seize a treasure fleet and, though not the massive prize everyone expected, those involved were paid out handsomely for their trouble."

"It is a matter I have considered at length," Leyton commented dryly, "though to little benefit."

"So why did you not join the *Bonetta*?" King insisted.

"There were a number of reasons and, I must own, the blame lay mainly with me," the older man confessed. "You see I was young and relatively comfortable in my present post. At that time it seemed promotion was bound to come; all I need do was wait. And I was equally aware another officer was in position."

"*Bonetta* already had a first lieutenant?" King clarified and Leyton nodded.

"Had I asserted my case, reminded him how well we worked together and made it plain I would be his ideal second in command, Captain Moore might have been persuaded to dismiss the fellow. But he was too much the gentleman to do so off his own bat, and I too much the fool not to insist."

* * *

Cranston handled the wooden fid like the expert he was. With a length of line in one hand and the tool in the other he swiftly unravelled and separated the three primary strands, then glanced up at his audience.

"It's important not to go too deep," he explained, "Otherwise you'll only waste line."

Longdon nodded as he worked his own fid and produced a result not too dissimilar to his teacher's. The lad had watched splicing on numerous occasions but the practice always mystified him; this was the first time anyone had taken the trouble to explain it, and he didn't want to miss a word.

"Shake the strands out like so," Cranston continued, making a small whip from his line before gathering the fibres together once more. "Then you got a middle, larboard and starboard, see?"

He held the length up and again Longdon nodded mutely.

"Then you decides how large you want your eye to be," the seaman continued, folding the line back on itself, "and digs the fid in at that place."

Longdon duly inserted his own tool and the line separated easily.

"Stick your centre strand in the middle, and pull it through tight," Cranston continued while casting a subtle glance at his student. "Then tuck your larboard through the next one up from the middle, an' the starboard the next down – see?"

The fingers appeared gnarled and clumsy but worked the line with amazing agility; Longdon, with a slimmer hand and a full set of nails, found the process far more difficult but managed it eventually.

"Now you got your eye, and you're started," Cranston continued when the boy had caught up. "An' all you 'as to do is continue weaving your line in so – middle, larboard, starboard."

Again the fingers moved as if of their own volition; separate strands were fed in turn until they became a part of the rope. Longdon watched in fascination, then addressed his own work. His eye looked sloppier, but the basics were there and as he eased the strands in he sensed it was becoming tighter.

"You got it," Cranston confirmed with apparent satisfaction. "Now do a dozen more and you'll be able to splice an eye in y'r sleep."

"I'm obliged," the lad told him with transparent honesty.

"No need," the seaman chuckled. "I've shown how it's done, only you can decide to learn. Now, how's about splicing two lengths together?"

* * *

"So I gets the day off then?" Alice supposed.

"I wouldn't say the *day* off," her mistress replied, puzzled. "Sure, I am only dining with the captain, so will need one meal less. Besides, I have done so before," she added. Ireland was already over a week behind them and a considerable amount of routine had built up in that time. It would be broken by this meal, and the woman was in no way sorry.

"Never went to all this trouble in the past." The girl pointed to the collection of pots and jars assembled on the washstand.

"I had no idea of our host's status then," Lévesque explained as she dabbed a small measure of carmine into a bowl of white powder. "Several thousand invested in 'the funds' it would seem, and a deal of property into the bargain."

"How'd you find that out?" the girl asked suspiciously. "An' in Cork of all places?"

"We've been doing this some time." The woman was considering her face in the mirror. "And whether for good or bad, have put a deal of money through the banking system. After a while they starts to treat you differently – even if you do happen to be a woman."

"How queer," Alice mused. "From the looks of 'im you'd say he ain't got two beans to rub together. An' 'e eats an' drinks like a monk."

"Maybe so, but I understand Captain King has a fine house, plenty of land and several paying tenants."

"Then 'e's takin' a bit of a chance," the girl scoffed. "Entertaining a pretty young lady in 'is quarters – not what I'd expect from an upright cove."

"Oh, there will be others I have no doubt. But it is him I shall be focusing upon. And for all his appearance, think he'll turn out like men everywhere." The woman spoke slowly as she dusted the rouge onto her face. It was a delicate operation; too much and she would look like a whore from the last century, but the right amount should add a measure of interest to what was an otherwise pale complexion. "And like men everywhere, he will have a weak spot which I fully intend to discover, then exploit."

"Why does that not surprise me?" Alice chuckled. "And when you do, will it be of any use?"

"Of any use? Do you mean will we benefit?" She looked at her reflection again and nodded to herself. Then, rising from the chair, turned back to where the dress was lying on her bed. "Oh, I think we might..."

Alice, who had been standing while her mistress worked, noticed the movement and shuffled across the small space. Collecting the dress in her hands she began to gather it together until the garment was little more than a tight ring of material. Without a word, Lévesque knelt on the bare boards, being careful not to ladder her white silk stockings, before raising her hands and passing them gently through the circle of cloth her maid held above. Then, standing slowly as Alice released the material, the dress was allowed to flow down about her.

"That's a lovely bit of silk," the girl said, smoothing the fabric down. "But then it ought to be, the amount it cost. I sometimes reckon if we stopped buyin' you fancy gowns we might 'ave enough to get by on without working no more."

"Sure, but I look on such things as an investment." Lévesque glanced down at the intricate lacework and embroidered seams. It was not the latest in fashion perhaps, but more than enough to dazzle a simple naval officer. "And one worth making if we are to prosper."

"Might be an' all," the girl allowed, "'cept it always seems to be you what gets to wear 'em."

* * *

"And the damned brig is falling behind again," Taylor added.

Croft glanced back; the wind was constant if surprisingly light and with a sea about as flat as the North Atlantic could manage, there was no excuse. "Any trouble from the others?" he asked and Taylor shook his head.

"Good as gold; *Lady Camden* keeps a steady pace and I reckons we're holding the schooners back. If it weren't for matey astern I'd say we could add another knot to our speed."

It was a nice point; Captain King had made it clear that, should the brig fall into difficulties or suffer damage, he would leave her behind. But though she was slow in stays and had a suit of sails that might have come from a dozen different vessels, her master was a seasoned mariner and clearly doing his utmost to maintain a reasonable speed. For as long as that continued, there was little they could complain about, although neither could they raise the pace any.

"Otherwise I reckon you can look forward to a peaceful watch."

Croft nodded; the horizon was clear and the sun bright, though his waistcoat was still necessary. Forward, on the forecastle, a youngster was being shown how to tie a Turk's head and further aft the carpenter's team were making repairs to one of the gratings. He, too, had not made such a northerly crossing before and had to admit to enjoying the experience, so a quiet watch would be welcome.

"You'll find the servant girl below," he said as Taylor turned to go.

"Who, Alice?" The younger man was surprised. "Is she not attending her mistress?"

"There's a meal being held in the great cabin," Croft told him as he wiped the traverse board clean, "and Miss Lévesque is amongst those invited."

Taylor was careful to make no comment. The second lieutenant could be a queer old fish; most times he was a pleasure to serve alongside, hardly the life and soul of the gunroom perhaps, but a sound colleague who did his job well and could be relied upon. But some subjects were taken extremely seriously and anything concerned with the captain fell into that category. From forward came the sound of the ship's bell being struck eight times.

"I must say I'm ready for a bite myself," the younger man remarked.

"Very well, Mr Taylor, I have the ship."

The third lieutenant turned to go but Croft stopped him.

"A word to the wise," he said, his tone suddenly urgent. "The girl, Alice..."

"Yes?" Taylor blinked.

"She usually leaves early to see her mistress fed." Croft had stepped closer until he was less than a pace away and continued in barely a whisper, "Though clearly will not have the need today..."

It was odd for Croft to impart mundane information and stranger still that he did so in such a furtive way.

"Take my advice; give her a wide berth."

"A wide berth?" Taylor repeated.

"Her and her mistress," Croft continued, equally low. "I have nothing to base my suspicions upon, but there is something about the couple that strikes me as odd."

"I see," the younger man muttered. "And have you mentioned this to the captain?"

Croft stepped back and appeared mildly awkward. "As I say, there is nothing specific. But I have spoken with Mr Leyton and he is of the same opinion."

Now that just about capped it all; it was one thing for Croft to suspect the girl – although heaven alone knew of what offence – and feel the need to pass a warning. But what truly amazed Taylor was that Croft and Leyton had discussed the matter. For most of the trip any words exchanged beyond their duties were either overly polite or mildly barbed, so much so that Marine Lieutenant Piper believed one of them harboured some form of grudge. But whatever the case, Croft's warning was sincere, and Taylor sensed he would be a fool to ignore it.

"Thank you, sir. I hear what you say and shall treat both with the utmost caution," he promised, then turned again and finally left the quarterdeck.

* * *

Despite his initial offer, and King having met with Gilroy on several occasions when in Cork, there had been no further mention of them dining aboard the former Indiaman. So, given that it appeared to be a lost cause, King had decided to host this private party himself.

And, as he sat back at the head of the table, he was glad. It was by no means a grand affair, such things went very much against the grain, but still an improvement on the twice-weekly meal he was accustomed to sharing with one or two selected officers. It had also started at three, traditionally the time when a Royal Navy captain dined, and so was unlikely to have the same gravity as one staged later in the day.

Still, his guests, and King had been especially careful with his selection, had done their best to appear smart. Leyton wore what appeared to be a brand-new uniform while Marine Lieutenant Piper was resplendent in his customary scarlet and white. Manning's black jacket was also well cut and had never seen the rigours of surgery and King himself had donned a full-dress tunic. He had even gone so far as to dispense with his beloved trousers and squeeze into a pair of britches complete with stockings, while both midshipmen were presenting as well as creatures from their dark domain might. But although each man had gone to special pains to appear smart, none came close to competing with the vision that was Amanda Lévesque.

Whether by accident or design, she had appeared from her quarters off the great cabin just as the last male guest arrived and immediately stunned all present. And now, as she delicately sipped at her soup to his left, King supposed that, if nothing else, she made an attractive addition to the dining table.

"So you are staying in Halifax?" Piper, the marine, was asking.

"For a while," Lévesque admitted. "Sure, I grew up there and my parents still keep a house in town."

The casual reference fitted perfectly with what King had already learned about the woman; she must indeed be of wealthy stock, something that would have made her recent rejection in marriage the harder to bear.

"And what took you to England?" Piper continued, "It were hardly the season to visit."

"It was partly social, partly business," the woman replied. "Tell me, Mr Piper, have you been to Canada before?"

All present heard the exchange, but King guessed only he knew how skilfully Lévesque had fielded the question. And again it was a perfect answer; a solitary woman at a table full of men might feel tempted to tell something of her story if only to gain their sympathy. But if she truly wanted to keep her shame a secret, it must be shared with as few as possible, and Lévesque was holding her course like a seasoned quartermaster.

However, it seemed Piper was not to be put off and, once he had denied all knowledge of Canada and the continent in general, doggedly returned to the previous subject.

"I assume that would be a family concern, Miss Lévesque?" he asked.

"Forgive me..." she began, apparently confused.

"You mentioned business in England; do I take it you have family interest, or are you one of these new-fangled women who dabble in such things on their own account?"

King was sure he saw Lévesque bridle slightly, even if her reply remained composed.

"Sure, my father is in finance," she stated. "I assist him on occasions and have done so for as long as I can remember."

They had mainly finished their soup and there was a pause while the dishes were cleared.

"And where did you learn such expertise?" It was Leyton this time; King was mildly surprised to notice his second in command entering the conversation.

"It is as with any family trade," she smiled, then nodded when a steward offered to fill her glass once more. "When you live in such an environment, an understanding is acquired along with your ABCs."

The next course would be something of a deviation from the norm. Sturridge appeared at the head of a short line of stewards carrying tureens and began to fuss about as they placed these down on the table. King was taking something of a risk by serving a made meal; roasted meat being far more common and there were sufficient sheep, pigs and even geese in his personal store. But he was starting to miss Aimée more than he imagined and wanted a small reminder of her.

In the part of France where she was born they casseroled chicken in a way King found truly delightful. He had explained this to Sturridge who claimed to have produced similar and had most of the ingredients to hand. Consequently, King entrusted him with four of his hens and now was more than interested to see if the risk had been worthwhile. Then the first of the lids was removed and the scent told him the man had been as good as his word.

"And your father's speciality?" Piper was at it again while the plates were being distributed and King was about to steer the conversation away when Lévesque answered more readily.

"Investments mainly," she replied. "We have an interest in various ventures and a select number of clients who are looked after exclusively."

"That would sound to be important business," Manning remarked as the steward serving wine circulated again.

"Oh I can assure you it is, Doctor," the woman confirmed.

"Sure, there is a strict limit on the amount we take from any one investor, but that way we are certain of providing a reliable service."

"Don't want to take too much, eh?" the marine supposed.

"We don't want to take anything at all, sir," she replied promptly. "And the limit is a minimum, to prove they take the matter as seriously as ourselves. No investor will be accepted unless they agree to commit at least one hundred guineas."

"And for that, what do they get, pray?" Piper was leering mildly now and King cleared his throat in preparation but again the woman was there before him.

"For that, they get our full attention, Lieutenant Piper," she told him coolly, and might even have given an answering look, for Piper appeared to colour slightly. "Along with a return far more attractive than anything available on the three percents."

* * *

The ship's bell was struck four times and Hedges trooped off with two seamen to measure their speed. Croft had been on watch for two hours; in the same time again he could rest and would have no further duties for some while. Beneath his feet, the captain's party was in progress and a less responsible officer might have positioned himself nearer the skylight, where he could have kept track of the conversation. But Croft had no wish to eavesdrop and was secretly relieved at not being invited.

"Little more than three, sir," Hedges reported as he returned, and the second lieutenant made a note on the traverse board. At that rate it could be the following month before they sighted the next piece of land and, if the brig at their tail did not pick up, possibly longer. Which might mean they were less likely to be accepted into Admiral Warren's squadron and Croft was just considering the ramifications when a call from the masthead broke into his thoughts.

"On the larboard beam," Hacker, at the main top clarified, "though it's little more than a smudge at present."

"Signal from the *Lady Camden*," Hedges broke in. "Sail in sight to the south."

"Very good, acknowledge," Croft murmured, before turning and starting to pace down the length of the quarterdeck. For there was little more he could do; summoning the captain would be premature: a sail was simply a sail after all and, unless it could be identified or drew closer, meant little. It may be an independent British merchant making the same passage, in which case, were the convoy spotted and identified, they could have an addition to their charges. Or it might be an outlying escort for the next official convoy. That was a far better proposition and meant the pressure of being the lone bodyguard would be taken from them. But until the sighting became more recognisable, it was better to keep it to himself. A chorus of laughter rose from the skylight and Croft stopped pacing and resumed his usual position by the binnacle. He would send for Captain King once there was a need, until then he may as well enjoy his dinner.

* * *

The meal in the gunroom had also been going well. Taylor had come down to find those at the table finishing what appeared to be a rather splendid duff. But he had soon caught them up and a reasonable portion was left for him. And now, as the stewards served coffee and the men cracked jokes and nuts, young Alice, usually an early leaver, was holding forth.

"Why, you can keep your men of business," she was telling an enthralled audience. "There ain't nothing like my mistress when it comes to findin' a bargain."

"And does she deal directly with stocks?" Dennison, the purser, and only professional capitalist present, asked.

"Oh I wouldn't know all them details," she laughed. "But I sees the money she turns, and it would make your eyes water."

"So Miss Lévesque is a rich woman?" Marine Lieutenant Cross pondered.

"She's warm enough," Alice supposed, "though most of 'er money belongs to other folk."

"An excellent arrangement!" Manton, the sailing master, remarked to a round of laughter.

"No, there's nothing like that," the girl was serious. "My mistress is as 'onourable as the day is long. She makes fortunes for her clients and every penny is paid out regular an' in full."

"So how does one become one of your mistress' clients?" Cross asked, and Taylor felt this was more than idle speculation.

"Well there's a thing," the girl told him. "Money comes from money; you don't just join up and start raking it in, there's got to be han investment."

"Which is?" Now Taylor was sure the marine was in earnest.

"Starting stakes is high if you goes through my mistress, but I can help out."

"Help out?" Cross asked. "In what way?"

"Well I'll 'ave a talk with her, see what's about and she lets me put a bit in myself from time to time."

"An odd arrangement," Dennison sniffed.

"Works for me," Alice declared. "Year or so from now I won't be washing no clothes nor scrubbing tables."

There was a pause while the men considered this, then Cross spoke again.

"So how much?" he asked, and more gently this time, "If you were to oblige us?"

"You put down ten beans an' I'll see you alright," the girl announced smiling coyly. "Alright in every way."

* * *

"Are you certain?" Croft bellowed.

"Sure as can be, sir," Hacker replied. "Making directly for us and coming up fast. She's showing royals and steering so as to cut us off."

It was about the worst news there could have been. Almost as soon as the sail was sighted it had altered course and was quickly revealed to be a warship. Such a vessel was hardly unusual and, whatever the nationality, sighting a small convoy would cause any to investigate. So, all thoughts of resting after his watch must be dismissed; even if they held their current heading it would be several hours before the sighting closed on them and Captain King might well think it better to lead his charges away. But there was no sense in prevaricating further; now the ship was a known entity the captain must be informed which would signal an end to his little party. Croft turned to the nearby messenger and was about to send him down to the great cabin when Hacker called out again.

"Deck there! I think I seen another one!"

"Where away?" Croft asked.

"Directly astern of the first," the lookout replied, "which is why I couldn't make it out until now. An' there may be a third an' all."

Chapter Nineteen

Once more, King was frustrated by his inability to go aloft. The quarterdeck was crowded, every officer had been summoned either by the message to the great cabin or on hearing the general commotion and now stood in expectation. And rather than taking the role of a leading man who knew the script perfectly, King felt like some jobbing actor thrust on stage without lines and expected to perform; to make a speech or some bold declaration that would convince his audience the current dilemma was in capable hands. Yet their main masthead was adamant the two vessels bearing down were warships, while Bovey, at the fore, thought them merchants. Summers had gone aloft with a glass and should shed more light but, until they knew exactly what they were up against, King felt the lack of a prompt.

"I would have alerted you earlier, sir," Croft assured him, "but there seemed little to be done about the situation and could not be certain we had even been sighted."

"Of course," King replied, glad that at least one man appreciated his predicament. Once they could identify the vessels it must ease matters; were they definitely merchants he would allow them to close. Two or three sailing independently could have been separated from another convoy and would have every right to seek shelter amongst his but, should they prove potentially hostile, he must run. The wind was steady and in the south; turning to starboard would bring it on their quarter and, though that meant a more northerly course, must surely stretch the chase out until nightfall. Quite what would happen to the brig at their tail was another matter; if it came to it they would just have to leave her in their wake, but King preferred not to pursue that tack further.

"Nearest is hull up now." Summers' voice drifted down from the maintop. "She'll probably be in sight from the deck afore long. And I'd say she was a warship right enough."

"What of the other?" Leyton's voice rang out as King moved across to the larboard bulwark. The horizon appeared clear, but something might still be out there he could not pick out.

"Nothing more I can say," Summers continued. "She must be

a mile or so behind the leader and I cannot be certain of anything beyond her."

For two – or possibly three – to sail so widely separated suggested they were searching for something. Possibly nothing more than their old convoy, or they could have more sinister intentions.

"I have them!" It was Taylor, the third lieutenant. The man was standing less than five feet away and pointing positively just forward of the larboard beam. King stared hard at the place but the horizon seemed as empty as ever. Then just the flicker of grey caught his eye and slowly the form of a sail came into view.

And it was strange what a difference making visual contact made; suddenly the sighting was so much more than a vague image mentioned by others. Now it had become a ship, a physical being and one heading for them at the greatest possible speed. That fact, combined with Summers' estimation of it being a man-of-war, finally prompted King to act, and as he turned from the sight it was hard indeed not to appear dramatic.

"General signal to the convoy; 'hostile sail in sight'." Hedges began frantically scribbling on his message block as King continued. "Make sure you get an acknowledgement from each one – *each one*, do you understand? Then follow up with 'make all sail commensurate with the weather'."

That would do for now, once every vessel was aware of the situation he could order an alteration of course, but to do so before might split the convoy prematurely and prove disastrous.

"Mr Manton, what sail can we carry and remain solid?"

"We can shake out the reefs in the tops'ls," the sailing master began, pulling at his chin as he spoke. "They was only there to keep our speed down. Then add t'gallants and possibly royals, though you did mention keepin' things solid, an' that might be pressin' matters rather."

"Very well, t'gallants it is." King glanced up, they were also carrying staysails as *Tenacious* was on a broad reach; once they turned, the fore and aft sails would become less effective, but there was no sense in striking them.

A pipe sounded, followed by a series of bellowed orders and soon *Tenacious'* forefoot was digging deeper into the Atlantic swell as her speed increased.

"Most have acknowledged." Hedges spoke as the last piece of canvas was hauled tight. "But then the *Mary Jane* is always a mite slow in replying."

"Slow in that an' everything else," the senior marine lieutenant added.

"Thank you, Mr Piper," King snapped. It would never be possible to suppress all discussion on the quarterdeck but the marine's comment was unfair. The elderly merchant might not be quick in responding to messages and no one could call her pace brisk, but her master was a good seaman and had consistently wrung every possible knot from her tired hull. Despite this, they might have to leave her behind and, should that be the case, King was certain it would not be on Piper's conscience.

"Take us five points to starboard and signal that to the others," he ordered.

"Very good, sir," Hedges replied, adding, "and the brig has acknowledged."

Tenacious leant into the turn and King could feel her pace increase further as the wind crept abaft the beam. To starboard, the convoy was also altering course, but the two schooners were taking flight and had almost drawn level with the more bovine *Lady Camden*. The *Mary Jane* was yet to respond; she had been carrying more canvas than any other and drifted further behind as he watched. He turned his attention to the sighting to larboard, which was now considerably further aft, then collected the deck glass from the binnacle. Such things were especially hard to use with one hand and rarely of any benefit. After resting the instrument against a ratline the leading ship became more defined but nothing of value could be learned and it remained little more than a sail on the horizon. He stared for several seconds, straining every sense to detect something of its identity or purpose, and failing.

"*Lady Camden*'s made the turn," Leyton commented; King's gaze swung back. Yes, the entire convoy was now on a more northerly heading; even the *Mary Jane* had clumsily swung her stubby hull around and, if not spray, at least there was a greater disturbance at her bows.

So now it had become a stern chase; there were several hours before nightfall and the moon had been particularly bright of late so any cover was questionable. But King supposed such a dramatic alteration in course might dissuade some followers; certainly, if the sighting had been a friendly force, intent only on closing and speaking with them, he may have put them off. And if he were indeed facing yet another group of raiders the manoeuvre would have bought a little time. A little, no more, he gloomily acknowledged. And probably not enough.

* * *

"Well I'd say that went broadly to plan," Lévesque announced as she eased her right leg free of its stocking. "Nothing from Captain Tom, though I still reckon he'll be worth a touch later, and I have yet to make any impact on the doctor fellow, Manning."

"'Im?" Alice seemed appalled. "'E surely ain't worth the trouble!"

"Now that's where you're wrong," her mistress declared while addressing the other stocking. "Sure, our Mr Manning is a dark horse and has a thriving medical practice. Exactly what he is doing aboard a ship like this I have no idea."

"Bank told you that an' all did they?" Alice asked lying back on her mistresses' bed.

The woman paused and fixed the girl with her eyes. "It came up in our conversation, but any information is valuable."

"Well don't look at me," the girl sniffed. "I ain't got the mind for such things."

"There are times when I wonder quite what you are good at..."

"Do you now?" Alice pouted as she luxuriated in comfort. "Don't forget I supports you in other ways..."

The woman considered her for a moment, then continued the account. "Anyway, there was more than a spark of interest elsewhere."

"Really?" the girl sniggered. "One of the midshipmen's a Baron is he?"

"No, it came from Mr Piper."

"What, you mean the soldier man?"

"Marine Lieutenant," her mistress corrected, "and worth a bob or two if I'm any judge."

"Did he bite?"

"He has not yet, but we were rudely interrupted." She tossed both stockings onto the washstand and began to unbutton her petticoat. "I'll arrange a meeting in private and am sure we can work out a suitable arrangement..."

"Another one of your appointments?" the girl suggested,

213

chuckling again.

"It seems the agreed form," the woman allowed. "Sure, it is strange how men find it easier to trust a woman once they believe her seduced..."

"And long may that continue!" Alice sighed. It was one of the advantages of not getting all spruced up: there was no need to undress afterwards, although she was always happy to watch her mistress disrobe.

"But at least my work is carried out in secret," Lévesque added, turning her attention to the smock.

"Well you won't find me doing nuthink in public," the girl grunted. "Besides, I don't look on it as work. An', as it 'appens, I ain't done so bad neither," she added thoughtfully.

"You?" The woman paused with the garment over her head.

"Dennison the purser were interested," Alice announced while contemplating the woman. "And I reckon the other soldier boy's keen as well."

"That would be Mr Cross," Lévesque informed her. "Another marine lieutenant though junior to Mr Piper."

"Might be lower in rank but 'e's warm enough; turns out 'is father's worth several votes an' they got three howsis."

"So you *can* carry out research!" her mistress exclaimed.

The maid shrugged. "I thinks of it more like gossip."

"Call it what you will but if I'd known I'd have made sure he was invited upstairs; we could have trimmed him for a darn sight more!"

"Don't make much of a difference," Alice pouted, "I reckons I turns over as much and no need for fancy dresses."

"Sure, but you have to work the harder for it."

"Like I say, it ain't work," the girl told her smugly, "not if you enjoys it."

"Well, there'll be little chance of any enjoyment for a while." Lévesque had selected a plainer smock and slipped it over her head as she spoke. "Everyone has gone on deck and seems mighty excited about something."

"Think there'll be another battle?" Alice asked, her interest in the woman now fading.

"I should say so; that or a storm."

"I'd prefer a battle."

"Really?" She was amazed.

"As long as I'm not personally involved," the maid qualified. "Storms make me sick."

"Well, if there's to be fighting, they'll no doubt want this space, so we'd better prepare to make ourselves scarce."

"It's a shame." The girl rolled her eyes with renewed interest. "I were hoping you an' I could 'ave a bit of fun tonight."

"We'll have to see about that," the woman pulled a stern face as she reached for a dress. "Though frankly, I doubt there'll be much in the way of enjoyment aboard this ship, not for a while at least."

* * *

Six hours later the sky had begun to darken although all was very much clearer. The pursuing ships had gained considerably, they were in plain sight from the deck and appeared to be heavy frigates. Furthermore, whatever supposedly seen beyond the second must have been nothing more than an aberration as there were only two. But as all aboard *Tenacious* were uncomfortably aware, two would be enough.

Their stalkers were almost directly astern and less than three miles off the last in convoy which, predictably, was the brig. Though still showing every stitch of available canvas, the *Mary Jane* had been consistently falling back and was bound to be the first taken. *Tenacious* was next in line, probably another three miles ahead and checking her speed to remain so while, just off her larboard bow, Gilroy's merchant fought for every knot. However, the schooners were almost out of sight. Having taken King's signal to heart, the pair had packed on as much canvas as their tall masts could bear and were nearly over the horizon. They could change course once darkness fully descended and seemed likely to complete an otherwise uneventful passage to Halifax in safety. But King's concerns were not for them, his thoughts lay with his other two charges.

Despite being under considerable pressure, the *Lady Camden* was holding up well and, providing nothing important split or carried away, was set to meet nightfall considerably out of reach of the oncoming raiders. The brig was another matter however and, despite making it clear he would do nothing to assist the plucky little craft, King felt more than a measure of responsibility for her. And it was clear his feelings were shared for, as he continued looking back over the taffrail, another voice broke into his thoughts.

215

"Game little blighter, it's the pity we cannot do more."

King turned at the sound and was surprised to see Leyton beside him when he had thought the visitor to be Croft.

"I did explain on taking her on," he muttered softly as his gaze returned to the merchant.

"Indeed," Leyton agreed. "And I am certain no one shall pass judgement."

Actually, the prospect of being called to account had not entered King's head; his concerns were for the men aboard the small vessel. He had only met her master briefly, but now felt he knew him better by his seamanship which had been impeccable throughout. Though slow with signals and not blessed with the sleekest of craft, at no time was anything other than the best obtained from a vessel that resembled a millstone, both metaphorically and in her sailing abilities. Admittedly King had frequently cursed the *Mary Jane*'s constant lagging though he held nothing but respect for those aboard who had worked so hard to see her safe. And now that effort looked likely to be wasted; in under an hour the enemy would be in range and, whether they chose to board or pick her to pieces with cannon fire, their backmarker would be lost.

But at least such an act would confirm their pursuers' identity and intent. Their type could hardly be in doubt although there remained a chance the warships were nothing more than neutrals on a jaunt, and what would brighten up a boring passage better than putting the wind up a handful of British shipping? The idea was not inconceivable, yet King had dismissed it long since. The Americans were the most likely culprits but would surely not go to such lengths; besides, their infant navy was hardly large enough to allow two such powerful ships to sail in company this deep into the North Atlantic. And other neutrals seemed equally improbable; in fact, the more he considered the matter, the more certain he was they were facing French raiders.

"Will you fight them?" Leyton asked and King was aware such a question would have annoyed him in the past.

"I shall have to," he replied calmly, "though doubt there is much I can do against such a pair."

"The *Lady Camden* might be of use," the older man suggested. "John Company vessels have been dressed as warships in the past..."

"In force, perhaps," King sighed. "But the French will have

seen the schooners and no doubt already assessed the brig for the drogher she is; there can be no doubt in anyone's mind that they have chanced upon a minor convoy and one that includes something truly substantial."

Slowly others joined them and soon most of *Tenacious'* officers were assembled at the taffrail. Dusk was falling fast yet enough light remained to show the *Mary Jane*'s final moments. Sharp flashes flared briefly from the leading frigate but there was no sign of damage and neither did the brig's course deviate in any way. The group aft remained silent and there was little more than a groan when further shots were released, and this time part of the brig's foretop yard was knocked away. The vessel wavered slightly yet soon regained her heading and continued as before if slower still.

But if anything the French were increasing their pace; the leading ship had eased to larboard and appeared to be forereaching at considerable speed. There were no more shots from her chasers but, once she had gained further, she yawed steeply and a ripple of flame ran down the length of her hull.

"A broadside!" Marine Lieutenant Cross muttered in surprise, and it did seem extreme measures for such a paltry prize.

"And why not?" his senior asked. "The Frogs won't expect a tub like that to be carrying anything of value; better to sink her or set her aflame than waste a prize crew."

King bristled slightly; he could not blame the others gathering but wished the marines at least would be less dispassionate in their comments. He glanced down and was surprised to note he still wore his full-dress tunic from that afternoon's dinner. If action came that evening he would meet it in britches and stockings, which would be novel indeed.

"She seems to have survived," Taylor remarked more hopefully as the leading enemy frigate returned to her original course. From their viewpoint there had been little apparent damage; the *Mary Jane* was stubbornly slogging through the dark waters at what for her was considerable speed and appeared almost contemptuous of the heavy warship off her quarter. But such a situation could not last; before long the frigate yawed again and this time her broadside had more effect.

With a tumbling of sail that made the sea officers hiss and groan, her fore came down, dragging the main topmast with it. The small craft veered from such sudden imbalance and, whether by accident or design, presented her larboard broadside to the warship. The remaining canvas briefly reflected a series of dull flashes and King wondered if she had caught alight until Croft, ever vigilant, produced the answer.

"She's firing on them!" he shook his head in wonder. "A merchant brig, firing on a frigate..."

"Did you ever hear of such a thing?" an unknown voice questioned and there was a rumble of agreement from the rest. But such arrogance could not endure, and neither would it go unpunished. Whatever damage the brig's pop guns might have caused, the heavy frigate retaliated in force and its third barrage was by far the most effective.

When the smoke had cleared the merchant was revealed to be lacking all spars and even her hull appeared oddly out of shape. Then the first of the flames rose up and soon the entire vessel was enveloped in a mighty conflagration.

The group watched, stunned and horrified, as the merchant was quickly consumed, then Leyton broke the silence.

"That was surely avoidable," he said, and he spoke for them all.

Chapter Twenty

It was well past midnight but, as King predicted, not inordinately dark. The moon had risen some hours before and was almost full while the crystal sky was so filled with stars he felt the gods must be determined to illuminate *Tenacious'* downfall. And that was still the likely outcome as he was uncomfortably aware; the brig's smouldering remains lay many miles in their wake and both schooners might be halfway to Halifax for all it mattered, but at least the situation close at hand was far simpler if no more hopeful.

The wind was staying strong and the *Lady Camden* had every usable sail set and trimmed to perfection while the occasional splash to leeward suggested Gilroy had ordered any unnecessary weight jettisoned. With the addition of royals, *Tenacious* would raise slightly more speed but that was immaterial and once more the theatrical allusion seemed unavoidable; he had been cast in a supporting role and King was determined to play the part to the final curtain.

Behind them the French were less encumbered and, though the nearest remained comfortably beyond effective range, the distance was steadily diminishing. He reached into his tunic pocket for his watch and stared briefly at the white dial. At such a latitude the nights barely lasted eight hours; in less than two there would be a considerable lightening in the sky with full daylight shortly after. And by then the French should be close enough to open fire; it was a dismal prospect and King was suddenly reluctant to wait any longer.

Once more he was standing by the taffrail but this time quite alone and the thoughts were allowed to tumble through his troubled mind without interruption. He could indeed wait, let the enemy creep closer and, when the time finally came for action, react; such had been his policy in the past and the ploy usually served him well. But on this occasion stretching matters out seemed unnecessary; not only would it mean straining men already primed for combat, but the end result was far too predictable. Alone, *Tenacious* might have coped with one of the heavy frigates and possibly avoided becoming a complete wreck in the process, yet to willingly meet twice that force and still retain any hope of victory would be foolish in the extreme. However, there remained the chance he might damage one or both to the extent they were unable to proceed, and even the loss of a major spar was to be avoided this deep into the North Atlantic.

To do so would mean exploiting his ship's capabilities to the full and, of these, speed and manoeuvrability came close to the top of the list. But to use them fully he must first free himself from the constraints of the heavy merchant; the former HEIC ship could do little other than offer a token defence while her large and unwieldy hull would be a positive obstacle in any close action.

He stared back at the enemy, silently calculating distances while unconsciously planning exactly how he might take them on. They were sailing in line ahead but a good distance apart so there was the possibility of treating both to separate broadsides. His fingers twitched in anticipation and he thrust his hand into a pocket, making a fist and digging the nails deep into his palm. The French had the windward gauge and must consider themselves practically unassailable for there could be few surprises in the present conditions, yet still he sensed aggressive action on his part would be unexpected. Even if he failed to damage the enemy significantly, anything he did in advance of their attack must surely extend matters and, while he was fighting the French, the *Lady Camden* could continue in her steady bid for freedom.

He might only slow their approach for a while, and perhaps at the cost of destroying his own ship in the process, but the extra time could see them to daylight when a rescuer might be sighted. And even if not, even if they fought in near darkness, naval combat was rarely subtle. There would be the glare of cannon fire, possibly flames, and maybe an explosion – King shivered slightly at the thought – such a display could attract the eyes of passing ships and also bring assistance.

The actual form of attack remained a mystery yet he was strangely confident, if not of victory, then that he would account for himself well enough. First, they must clear for action, then turn about, add the royals and make straight for the enemy. Every move would be obvious, but it would be the French sitting in wait while he took the initiative which was an agreeable change. Both enemy vessels had the wind on their larboard quarter; there should be room enough to sweep down close-hauled on the starboard tack and the very edge of a luff. If he aimed as if to pass the nearest, then turn hard to larboard, there was every chance of landing a decent broadside on her prow. But the same trick would not work with the second; she would surely come up and *Tenacious* might be trapped between the fire of both.

At best it would be broadside against broadside, but the likelihood of the first enemy turning back and raking them across bow or stern was high. King swallowed; it all seemed horribly predictable. Exactly how long *Tenacious* could hold out in such conditions was debatable, but he would be surprised if the enemy's advance and their final capture of the *Lady Camden* were delayed by more than a couple of hours.

And was that truly worth the loss of one of His Majesty's frigates along with a large proportion of her crew? If it meant a wealthy merchant went free, then the answer was undoubtedly yes. Ignoring the military officers and their families, the *Lady Camden* carried a small fortune in goods essential to the maintenance of one of Britain's colonial outposts. Such necessities would be welcomed by the resource-starved French, which would effectively double the value of their loss. But he was assuming help would arrive in the short time he was proposing to buy and, deep as they were in the North Atlantic, the likelihood was slight indeed.

But even as he debated King knew there was truly little choice. To do nothing, to simply wait for the enemy to strike – strike and probably destroy his ship as easily as if he had taken the offensive – was a prospect too terrible to contemplate. No, he would have to act, even if doing so invited disaster. But as he finally turned from his solitary vigil and bellowed the order that would set the wheels of destruction in motion, he was still very undecided.

* * *

Lévesque expected interruption long before this but, when night fell and action still seemed far away, she had finally given in to the temptations of bed. So when the ship suddenly began to vibrate to the sound of whistles, shouts and the banging of mallets it came as a shock. She had been sharing the small space and the bed it contained with Alice and leapt from the sheets in sudden guilt. But the men that came tumbling through the door and began clearing away both cannon had no thought for them.

"Get some clothes and a bottle of water," she told her maid while grabbing at a heavy dress herself and flinging it over her head. Her shoes were nearby and she forced her foot into one while desperately fastening buttons. With a crash, the outer bulkhead was brought down, opening the entire deck to others working with the same grim determination and it was obvious that soon *Tenacious* would be a true warship.

"We're not going downstairs," Alice announced, "not after last time."

"There's no choice," Lévesque replied. Something about the speed and efficiency of the transformation had impressed her. Most of those involved were common sailors; rough, rude men who would hardly warrant her attention in the normal course of events. She accepted they could manage a ship and so convey her to places in relative safety but had never credited them with any true skill or sense of purpose. But as the work continued at speed, with few orders and little instruction, it was obvious they knew far more than how to set a sail. And soon, she realised, they would be fighting for their lives – along with the lives of all aboard – while she and Alice cowered in the darkness below. And suddenly her own particular way of life seemed remarkably squalid.

* * *

Tenacious had turned for action and was increasing her speed as the fresh canvas began to fill. Soon she was fairly racing through the luminous waters with the oncoming French gaining clarity with every passing minute.

"Hoist our colours," King ordered softly, "And be ready to strike the royals on my word."

Those at the guns remained divided between both broadsides; he was still relatively certain of his tactics yet felt unwilling to commit the crews, as if doing so would somehow convey his intentions to the enemy.

"Nothing showing on the Frenchies," Manton muttered to the quarterdeck in general but no one commented. For no ensign was necessary – the utter destruction of the *Mary Jane* had been indication both of their opponent's nationality and intent.

"They'll be coming into range of our chasers shortly," Leyton remarked almost apologetically.

"I am aware of that," King replied in a surprisingly mild tone, "but do not intend to open fire yet awhile."

Tenacious was now travelling as fast as she could in the

conditions; a rare event and one King found both refreshing and stimulating. The binnacle lamp was casting shadows on the sailing master's face making his features appear quite grotesque. And the marines, standing erect along each gangway, looked equally odd in the half-light; the red of their uniforms had become all but invisible though their crisp duck trousers gleamed brightly and the lines of pipeclayed leatherwork appeared to be floating unsupported. He pulled himself together; they were about to enter an action that would probably account for his ship and most aboard her. In an hour from now, he could be nothing more than a mutilated corpse floating in the midst of a vast ocean, yet his mind was playing with odd thoughts and strange notions.

There was a basic plan, but no more, and it lacked one all-important aspect – the element of cunning necessary in any successful frigate action. What would come after his initial strike was also very much in doubt and King fidgeted awkwardly as he privately acknowledged the fact. And it was then that inspiration struck.

"Mr Manton, I shall wish to turn to larboard shortly," he said, taking care to speak clearly.

The sailing master considered for a moment then nodded his head. "Very good, sir."

"And wish to appear as if I intend to rake the enemy's bows."

"I can bring us closer if you've the wish," the man offered.

"I am sure you can though that will not be required; I have more to ask."

"Very good, sir," Manton's reply was suitably cautious. "You'll be expecting the Frenchie to turn no doubt?"

"I will," King confirmed, "and almost certainly to the west; to avoid my apparent intention and bring her own broadside to bear. In truth, I shall be banking on it."

"Yes, sir." For the leading frigate to steer any other way would force her to wear; something best avoided with an enemy bearing down and another warship on her tail. But still it was a bold gamble.

"Once she has, I want us to turn also."

"Further to larboard," the sailing master supposed.

"No, to starboard," King countered.

"And tack, sir?" the man asked in doubt.

"Not to tack, I believe there to be room enough to pass with her on our larboard beam."

There was another pause while Manton considered further. It

was a tall order and one that took some thinking about. In theory, King was asking the senior warrant officer to carry out a complex calculation in his head. And not only must he deal with known facts, there was the speed and exact heading of an oncoming enemy, which could only be guessed at. But both men knew better; Manton had been a seaman for most of his life and knew exactly how much could be left to instinct.

"I understand, sir," the sailing master replied at last. "Much will depend on the Frenchman's pace, but if she strikes some of her canvas I think we might do as you ask."

Suddenly it all felt very clinical and King sensed a cold wave of doubt wash over him; what he had suggested was barely possible. Four times out of five such a manoeuvre must fall flat; *Tenacious* would luff up, be caught in irons and ultimately fall to the combined fire from both enemy frigates. He would be gambling everything on that fifth chance, but then chance really had no place in the equation.

In the short time he had been in command, both ship and crew had improved beyond measure. More than that, he now felt he knew them well enough to predict exactly how each would behave and what could be expected. It was a harsh demand to be sure, and one that might not be met, yet inwardly he sensed it within reach, and that he would not be disappointed.

* * *

"Seems the French are being cautious," Summers remarked to Brotherton. The pair were standing between both batteries of cannon just aft of the forecastle and had spotted the leading enemy ship taking in her royals. "Reckon they know what they're in for."

"Why doesn't the captain do the same?" his friend enquired.

"Oh, he will, no doubt about it." The older lad was positive. "But right now we need to be a mite closer."

"And then?" Brotherton asked, half dreading the answer.

"Well, if we stays as we is, we'll pass with the nearest easily to larboard," Summers continued after a moment. "Yet I know Captain King of old and doubt it will be that simple."

"Then we're going to turn?"

"I'd say, and to larboard though not for a spell; we need to get a lot closer and as quickly as possible, so the royals will be staying a while longer. Then expect the starboard battery to be made ready."

Brotherton nodded, it was what he expected. *Tenacious* would be passing across the bows of the oncoming Frenchman, the classic crossing of the T; he had heard of the ploy and now it was being played out before him. And the nearest enemy was taking in her topgallants now; a sensible move but one that made *Tenacious'* vast expanse of sail seem even more apparent.

"Strike royals!" Manton's voice roared out from the quarterdeck and was followed by that of the first lieutenant.

"Ready *larboard* battery!"

The nominated topmen made a rush for the shrouds as the transient gunners moved across to their larboard weapons.

"Shows how wrong you can be!" Summers grinned when both midshipmen had finished supervising the change.

"So we're not going to turn?" Brotherton asked.

"Apparently not, though it is strange for sure, and hardly like Captain King to miss the chance of even a long-range raking."

The slight reduction in sail was a concession at least, but they were still going into action at a cracking pace and dangerously over-canvassed.

"Three points to larboard!" Manton's voice again and this time both lads looked concerned.

"We *are* turning!" Brotherton exclaimed.

"Yes, but surely too soon," Summers replied.

"And the wrong battery is prepared…"

"Captain King will have a plan," Summers maintained. "He always has, though I could wish he had shared it with us…"

* * *

It would be close and fast, King decided as he stared forward: damned fast.

"Be ready to turn back on my word," he ordered and glanced cautiously about. The moon had almost set and dawn was still no more than a promise yet those about him stood out plainly in the starlight. And they were primed; he could almost reach out and touch the tension.

"The enemy is turning to the west." This was Leyton again and, again, King found he did not resent the observation. The nearest frigate had indeed put her helm over, but *Tenacious* was blasting

225

towards her with a veritable cloud of spray rising from her stem. There had been no time to explain the niceties of the situation to those at the guns but Croft was in charge and could be trusted to carry everything through correctly. And now, with the enemy committed to her turn, their manoeuvre must surely follow. He glanced speculatively at Manton and received a nod in reply.

"I think it time, sir."

"Very good. Take us back to starboard – hard as you like and as close to the wind as she will carry!"

Tenacious heeled steeply as she was thrown into the manoeuvre and a hand at the nearby carronades fell sprawling across the deck. But the ship responded well and was righting herself just as the enemy frigate fired her opening broadside.

It struck them fine on the larboard bow; not quite a rake and decidedly healthier than if they had waited a minute or so longer. For several seconds there was confusion; two marines on the forecastle had been swept aside as if by an invisible broom and a mass of deadly splinters was sent flying in search of victims. Robson, Cranston's late mess captain, had been stationed near a forward chaser and was wiped away by an eighteen-pound round shot that also wounded two others but, in all, they seemed to have got off lightly. Principally their sailing abilities were not affected, and neither was their capacity to strike back.

And now it was a race; *Tenacious* quickly settled on her new course and, as she held as close to the wind as Grigson, the quartermaster, dared, seemed to be eating up the short distance between her and the frigate. King stared over the larboard bow; the enemy was coming up fast. Had she not shortened sail *Tenacious* would have ploughed straight into her side. As it was...

As it was he felt they had a chance.

Time's true measure ceased; in seconds it seemed they were about to pass in front of their enemy and her jib boom would be less than a cable from *Tenacious'* yardarms. King watched, too fascinated to move; Croft was biding his time as well he might; a rushed broadside would only be a waste of shot. But finally they were in position and *Tenacious'* larboard battery could be released.

When in action, no sailing master likes to hold a ship so close to the wind and, even before the smoke had blown clear, Manton was easing them round. King noted the ship was continuing to respond well. As were her gunners; those at the larboard battery were steadily serving their weapons even though each probably braced themselves for the fire that must surely come from the enemy's larboard cannon. As *Tenacious* hurtled by the stunned Frenchman, Piper's marines took potshots from the larboard gangway and quarterdeck. And then, mercifully, they were past.

"We're clear!"

It was Hedges, the signal midshipman, but he had voiced the thoughts of many. *Tenacious* had swept down the Frenchman's side and received nothing other than musket fire for such presumption. It was what King had hoped; the shock of a raking, combined with his opponent's larboard battery being unattended had been enough for such an audacious move to succeed. Although now he must pay the penalty.

* * *

O'Grady and Lovemore were finished with their duties; the larboard gun had been quenched and cleared; now fully charged with powder and shot, the beast was being hauled back to face the enemy. Cranston was a new addition to their team and had been stationed amongst the tackle men, even though he had served as gun captain in another vessel. And as he also came to a halt, the three stood together and regarded their enemy.

Since delivering the recent raking, all had been too intent on their work to consider the Frenchman but now, as the smoke steadily cleared and with the first signs of dawn picking out their target, they began to wonder. *Tenacious* had gained a little to windward but remained less than half a cable from the frigate's two stern guns, yet the weapons – indeed the entire ship – seemed strangely inactive.

"Belike we hit her hard," Lovemore supposed as Longdon, another tackle man, joined them. All could guess that such a devastating barrage would have caused significant damage, with the majority inside the hull and hard to spot.

"So this might be easier than we'd thought," the boy suggested, but it was clear he was the only optimist amongst them.

* * *

The temptation to continue, to leave the first frigate behind and make for its partner, had been strong. In the time it would take they might have been ready to meet the second in reasonable order. But King knew he had to do more; one sound broadside could never be enough, he must damage his first opponent to the extent it could not continue to sail.

"Very well, Mr Manton, take her about!"

Tenacious flew into the tack at considerable speed, even King, who had been expecting it, lurched sideways and was only prevented from tumbling to the deck by the solid body of Leyton standing nearby. But the manoeuvre had been slick and fast; soon they were taking the wind on their beam, then their quarter, and then they were racing back for the Frenchman.

In the time they had taken to turn, the enemy had steered marginally to larboard. Which was good, King assured himself; every second they could delay their opponent made the merchant's eventual escape more likely although there was now the very real danger of receiving a raking themselves.

"Ready starboard battery; target the tophamper and reload with bar!"

The enemy frigate was coming up fast on the starboard bow, he needed to close, but not at the expense of meeting their broadside head on.

"Two points to larboard!"

The ship settled quickly and King considered his adversary again. The light was still poor and he could see little sign of damage but no ship can take the punishment already inflicted and remain intact. And it would be tempting to add to it; to strike once more at the hull. But he had no interest in killing the ship as such, a wound sufficient to make her lame would suffice.

"Here it comes!"

The cry came from forward and heralded the next French broadside. For several seconds the ship was thrown into confusion as shot and splinters tore about her decks striking men and material with an equal lack of regard. The launch, mounted on skids with the spare spars and filled with water to serve against fire, was hit twice and separated into its component planks, soaking all nearby and deadening the powder in an open salt box. Several were struck down by round shot and many more fell to splinters, while solid belly blows pummelled into the hull that caused the entire ship's frame to ring like a deadened bell. But despite it all, *Tenacious* remained viable and would soon be able to return the compliment.

King, along with all on the quarterdeck, waited. They were

gaining slightly on the Frenchman, but not to the extent it would be possible to cross her hawse, yet still Croft seemed to be delaying. And it was only when King was about to issue the order himself that the starboard battery was released.

And the pause had been worthwhile. Even before the smoke was fully clear it became obvious the broadside had been well laid and their enemy comprehensively bracketed. Round shot might not be the ideal projectile against masts and yards, but enough must have passed through the cat's cradle of line and spars to cause some damage. And yet it seemed the enemy frigate was in luck. A glow was growing in the east though the light was still poor and, at such a distance, it was impossible to be certain. But as the seconds passed with no change noted in the frigate's tophamper, it appeared the French ship had escaped serious injury.

For a moment King was stumped; he had been expecting something, even a minor spar carrying away would have been some reward and must make his next move easier. Their efforts so far had wounded one ship to some extent while deviating it slightly from its path, but the French remained heading in the general direction of the fleeing merchant and seemed as likely to catch her as ever.

"Wear to starboard; take her about once more."

It was a relatively obvious option so had been the last he wished to take, and not without risks. But he must drag the first Frenchman south and bring *Tenacious* within reach of the second, while there was also the very real opportunity of releasing his larboard guns, even at the risk of exposing his bow to further fire. And no one ever claimed frigate action to be without danger; it was something that must be acknowledged and accepted, then balanced against possible gain. Whether he had chosen correctly was to be seen but turning so would at least give the chance of firing once more on the nearest enemy while bringing its partner within striking distance.

Yet still King had given the order with the greatest reluctance; it was not ideal and must eventually place *Tenacious* within the crossfire from both ships. If she did indeed become trapped he could do precious little and all must then be down to luck. Luck and her gunners.

Chapter Twenty-One

Tenacious had turned, and turned fast; she did so in relative safely but, once round and heading south, the enemy were straight on her tail. For the first frigate had turned also and now lay on the British ship's larboard quarter while her partner, the untouched southerly warship, was less than a mile ahead and off their starboard bow. *Tenacious* remained on the starboard tack and both ships were temporarily out of reach. He might continue so and simply meet up with the second vessel but the need to drag the more northerly frigate south remained strong; slowing slightly would bring it into range but equally delay meeting up with the untouched enemy. They would have to veer, release a broadside, then revert to their previous course.

"Ready larboard battery," Croft's voice came up from the waist; he was equally on top of matters and thinking along a similar path. "Aim high and reload with bar!"

King looked to Manton, standing solidly by the binnacle. "Very well, Master, take us four points to larboard."

Once more *Tenacious* thundered into the turn, spray flying from her stem. Yards were hauled about in concert with the wheel and at no time was there more than a flutter of canvas. Then the first frigate was closer to her beam, within the arc of their guns and the range well under a mile; the larboard battery, still charged with round shot, should reach them with ease.

Tenacious' broadside was despatched in a shattering roll of thunder and no gunner paused to survey their work but rather threw themselves into serving their hungry charges like so many mother sparrows. The French must have registered their turn and had been sweeping larboard to meet them, so received the barrage over their starboard bow, and this time, surely, there would be visible damage. But as all on the quarterdeck strained for the reward of even a torn sail, they were disappointed. Dawn was undoubtedly rising; daylight could not be far behind and the enemy's tophamper was relatively easy to define. Yet every stick and stitch was apparently untouched and it seemed that, once again, *Tenacious* had been unlucky.

Croft knew none of his men had failed in any way; despite violent manoeuvring and persistent attack, each had done their duty impeccably and nothing but well-timed, seemingly accurate broadsides had been despatched. But only one had made any visible impact; admittedly that had been a devastating blow although since then the enemy seemed to be living a charmed life.

Summers was looking to him; his face bore smears of grime and part-burned powder but the look of incomprehension was obvious.

"We shall be firing bar from now on," Croft reminded. "That must surely bring better results."

"But will it have the distance?" Summers insisted.

"I should say so," the answer came quickly and Croft intended it to be reassuring, but the midshipman appeared unconvinced. And the lad was probably right; for all its effectiveness in destroying tophamper, bar shot lacked the reach of round and was notoriously inaccurate at anything longer than point-blank range.

They were coming close to having the next broadside ready, even now two gun captains had their pieces prepared, but enemy fire could also be expected and Croft suspected it would come sooner than later.

And so it turned out; with a ripple of flame that was already less visible in the growing light, the nearest frigate released her broadside and all with time to notice braced themselves for the onslaught.

It landed hard and surprisingly low, peppering the British frigate's hull and upper decks, turning bulwarks to matchwood and destroying all in its path with blatant disregard. Croft was no stranger to action and prided himself on an agreeable lack of sensitivity yet still the sight, sound, and smell of it all threatened to make him retch. But there was no time for such foolishness; though some gunners lay wounded, the rest had dutifully continued to work and, despite the devastation, several now signalled their pieces ready.

"Fire!"

As he bellowed the order, Croft choked on he knew not what, but the gun captains were as primed as their weapons and a broadside of sorts rang out amid the screams. For it was not complete; a number of cannon lacked full crews and at least two weapons were little more than smoking wrecks, yet *Tenacious* had replied. And now Croft had to see that she did so again and, whatever the distraction, would continue until told to stop.

* * *

The first reports of damage had yet to arrive, but King already knew *Tenacious* had been hit hard. Several men were missing at her cannon and he could see at least three of the weapons themselves were no longer of use; two having lost their carriages while the barrel of the third lay across the body of a loader. As far as the frigate's hull was concerned, he knew nothing, although many of her fixtures had been battered beyond recognition. In the waist, Croft and Taylor were doing their best to restore order but he could see neither midshipman.

"The braces look to be sound." This was Leyton; he was close by but with the din of their recent broadside still ringing, the man had bellowed to be sure of being heard. King nodded; with the ship still under relatively heavy canvas any weakness on that front would have been instantly noticeable yet *Tenacious* was sailing sweetly.

"We'll have the t'gallants off her," King announced, and Manton shouted the order. It would be an annoying distraction when they were still reeling from the French barrage, but King felt the time for speed was coming to an end and extra canvas must be more liability than benefit.

"Message from the bo's'un." It was a young voice and King turned to see a boy of no more than twelve standing confidently before him. "We've lost several of the larboard shrouds, but he's a team workin' on 'em."

"Anything else?" King asked.

"No, sir; he says the rest is just piddlin' stuff," the child informed him earnestly.

"Guns are still being served," Leyton interrupted, "but they'll be ready to fire again in no time, we might get another broadside in."

King glanced across at the nearest frigate; he had forgotten to register the results of their last barrage and, now that he did, was initially disappointed. Once more it seemed the French had escaped

232

any visible damage, until he noticed her jib fluttering slightly. As he continued to watch, the sail was brought in, along with the forecourse, and the ship herself fell off the wind slightly. It wasn't a mast or even a major spar, but at least their efforts were finally having some effect.

And due to the Frenchman's slowing pace, she was steadily moving off their larboard beam and in time would be out of reach. But of greater importance was the second ship, now more clearly visible in the growing light and fine on *Tenacious'* starboard bow.

"We will shortly have to attend to the starboard battery as well," King announced; it was a lot to ask of men who had already given much.

"That we will, sir," the first lieutenant agreed.

"Ask Marine Lieutenant Piper to supplement the gun crews; I cannot see us needing muskets for a while."

Their next opponent was partially hidden by *Tenacious'* foresail; King ducked down and regarded her in time to see two jets of fire erupt from the enemy's chasers. She appeared as heavy as the frigate he had just met and was also relatively close by. But dawn was breaking fast; a sliver of sun could now be seen on the eastern horizon; as it rose the breeze would drop and their speed must reduce further. Both *Tenacious'* chasers returned the fire but there was no visible damage and King stood up once more before glancing over to his charge.

The *Lady Camden* was in sight though a good distance off. She was still showing all available sail and drawing away with every second. Watching her, King realised that, whatever happened now, he had partly achieved his main objective and bought the merchant some time.

Nearer to, the first frigate was steadily creeping out of *Tenacious'* ark of fire but appeared to be turning and adding sail once more; shortly they would have to face attention from that direction as well. It was an unpleasant prospect but one he had anticipated and at least it would mean both ships would have been stopped.

"Mr Morales reports three 'oles just above the waterline; they are being attended to, sir."

This was one of the carpenter's team making a report to Leyton. After the urgency of the last few minutes, it was odd how everything suddenly seemed to be happening incredibly slowly. And there was Summers, King drew a sigh of relief as he noticed the young man approach although his face was badly bruised and bleeding slightly.

"Mr Croft says we've lost three guns from the larboard battery." The midshipman's report was articulate enough, yet he appeared strangely distracted. "Starboard battery is served and ready."

"Very good, Mr Summers," King told him. "And how are you loaded?"

"Bar shot, sir – as you ordered."

They were closing rapidly with the new target; soon she would be within the arc of their starboard guns although the range remained long.

"Ask Mr Croft to continue for as long as we may reach. And remind him I will shortly be requiring both batteries."

"Both batteries, yes, sir," the lad repeated.

"Are you injured, Michael?"

"A bit dazed, sir," he admitted. "But Brotherton's hurt and has been sent below."

"Then Mr Croft will be needing your assistance, you'd better return."

The lad left and King glanced up at the main masthead. The light was increasing steadily but there had been no report from the lookout. His attention returned to the deck. It might all have been a waste of time, yet he still had to see matters through to their inevitable conclusion.

"Mr Manton, we will shortly be turning to larboard." The sailing master jerked to attention at the sound of his name.

"Very good, sir; do you propose to run us alongside the Frenchie?"

"No," King replied, and he drew breath before continuing. "No, I want us broadside on and hope to reach the first frigate as well."

The implications were obvious; *Tenacious* would be placing herself between the two enemies and taking on both simultaneously. Such a move would put an end to any thoughts of a victorious outcome; even if friendly ships were sighted none could arrive in time to intervene. The best anyone could hope for was to string matters out long enough for the *Lady Camden* to escape.

Manton was obviously considering this as he paused, and King noticed Leyton was also strangely silent. Then the sailing master

234

pursed his lips and gave a slight nod. "I understand, sir."

King looked to his first lieutenant and unconsciously prepared himself for any amount of protest. But it was clear he understood as well.

* * *

"Sure, you got your battle," Lévesque told her maid.

Alice shivered slightly and pulled the light cotton shawl more tightly about herself, although the orlop was surprisingly warm and a distinct lack of fresh air made the atmosphere extremely close. But there was no mistaking what was happening a mere twenty feet away, and the sight was enough to chill anyone with a modicum of sensitivity.

It seemed no time since the first casualties had been delivered to the sickbay and Manning and his assistants began to work. And both women had watched until the combination of surgical procedure blended with plain butchery had utterly appalled them. But though the surgeons were fast and skilled in their craft, they could not meet the constant flow of fractured bodies that now lay sprawled on the deck in various levels of destruction. The sight was mercifully dulled by a lack of light, but nothing could mute the sound of corporate pain and the very air was thick with the scent of desperation.

"Reckon we'd 'ave been better off on deck," the girl grumbled.

There was a deep rumble as the sound of yet another broadside vibrated through the warship's timbers; Lévesque waited until the thunder ceased.

"If we'd have been on deck," she said at last, nodding towards the wounded, "we might have ended like them."

Alice closed her eyes at the thought and, mildly relieved by the action, proceeded to keep them tightly shut.

* * *

Tenacious had taken up what would probably be her last station and, for the moment at least, could fire both batteries at the enemies gathering about her. Dawn was breaking properly now and in the rapidly increasing light, King continued to watch from the quarterdeck. Croft had been sensible enough to allow individual fire and the broadsides were becoming more ragged as faster, or more complete, gun crews drew ahead. Much had been written about the spirit-breaking effect of volley fire but King was not interested in eroding his enemy's morale; by giving the gun captains autonomy, each team was working at its maximum speed, with only the six-pounders in the bows being allowed to grow cold.

But it could not last long; that was becoming increasingly obvious. *Tenacious* was firing specialist shot; two heavy spheres connected by a short bar and designed to wreck an opponent's tophamper. It was wicked stuff that would equally tear through flesh and light fixtures but lacked range and, as both enemy ships were hove to on the very edge of its reach, King wondered if every charge was reaching its target. Although some damage had already been done; the first frigate, which was currently benefiting from *Tenacious'* larboard battery, had recently lost her mizzen topmast while her main top looked decidedly shaky and the second was suffering from a foreshortened bowsprit, the jib boom having been removed by a lucky low blow. But such damage would hardly slow heavy frigates; once this annoying escort had been dealt with, they would soon pick up sufficient speed to catch the fleeing *Lady Camden.*

And that time could not be long in coming, as any free to consider the prospect would know. Rather than target *Tenacious'* masts, the French were firing deep into her hull. King could feel an almost constant tremble through the soles of his shoes and knew it to be caused as much by the impact of enemy round shot as their own cannon fire. And the enemy's steady bombardment was equally showing results. The gun crews, already depleted from the need for both batteries, had been reduced further: several cannon were being manned by less than half their normal complement and marines were hauling on tackle and loading shot with a will. The sea soldiers might lack the dexterity and experience of regular hands but no one could fault their enthusiasm.

There had been material damage as well; the enemy gunfire had reduced most of the frigate's chains to splinters; shrouds and odd lengths of line hung loosely from above and her sails were little more than ribbons fluttering gently in the breeze. But King supposed such damage did at least relieve him of a measure of responsibility – there would be no manoeuvring until repairs were made, although he had long since abandoned hope of moving *Tenacious* again.

Shortly Croft would return to round shot; he could pass an order to that effect but trusted the man implicitly and would prefer not to interfere. They would continue to aim high in the hope of a lucky hit but the prospect of severely damaging either of his opponents' tophampers now seemed small. Every few seconds a further belly blow dug deep into their lower hull and men were continuing to fall with sickening regularity. Hedges had followed Brotherton to the orlop and the shattered body of Guppy, the master-at-arms, had recently been flung over the side by a group of seamen keen to compete for the task. With his men otherwise engaged, Cross, the junior lieutenant of marines, was standing bemused but inactive and Piper, his senior, was unaccountably absent. If the enemy's fire continued so, *Tenacious* could sink beneath their feet, although King suspected her guns would have fallen silent long before that might happen.

For he would strike. It was an option he had been considering for some time and one that carried little horror as King had surrendered a ship before. As soon as no further damage could be inflicted, it would be the most sensible course.

"Two guns unmanned to starboard," Leyton began, then paused as a nearby carronade was despatched. "And another on the larboard," he added when the ringing died.

King nodded but made no attempt to reply. The first lieutenant was right and their firepower would continue to decrease as the casualties mounted. But for as long as they could injure the frigates, and delay them to any extent, they must continue.

The sun was up now; even through the smoke of battle, he knew it would be another clear and bright day, possibly with a hint of warmth even so far north. And the sea was also starting to rise; the previous calmness they had enjoyed was coming to an end; soon their guns would find it harder than ever to reach the enemy. King closed his eyes for a moment and drew breath; it seemed the time had arrived.

"I shall have to strike," he stated when conditions allowed.

"Let us hope they respect it when we do," Leyton replied as a block crashed to the deck a few feet from where they stood. "I doubt the *Mary Jane* was shown such courtesy."

King disagreed, from the little he knew of the brig's master, surrendering would have been the last thing on his mind. But it was not the time for debate; a hand was approaching, and King thought he recognised one of the carpenter's crew.

"Message from Mr Morales," the man announced, knuckling a forehead that was bleeding from a shallow gash. "The well's rising steadily and we're down to one pump."

"Very good," Leyton replied. "How long might we remain afloat?"

The man shook his head. "Not for me to say, sir; Joe's doin' all he can to sort matters but they're hitting us pretty regular."

King absorbed the information with no change of expression and when the two nearest carronades were despatched simultaneously he hardly noticed. Leyton dismissed the hand and turned to speak to his captain but he appeared lost in thought. And, taking his lead, the older man remained silent also. For speech was truly unnecessary; both knew the time for surrender was imminent.

Chapter Twenty-Two

Cranston and Lovemore were hard at it. With the remaining gunners distributed between both batteries, only luck had seen the pair working on the same weapon. But the tie mates were glad to be together and their cannon was being served faster than many others.

"They're aiming low," Cranston shouted. He had delivered the heavy chunk of bar shot and now his friend was ramming it home. "Odd for a Frog."

"Aye," Lovemore agreed briefly, before picking up the train tackle and, with Cranston on the opposite team, the beast was hauled back to its firing position. One advantage to the ship being all but stationary was little need for the gun captain to take aim. Bar shot was notoriously inaccurate and the range long; the only thing required was for the weapon to be pointed in the enemy's general direction.

Their cannon spoke and both men moved in with the others to repeat a process already carried out a dozen times. But as they worked a wave of enemy shot thundered against *Tenacious'* side. Lovemore instinctively ducked and dropped his rammer. Three men had been knocked down horribly at the next piece and he recoiled from the sight only to look back to his friend and notice him strangely absent. He glanced about in disbelief while the dust and splinters continued to fly. Cranston had been to the other side of the weapon, they had been speaking barely seconds before, but now the man had simply disappeared. Then Lovemore leaned over the gun's warm barrel, saw his tie mate, and immediately knew him to be dead.

* * *

Lévesque had decided enough was enough. Their dark corner of the orlop might be comparatively safe but being close to so much agony was a torture in itself. Alice seemed relatively composed and might even be dozing, but she had been unable to close her mind to the suffering and quietly eased herself upright. It was a low deckhead and the light from a dozen lanthorns barely made an impression on the dense gloom. As she took a few paces forward she noticed the injured had gathered themselves into groups as if for support. For a moment she searched for some figure of authority in the hell hole, but the surgeons were literally up to their arms in their work, and their assistants had more than enough to do in bringing fresh meat to their table. And through it all came the constant murmur of moans and pleadings; prayers, sobbing and an occasional call for a far-off mother that chilled her very soul.

"Have you water?" The voice came through clearly despite the competition and she found herself looking down and into the eyes of a young boy. He was amid a cluster of men, yet seemed somehow detached, as if not of them.

Lévesque bent down and suppressed a retch as the sudden scent of sickness overwhelmed her. "I might find you some," she supposed.

"Oh please!" he beseeched, and the cry was taken up by those close by. She stood once more and looked about, then noticed a small pail to one side and, stepping carefully between the bodies, made for it. The thing was full but in the near darkness she could not be sure of its contents. There was a small ladle though and a cursory sniff seemed to confirm nothing worse than ship's water. On turning back she found she had lost sight of the boy's group, but several waving hands attracted her attention and she picked her way back.

"Here, I'll give you a sip," she announced, bringing the dripping ladle out. The boy half raised himself and gulped wildly. Much of the water washed over his face and chest but enough seemed to be taken in and, after three servings, he was sated and fell back.

"If you please, miss," another begged, and the woman turned her attention to him. Others were equally thirsty, soon the ladle was coming out partly filled and finally she was tipping the last drops from the bucket straight into the mouth of a wounded marine. But when she was finished they all seemed the quieter and, as space had been found for her, she settled herself amid the mass of tortured humanity.

"It's my arm," the boy announced. "I think it broke, it hurts plenty."

"I cannot help you," she told him softly.

"Sawbones'll sort him," a seaman grunted.

"Aye, probably cut it off and save further trouble," another agreed.

The lad's eyes widened in horror and Lévesque smiled reassuringly. "If it's broken it can be set," she assured him.

"I hope so," the lad groaned. "Can't be an officer with only one arm."

"Is that what you want?" she asked.

"'E's han officer already," a seaman interrupted. "Young gentlemen, they calls 'em, and due for better no doubt."

"Though there ain't no difference really," the marine, who had a splinter in his shoulder, supposed. "Still gets hurt jus' the same as us an' we all ends up together."

"I'm a midshipman," the boy confirmed.

"I know what that is," she assured him, "and that you will indeed be an officer. Plenty have but one arm, you need only look to your captain."

"An' it didn't do Nelson no 'arm either," another announced with a little more understanding.

"Aye, Nelson – no arm!" the marine repeated and a ripple of strained laughter flowed about the small group.

Lévesque smiled; if nothing else it was a change from the atmosphere of a few minutes before. Then she caught the eye of the youngster again.

"Sure, you need not worry," she said. "The surgeon will do the right thing and you'll end up an admiral whatever."

"My father's an admiral," the boy told her a little wistfully.

"Your father?" she asked.

"Admiral Brotherton," the boy confirmed, "only he spends most of his time working."

"And is not being an admiral work?" she laughed.

"Probably, but he doesn't go to sea no more," the boy sighed. "Much of the time he's in parliament or the stock market. And there's the bank of course."

"The bank?" she repeated, her interest awakened.

"My uncle owns Welbys and father is one of the directors," Brotherton told her and she nodded with approval.

"Is he indeed?"

* * *

Brotherton had given little in the way of support but, since he was sent below with a shattered right arm, Summers found he was missing the lad. Having both batteries in action simultaneously was as much a draw on the officers as men and, with enemy shot arriving from both sides, keeping every weapon adequately manned proved a job for more than one. Taylor and Croft were doing their best, of course, but with the smoke, dust, and general confusion it was hard to keep track of every team.

Then Croft's face suddenly appeared almost next to his, making him jump slightly despite the turmoil. "Switching from bar to round." The words had been shouted in a brief pause between cannon fire. Summers mumbled a reply but a nod was sufficient and the second lieutenant moved on to inform Taylor. There had been no order from the quarterdeck but every reason to make the change. They had been blessed with little more than a gentle swell, yet both enemies were drifting away and the greater range of round shot was needed.

He turned to the nearest cannon in the forward battery, now his sole responsibility since Brotherton's departure and, so intent were all in their work, had to physically stop another round of bar shot being loaded. The chunk of iron was swiftly swapped for a ball from the garlands and Summers repeated the procedure at the next weapon. But when he reached number eight he paused; a man had fallen: his body was lying still and apparently ignored. The cannon was still being served but rather than its usual crew, no more than five were attending it. Summers stepped swiftly to one side as the weapon was heaved in and fired. Then, as the gun's crew began working once more, he bent down and lifted the corpse himself.

It was warm – hot even – and had been living tissue barely minutes before. But there was no helping the fellow; it would be kinder to despatch him over the side and, without a word to anyone, Summers heaved the body upright.

"Leave him!" The order was harsh and unexpected, especially as it came from a regular hand and usually the gentlest of fellows. "Leave him I say!"

Summers paused, then moved the corpse a little further to one side and against the next cannon which had a damaged carriage and had long been silent.

"Leave him there, Mr Summers," Lovemore repeated, this time slightly softer. Summer's eyes turned to the rest of the gun's crew; he realised they had paused also and were watching him intently.

"It's Cranston," Lovemore explained. "I'll deal with him. An' he ain't goin' over the side."

Then Summers understood and, after lowering the body gently down, moved on.

* * *

Tenacious' guns were continuing to fire; ringing barks that repeatedly punched through the chorus of orders, prayers and curses as her men continued to fight. And there was movement; lads with powder raced across the crowded decks, the weapons themselves, now hot with justifiable anger, reared back in brutal recoil while blocks, line and odd pieces of tackle tumbled from above in a constant trickle of savage rain. A circle of white sun sat on the horizon like a stalker preparing to strike and, of all distractions, it was this image that seemed to penetrate King's tired brain where it cut and twisted like a cruel knife.

For this was the dawn he had held out for; the birth of a day that might have brought salvation in any form from friendly sail to wicked tempest yet was delivering nothing. There were fresh lookouts at the frigate's fore and main tops; seamen with eyes primed to spot a stitch of canvas an inch above the horizon and midshipmen equipped with glasses ready to judge the country and intention. But all were quiet and, apart from the group by *Tenacious'* binnacle, the only ones still and seemingly impotent.

And with the dawn, a fresher wind had risen, one several points off the old and large enough to encourage a slight increase in swell. In time it would turn the frigate as she fought and rob her of targets.

"We might launch a quarter boat," Leyton supposed in a rare portion of silence. King heard but felt unable to comment. Indeed speech itself would be a challenge while any measure of rational thought lay way beyond him. But he forced his mind to focus and evaluate both the suggestion and their entire predicament.

They might indeed launch a boat; it would take no more than the muscle of twelve strong men to haul the frigate back and keep her in play until the whole horrid episode came to an end. But with dawn now upon them and help so obviously absent, King felt even such small effort would be wasted. He looked across at the nearest enemy. She remained off their starboard beam and was being held back by *Tenacious'* near-constant fire. Likewise to larboard, the first frigate they had so soundly punished was further off; barely in range in fact and treating them with understandable caution. Neither French ship showed signs of significant injury; the most that could be said was a few spars had been knocked away and there might be damage to their hulls. But King knew better; he had raked the first and knew from experience what terrors such treatment could inflict; it was likely that at least a quarter of the crew had been disabled by that single barrage, to say nothing of the harm to equipment and frame. And even the nearer enemy, the one that had managed to avoid *Tenacious'* venom close up, must be hurt: no warship can withstand sustained fire from eighteen-pound long guns and remain untouched. He could not begin to gauge the devastation *Tenacious* had wreaked but would chance it to be great and was certainly sufficient to keep both at a healthy distance.

But that hardly solved his present dilemma; though she had masts, four of *Tenacious'* chains had been shot to splinters; all that was keeping her masts in place were a few remaining shrouds and habit. His ship could no more take to the wind than she might fly, and the damage to her hull was equally bad. Morales had done his best but there were places where tingles overlapped and the ship was only being kept afloat by a relay of sweating men at her one remaining pump. He turned and faced Leyton and guessed his desperation to be obvious.

"Or we could strike," the first lieutenant spoke as a nearby carronade was despatched, yet King heard every word. And he was about to respond; not with an eloquent answer perhaps – one simple nod of the head would have been enough – but a shout from the maintop stopped him.

"Deck there!" It was young Vernon's voice and, though it hardly carried the news he expected, King felt a warm wave of pure relief wash over him. "Nearest Frenchman's underway!"

The breeze was steadily building and, though it cleared any hanging smoke, fresh was constantly being produced by *Tenacious'* cannon and King could make out no fine detail on the enemy frigate. Then something more definite caught his eye; her main, which had been backed, swung round and the topsail billowed briefly; the ship was unquestionably in motion. And this was no small adjustment; her guns had also ceased to fire. Then, even as he watched, more canvas was added.

He swung around. The other frigate was also moving; more slowly perhaps, but there was definite progress and *Tenacious'* gun captains were already struggling to bear on her.

"The Frogs are beating it," Manton announced.

"Belike we were not the only ones waiting for dawn," Leyton agreed. But King said nothing, his brain felt swamped and was incapable of interpreting the recent developments. Fortunately Leyton seemed more attuned.

"There'd be no benefit in taking us," he stated with mild resentment. "We're nothing but trouble. Whereas..." His eyes turned westwards to where the *Lady Camden* could still be seen as she made her escape.

King supposed that was reasonable: the French had been bloodied enough. A solitary British frigate had proved far harder to take than they could have anticipated and was fighting still. Besides, both ships were already damaged; it would only take one lucky shot – a mast to fall or an important yard carry away, to wreck any thoughts of capturing the merchant.

"But they can't just bugger off," Manton announced, apparently in disappointment.

"And why not?" King's voice cracked slightly as he finally spoke, but now the thoughts were flowing freely again. *Tenacious'* guns had ceased to fire; already their targets were beyond reach and an eerie silence seemed to ring about the suddenly still ship. "What use would a beaten-up frigate be to them?" he continued. "They might set us alight, but there would be prisoners to deal with and wounded to attend. The French are far from home and on a mission to take prizes, true prizes that will not only weaken us but bolster their economy. Given the option of capturing a warship – one that is already on the verge of sinking – and a ripe merchant, which would you choose?"

Manton seemed to accept this and Leyton drew a deep sigh.

"Do you think they'll catch the merchant?" he asked, and King turned westward once more. Both enemy ships had picked up speed and, though battered, were heeling slightly in the freshening breeze.

"I'd say they had several knots on her," he said. "So yes, it is likely."

"We could hardly have done more."

King smiled, "I suppose not." He glanced at the remains of his ship. Now her guns had ceased to fire and the smoke was properly cleared he could see far more. And it was a terrible sight; her sails hung in shreds, untamed lines snaked from above while every inch of deck and bulwark seemed scarred, stained or shattered from the impact of countless enemy shot. The men, so recently toiling tirelessly, had finally relented and their worn-out bodies hung limp while the flapping of wayward canvas and a gentle swish of water from the pump-dale told their own story.

"Though, if we are to see harbour safely," he added, "I'd say there was a measure of work ahead."

Chapter Twenty-Three

With the sudden absence of any need to fight, the men seemed confused and oddly lethargic. Most sat or lay in small groups drawing on each other for support; talking softly, mindlessly and hearing only the deep, ringing echo of past cannon fire. There was no Guppy to chivvy and no equally spent officer intruded on their need for rest. Some, the minority, remained at work, clearing wreckage or splicing line, often at random, but most simply gave in to exhaustion while a few stared silently out to sea or up at the clean blue sky. And several gently sobbed.

But it did not last; within minutes strength was returning. A line formed at the scuttlebutt, minor injuries were attended to and a measure of order emerged. Then, though *Tenacious* still wallowed helplessly in the rising swell, the work began to bring her back to some semblance of normality.

Shot holes were plugged with a deal more care, some sense could be made of her tophamper and when a triumphant carpenter announced their second pump back in operation there seemed a modicum of hope. But still King, who was apparently everywhere and ever willing to listen to problems, was privately finding it hard to be positive. Realistically they had lost; he and his crew were free men still only because the enemy had greater priorities. And equally their main object had not been met, even before the *Lady Camden* reached the horizon, she had been caught and, after the briefest of struggles, swiftly claimed.

As he took a rare rest against the shattered remnants of the binnacle and accepted a cup of lukewarm chocolate from his servant, King felt the pressure begin to tell. *Tenacious* had so recently been a well-run ship and, as most of her heads of department had been spared, much of the repair work would continue without his intervention. Earlier the boatswain had reported the tophamper to be repairable; only the lack of support from shrouds and stays prevented them from getting underway. And much of the damage to the hull could be addressed while the twin pumps were finally making progress on the level in the well. Morales and his mates would eventually start work on the damaged chains although, even when completed, *Tenacious* was unlikely to take full sail. But progress could be expected and, though the journey would be longer than planned, they should finally raise Halifax. Yet still the feeling of anti-climax remained.

Several hours after its appointed time and just before they saw the merchant captured, a scratch breakfast had been served and, after another brief rest, the work began once more. And now, with beef boiling in the cauldrons and the promise of a double-shotted duff to follow, the men were rallying to the extent that it seemed possible – probable even – the ship would be secure before nightfall.

Which would be the best time for yet another round of inspections, King decided as he drank deeply from his cup. Remaining positive when his command resembled a wreck would be a hard task for any captain; in a few hours so much more should have been achieved and it was always easier to praise progress. But there was one department that had yet to receive his presence and, though his least favourite duty, he knew it must be addressed without delay.

"I shall go below and inspect the sickbay," he said, placing the empty cup on the binnacle lid. Leyton turned from speaking with the purser.

"Very good, sir. Shall I order Up Spirits at the appropriate time?"

King paused; an extra tot of rum had been issued before breakfast; another now might prove too much for some younger heads. But all had fought well and were continuing to work like Trojans; to deny their mid-day grog would be cruel indeed.

"I hope to return by then but do so if I have not." King turned to go and, with the movement, realised quite how stiff he had become. "And ask the cook if we have fruit; apples were taken aboard at Cork I believe or, if we have oranges, so much the better; but see every man receives something." There was a strange taste in his own mouth, as if he had been sucking copper coins and, with no enemy on the horizon and much still to be done, small indulgences were definitely in order.

"They fought well," Leyton chanced, and King sighed.

"They did," he agreed, "though 'tis a pity we could not save the merchant."

* * *

248

Manning had performed his last operation several hours before. Since then, and with only the briefest of pauses for burgoo and coffee, he had been making continuous rounds amongst his patients. And some had died; such a thing was expected so he tried to ignore the fact even though it was becoming increasingly easy to move about the orlop's deck. But others were more stable and a few showed definite signs of improvement. Brotherton was one; Manning fingered the tight bandage about the boy's arm: the splints were holding in place and, as far as he could tell, the bone remained correctly set.

"You are being careful not to move it?" he checked, and the lad rolled his eyes.

"I am, father," he replied, slurring slightly.

Like most, Brotherton had been given a liberal dose of laudanum. In many cases this was palliative in the true sense of the word; those with internal injuries or any who had lost more than one limb were not expected to recover and it was simple kindness to dull their pain. But Manning hoped Brotherton would improve and to do so he needed rest. The lad's quarters had been commandeered to form part of the sickbay but the drug might allow him to sleep even amid the misery of the crowded canvas-covered deck.

"I am glad to hear it," the surgeon told him, rising once more. "In which case, I think we might save the arm."

"Good news indeed." It was Tom King's voice and Manning jumped slightly on hearing it.

"Have you come for an inspection, sir," he asked. The pair had been close friends for many years, yet the honorific was important in such a public setting.

"I would welcome your report, Mr Manning."

"We received thirty-eight wounded in all," the surgeon began, "of which twenty-six are still with us."

He waited while his friend absorbed the information; it was a fair proportion of *Tenacious'* crew and, when those disposed of on deck were added, a hefty butcher's bill. King took the news with no visible change of expression, although Manning understood him well enough to know he was deeply shocked.

"Is there anything you need?" he asked, and Manning shook his head.

"We have all for now; perhaps some of my patients could be taken into the sunlight when there is space on deck, and a few might return to their messes when they are established."

"I shall send someone to organise that," King promised before turning his attention to the midshipman. "I see you have caught a wound in the arm, Mr Brotherton," he said. "Careless of you in the extreme."

The lad looked up in mild wonder but made no response.

"I believe I was able to save the limb," Manning interrupted. "Only time will tell, of course, but the bone appears willing to set and should knit properly."

King turned to him, and the surgeon blushed slightly. King himself had been in a similar position when Manning's efforts failed; the arm became infected and needed to be removed. "I trust you will be successful, Robert," he told him formally.

* * *

Lovemore had fulfilled his final obligations to Cranston. Under the direction of Wilson, the sailmaker, he had attended to his old tie mate's body, placing it in one of the hammocks that had caused so much trouble and adding two eighteen-pound shot for weight. Then, as an afterthought, he slipped in the piece of scrimshaw his friend had been working on before sewing the canvas up tight. Wilson then added the final 'snitch stitch' through the nose after which the neat parcel was placed with others of its kind. And now it lay on a grating where it formed part of a poignant line that caused many to pause in their work. It was generally accepted their late shipmates would be despatched during the next day's forenoon watch and though none wished for the traditional time to be brought forward, all would be privately glad when the deed was done.

"Would you have sorted the old fellow out?" O'Grady asked when Lovemore re-joined his messmates.

"I have at that," the seaman confirmed and closed his eyes briefly when the Irishman delivered a gentle hug that came from them all.

"We've been detailed to clear the scuppers on all decks," Wainwright told him more practically. "You and Longdon can take the starboard upper and work aft from the fo'c's'le."

Lovemore and the lad duly made their way to the first of the drains that lay choked with the debris of battle and set to with brushes and bare hands until most of the splinters, dirt and general filth was removed.

250

"A dose of water should set things off now," Lovemore announced and Longdon obediently dropped a wooden pail over the side. Lovemore trickled a little of the seawater down the open drain and both began scrubbing feverishly to clear the last of the detritus. When they were finished and the dale lay clear and steaming in the gentle sun, he turned to the boy.

"We'll need vinegar now," he told him.

"Of course," Longdon agreed. "Cranston used to swear by the stuff."

"An' he were right."

"Said if I washed my face in it I might lose me freckles," the lad added.

"I couldn't speak for that, but it cleans up most things lovely."

"He taught me a lot," Longdon contemplated a little sadly.

"And you've come on well because of it," Lovemore assured him.

"But now he's gone..." the lad began.

"Now he's gone, I'll carry on where he left off," the seaman announced. "I might not be the Jack he were but can still teach you a thing or two, and it will keep me amused."

"I'd like that," Longdon said.

"I'd like it too," Lovemore agreed. "Now light along and fetch that vinegar."

* * *

They passed the night safely enough and by the following day, when an element of order had been established and the aft grating was free of its canvas packages, the ship finally began to move of her own volition. The larboard fore channel had been repaired and, though not the neatest of jobs, was serviceable enough and enabled them to show a topsail. Almost as soon as she gained way, the officers' spirits lifted. Though not quite a defeat, the recent action had equally been no victory and some, the more earnest amongst them, felt vaguely responsible. But once they had a controllable ship to manage their attitude changed, and orders began to be issued with more positivity while the general hands remained resolute throughout.

But then the lower deck's view of the recent action was far more realistic; most accepted they had indeed been beaten yet were philosophical enough to include the odds in their assessment. And there was equally no doubt in anyone's mind that the ship had fought well and been a credit to the service while the act of bringing *Tenacious* back to order was steadily cementing her as a favourite in many hearts.

And when the main and mizzen chains were repaired to the extent that all masts could show some measure of canvas, a reasonable speed was achieved. There followed a small storm; nothing approaching what the North Atlantic was capable of but enough to test their recent repairs, and when that was successfully ridden out the terrible memories began to fade. There were constant reminders, of course; empty places on mess benches, pumps were still required for two out of every four hours and all parts of the ship bore the marks of a truly desperate action. But order and routine, the panacea of so many disasters, steadily worked their magic and, ten days after her masthead witnessed the *Lady Camden*'s capture, life aboard *Tenacious* was close to normal.

Consequently, when Amanda Lévesque tapped upon the door to the great cabin just as King was settling in an easy chair with a cup of chocolate, it was perfectly natural that he should ask her to join him. Their time aboard the frigate was starting to establish the familiarity of shipmates while surviving a storm, three actions and even the loss of the merchants had forged, if not friendship, then an acceptance of the other.

"I shall speak to the purser to see if further soap can be provided," he promised, adding, "and authorise an additional candle, though you will be careful to keep it, and any other light, covered."

"I will indeed," she promised, "and truly did not wish to complain, but the light in my cabin is so poor."

"Your quarters were only intended for sleeping," King reminded her. "Perhaps you should spend more time on deck?"

"Sure, if that would be agreeable I would appreciate the privilege."

"Remain on the quarterdeck," King said, softening further, "avoid addressing the officer of the watch or distracting any working seaman and I am certain you would be welcome. I shall make a note to that effect."

"That is kind indeed, Captain," she said, taking the proffered cup, "and I will endeavour not to be a distraction."

King took a second to digest her last remark, along with the

252

coquettish look that accompanied it, before deciding no reply was necessary.

The woman sipped cautiously at her drink, then looked afresh at King as if he had become less a man and more a proposition. "It is good to see your boat is moving once more," she said.

"I am extremely pleased with the state of our repairs," King confirmed, "though there will be a deal more to do once we raise Halifax."

"And when will that be, do you estimate?" she asked before sipping again.

"Such a thing is hard to judge, though I should chance by the end of the month."

"A pleasant time to arrive!" She sighed and leant back in the chair.

"I was forgetting, it is a place you know well."

"Know and love it; sure the country is beautiful but I always think it is the people that make any place special."

"It is something I had not considered," King admitted, "though take your meaning."

"Bluenosers are a mixed lot for certain, some have the nature of prospectors, others appear more, shall we say, intellectual? But all share a common trait."

"Which is?" King asked, more from politeness.

"Absolute honesty, Captain," she told him firmly. "Sure, I have never met a country so straight as Canada, and those from Nova Scotia are the most trustworthy of them all."

"I am delighted to hear of it."

She leant forward slightly and King was conscious that her dress was highly embroidered; when at sea, most wore faded uniform or slops and it was refreshing to look on clothing that had a measure of beauty about it. "May I ask, Captain; do you have much dealing with men of business?"

"There is a small concern that manages my estate," he admitted, "as well as what funds I have to invest."

"And do you trust them totally?" she asked.

"In the main I do."

"Only in the main?"

"I must confess to not being the best at figures," he grinned ruefully. "I can shoot the sun and work out longitude but matters of a financial nature leave me cold. Thus I employ bookkeepers and those with more legal minds to check all and set my concerns at rest."

"And I suppose they have your confidence." It was more statement than question, but the woman added a smile to make it gentle.

"I think between them I am safe," King chuckled.

"Then you are indeed fortunate," she sighed, resting back once more. "Sure, there are many who think they know it all and take chances. For I will not lie to you, sir, money can be made from the simplest of investments but is lost far more easily. One proposition might return a fortune, another leave you penniless; the difficulty is telling between the two, which is where trust becomes especially important."

King took another sip at his chocolate and smiled again. He had been away from home for well over a month and encountered obstacles of many shapes and sizes. But now, and with each successfully negotiated, it was pleasant indeed to find himself talking in such a relaxed way with an attractive woman wearing such a pretty dress. Nevertheless, the instincts that had guided him to that point remained and, though undoubtedly enjoying the moment, he was equally conscious of a well-remembered sense of foreboding.

"I assume you are proposing to manage my investments," he said, his tone still light.

"Nothing of the sort." The denial came as a surprise and, as she placed her cup down with an air of finality, King wondered if he had judged her unfairly. "My father's company has a select number of invited clients, all of whom are grateful for the personal attention they receive. But I do not concern myself with them any more than I sweep the floor or attend the mail." Again she sat back but this time King had the impression that something once offered was now denied.

"I am sorry, I merely supposed..."

"Sure, it is a common mistake," she admitted and slowly the smile returned.

"So you do not advise on business matters," he confirmed and though he noted the slight gleam in her eye, it now failed to bother him.

"The purchase and sale of stock holds no fears for me," she admitted, "and even if I still delight in seeing a healthy return, no longer undertake such work for anyone."

"Then some private clients are entertained?"

"Those I know well," she agreed. "I might find my way around any man's affairs but have found intimate knowledge to be vital if I am to provide all he truly requires."

She had finished speaking but her mouth remained slightly open and suddenly King realised he was staring at it like a child might sweetmeats in a jar.

"And any recommendations would be totally discreet?" he checked.

"Captain," she said, and now the tip of her tongue had appeared and was exploring those lips so tentatively. "Were I to do anything for you it would remain between ourselves. And purely on a personal basis."

* * *

"I'd chance you'll spend much of your time here," Summers sniffed, but Brotherton shook his head.

"As little as possible," he replied.

Most of the wounded had either returned to their messes or been consigned to the deep with only a few long-term patients left to clutter *Tenacious'* official sick berth. Consequently the partitioned areas that formed the warrant officers' cockpit had been restored and the midshipmen were returning to their old home.

"Mr Manning said I can do most things, though not move my wing," the younger lad continued. His entire right arm was strapped to his chest and immobile, yet he could still drag the small bag of dunnage to his usual corner. "So I intends standing my watches."

"Commendable," Summers told him, "and giving orders rather than carrying them out will be good training for when you become a proper officer."

"Who's becoming a proper officer?" Hedges demanded, entering the berth. At the sight of the senior man, Brotherton took a step back, but Summers simply grinned.

"It's Brotherton," he lied. "Captain's putting him up for a board as soon as we reach Halifax."

Since failing his fifth examination, Hedges had been famously sensitive about younger midshipmen being promoted ahead of him and he eyed Summers with outright hostility.

"He did what? But the chit ain't more'n sixteen – you need to be eighteen to pass for lieutenant!"

255

"And that's not all you need," Owens, another passed midshipman, pointed out as he followed Hedges in. "If age were the only requirement, we'd have both been on the quarterdeck years back, ain't that right, Sam?"

Hedges avoided the grin and turned his attention back to Brotherton. "So why are you being put forward?" he demanded. "Is it on account of the arm?"

"That's right," Summers agreed for his friend. "Brotherton breaks his arm, so the captain thinks he'll reward him with a commission."

"Well I caught a splinter in my leg, yet no one's offering me sight of a board!" the older man bleated. "I tell you, it ain't right!"

"And I tell you it ain't true," Owens assured. "Don't you know when you're being bobbed?"

"It could easily have been," Hedges grumbled as a grinning Summers led Brotherton from the berth. "Talk was the child were due to gain a fin, it would be just like the old man to take pity. And having an admiral for a father would no doubt have helped."

"In a bad skin today?" Owens enquired when they were alone.

"You would be if you'd failed as many boards as me," Hedges grunted.

"I'm not far off!"

"So what do we do?" the older man demanded. "Spend the rest of our days in the company of children, then watch them race past us to commission rank? There are boys I served alongside commanding squadrons while we prance about in monkey suits!"

"No point in bitching about it," Owens assured him as he set his ditty bag down and began to unroll a hammock. "Everyone says passing a board is more a matter of luck."

"Luck?" Hedges scoffed, "I think not; it's about as straight as a round of under and over: you have to know the right people. Like Brotherton – what are the chances he'll still be in the cockpit a year from today?"

"Whether he is or not won't make a lot of difference to me."

"That's a new tack; most times the subject puts you in a fair old cag."

The younger man gave a wink as he separated the nettles of his hammock. "Maybe I've found another way," he said.

"Another way? You mean you've got yourself some interest?"

"Better than that," Owens looked about the empty room and

256

continued in a softer voice. "I've discovered a passage out."

"Out? Out of what?"

"Out of the Andrew." He gave a quick grin. "Soon as we fetch Halifax I'm swallowing the anchor."

Hedges considered the man for a moment, his expression changing from wonder to mild admiration. "No half pay for us, you know," he reminded.

"There won't be no need," Owens assured him. "I shall be supporting myself."

"So what's the trick?"

"No trick," Owens confirmed. "Have you come across Alice, the Canadian mort's boot catcher?"

"I know her," Hedges admitted, colouring slightly.

"Then I'm surprised she hasn't mentioned it to you, though would hazard funds might be involved."

"I have funds, leastways, I might raise some."

"Then join me," Owens entreated. "With the income Alice predicts we'll be living like hogs in butter."

"I'm not so sure," Hedges pondered. "They seem a rum pair."

"Your choice, but I don't intend spending my days in a cell like this," he said, glancing about at the shabby quarters. "We'll be warm for life and shall want for nothing."

* * *

Croft had come up to stand the afternoon watch when he noticed Leyton on the quarterdeck. And once he had formally taken over from Taylor, the first lieutenant approached.

"Ship is handling well enough," he said and Croft nodded. The latent animosity between them had all but diminished; Croft might still resent being demoted to second officer, and Leyton remained conscious of him effectively waiting for his position, yet an understanding was forming between the two based on mutual respect. However as both officers were of a taciturn nature; neither socialising nor welcoming conversation, they still rarely discussed anything other than ship's business.

And this occasion appeared to be no different; after commenting on the novel arrangement Amon had made to brace the mizzen – setting the catharpins lower and so extending the futtock shrouds – the conversation dried and Croft fully expected Leyton to go below.

But he stayed; stayed and seemed keen to talk further, even if he appeared uncertain of how to begin. And it was not until two bells had been sounded, and the watch was a quarter through that inspiration apparently struck and he turned to Croft once more.

"Actually, James, there's something I wished to discuss with you..."

* * *

King felt his recent conversation with Lévesque had gone very well. Initially he had mistrusted the woman but it would not be the first friendship to develop from inauspicious beginnings and, if what she predicted came about, he should do exceedingly well from the arrangement.

Money, or the lack of it, had been a persistent problem with him; in the past whenever a windfall came his way it had disappeared almost as quickly. His current wealth was the product of a succession of lucrative prizes and, with Aimée's guiding hand, much of it had been quickly invested in his estate. But a sizable amount remained that was doing little, so even a modest increase would be welcomed although, if the Canadian's predictions proved correct, it could be so much more.

But thoughts of money and his home had awoken many other notions. There had been no word from Aimée for several weeks; she had thought herself with child and it was possible, likely even, further news awaited him when they finally brought *Tenacious* in. And if she were indeed with child, it would alter matters considerably; young Robert was a delight, but two children would be twice as hard to be separated from.

They must be raising Halifax before long; once there, and providing he avoided censure for losing the *Lady Camden*, *Tenacious* would be taken in for repair. Morales claimed their damage to be significant yet relatively simple to address; the frigate's hull had been damaged below the waterline but much should be accessible with a little lightening, and mast and spars were comparatively easy to replace. With luck, the ship could be returned to sailing order within a few months but in such a time he could have made the journey back to England and be with Aimée for the birth. Considering his assurances to Trenchard at the Admiralty, it would be the end of his career, but that bothered him little. The recent battle had left him with distinct feelings of anti-climax which were likely to be reinforced when they reached port. Were his actions judged insufficient he might be admonished, or even dismissed the service and could find himself returning to England whether he liked it or not.

A shout from his marine sentry broke into his thoughts and King arose as Robert Manning entered the great cabin.

"It's good news," his friend announced, taking the chair indicated. "Reynolds and Stokes have been returned to their messes; I am gradually regaining my sick berth."

"Good news, indeed, Bob," King told him. "And you think the others will last until Halifax?"

"I am practically sure of it," Manning beamed, "though what befalls them then is anyone's guess."

"I think a lot will be discovered when we make port," King agreed more seriously.

"You are concerned about the recent action?" the surgeon asked.

"A little; we might have survived but only due to the French choosing to take the merchant."

"But they were odds of two to one, Tom!" Manning declared.

"Maybe so."

"So you're thinking of returning to England?" his friend chanced and King grinned.

"It had crossed my mind; am I so obvious?"

"Not to most, perhaps, but we have known each other a fair while."

"You must admit it is an attractive option."

"Oh, I cannot blame you." Manning sighed. "To many, it must seem you have all a man might desire; a naval career and a fine and loving home life, but such a thing is rare indeed."

"Think you so?"

Manning shrugged. "I can recall few successes. We have to accept we are either sea or land animals, there can be no compromise."

"You may be right."

"I am convinced of it. And equally that only you can choose which you might be."

259

* * *

"I were surprised to learn you was eating alone," Alice announced as she carried a tray into her mistress's quarters. "What with the mileage made with the captain I thought the pair o' you'd be dining together."

"Sure, but I figured it better not to press matters," Lévesque replied as she seated herself at the small table. "You see, Alice, catching a man is like reeling in a fish; sometimes you have to play him a little first."

The maid sniffed and set the meal down with a clatter. "I wouldn't know about that," she admitted. "And it certainly ain't the way I does it. Still, I reckons we both done alright on this little tub."

"I think we have," the woman agreed as she contemplated her meal. "But then ships have proved fruitful in the past. You truly cannot beat a captive audience."

The girl nodded. "It's like catchin' fish in a barrel."

Chapter Twenty-Four

"I might signal for a pilot," King suggested when the vast harbour came into view. In addition to a number of small islands, there were several marked channels and the probability of conflicting currents would be high.

"There is truly no need, sir," Leyton replied. "I have navigated these waters many times and our anchorage is easily found."

"Very good," King grunted, and in truth he was happy for his second in command to take charge. Bringing the ship in without waiting for assistance would save time while also leaving him free to examine such a large and interesting port.

The harbour mouth was indeed immense and there were a few buildings already in sight. *Tenacious* benefitted from a fair wind on her beam and, even with her motley rig, was making steady progress. While King watched he allowed his mind to wander. It was almost three weeks since the battle; if the two schooners had made port safely, there would be those ashore who must already have written their escort off as lost. He smiled to himself as he anticipated something of a victory in proving them wrong, even if it then meant admitting defeat in having lost his primary charge.

"Point to larboard." Leyton's voice broke into his thoughts and King turned his attention to him. The man was at the conn and appeared the very epitome of efficiency. A large island was passing to starboard and, when the interrogative was raised, Leyton ordered that day's private signal and their number without reference to him. But then in essence little had changed, King reminded himself; from the outset, the elderly lieutenant had shown a self-assurance that was dangerously close to arrogance. Having to nursemaid a previous captain might have encouraged such an attitude, although King suspected it was an inherent part of his nature. But strangely he no longer felt annoyed; they had come to an understanding and the basis of a good working relationship was definitely in place, possibly even friendship.

It had been much the same story when he first encountered Croft, King remembered. Both men shared several traits and were considerably older than himself: a strange coincidence. But quite how Leyton would have accepted effectively being demoted to second lieutenant was another matter, and one he was glad never to have put to the test.

"Little appears to have changed since my last visit," Leyton announced, turning to his captain. "The port is well served with a building slip, mast ponds and a careening wharf. The merchant anchorage is off our starboard bow."

King obediently turned his attention there and looked for the two schooners amidst the collection of assorted shipping. And it was then that another sight caught his eye, one that made him go cold, then hot in equal measure.

"And there, if I'm not mistaken, is the *Lady Camden*..."

Leyton followed his pointing finger and the older man's small gasp of surprise gave King a moment of pleasure. "So it is and be damned!"

There was always room for mistakes, of course; one seven-hundred ton former Indiaman could look very much as any other, although they had escorted this particular ship for many miles and knew her well. Besides, she was showing signs of damage; there were several obvious tingles on her hull consistent with having recently been in action and just forward of her larboard quarter gallery two gun ports had been knocked into one.

"Signal from the dockyard," Hedges' voice rang out. "They're directing us to an anchorage."

"I shall be meeting with the C-in-C," King announced, "so shall need to shift my coat."

"Of course sir," Leyton replied, his composure now restored.

King turned and made for the companionway where he met Manning coming on deck with their health certificates.

"Our merchant's in port," he announced briefly.

"What the *Lady Camden*?" the surgeon questioned. "How ever..?"

"I have no idea, either she overpowered her prize crew or was recaptured; no doubt we'll learn the full story once ashore."

But the question was still reverberating about King's brain as he slipped down the companionway and made for his quarters. The coach, that had become his sleeping cabin, was to the right; to the left lay the temporary door to his passenger's quarters and between them, a marine private stood guard. King muttered a brief good morning to the sentry and was making for his entrance when Lévesque's door suddenly flew open. King paused, the woman may not be aware they would shortly be anchoring; she would have baggage to prepare and probably wish to alert her maid.

However the person who emerged somewhat furtively was not Amanda Lévesque. Instead, without a tunic but wearing a look of acute embarrassment, was James Croft.

* * *

The quick interrogation of his second lieutenant revealed little and there was no chance to probe further. Croft claimed personal business with Lévesque but was uncharacteristically vague. King could only guess what this might be but at that moment the woman herself appeared. And he had rarely seen anyone so white-hot with anger, yet she too refused to elaborate. Croft had used the distraction to make off before any hope of explanation was ended by the deal door being slammed in his face. And to make matters worse, everything had taken place under the amused eye of the marine.

But he was wanted on shore and could not delay; by the time King had swapped seagoing trousers for britches and hung the heavy full-dress tunic about his shoulders, *Tenacious* was coming up to her anchor and his gig had been prepared. Manning accompanied him to the shore but, such were the thoughts running through his head, simple conversation was beyond him and the pair were rowed to the nearby wharf in dull silence.

Once the surgeon had been left to hand in his certificates and arrange the transfer of those still wounded it called for a near physical effort from King to clear his mind of all distractions. Shortly he must meet with his new Commander-in-Chief and had both written reports as well as a practised verbal account of his actions, including the loss of the *Lady Camden*. He had never expected it to be a pleasant interview and yet, with the ship herself riding boldly at anchor not half a mile from the port admiral's offices, King now felt it was him who deserved an explanation.

The solid stone building was mercifully cool and, after waiting for less than two minutes, he was shown into a large, airy room on the first floor. An open window looked out on the harbour and there was a pleasant breeze, yet when King was ushered to a table that already held three senior officers, he was still inordinately hot.

He shook hands with the others; John Borlase Warren was an old acquaintance although they had met only briefly, at the time King was a mere lieutenant in a ship attached to a squadron under Warren's command. Since then the man had aged considerably and was now resplendent in the uniform of a vice admiral. The second was named Saunders and a fellow senior captain, although not one he recognised. But there was no doubting the third: Harry Gilroy of the *Lady Camden*.

He was someone King had long since regarded as lost and, from his look of amused surprise, Gilroy might have been harbouring similar thoughts about him.

"Well, Captain, I have to say we were astonished to see *Tenacious* come in," Warren began when the introductions were over and they could be seated. "Though equally delighted of course," he added.

"And I am every bit as pleased to be here," King admitted. It soon came out that Saunders, the unknown captain, had the frigate *Veritas*, but King was no more the wiser as to his presence.

"Captain Gilroy has explained much about your very gallant action, though from his description we had rather written you off." Warren continued.

"It did seem as if *Tenacious* had been left for dead," Gilroy confirmed. "Our captors were convinced she would not last the night."

"The damage was extensive," King admitted, "but we were able to make rudimentary repairs."

"Clearly," Warren agreed, "and it is to your credit. I will await your written report, but might say now that you appear to have done everything to defend your charges."

"The *Mary Jane* was lost," King found himself conceding, but Warren seemed prepared to overlook that.

"Which is regrettable, of course, though *Speedwell* and *Nancy* made harbour two weeks back and are already heading south with a fresh cargo."

"I am pleased to hear of it," King replied while casting a furtive look at Gilroy. "Though truly sorry we failed to stop your ship being taken."

Gilroy grinned and shook his head. "Lord, Tom, you could not have done more. They were odds of two to one and few would have condemned you for making a run for it. Yet, as Sir John has said, you fought a gallant action."

"To little effect," King insisted. "Our masthead saw you captured, but..."

"Oh we were taken alright," Gilroy agreed. "I did what I could, but they were warships; I were forced to strike."

"Which brings no dishonour," Warren hurriedly assured them all.

King waited; there had to be more, yet it was as if the other three were enjoying keeping him in suspense. Finally he could take it no longer.

"So, how do I find you safe at anchor?"

"I have to own to that," the unknown Saunders admitted with a smile. "The Frogs were reported as being in the area, presumably awaiting the next convoy. I had been searching for them in company with Dodgson of the *Asterias*. We sighted both and their capture a good distance off and, though we gave chase, they had the wind in their favour. To be honest I would have been happy just to retake Harry's ship but the French were easily caught and, once we closed with them, it were clear why."

"One is in our yard as we speak," Warren announced. "Fine ship, Toulon built and from the best timbers, but it's doubtful she'll ever see service under our flag."

King looked between the two, still too confused to speak.

"Hull's more akin to a colander," Saunders agreed. "She could sail but had been holed by your shot so often there was no fight left in her."

"I had tried to disable her tophamper," King confessed, reddening slightly.

"From what I could see, the range were long..." Gilroy interjected.

"While in the smoke of battle..." Saunders added and all bar King nodded wisely.

"Whatever, she was captured and due mainly to your actions, Captain," Warren declared. "'Tis a pity you shall not share the prize, but we all know the rules well enough."

King gave a rueful grin, he surely did; only those actually in sight when an enemy struck would be included in any compensation although it was hardly fitting for Warren to commiserate; as Commander-in-Chief, he would benefit from a substantial share while safe ashore in Halifax. "In truth, I am glad to see all safe," he admitted.

"The other frigate caught ablaze and later exploded," Warren explained. "Though there will be head money to be paid for that as well."

"Quite what the prize courts shall make of my ship is another matter," Gilroy sighed. "Belike, it will go to this fellow as well for she was undoubtedly in French hands when retaken," he added, glancing at Saunders. King did a rapid calculation; it was not uncommon for such a merchant to carry several hundred thousand pounds worth of cargo. It would be less on the outward leg of a voyage but, even allowing an eighth for the admiral, both captains would be set for life.

"I cannot say I mind," Saunders confessed, "and am assured the money shall not come from your pocket, Harry."

"Oh I were employed as master, no more," Gilroy agreed, "and have already made a pile from my time with John Company. It is simply a relief to be a free man again and able to enjoy it, though you might consider a private consideration to Tom here," he added.

Saunders went to reply but King was ahead of him.

"That will not be necessary," he said. "I also have fared well in the manner of prizes and want for nothing."

"Maybe so, Captain," Warren mused, "though your people may not be as well provided for, and we must see to their needs as eagerly as our own."

"Of course," King agreed, blushing once more.

"I am sure a small allowance can be arranged and will speak to Dodgson about it." Saunders assured. "In truth, we have fared so well it will not be noticed, and you are certain you do not wish to be included, Captain?"

"I am, sir, I have all I need."

And suddenly he felt that was indeed the case; in the space of an hour all worries over the loss of an important merchant had dissolved while his action with the French frigates, something he had feared would be dismissed as unnecessary, was being fully appreciated. And to be able to make such a statement in the presence of three undoubtedly wealthy men was equally satisfying, especially when it was the truth. Whatever happened, King's personal funds were substantial and sure to last him and his family for many years to come. Besides, if Amanda's promises were born out, they would shortly increase a good deal further.

With a damaged ship freshly at anchor and a markedly reduced crew, Leyton had more than enough to see him occupied, yet he had found time to send for Midshipman Summers and the captain's absence was a major factor in his doing so. For this was something he was keen to handle alone.

"I have mentioned before how well I feel you behaved in the recent action," the first lieutenant began when the lad joined him in the gunroom. With Dennison and Manning also ashore, Croft, Taylor and Manton otherwise engaged and Piper dead, Leyton had been confident of a measure of privacy. Should Marine Lieutenant Cross choose to interrupt he would be asked to leave and there was good reason to think the servant woman would not be bothering them again. "The captain shares my opinion and we have agreed to put you forward at the next board."

Summers' mind had been on bedbugs; the day before Wainwright reported an outbreak in his mess and the midshipman was making plans to deal with them when he received the summons. But all thoughts of parasites were instantly dismissed as he digested the first lieutenant's words. "A board?" he repeated weakly. "You mean..?"

"I mean you are being offered the chance to stand for a commission," Leyton told him bluntly. "There is no guarantee you will pass, of course, but the experience will be beneficial in any case and besides," now the man's eye held the suggestion of a twinkle, "Halifax has a reputation for being short of lieutenants..."

"But I am not quite of age," Summers began.

"Which will hardly make you unusual," the older man grunted. "The stipulation is for candidates to *appear* to be of eighteen years; were they overly pedantic our wardrooms would be empty indeed. So what do you say?"

"I-I'm not sure, sir," he stumbled, "surely Hedges – Mr Hedges or Mr Owens should take precedence?"

"They have both had their chances and plenty of them," Leyton snorted, "it is time for a younger man to try his hand."

"I see, sir," Summers declared, yet it was clear he did not.

"Look, let me make it plain," he rested both arms on the table and fixed his eyes on the young man opposite. "We have a measure of work ahead of us; the ship must be seen through the dockyard and then is likely to be under Admiral Warren's flag and expected to take on a variety of tasks. Some may be independent and all will call for an efficient crew with suitable officers to command them. As I have said, lieutenants can be hard to find this far from home, and I have a suspicion we shall shortly be one down."

"Someone is leaving?" Summers questioned.

"I shall not say more." The older man's sudden bark made Summers jump. "It is a matter even the captain is unaware of, but you can see that *Tenacious* cannot be left without an efficient officer force."

"You don't think Mr Hedges will object?"

"I could not care less if he does," Leyton snorted. "I have a notion you will pass your board with ease, in which case you will be his superior officer. And even if you do not; if you encounter a bunch of nincompoops who could not recognise potential if it were pointed out with a stick, anyone who thinks to cause trouble will be unlikely to see another board themselves and that fact shall be made clear."

"I understand, sir."

"And you will excuse me for saying so, but do not let this be your final step." Leyton's tone was still rich with feeling. "Even to be considered for the rank of lieutenant is an honour for it is one the Royal Navy relies upon. But do not linger; the moment you get the whisper of a chance to be made commander, grasp it and cling on tight until you are made post. Only then can it be said your career has been a success."

Now Summers was decidedly uncomfortable; he had never heard *Tenacious'* premier speak so. It was as if his progression were being taken personally; Leyton seemed determined that a midshipman he barely knew should succeed where he had so obviously failed and sensed his future career was to be followed by this enigmatic officer.

"The Captain and I discussed this yesterday morning; he will be enquiring of the next board while ashore," Leyton continued and his voice was slowly reverting to the solid, precise tone that was far more familiar. "He would have spoken to you himself, but needed to report to the C-in-C."

"Of course, sir."

"Though I would predict you will be made acting lieutenant in the meantime," Leyton added, almost as an aside. "It should allow you to accustom yourself to the position, as well as closing Hedges and Owens down if they do seek to cause trouble."

"And if I do not pass, sir?" Summers questioned.

"Do not think that way, boy!" Leyton all but shouted, his face suddenly livid. "Go with a positive attitude, it is what they will be looking for almost as much as an ability to command. And remember what I have said, this is a step, nothing more. Take it but do not stop until you are made captain. On no account allow yourself to become comfortable."

* * *

"You wished to speak with me, sir?"

"Yes, James," King stood up from behind his desk and indicated the chair opposite. "Take a seat." *Tenacious* was now under the care of the dockyard and work had begun in earnest; there was already a strong scent of marine glue in the air and her hull vibrated to the sound of constant hammering. But it was a noise the ear quickly became accustomed to and, ironically, ensured a measure of privacy in the great cabin. Which was something King especially appreciated as he sat and considered his visitor for a moment. He had known from the start this would be a difficult conversation and not one he had been looking forward to. "It was with regards to the woman, Lévesque," he began.

"Nothing has been heard of her, or her maid," Croft replied quickly. "And it has been almost a week, so I doubt anything will."

King regarded him a little longer before speaking again. "We are all aware of that and, truly James, I had thought you would know more."

"Me, sir?" the elderly lieutenant exclaimed, and King gave a heavy sigh.

"I'll make no bones about it; you left her quarters as we were about to anchor – I saw you myself. And the pair slipped ashore shortly afterwards, ostensibly to send a message to Miss Lévesque's family, but neither she nor her maid have been seen since. Their dunnage remains on board and as far as anyone can tell there are no financial institutions nearby with an owner named Lévesque. Now, I am not interested in any private arrangements you may have had, but if there is something you can add to this conundrum I should like to hear it." He paused, then on noting Croft's expression, added, "And if it makes matters easier, this can remain between the two of us."

The lieutenant nodded once, then seemed to be taking stock.

"You will permit me to start from the beginning?" he asked.

"I should like that most of all," King confirmed. "And have no fear of time, this has to be addressed in full."

"Very well, then I suppose the roots lie with my change from first officer to second."

King eyed him warily; if Croft was intending to complain about his current position he had chosen the wrong moment.

"To be frank, it was a novel experience, but one not without advantages. I learned a lot about responsibility, or rather the lack of it. To my mind such a thing can be likened to an annoying noise," he said as the hammering grew slightly louder. "If constant it is hardly noticed, only with change are you reminded of its presence. When a first lieutenant, my time was fully committed to any number of official tasks, all of which I would be answerable for, but as second officer I was less in demand and own to enjoying the break. I did, however, retain the insight gained from the more responsible position and found it to be of immense benefit. Forgive me, sir, but I believe you never served as a first lieutenant?"

"That is true," King admitted softly.

"Then perhaps you will permit me to observe that no band of officers can be led successfully unless their attributes, and deficiencies, are fully known, so it is the duty of a first officer to thoroughly acquaint himself with his juniors."

"I believe that to be the same for any captain."

"To some extent I am certain," Croft agreed, "though you must allow a captain does not enjoy the close contact usual when sharing a mess. But whatever the case, I was given time to study those aboard *Tenacious* in detail and had experience enough to assess them properly: Dennison with his penny-pinching ways and interest in the younger hands and our late Mr Piper's partiality for the bottle – qualities I am certain Mr Leyton has noted, as every premier should. But I was also able to observe the passengers, possibly in a more dispassionate way than any other. And I suspected the woman, Lévesque, to be a charlatan from the start."

"I see," King declared, crossing his legs, and clearing his throat. "And on what do you base your accusation?"

Croft's eyes fell and the customary firm composure relaxed as he considered this. "I took from her language that she was knowledgeable about financial matters though could not fully comprehend the manner of business her father's firm conducted. The profits intimated seemed foolishly high; only one totally ignorant of such matters could be taken in by them, and sea officers are not known for being fiscally astute..."

His usual poise was returning but still he seemed unable to look King in the eye. "I was also aware of a measure of more basic commerce on the part of her maid, who seemed to be accommodating members of the lower deck and some junior officers on a regular basis; later I had reason to believe several gunroom officers were conducting similar transactions with the lady herself."

King moved awkwardly in his seat but remained silent.

"I might add it is my belief the recent applications from Hedges and Owens to leave the service are also directly connected with the two women and have nothing to do with Mr Summers' forthcoming board."

"Then why was I not informed?" King asked.

"I felt unable to speak with you for a number of reasons, sir."

"Unable?" King repeated in mild disgust.

"At the time you seemed to be paying the lady a deal of attention yourself and I had nothing firm to base my suspicions upon. Oh, I might have denounced the maid, and doubtless she would have been dealt with, but that could have hidden a far more devious crime, and one I was determined to reveal."

"But you had no proof?"

"Nothing beyond my instincts," Croft admitted, and King smiled slightly at the word, then nodded.

"I did, however, share my concerns with Mr Leyton, who proved agreeably supportive. We decided one of us should confront the woman before reaching Halifax, and I had been doing that very thing when you saw me leave her quarters."

"You were accusing her of..."

"I was accusing her of nothing, sir," the older man interrupted. "That way lies danger indeed, especially as all I had were suspicions. But once confronted she proved surprisingly honourable."

"Honourable?" King raised his eyebrows; it was an odd choice of adjective.

"I mean she did not attempt to deny anything; instead the woman proved most helpful and revealed far more than I had expected."

"And can you share that with me now?" King asked.

"Not in detail," Croft replied, his usual composure once more in evidence. "Suffice to say she had entered into several financial arrangements with officers aboard this ship, many of which appeared to involve a degree of sexual favours on her, or her maid's, part."

"I see..."

"It was an achievement she appeared inordinately proud of," Croft reflected. "I drew the impression each encounter was regarded as some form of personal victory, though goodness knows why that should be."

"But not all took advantage of her... favours?" King confirmed.

"That is so," Croft agreed. "It was by no means universal; a few were only interested in the financial aspect and it appears there is one amongst us who has little taste for the fairer sex."

That would be Dennison, King decided; the only interest the purser had was for money, or so he had thought until Croft's recent revelation.

"Well, at least she was willing to cooperate," he mused. "But when last seen, Miss Lévesque did appear somewhat agitated."

"I would say extremely angry," Croft replied as he raised his head. "You see, she had expected to win me over as easily as the rest. But, after hearing her story, I remained set to expose them both."

"And would you have done?" King asked.

"Oh yes," Croft confirmed, his expression softening slightly. "Some might say I am doing so now, though I did agree to remain silent a good while and assume this remains strictly between ourselves."

King nodded and waited.

"The arrangement was accepted, if grudgingly, which is what I assumed. You see publicity would be the worst thing for a woman of Miss Lévesque's ilk. People like her only survive through anonymity and I also reckoned whatever they planned to make aboard *Tenacious* was a fraction of the pair's usual earnings. The ship was principally a means of transport; if they could turn a penny as well it would be an advantage but not one worth risking their regular livelihood for. I might add that, wherever they are now and however engaged, it will doubtless be under another name, yet if their descriptions and *modus operandi* became known little effort would be needed to smoke them."

"You seem to have given this a deal of thought," King commented.

"As I have stated, the position of second lieutenant is less taxing than that of first."

There might have been a minor barb in that statement, but King felt they should move on. "I do not understand why Miss Lévesque should assume you could be manipulated," he prompted.

"I'm afraid the lady had a somewhat fixed view of men," Croft stated. "A number of inducements were mentioned, but I refused them all and it was then that her temper became fully aroused and she threatened to accuse me."

"Accuse you? Of what?"

Croft blinked. "Succumbing to her offers," he said.

"It would be a thing hard to prove either way," King supposed.

"Possibly, though I told her to do her worst and be damned." Croft's tone carried a measure of pride now and he definitely smiled. "You see there was little she could do to hurt me; I have money enough from previous commissions to provide a comfortable retirement and little desire for more. And she was quick to accept there might be two officers in the same gunroom with no eye for the ladies."

At the last statement King swallowed but made no comment.

"Then I asked for all money to be returned."

Now King was watching the man with frank fascination, but it appeared Croft's interest had returned to the deck between his feet. "However high her temper, she was no fool and, I say again, whatever they hoped to make was small beer and not worth risking future income for."

"I should think not," King agreed, somewhat sadly.

"I had expected perhaps a few guineas, I did not anticipate this." He looked up and reached into his tunic pocket, then brought out a package of papers bound with black ribbon. "These are personal cheques written in favour of Miss Lévesque. In theory, they must be presented at the bank in question but a good deal of leeway can be allowed, especially when distance is involved. Suffice to say, she would have had little trouble cashing them with a small loss at any number of Canadian clearing houses."

"I see," King grunted as his attention turned to the tight

273

bundle. "And what do you propose to do?" he asked.

"They shall be kept safely," Croft replied, returning the package to his pocket, "and about my person whenever possible."

"For how long?"

"At least while we remain in Canada." His eyes now met King's. "With a woman like Lévesque you can never be sure what might occur; she could have second thoughts or even be planning revenge. With these drafts, there is a measure of security – proof if you like of her misdeeds. And as long as I have them I am safe, while those officers to whom the notes initially belonged shall not suffer any loss."

"And you know who they are?" King supposed.

"The officers? Not in detail," Croft admitted. "The outer draft is from Mr Dennison, and it appears he failed to pay the full amount. I have not opened the package and neither do I intend to."

"I understand," King said. "So what happens now?"

"Nothing, sir," Croft blinked. "The woman has gone, and I hope will not be returning. There is little to distract us from seeing *Tenacious* back to being an efficient ship."

For a moment there was silence, even the noise of hammering had stopped. Then it was replaced by that of a saw apparently being wielded by a lunatic.

"I think you have behaved remarkably well," King announced, his voice rising above the din, "and several aboard have reason to offer their thanks. Though I would gauge they shall not know their good fortune for some while, nor who to attribute it to."

"And probably better that way," Croft replied after considering for a moment. "When they do realise, any number of conclusions might be drawn but in some cases it could serve as a warning, and one they would be wise to take heed of."

"Indeed," King agreed.

"It is the pity I could not do the same for the junior officers and those on the lower deck," Croft continued. "I understand her servant made several minor transactions but these were for coin and there was little opportunity to correct matters. I might have asked for the money though to do so seemed somewhat sordid and could have weakened my position."

"Of course."

Such trades were common amongst seamen and those involved would probably already consider themselves sufficiently recompensed. But there was one thing that still concerned King and he sensed it best addressed immediately.

"As I have said, you acted well, James, and with real courage."

Croft waved the suggestion away but King was not to be deterred.

"No, I am right in my meaning; to face an enemy in combat might be considered brave, but the woman could have destroyed you as easily as any involved in her little scheme."

"I did not fear her," Croft maintained.

"That is obvious and does you credit."

"No, you mistake me," the older man corrected. "I did not fear anything she might say or do; no money had been passed and neither was I compromised in any way."

"Nevertheless you had revealed much about yourself," King pointed out. "And it was personal information of possible value to someone with evil intent."

"If you mean the woman could have threatened to expose me, she did exactly that, though to little benefit. For, as I told her, favouring your fellow man is no crime, only when some form of act is committed does it become illegal and penalties encountered."

"But such a thing might affect your future promotion?"

Croft shrugged. "I have few ambitions in that direction and besides, many senior officers are of such a disposition," he paused, then appeared to relax and the faint smile returned. "Though I am not one."

King blinked; his friend had just admitted to a significant and personal trait, only to deny it almost immediately. "Forgive me, I do not..."

"You see I had lied," Croft declared with an element of satisfaction. "Yet Miss Lévesque accepted my story as readily as if it were written in the Gospels."

King raised an eyebrow. "And that does not bother you in any way?"

"None whatsoever, for she had done the same and with every intention of robbing my brother officers. I merely administered a dose of her own medicine and regard it as a fitting return for the evil she had intended."

"Fitting indeed," King agreed. "The biter bit."

"As you say, sir, though I might add, I think it strange."

"In what way?"

Croft now fully met his eyes. "That such a woman should be fooled so; for all her guile she proved as naïve as any one of her intended victims."

"You are right, I am certain," King sighed, "it simply shows how gullible any of us might be."

Epilogue

The repairs to their damaged pump had seen them as far as Halifax but a new unit was necessary, and King had been doing his duty by standing before it and making agreeable noises while Joe Morales extolled the machine's virtues. It was, it seemed, of the latest design; alone it could shift over a ton of water in under a minute, which was undeniably worthy of comment. But when the carpenter finally left, King breathed a sigh of relief. The pump was just one of many repairs and improvements carried out in a particularly busy couple of months.

Tenacious' entire hull had been addressed and, though she needed neither a careen nor the dry dock, she was now fully watertight and likely to remain so for several years. Her tophamper would shortly be resplendent with new fore and main topmasts; replacement yards had also been ordered, and all chains and channels were in the process of being rebuilt with fresh deadeyes fitted where necessary. The first batch of the new cordage had also been delivered which Amon reported to be of a far higher standard than any currently available in England. Even now the painters were making a start on covering the ship's scars with the first of several layers of oil-rich paint and it finally seemed possible she would return to her previous degree of excellence.

And there had been developments in other areas. There had been no news waiting from Aimée on their arrival and several weeks passed in apparent silence causing King to be close to the end of his tether with worry. Then, less than a week ago, five letters arrived aboard the same packet confirming she was well and that he was indeed due to be a father once more. Even now he felt mildly stunned, although the slight muzziness might also be blamed on the celebratory dinner the gunroom had held for him the previous day. The last letter was written a little over three weeks before at which time all had been progressing nicely. More than that, it carried firm indications that she intended joining him on station as soon as her confinement was over. That must still be many months in the future of course, but the thought was enough to cheer him considerably. With Warren ensconced as Commander-in-Chief, King was relatively certain of remaining on the North American Station a goodly time, yet there would be a home and family close by which was a luxury denied even to some admirals.

Replacements had been found for some of their casualties and, in the main, were experienced seamen. *Tenacious'* present complement might not be quite up to when they left Falmouth but the people themselves were in a far better frame of mind. Both senior midshipmen had applied to leave, with only Owens, the younger of the pair, relenting at the last moment. Rumour had it Hedges was now serving aboard another warship based at Quebec although King could not care less; he had taken on two additional midshipmen and now had an efficient corps of junior men, many of whom would make excellent commissioned officers, which was all any captain should wish for. Taylor had grown in confidence and expertise while Croft continued to carry out his duties with quiet competence and nothing more had been heard of their former passengers.

Thoughts of his officers naturally brought King's mind on to Leyton. The man was currently absent, a strange event in itself, and more so that he was ashore on a personal matter. Throughout *Tenacious'* refit he had been a constant presence, ready to advise on problems of any magnitude and often already at the scene when King arrived to inspect. The man had undoubtedly earned the right to be missing and King hardly batted an eyelid in granting the absence, yet it had been relatively urgent and he was intrigued to know what had tempted him from a project that previously demanded his entire attention.

So it was fortunate that he noticed Leyton clambering through the entry port, just as he was returning from inspecting the pump, and it seemed entirely natural for them to make their way straight to the great cabin. For that was another oddity; the first lieutenant's mystery appointment had clashed with their customary morning meeting and King had much to tell his first officer.

But once finished, and the details of the pump, along with Summers' recent suggestion for watch changes and Dennison's request to return a batch of tallow, had been fully explored, King sensed an element of anti-climax and looked to his second in command.

"I think that is about it," he admitted, "do you have anything to add, William?"

"I do, sir," Leyton admitted. "I shall be leaving the ship

forthwith."

King rocked back in his chair; there was little the older man could have said that would have shocked him more and he felt as if a physical blow had been delivered.

"Leaving? But why?" he asked feebly. "I know we've had our differences, though assumed all to be behind us and I could not have asked for better support with the refit."

"I am glad to hear of it," Leyton acknowledged, "but it has been my intention to go for some while, though nothing you have said or done is the cause. In truth, I have been glad to serve under you; it was pleasant to finally discover a captain worthy of the title and I shall always remember my time aboard *Tenacious*."

"Then I take it this has been planned," King clarified, still reeling slightly. "So why the sudden appointment ashore?"

"I had intended to surrender my commission when all repairs were completed," Leyton explained. "It was in my mind to seek retirement; a few of my age are being offered the rank of commander when going ashore for the last time, rather on the lines of a yellow admiral, and I own it is a rank I had always aspired to. Nova Scotia is also a favourite of mine and seemed a good place in which to end my days. However, my summons was to the port admiral's office and rather upset my plans."

At this, his composure crumbled slightly. Leyton was not alone in keeping a tight rein on his emotions; in common with many officers from the last century he seldom showed any degree of feeling, yet now his expression changed from one of mild confusion to almost abject despair.

"Would you care to tell me more?" King enquired gently.

"I am to be made commander," Leyton confessed at last, "though it is not retirement but true promotion. It seems my previous conduct with Captain Moore put me in good stead; he is in regular correspondence with Admiral Warren and commended me most highly. Likewise, the late Captain Wheatstone was considered something of a problem by the Admiralty and my attention as his first officer was also noted."

"You were well mentioned in my own report," King admitted softly, and Leyton nodded in acknowledgement.

"Which I would chance was enough to tip the balance. Despite my age, I will be commissioned from the first of the month. There is no command for me at present, but I have been assured the next available vessel shall be mine to manage as I see fit. Until then I will be happy to continue assisting in the refit if you shall have me."

"I would like nothing better," King admitted, "though suspect James Croft will wish to assume many of your responsibilities."

"He is a good officer and has supported me well; I doubt I could have behaved so nobly in his position. And at least you shall have Michael Summers."

"Yes," King agreed, "I have never seen a man take to responsibility so readily and am sure he will do well in his board."

"And if he does not there are several months of work ahead," Leyton remarked. "If no one suitable is available in Halifax I would chance it possible to send for another from home."

"There is a man I have served with before who would fit perfectly, were he available," King agreed.

"I am glad to hear of that also," Leyton declared, softening further.

"And I am glad for you, William. Indeed no one deserves command more."

"Thank you, sir; it is something I had thought would never come," Leyton admitted, "but shall be pleased to leave Mr Croft in my stead. In truth, this would seem to be the ideal solution for all," he added and now both men were definitely smiling.

Selected Character List

(positions are as at the start of the story)

HMS *Tenacious*

Ralph Wheatstone	Captain
William Leyton	First lieutenant
Taylor	Third lieutenant
Manton	Sailing master
Piper	1st Lieutenant of marines
Cross	2nd Lieutenant of marines
Dennison	Purser
Hopper	Surgeon
Guppy	Master-at-arms
Samuel Hedges	Senior midshipman
Owens	Midshipman
Hanson	Midshipman
Brotherton	Midshipman
Vernon	Volunteer
Sturridge	Gunroom cook
Amon	Boatswain
Joe Morales	Carpenter
Wilson	Sailmaker
Grigson	Quartermaster
Bovey	Seaman
Wainwright	Seaman
Robson	Seaman
Houghton	Seaman
Longdon	Boy, second class
Amanda Lévesque	Passenger
Alice	Maid to Lévesque

The *Merriweather*

Lovemore	Seaman
Cranston	Seaman
O'Grady	Seaman
Hacker	Seaman

The *Lady Camden*

Harry Gilroy	Master

Also

Thomas King	Senior post captain
Aimée Silva	King's common law wife
James Croft	Former first lieutenant
Robert Manning	Ship's surgeon
Michael Summers	Midshipman
Admiral Garston	Port admiral Falmouth
Vice Admiral Cox	Admiral commanding the convoy
Admiral Carson	Port admiral Cork
Vice Admiral John Borlase Warren	C-in-C North American station

Selected Glossary

Andrew	*(Slang)* The Royal Navy. From Andrew Miller, an enthusiastic impress officer who was said to have recruited so many the service had become his personal property.
Back	Wind change; anticlockwise.
Backed sail	One set in the direction for the opposite tack to slow a ship.
Backstays	Similar to shrouds in function, except that they run from the hounds of the topmast, or topgallant, all the way to the deck. (Also a useful/spectacular way to return to the deck for a topman.)
Backstays, running	A less permanent backstay, rigged with a tackle to allow it to be slacked to clear a gaff or boom.
Barky	*(Slang)* Seamen's affectionate name for their vessel.
Barrel fever	*(Slang)* Illness brought about from excessive alcohol consumption.
Being	Old English term for home.
Bitche	A French town that housed one of the worst punishment prisons of the Napoleonic Wars.
Bilboes	Iron restraints placed about an offender's ankles, allowing him to be of some use, picking oakum, etc.
Binnacle	Cabinet on the quarterdeck that houses compasses, the deck log, traverse board, lead lines, telescope, speaking trumpet, etc.
Bluenoser	*(Slang)* A citizen of Nova Scotia (and occasionally New Brunswick).

Block	Article of rigging that allows pressure to be diverted or, when used with others, increased. Consists of a pulley wheel made of *lignum vitae*, encased in a wooden shell. Blocks can be single, double (fiddle block), triple or quadruple. The main suppliers were Taylors, of Southampton.
Board	Before being promoted to lieutenant, midshipmen would be tested for competence by a board of post captains. Should they prove able they would be known as passed midshipmen but could not assume the rank of lieutenant until they were appointed as such.
Boatswain	*(Pronounced Bosun)* The warrant officer superintending sails, rigging, canvas, colours, anchors, cables, and cordage etc., committed to his charge.
Bob	*(Slang)* A trick.
Boom	Lower spar to which the bottom of a gaff sail is often attached.
Braces	Lines used to adjust the angle between the yards, and the fore and aft line of the ship. Mizzen braces and braces of a brig lead forward.
Brig	Two-masted vessel, square-rigged on both masts.
Bumboat	A shore-based open boat that unofficially sells various provisions and supplies to men aboard an anchored vessel, often in exchange for pay tickets or items of clothing or jewellery.
Bulkhead	A partition within the hull of a ship.
Burgoo	Meal made from oats usually served cold and occasionally sweetened with molasses.
Bulwark	The planking or woodwork about a vessel above her deck.
Cag	*(Slang)* A state of sulkiness or ill humour.

Careening	The act of beaching a vessel and laying her over so that repairs and maintenance to the hull can be carried out.
Carronade	Short cannon firing a heavy shot. Invented by Melville, Gascoigne and Miller in the late 1770s and officially adopted in 1779. Often used on the upper deck of larger ships, or as the main armament of smaller.
Cast up	*(Slang)* Cast up one's account – to vomit.
Chains	Small structure built to either side of a hull to provide a wide purchase for the shrouds of a mast. See Channel.
Channel	(When part of a ship) Projecting ledge incorporated in the chains that holds deadeyes from shrouds and backstays and can be used as a platform for heaving the lead. Originally chain-wales. See Chains.
Chit	*(Slang)* Child.
Close-hauled	Sailing as near as possible into the wind.
Clink	*(Slang)* Money.
Companionway	A staircase or passageway.
Course	A large square lower sail, hung from a yard, with sheets controlling and securing it.
Cove	*(Slang)* A man, occasionally a rogue.
Crows of iron	Crowbars used to move a gun or heavy object.
Cull	*(Slang)* A man.
Cutter	Fast, small, single-masted vessel with a sloop rig. Also a seaworthy ship's boat.
Dale	Drain aboard ship, larger than a scupper.
Deadeyes	A round, flattish wooden block with three holes, through which a lanyard is reeved. Used to tension shrouds and backstays.
Ditty bag	*(Slang)* A seaman's bag. Derives its name from the dittis or 'Manchester stuff' of which it was once made.
Dunnage	Officially the packaging around cargo. Also *(Slang)* baggage or possessions.
Fall	The free end of a line on which the men haul.

Fetch	To arrive at or reach a destination. Also the distance the wind blows across the water: the longer the fetch the bigger the waves.
Forereach	To gain upon or pass by another ship when sailing in a similar direction.
Fin	*(Slang)* The stump of an arm or leg.
Frumenty	A pudding of French origin made from wheat, dried fruit, and egg, heavily seasoned and served with rum and cream.
Futtock	A lower frame in the hull of a ship (similar to a rib). Futtock shrouds run down from the edge of a top to the mast.
Glass	Telescope. Also, hourglass: an instrument for measuring time (and hence, as slang, a period of time). Also a barometer.
Gullion	*(Slang)* Literally a bastard's bastard.
Gunroom	In a third rate and above, a mess for junior officers. For lower rates, the gunroom is the equivalent of the wardroom.
Go about	To alter course, changing from one tack to the other.
Hawse	Area in the bows where holes are cut to allow the anchor cables to pass through. Also used as a general term for bows.
Hawser	Heavy cable used for hauling, towing or mooring. Hawser laid describes a type of line.
Headway	The amount a vessel is moved forward (rather than leeway: the amount a vessel is moved sideways).
Heave to	Keeping a ship relatively stationary by backing certain sails in a seaway.
HEIC	Honourable East India Company.
Impress Service	A branch of the Royal Navy that specialised in recruitment.
Interest	Backing from a superior officer or one in authority, useful when looking for promotion.
Jaunty	*(Slang)* Master-at-arms.
Jarvie	*(Slang)* The driver of a Hackney coach.

Jib boom	Boom run out from the extremity of the bowsprit, braced by means of a Martingale stay, which passes through the dolphin striker.
John Company	*(Slang)* The East India Company.
Jury mast/rig	Temporary measure used to restore a vessel's sailing ability.
Landsman	The rating of one who has no experience at sea.
Lanthorn	Large lantern.
Larboard	Left side of the ship when facing forward. Later replaced by 'port', which had previously been used for helm orders.
Leaguer	A long cask with a capacity of 127 imperial gallons, normally used to hold water.
Leeward	The downwind side of a vessel.
Leeway	The amount a vessel is moved sideways by the wind (as opposed to headway, the forward movement).
Liner	*(Slang)* Ship of the line (of battle). A third rate or above.
Linstock	A forked staff to hold a lighted slowmatch. Using a linstock enables a gun captain to fire his weapon from a distance, without the aid of a gunlock.
Lubber's hole	*(Slang)* Entrance to a fighting top. In theory, a new seaman can only use a lubber's hole seven times, after which he must always come up via the futtock shrouds.
Luff	Intentionally sail closer to the wind, perhaps to allow work aloft. Also, the flapping of sails when brought too close to the wind. The side of a fore and aft sail laced to the mast.
Make and mend	A period when seamen are allowed to attend to their kit or hobbies.
Nugging house	*(Slang)* A brothel.
Orlop	The lowest deck in a ship.

Packet / packet service	The Post Office maintained a number of fast sailing vessels to maintain communications and carry light cargo.
Patter	*(Slang)* To talk.
Peter Warren	*(Slang)* Petty warrant, a term usually applied to victuals served while a ship is in harbour (and supposedly fresh).
Pipeclay	Compound used to polish and whiten leatherwork.
Point blank	The range of a cannon when fired flat. (For a 32-pounder this would be roughly 1000 feet.)
Pusser	*(Slang)* Purser.
Pusser's pound	Before the Great Mutinies, meat was issued at 14 ounces to the pound, allowing an eighth for wastage. This was later reduced to a tenth.
Quarterdeck	In larger ships the deck forward of the poop, but at a lower level. The preserve of officers.
Queue	A pigtail. Often tied by a seaman's best friend (his tie mate).
Raffle	A tangle of line, canvas and cordage.
Reef	A portion of sail that can be taken in to reduce the size of the whole.
Rigging	Tophamper; made up of standing (static) and running (moveable) rigging, blocks etc. Also *(slang)* clothes.
Rino	*(Slang)* Money or coin.
Running	Sailing before the wind.
Salt box	A wooden box kept to the rear of a cannon and used to house spare cartridges. To guard against moisture it was lined with salt.
Salt junk and sixpenny	A soubriquet awarded to Vice Admiral Collingwood (*1748-1810*), an officer known for his mean table and one rumoured to pay sixpence a gallon for his wine.
Salt horse	*(Slang)* Salt beef.
Save-all	*(Slang)* One who is careful with money.
Schooner	Small craft with two or three masts.
Scran	*(Slang)* Food.

Scupper	Waterway that allows deck drainage.
Sheave	The inner wheel of a block usually turned from *lignum vitae*.
Sheet	A line that controls the foot of a sail.
Shrouds	Lines supporting the masts athwartship (from side to side) which run from the hounds (just below the top) to the channels on the side of the hull.
Smoke	*(Slang)* To discover or reveal something hidden.
Soft tack	Bread.
Stay sail	A quadrilateral or triangular sail with parallel lines hung from under a stay. Usually pronounced stays'l.
Stern sheets	Part of a ship's boat between the stern and the first rowing thwart and used for passengers.
Strake	A plank.
Swallow the Anchor	*(Slang)* To retire from the sea.
Tack	To turn a ship, moving her bows through the wind. Also a leg of a journey relating to the direction of the wind. If from starboard, a ship is on the starboard tack. Also the part of a fore and aft loose-footed sail where the sheet is attached, or a line leading forward on a square course to hold the lower part of the sail forward.
Taffrail	Rail around the stern of a vessel.
Tarpot	*(Slang)* One of many terms for an elderly seaman.
Tingle	A lead or copper patch used to temporarily repair the side of a ship. It would be spread with tallow and nailed into place.
Tophamper	Literally any weight either on a ship's decks or about her tops and rigging, but often used loosely to refer to spars and rigging.
Trick	*(Slang)* A period of duty.
Tumblehome	Describes the narrowing of a large ship's hull as it rises above the waterline.
Turk's head	An elaborate knot.

Twickenham Set *(Slang)* Derogatory name for lesbians.

Under and over A fairground game where players are easily cheated.

Veer Wind change, clockwise.

Waist Area of the main deck between the quarterdeck and forecastle.

Watch Period of four (or in case of a dog watch, two) hour duty. Also describes the two or three divisions of a crew.

Wearing To change the direction of a square-rigged ship across the wind by putting its stern through the eye of the wind. Also, jibe – more common in a fore and aft rig.

Windward The side of a ship exposed to the wind.

Yellow (admiral) The rank of admiral was achieved solely through seniority. Following a man being made post (captain) he gradually rose on the captains' list as those above him died, retired, or were promoted. On attaining flag rank he would normally be appointed rear admiral of the Blue Squadron, the lowest level of flag officer other than commodore. But should the officer be considered unsuitable for such a position, he would be appointed to an unspecified squadron; what was popularly known as being yellowed, and a disgrace to him so honoured.

About the Author

Alaric Bond has had a varied career, writing for various periodicals, television, radio comedy as well as the stage. He now focuses on historical nautical fiction with sixteen published novels, thirteen of which are in his acclaimed 'Fighting Sail' series.

Set in 'Nelson's Navy' of the Revolutionary and Napoleonic wars, these have no central hero but feature characters from all ranks and stations; an innovative approach that gives an exciting and realistic impression of life aboard a warship of the period.

Hellfire Corner is the first in an intended new series and marks a change in emphasis, although future 'Fighting Sail' instalments are planned.

www.alaricbond.com

About Old Salt Press

Old Salt Press is an independent press catering to those who love books about ships and the sea. We are an association of writers working together to produce the very best of nautical and maritime fiction and non-fiction. We invite you to join us as we go down to the sea in books.
Visit the website for details of all Old Salt Press books:

www.oldsaltpress.com

The Latest Great Reading from Old Salt Press

Rick Spilman
Evening Gray Morning Red

A young American sailor must escape his past and the clutches of the Royal Navy, in the turbulent years just before the American Revolutionary War. In the spring of 1768, Thom Larkin, a 17-year-old sailor newly arrived in Boston, is caught by Royal Navy press gang and dragged off to HMS *Romney*, where he runs afoul of the cruel and corrupt First Lieutenant. Years later, after escaping the Romney, Thom again crosses paths with his old foe, now in command HMS *Gaspee*, cruising in Narragansett Bay. Thom must finally face his nemesis and the guns of the *Gaspee*, armed only with his wits, an unarmed packet boat, and a sand bar.

Linda Collison
Water Ghosts

Fifteen-year-old James McCafferty is an unwilling sailor aboard a traditional Chinese junk, operated as adventure-therapy for troubled teens. Once at sea, the ship is gradually taken over by the spirits of courtiers who fled the Imperial court during the Ming Dynasty, more than 600 years ago. One particular ghost wants what James has and is intent on trading places with him. But the teens themselves are their own worst enemies in the struggle for life in the middle of the Pacific Ocean. A psychological story set at sea, with historical and paranormal elements.

Joan Druett
Tupaia, Captain Cook's Polynesian Navigator

Tupaia sailed with Captain Cook from Tahiti, piloted the *Endeavour* about the South Pacific, and was the ship's translator. Lauded by Europeans as "an extraordinary genius", he was also a master navigator, a brilliant orator, an artist and mapmaker, and a devious politician. Winner of the New Zealand Post General Non-Fiction Prize.

Alaric Bond
Hellfire Corner
(The Coastal Forces Series)

Autumn 1941 and a fierce war rages amid the treacherous waters of the Dover Strait. It is fought by the gun and torpedo boats of Britain's Coastal Forces: fast, frail vessels that do battle against the best of Germany's Kriegsmarine including the notorious E-boats.

Antoine Vanner
Britannia's Innocent
The Dawlish Chronicles: February – May 1864.
Political folly has brought war upon Denmark. Lacking allies, the country is invaded by the forces of military superpowers Prussia and Austria. Cut off from the main Danish Army, and refusing to use the word 'retreat', a resolute commander withdraws northwards. Harried by Austrian cavalry, his forces plod through snow, sleet and mud, their determination not to be defeated increasing with each weary step.

Seymour Hamilton
River of Stones
Only three stones of power remain, and only the eight descendants of Zubin can wield them. A ruthless and power-hungry man is intent on stealing the stones, murdering the three leaders of the fleet, and torturing the secrets of navigation from their children. Grand master Astreya gives his daughter Mairi command of a ship with instructions to keep the younger members of his family far from danger. However, safety is elusive. Mairi must face political turmoil ashore, resolve conflicts with her twin brother Trogen, and lead her young crew through storms, dangerous passages, and battles at sea before she can discover the secret that will lead to the river of stones.

V E Ulett
Blackwell's Homecoming
In a multigenerational saga of love, war and betrayal, Captain Blackwell and Mercedes continue their voyage in Volume III of Blackwell's Adventures. The Blackwell family's eventful journey from England to Hawaii, by way of the new and tempestuous nations of Brazil and Chile, provides an intimate portrait of family conflicts and loyalties in the late Georgian Age. Blackwell's Homecoming is an evocation of the dangers and rewards of desire.

295

Printed in Great Britain
by Amazon